Also by Holly Huntress

The Broken Angel Series:

Broken Angel
Condemned Angel
Forsaken Angel

Unbound

∘Book One∘

Holly Huntress

First edition: December 2021

Unbound by Holly Huntress
Cover design and map art done by Holly Huntress

This book is dedicated to all my
friends and family who have
supported my dream
of writing...thank you.

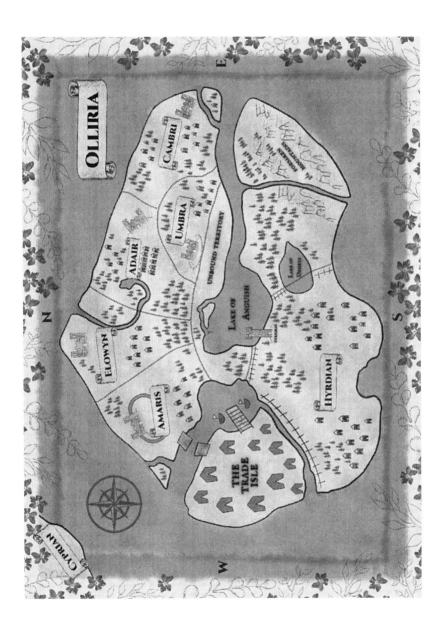

PRONUNCIATION GUIDE

Characters

Mylah – My-luh
Emil – Eh-meel
Vita – Veet-uh
Castien – Cast-shien
Elias – Eh-lie-us
Edris – Ee-dris
Torin – Tore-in
Haldor- Hall-door
Lachlan – Lock-lan
Ailsa – Ail-sa

Places

Hyrdian – Her-i-dee-in
Adair – Uh-dare
Elowyn – Ell-oh-win
Cyprian – Sip-ree-an
Olliria – Oh-leer-ee-uh

Other

Shreeve – Sh-reeve
Hosath – Hose-ath

One

"Two more were found dead across the border between Adair and the Unbound territory this morning," a voice echoed up through the council chambers. Mylah leaned forward, peering over the balcony railing until the owner of the voice came into view. He wore the forest green Adairian uniform, but Mylah did not recognize him.

She leaned back, watching from her assigned seat in the upper gallery as King Florian and the fourteen advisors who made up his council shared an uneasy look. The king sat upon his simple black and gold throne built into the platform at the front of the room. Mylah studied him as he opened his mouth to speak. His brown hair had recently been cropped short to allow his gilded crown to sit comfortably on top of his head. The forest green train of his royal robe bunched at the base of the throne where an unused footstool had been placed.

Mylah's eyes flicked to the queen at King Florian's side, Queen Aurelia. Her braided hair, black as a starless night sky, sat piled on top of her head. The sun that streamed in from the windows up above them caused her deep brown skin to glow. Her hazel eyes were glazed and unfocused as per usual, uninterested in what the man before them said. Their two children, Princess Mina and Prince Ari, were too young to attend the council's meetings. Mylah had only seen them once from afar, but they seemed to have inherited most of their mother's traits.

Greyson leaned over to ask Mylah and Cassia, "Do you think it was an Unbound creature or a shreeve?" Greyson leaned over to ask Mylah and Cassia. His voice distracted Mylah from the conversation happening below and he raised an eyebrow at them in question.

"Obviously the shreeve, Greyson," Cassia snapped. "They're always trying to get more of our land."

"Pa told me that our quarrels with them have nothing to do with the land. He thinks it's a creature from the Unbound territory doing the killing, not the shreeve." Since the shreeve, who were human-fae hybrids, normally kept to their own kingdoms of Elowyn and Amaris, Mylah had never encountered them before, but she had seen depictions and heard about them. They were usually at least a head taller than most humans and were covered in blue and green markings. Their most distinctive feature was their eyes. An image from a book flashed in Mylah's mind, sending a shiver down her spine. There was color where the whites of their eyes should be, and their iris was another color.

"We will expand the patrol for that edge of the border, day and night." King Florian's commanding voice cut through the conversation in the upper gallery. "No citizen of Adair will be allowed out of town after sundown unless they are given special permissions." Mylah noticed some grimaces at that declaration. The king's sharp, hazel eyes missed nothing. He went rigid in his throne, glaring out over his council. Mylah chuckled as she watched them all sink into their own chairs. *To have such power...* she thought.

"Come on, let's get out of here," Greyson said, stealing her attention away from the lower gallery again. "The good part's over." Greyson stood but kept low as he half waddled out the doorway that led to the stairs, Cassia following close behind him. Mylah worried that they might miss out on some interesting information, but she decided to join her friends. Sighing in resignation, she turned and trailed behind Cassia.

It wasn't unusual for them to sneak out of meetings, but Mylah wasn't always happy to leave. Though, if she asked, her parents would fill her in later about the rest of the meeting. She enjoyed hearing what was going on in the kingdom but spending time with her friends had become harder and harder as more responsibilities fell on each of them.

The trio hurried down the stairs and out to the king's gardens. The gardens were enclosed by the castle on all sides, but with no roof, it gave them a breath of fresh air. Roses were the most common flower to be found in the gardens, but Mylah's favorite was the blue dahlias. The king had them specially altered by a witch since they didn't grow that color naturally. The king had at least two witches at his disposal, that Mylah knew of.

"Greyson, why don't you go fetch us some biscuits from the kitchen, I'm starved," Cassia said as they wandered down a path lined with daisies. Greyson assented immediately, as usual, always seeking Cassia's approval. Mylah understood – Cassia was much prettier than most girls their age. She was fifteen, a year older than Mylah and Greyson, and had glistening, warm, brown skin; fine, black hair that reached the middle of her back; and fierce, green eyes. All her features were soft and rounded. Mylah envied her.

It wasn't that Mylah was less attractive, but her own features were sharper and more defined like her father's, not quite as seamless as Cassia's. Mylah had rich chocolate brown hair, much thicker than Cassia's, and it fell in curls down past her shoulder blades. Her eyes were a dark grayish blue color, not nearly as intriguing as Cassia's eyes. Mylah could thank her mother for that combination, while her dad had brown hair and brown eyes.

Cassia noticed Mylah staring and offered her a dazzling smile.

"Now, Myles, it's not polite to stare," she chided as she flipped her hair over her shoulder and laughed.

"Sorry, Cass. I was just wondering whether you realize you have poor Greyson wrapped around your finger," Mylah said, watching as Greyson's slender, twig-like figure disappeared into the castle. His shocking white-blond hair blinked out of existence amidst the shadows of the doorway.

"Oh, don't be silly. He's wrapped around any girl's finger who gives him a second glance. He's too willing to please." Cassia giggled. Mylah thought that was unfair. She'd known Greyson her whole life and had never seen him act that way around anyone else. But, before she could say so, Greyson was hurrying back towards them, so she kept her mouth shut.

"Thanks, Greyson," Mylah said, smiling brightly at him. There was a permanent glimmer of innocence in his deep blue eyes, and she wondered how long he'd keep that before Cassia crushed his heart. Mylah knew it was bound to happen. Cassia had her sights set elsewhere, and poor Greyson would never stand a chance.

Mylah sat in the kitchen eating dinner with her parents that night, listening to them bicker about the meeting earlier. Nights after a council meeting almost always went that way, their voices steadily rising to fill their normally calm and cozy two-bedroom home. Mylah's mother was usually upset about something the king had said or done, while her father tended to go with the flow.

"King Florian needs to retaliate and show the Elowyns they can't get away with this!" her mother argued.

Mylah traced a whorl in the wooden dining table with her index finger, pretending not to pay attention, though she absorbed every word that was said.

"Yes, Vita, let's storm their castle while we're at it!" her father quipped.

"You know what I mean, Emil. Patrolling the borders is not enough!"

"I agree, but there is no evidence that the shreeve are responsible for these deaths. It could easily be an Unbound creature..." he trailed off as Vita began speaking again.

"It's madness. Next those shreeve will be invading farther onto our land and killing more of our people. They may not be as fast and as strong as the fae, but they certainly have the upper hand against us humans. Allowing them to gain any foothold on our land will be detrimental." Vita and Emil both glanced nervously at Mylah. She felt their eyes on her and looked up from her empty plate.

"What?" she asked.

"Nothing, Bun." Mylah cringed at her father's nickname for her. Bun, short for bunny, because she used to pretend she was a bunny when she was five. Unfortunately, though she grew out of that phase, the nickname stuck.

"Where did you and your friends sneak off to earlier? I don't think King Florian would be too happy to see his future advisors skipping out on meetings," Vita said, giving Mylah a disapproving look.

"The gardens. Greyson led the escape, I went along for the thrill of it all," Mylah joked, which made her father laugh, and her mother even cracked a smile. They both knew Greyson and how careful he always was. The only time he broke the rules was to sneak out of the council meetings. As children of advisors, Mylah, Greyson, and Cassia were all required to attend the meetings since they had turned twelve. They needed to be ready to take over for their parents someday.

"If it's the shreeve, do you think they're trying to start a war?" Mylah asked. Emil sighed, looking to Vita for help.

"You don't need to worry about that, Mylah," Vita used her soothing voice that was meant to ease all Mylah's worries. It had stopped working on her when she'd turned twelve and started attending the council meetings. It was hard not to worry when you were always being informed of everything that was going wrong in the kingdom.

"Yes, leave the worrying to the adults, Bun. You'll have plenty of time for it when you're older," Emil added.

"Very reassuring, Pa," Mylah laughed, but he was right. When she turned eighteen, she'd be an official member of the king's council, and when Emil stepped down, she'd take over as an advisor. Vita would step down from her role as an advisor eventually as well, and presumably, Mylah's future spouse would take Vita's place. Advisors had more say than other council members since the rest of the council was made up of the advisor's children. Occasionally the king allowed a few random citizens of Adair, picked in a lottery or by popular vote, to attend council meetings and voice their opinions.

A pounding on the door made them all jump out of their seats. "I'll get it." Emil hurried to the door. Curiosity had Mylah peering around the corner, attempting to see who stood behind the door. They didn't usually have uninvited guests after dark, and it left her wondering who could be out and about so late.

"Sir," Mylah heard, but then the voice turned to a harsh whisper. She caught a few words but couldn't make sense of any of it. "We need...the sprites...yes. There's no one else." A sense of disease began to settle into Mylah's stomach as a thick tension became palpable in the house.

After a few more minutes of chatter, Emil shut the door and turned back to his family. He held a leather-bound book in his hands and brought it to the table, setting it down gently. There were intricate swirling designs on the cover and words written in a language Mylah had never seen before.

"What is it, Emil?" Vita approached cautiously, as if the book would self-combust.

"A book."

Vita scoffed. "Obviously. What *kind* of book?" Mylah could tell from the look on Vita's face that she already had some idea of what kind of book sat on their table. Fear filled her eyes and worry shaped her features. Emil clenched and unclenched his fists nervously but when he spoke, it came out clear and without strain.

"According to the sprites who stole it from King Haldor of Elowyn, it contains information that could help us gain an advantage over the shreeve. If we can translate it, we can potentially keep them off our land, forever."

Two

Emil set to work translating the book the next day while Vita and Mylah went into the village to do some shopping. Vita had been on edge since the night before, and Mylah noticed her mother glancing sideways every now and then. Mylah's gaze swept the woods surrounding them, but nothing of note stood out.

As they walked, the woods thinned out and disappeared entirely where the village began. Shops and a few food stands lined the straight and narrow streets. Mylah knew the village well enough, but she didn't venture too often to the outer edges where most of the villagers lived. Her family mostly frequented the other advisors' homes which were separate from the village and set further into the woods.

Mylah caught herself staring at the bookstore, admiring the ornate covers displayed in the window. Vita stepped up beside her and squeezed her shoulder.

"We can take a look," she offered. Mylah nodded before pushing her way through the front door. It always stuck and took extra effort on the entrants' part. From the outside looking in, the store appeared to be an exotic and luxurious place, but the displays in the window were the only part of the store that were tended to. The rest of the store was basically a small barn with long shelves that created aisles. Books were piled at the ends of each aisle, all along the walls, and almost spilling off their shelves.

Mylah wandered through the bookstore aimlessly. Though she normally loved to look through the books, she found herself too distracted thinking of the book her father was at home translating.

"Psst." Mylah whipped around to face the towering bookshelf behind her where the sound had come from. "Mylah." She followed the voice to the next row over and found Greyson with an armload of books.

"What are you doing here?" Mylah asked. Greyson had always complained about reading in the past, saying he found it tedious and dull.

"My dad wants me to start reading up on warfare and fighting tactics. I've already started training," Greyson said, struggling to keep his pile of books from toppling over. Mylah reached out and took a few books from his stack.

"Warfare, huh? I guess my parents aren't the only ones worrying that a war is coming." Mylah cringed looking at the gruesome images depicted on the covers of the books in her hands.

"I guess. Anyway, I wanted to ask you something..." he was cut off by Vita as she hollered from the front of the shop.

"Mylah! Time to get going!" Mylah gave Greyson an apologetic look.

"Sorry. We can talk tomorrow, okay?" She placed the books she had taken back on his pile, nearly sending the whole stack toppling to the floor, and hurried out of the shop. Vita stood waiting on the cobblestone street, empty handed. She'd had as much luck as Mylah.

"Come on, let's pick up some vegetables and head home." Vita snaked her arm around Mylah's as they made their way to the vegetable stand. A sense of longing nagged at Mylah as they passed by the dress shop along the way. She paused, imagining herself at one of the balls in the palace, swaying to the beat of the song playing in her mind.

Vita nudged Mylah's arm, pulling her from her reverie, and steered her into the shop. Light scattered throughout the store, glinting off a diamond-encrusted chandelier that swung slightly from the ceiling. The fractals of light caught on the bejeweled gowns sending a cascade of rainbow glitter onto the walls and floor. Mylah held out her hand to catch some of the light and watched the colors dance across her palm. Her mother wasn't looking at the dresses, though. She gazed into the jewelry case off to the right. Mylah drifted to her side.

"May I help you with anything, Vita?" the shopkeeper said as she walked over to them.

"Good afternoon, Sissany! How nice to see you!" Vita beamed at her friend. "Could I please see that necklace?" She pointed to a heart-shaped diamond pendant on a silver chain. In the center of the heart, there was a sapphire. Sissany pulled the necklace out of the case and handed it over to Vita.

"That's one of our newer pieces," she said. Vita held it up to Mylah and nodded to herself.

"Yes, we'll take it," she said. Mylah gaped at her.

"Ma, no, I don't need anything."

"Nonsense, Mylah," Vita waved her off. "Charge it to Emil please, Sissany." Sissany had already packaged up the necklace and handed it over. "Oh, no. We don't need any of that." Vita unwrapped the necklace and clasped it around Mylah's neck.

"Ma, thank you, I love it." Mylah didn't understand what had prompted her mother to buy her the necklace, but she accepted it.

"It brings out the blue in your eyes," Vita said, smoothing down Mylah's curls. Her lips were pinched together, and her eyebrows furrowed as if she were in deep thought, but then she was on the move again, waving to Sissany as she strolled out the door.

Mylah caught up to Vita as she walked down the sidewalk. An unfamiliar carriage rumbled past headed in the direction of the castle. Mylah watched it for a moment, considering who may possibly be inside, but her attention snapped back to watching where she was going as she tripped over a cobblestone.

While Vita bought vegetables at a roadside stand, Mylah watched the villagers. A young couple strolled past, heading for the butcher, while another twosome stood directly opposite Mylah. The shorter of the two, an older man who held flyers, pinned her with his stare. The younger woman beside him, most likely his daughter or granddaughter, leaned heavily on a walking stick. Mylah recognized them as petitioners for the Hall of Hosath.

The hall was located in a rundown building on the edge of town. Mylah did her best to avoid it because the followers of Hosath tended to be a bit brash. A few weeks prior, one of them followed her halfway home before she was able to convince them she was uninterested in the sanctification.

"The day of sacrifice is nearly upon us! Hosath and Myda are waiting for you!" the older man croaked as a young boy hurried past them on the street. "If you don't make the sacrifice, your soul will die with you!"

Mylah wished her mother would hurry up so they could escape the onslaught of the man's declarations. She knew of few people in Adair who still belonged to the Hall of Hosath. Most of the followers wound up in Hyrdian, the land of the witches and warlocks, which was where Hosath originated. Mylah had never been outside of Adair, let alone across the continent to Hyrdian.

"You ready to head home, Mylah?" Vita stopped beside her, vegetables in a sack slung over her arm. Mylah nodded and they started towards home.

They left the range of the old man's voice and tension eased from Mylah's brow. Now they were surrounded by other villagers, ones who didn't make her as uncomfortable. She felt separate from them, though, because her only friends were the other advisors' children. Yet, she knew most of the shopkeepers by name. Her mother had been friends with a lot of them before she married Emil. Emil was born into an advisor's family, and he never knew any different lifestyle. Vita had lived in the village and worked in her family's shoe store. Her parents had since passed on, and their store had been taken over by another family. Mylah often wondered what it was like for her mother growing up, but she didn't talk about it often.

The one time Mylah asked her mother about her life before Emil, she brushed her off and told her to leave the past in the past. Whether it was shame or something else that kept Vita tight-lipped on the subject, Mylah had no idea, but she never asked her about it again.

That night, Emil noticed Mylah's new treasure.

"Bun, where'd that come from?" He looked pointedly at Vita who did not react.

"Ma picked it out for me, isn't it lovely?"

"Yes, it suits you well. It brings out the blue in your eyes," he said. "What's the occasion, Vita dear?"

"I wanted Mylah to have it," Vita said, holding his gaze.

"I guess Bun deserved a little treat after all the worrying lately. Of course, as do you, Vita." Emil grinned and pulled a box from his jacket pocket. "I picked this up the other day." He opened the box to reveal a ring with a brilliant oval shaped ruby encircled by tiny diamonds.

"Oh, Emil...you shouldn't have," tears sprung into Vita's eyes. "Truly." Emil took Vita's hand in his and placed the ring on her middle finger. "It's stunning."

"A perfect fit for you, my dear."

Mylah envied her parents' relationship and hoped that she could be so lucky to find someone who loved her as much as they loved each other. Though, at fourteen, she had yet to meet anyone who even kept her attention for more than a few seconds.

"Did you have any luck translating the book today?" Vita asked.

Emil shook his head. "None. I sent word to another advisor who helped me last time, but she had no clues for me."

"Why did they pick you to translate it, Pa?" Mylah asked, breaking into the conversation.

"It's a family tradition for Orson's to translate long forgotten languages," he smirked. "I, myself, have had some luck in the past with other works. I guess you could say I have a special skill for it."

"Can you teach me, so I can help too?" Mylah asked, perking up.

"Of course! I'd love for my Bun to take after her Pa and carry on the tradition!" His grin widened. "Come on, let me show you what I've done so far." He pushed away from the table, leaving a half-eaten meal behind. Mylah followed him to his office. "Take a seat." He waved to the armchair behind his desk. Mylah sat in front of the mysterious book.

"First, I like to interpret the title of the book because it will give us insight into the contents. From what I've seen in past texts, this is the original language of the shreeve. There are probably few, if any, alive that would be able to read it."

"So how are *you* supposed to be able to read it then?" Mylah would never think it possible if she didn't know how brilliant her father could be.

"I need to figure out a few of the characters' meanings and hopefully the rest will start to fall into place. Though, it could take months, or even years for that," he sighed. "That's why it's so important to spend as much time as I can working on this."

"What if you were able to find someone who still knew the language, or at least, had an understanding of it?" Mylah asked, tracing the whorls on the cover with her pinky.

"Well, that would speed up the process, for sure."

"So, we should be asking everyone for help with this." Mylah glanced up at him and noticed his skin pale as her words.

"No," Emil said forcefully, alarming Mylah. "No one but the advisors and the king can know that we have this. If the wrong person found out, we could be in trouble. This must remain a secret, Bun, understand?"

"Yes, Pa." She sat up straighter and clasped her hands in front of her.

"Here." He placed another book on the desk. "Start comparing the characters from this book to that one and let me know if you find any commonalities."

Mylah poured all her focus into the books, excited to be helping her father with such an important task. She scribbled down every similarity she spotted, trying to be as productive as possible. She wanted to be the one to figure out the puzzle that was the shreeve language and couldn't wait to see the look of pride on her father's face. Finally, Vita came into the room and closed the books in front of Mylah.

"Come, Mylah. It's time for bed. You can continue in the morning." Mylah responded with a yawn and headed to her room, dragging her feet as she went. She paused before her door as Vita's voice floated towards her from Emil's study.

"We shouldn't be keeping that in the house," she said.

"Just a few more days, dear," Emil spoke through a yawn. Mylah turned away from the conversation and pushed her door shut. She flopped onto her bed, closed her eyes, and let sleep overtake her.

Three

"Pa! Look!" Mylah jumped out of the leather armchair in excitement. "These ones match!" Emil leaned over the desk and inspected Mylah's discovery. They had been hard at work all morning in Emil's study trying to translate the shreeve book. Mylah never felt more at home than in her father's study, surrounded by books. It was small, but fit Emil's desk and two bookcases while leaving room for his chair and Mylah's that she often dragged in from her own room.

"Good job, Bun." He wrote down the character in his notebook. "Now, do you know what letter that character represents?"

Mylah glanced down sheepishly. "No."

"I didn't expect you to. This is a newer, though still unused language of the shreeve," he said, gesturing to the book that he'd translated many years prior. "Do you know the main purpose for the original language that the shreeve created?" Emil asked, and Mylah shook her head. Her cheeks heated at the thought that she hadn't been taught something that was so important to her father.

"Not to worry, Bun, it isn't widely acknowledged by our people. But, as you should know, the shreeve themselves were created by the witch Ailsa to garner peace between the fae and humans."

"I was taught that!" Mylah chirped, her eyes lighting with excitement. "They are a combination of human and fae, taking traits from both people. Like, shreeve are fast and strong like the fae, and some have magic!"

"You are correct! Of course, the first shreeve created knew that they were meant to keep the peace. But, as time went on, and the shreeve population grew, they began to want more than to be peacekeepers." Emil nestled into the back of his chair, making himself more comfortable.

"How come?"

"You tell me. Would you be okay if I told you that you had to give up any dreams of becoming anything other than a peacekeeper?"

"I guess I wouldn't like that much. I want to be a council member, like you and Mother."

"Well, the shreeve wanted something different too. So, they created a language that only they could understand so that they could begin organizing a revolution to break free from the kingdoms that held their contracts. It ended up working, and they gained their freedom, but they no longer had use for the language, which is in this book." He pointed to the book they were translating. "It changed over time, to what we're looking at now." He moved his hand to the already translated book.

"I get it!" Mylah grinned.

"I translated this book several years before you were born with the help of a shreeve from Elowyn." Mylah gaped at him. "Strange, isn't it? We used to interact with them more frequently and on better terms. They're not all as bad as you've been led to think." Mylah scrunched her nose, finding that hard to believe after all the stories she'd been told.

"Who was it that helped you?" she asked.

"His name was Wren. I met him while exploring the Unbound territory." Emil's eyes drifted to the book he'd previously translated, and a smile tugged at his lips as if some happy memory had surfaced for him.

"What did he look like?" Mylah broke him out of his reverie.

"Quite tall, a whole head taller than myself. He had a deep burnt-red iris surrounded by orange. His eyes were a lively sunset color. It was quite hard to get used to. He also had the blue and green markings on his skin, which was the same color as ours, pale and creamy," he chuckled. Mylah was in awe listening to him talk about the shreeve. "He had one distinctive marking on his neck, it appeared bird-like in shape, and when he turned his head, it would stretch so that it looked like its wings were flapping. That's how he got his name, Wren."

"Wow." Mylah's eyes widened in awe as she imagined Wren.

"I want you to remember that if you ever come across a shreeve, they are not people to be feared." Emil's voice lowered and his facial features pinched together, creating a stern look that had Mylah straightening her back.

"But they are killing our people!" she protested.

"The action of one is not to be blamed on an entire race. Sometimes when we show kindness to others, they will return it in ways we may not expect. Kindness is not weakness, kindness breeds strength and understanding."

Mylah chewed the inside of her cheek as she considered her father's words.

"Anybody want some lunch?" Vita poked her head into the office.

"Yes, please!" Emil jumped up and followed Vita into the kitchen, all residual seriousness of his conversation with Mylah gone.

After lunch, Emil and Mylah picked up where they left off with his story.

"So, how did you meet Wren?" Mylah asked as she scoured the pages in front of her.

"Exploring in the Unbound territory with Garrick Callister, actually." Emil leaned back in his chair. Garrick was Greyson's father. "We met a lot of interesting characters out there. Mermaids, sprites, pixies, and a few shreeve."

"I remember the stories you used to tell me about mermaids." He used to tell them as bedtime stories when she was younger.

"Yes, well most of those stories were rooted in truths." His eyes glimmered with mischief. "Garrick and I had quite the adventures in the Unbound territory when we were young."

"I'd love to hear more of those stories," Mylah said.

"Another time, right now we have to focus." He tapped the book in front of Mylah. She shook her head but went back to work.

Mylah poured all her focus into the book. After a few hours, she had a page full of notes that had her more confused than ever. Basic words like 'tree,' 'book', 'yellow', and 'day' were all she'd been able to decipher with the help of Emil's past translations. Nothing made much sense and it caused Mylah's head to pound from a tension headache.

"Emil, darling, Garrick is here for you," Vita said as she appeared in the doorway, jolting both Mylah and Emil from their intense focus. Mylah let out a breath of relief and the tension in her head eased slightly as her eyes left the book.

"Ah, yes. I nearly forgot he mentioned he might stop by today." Emil stood from his chair, stretching his limbs, and cracking his neck. He started to leave the room, but doubled back, making Mylah glance up at him. "Why don't you take a break from those books for a bit? Come sit with Garrick and I, maybe I can convince him to help tell some of those stories you were asking about." Mylah hopped out of her chair.

"Okay!" She followed him out of the room, and they sat at the kitchen table with Garrick while Vita prepared tea for them all.

Mylah was used to Garrick stopping by. He and Emil had been best friends since childhood. As she studied him sitting across from her, she noticed how much Greyson had begun to look like him. Greyson's older brother Crane had always been the spitting image of Garrick, with his strong, square jaw; russet-colored hair; dark green eyes; and broad, commanding shoulders. But, for much of his life, Greyson mostly resembled his mother. He'd inherited her hair color, her eye color, her less pronounced jawline, and slenderer frame, though he'd begun to slowly fill it out.

"How is the job coming along?" Garrick asked Emil, remaining vague. Mylah assumed it was in case someone was listening in, but she couldn't imagine anyone spying on them in their home.

"We've made some progress, not much, but it's better than nothing," Emil explained, helping Vita unload the tea cart onto the table. "Here, help yourself." He pushed a cup over to Garrick and set the teapot in the center of the table, along with the honey.

"I've been readying Greyson for war. I can feel it coming." Garrick leaned back in his chair with his full cup, sipping it slowly. "Crane enlisted in the king's army a few months back, the day he turned eighteen. He'll be sent to the outpost along our border with Elowyn."

"Elena must be a wreck," Vita chimed in as she sat down. "I know I would be if it were Mylah."

"Thankfully, he'll only be gone for a week at a time, once a month. They have enough manpower that they can rotate shifts frequently," Garrick explained.

"Not so bad then, that's good," Emil said as he swirled honey into his tea.

"But those men died..." Mylah murmured. She knew Crane well from spending so much time with Greyson and she worried for his safety. Vita gave Mylah a withering stare, making her blush and realize her error. Garrick needed reassurance, not reminders of the danger his son would be in.

"I'm sorry," Mylah said, casting her eyes down to the table.

"Don't be," Garrick waved off her apology. "Crane knows what he's getting himself into. He is a smart boy; I know he'll be fine."

"Do you remember the time we fought a troll?" Emil cut in, changing the subject. Garrick grinned and let out a low, rumbling laugh.

"How could I forget? I nearly lost an arm saving you from being lunch!" Garrick bellowed and he and Emil burst out into laughter. Vita watched them, smiling, and Mylah's heart swelled with happiness.

"Can you tell me about it?" she asked, and Garrick raised an eyebrow at Emil.

"Well, it's quite the story..." he began. "See, your father and I weren't always as smart and strapping as we are now."

"Don't be humble, Garrick," Vita chided, her lips fighting a smile. She turned her gaze to Mylah. "Your father and Garrick were sought after by all the young ladies in their time."

"Oh hush, dear. There was never anyone who could have outdone yourself and Elena," Emil said, clasping his hands over hers across the table.

"But that's a story for another time," Garrick cut back in. "Now, as I was saying, not so smart," he said as he pointed to himself and Emil. "We had heard talk of a troll terrorizing some dryads near the lake, and we decided to investigate."

"As it turns out, the stories were true. The troll found us and tried to turn us into lunch," Garrick said, shaking his head.

"If it hadn't been for our mermaid friends, he would have succeeded," Emil added. "They whisked us away to safer waters, and we trudged home to our lovely, understanding wives, living to tell the sordid tale." Mylah watched her mother narrow her eyes at Emil, and her smile widened.

"Yes, so understanding that your father and Garrick each slept outside for a week after that," Vita said, making them all laugh again.

The story went on and morphed into other tales as the sun set. The house was filled with laughter when they finally decided it was time for dinner.

"I should be going, Elena will be wondering whether I was taken by a troll again," Garrick joked. It was strange for Mylah to see him that way when he was usually so serious and reserved. Emil brought out a more lighthearted side in him.

"Thank you for stopping by Garrick. Next time bring Elena and the boys. We can do dinner." Vita hugged him.

He nodded and shook Emil's hand. "Good luck with the king tomorrow," Garrick said. "Let me know if you need anything."

"I will, thank you, Garrick."

Before bed that night, Mylah perched at her window, moonlight trickling through the trees and illuminating the ground beneath her. She gazed into the woods, imagining the Elowyn Kingdom that lay far beyond. She tried to picture Wren and others like him, going about their lives, but she had no idea what a normal day looked like for a shreeve.

"Bun, you should get to bed." Mylah jumped at the sound of her father's voice, her mind's image of Elowyn shattering. "I'm taking you with me in the morning to present our findings to King Florian." Mylah turned towards Emil and saw him leaning against her bedroom door frame.

"Really?" A rush of excitement and nerves washed over her. She'd never talked one on one with the king before. She'd only ever watched him from the upper gallery with Cassia and Greyson. Greyson...she'd forgotten she'd told him they could talk that day. *Oh well, he can wait until tomorrow,* she thought.

"Goodnight, Bun. Create outlandish dreams and tell me all about them." Emil closed her door as he left. Mylah smiled to herself. Her father had started saying goodnight that way when Mylah was eight and having nightmares. He had told her to never be afraid of her dreams because that was the one place that she had complete control. He reminded her every night by telling her to create funny, outlandish, crazy, or lovely dreams. She never quite took control of her dreams, but some nights she had more input than others. She hoped that she would dream of Emil and Garrick's adventures that night. She closed her eyes and fell asleep within minutes.

Mylah woke in the middle of the night to a crash. Her room was pitch black and it disoriented her. Her mind remained groggy, and she thought she was still asleep when her door flew open. Vita came rushing in, clutching the shreeve book. Her hair was undone and unruly as if she'd just jumped out of bed.

Vita slammed Mylah's door and shoved a chair in front of it before racing to Mylah's window and throwing it open. Vita breathed heavily and the moonlight shining on her revealed her ghostly complexion. Mylah rubbed her eyes, unsure if she was hallucinating. More bangs and crashes came from the other room and Mylah couldn't focus long enough to comprehend what her mother was saying.

"Quick, Mylah." Vita grabbed her arm, pulling her from the bed. "Take this and run to Greyson's house." She shoved the book into Mylah's arms and ushered her towards the window. Mylah could feel her shaking and her heart dropped as she finally understood that she was not imagining things.

"What's going on? Where's Pa?" Mylah asked, her voice still husky from sleep.

"No time for questions, my love. You must go." Emil began shouting in the other room and Mylah thought she heard a loud grunt.

"Are you coming with me?" she asked her mother.

"I need to make sure you won't be followed." Mylah's door opened but banged against the chair Vita had moved in front of it. "Go now!" Vita ushered Mylah out the window. Mylah was thankful that their house was one story, because she was barely able to catch herself as she dropped the short distance to the ground. The jolt woke her fully. Once she righted herself, she ran. She looked back in time to see her mother shutting the window.

After a moment, Vita turned, and a shadow loomed over her. Mylah sprinted to the closest tree and hid herself behind it. She peeked around the tree to see a man standing where her mother had been. The moonlight reflected off his eyes. Orange surrounding a gray iris; a shreeve. Mylah concealed herself again. When she struck up the courage to look back, he was gone. Her heart pounded so hard in her chest she assumed it would burst.

Mylah ran until she reached Greyson's house. She banged furiously on the front door, glancing over her shoulder every few seconds to be sure no one followed her.

The door flung open and revealed Garrick scowling down at her.

"What's the meaning of this?" He scanned Mylah who stood trembling before him, clutching the book, and his expression changed from annoyance to worry.

"The shreeve..." she began but couldn't finish. Once Garrick saw the book, he understood and ushered Mylah inside. Everything still had a surreal, dreamlike quality to it, even though Mylah knew she was awake. It muted her fear and kept her from panicking.

"Quickly," Garrick said, closing the door and leading Mylah into the sitting room where the rest of his family gathered, dazed and still half asleep.

"Mylah?" Greyson said, rubbing the sleep from his eyes.

"Crane, get your bow and head up to the roof. Shoot anything that moves," Garrick ordered, and Crane responded with a nod, leaving the room to follow his directive. "Greyson, take Mylah to the safe room and do not come out until I tell you." He gave Mylah a light push towards Greyson who took her arm and led her away.

"Elena, join them in the safe room. I'm going to sound the alarm," Mylah heard as Greyson steered her to a solid iron door. He opened it with some effort. Elena came up behind them and herded them inside. It was a room with no windows and all iron walls. Greyson closed them in the room and slid four locks into place, sealing them inside.

"Can you tell us what happened, dear?" Elena asked, reaching out to place her hand on Mylah's arm. Her hand was clammy and Mylah flinched away from the touch. "Take your time." Elena pulled her hand back and Mylah noticed it shaking. Elena clasped her hands in her lap to try to hide her unease, but it was written all over her face. Mylah looked away from her, she had enough going on in her own mind to worry about Elena.

Mylah wasn't even sure what *had* happened. Everything was a blur. She had no idea if her parents were alive, and what was real or imagined. She kept praying she'd wake up from the nightmare any second.

A wailing sound rose in the distance, barely audible in the solid iron room. Mylah knew what it meant: an invasion. The alarm had never been triggered in Mylah's lifetime. Tears slid down her cheeks as the three of them remained sitting in silence. Greyson sat pressed against her left side, lending her a small amount of comfort. Mylah turned into him and muffled her sobs against his shoulder.

Once the alarm stopped, Elena deemed it safe to exit the iron room. Garrick and Crane reentered the house soon after. Being in their house felt all wrong to Mylah. She should be home with her parents.

"Is it alright if I go home now?" she asked. Garrick exchanged a wary glance with Elena.

"You should rest, dear," Elena tried to divert the conversation.

"Yes, at home. I want to go home," Mylah demanded, her body shaking as she clutched the book to her chest.

"Unfortunately, you won't be able to go home tonight, Mylah," Elena clarified, causing anger to rise inside of Mylah.

"Why not? What about my parents? Where are they?" Mylah knew the answers, but she refused to acknowledge them.

"Mylah, dear, I'm so sorry." Elena looked to Garrick for help.

"They were killed," Garrick said, causing a weight to drop in Mylah's stomach.

"No..." She shook her head. "No, they can't be dead." A lump formed in her throat, and tears welled in her eyes, but she blinked them away. Her parents were alive, there was no reason to cry.

"I'm so sorry, Myles." Greyson placed his hand on her shoulder.

"Don't touch me," Mylah growled. Greyson stepped back, hurt flickering in his eyes. Mylah didn't have time to feel bad for her harshness. "I need to see them."

"I don't think that's such a good idea..." Garrick began.

"I need to see them," Mylah said more forcefully.

"Just take her Garrick. The girl deserves to see her parents one last time," Elena said. She took the book from Mylah's arms. "But we will keep this safe here while you're gone." The relief that flowed through Mylah as the weight from the book was removed from her arms almost brought fresh tears to her eyes. Her arms had begun to ache from how tightly she had clutched the book.

"Fine, let's go. Elena, keep an eye out, if you hear anything suspicious, go with Greyson back into the safe room. Crane," Garrick turned to Crane. Mylah hadn't noticed him in the sitting room gripping his bow. "Follow and keep watch. They didn't find the shreeve responsible, he could still be out there."

Mylah approached the front door of her home and her breath caught in her throat. The door hung awkwardly, broken off one of its hinges. She touched the wood gently and it creaked, threatening to topple completely.

"Are you sure you want to do this?" Garrick asked.

"I'm sure," Mylah lied. She would regret it if she didn't go in there, but she worried that she'd never recover from what she was about to see. Then again, she didn't *want* to recover. She wanted to remember this moment forever, so when she finally found the shreeve responsible and killed him, it would be so much more satisfying.

Inside, all the furniture had been displaced. Mylah went to her father's office first. The bookshelves were bare, and the books littered the floor. A pool of blood leaked out from beneath the desk. Mylah could see Emil's legs extended out towards the wall, the rest of him concealed by his desk. She remained rooted to her spot. A part of her screamed to run the other way, to get out of the house. But, instead, she took a deep breath and walked around the desk. A sob escaped her as she dropped down beside her father.

"Pa…" she raked her eyes up and down his still, lifeless body. She spotted the wound that had caused the pool of blood. Without realizing it, she lifted her hands to cover the wound on his abdomen. Some part of her felt as if she could make it all disappear if she willed it hard enough. Her eyes closed and she pressed down. *Please, please, please, come back to me…* Her sob broke the silence, and she opened her eyes to find nothing changed.

She lifted her hands to reveal the gash that seemed to be from a sword. He wouldn't have been able to recover even if help had come sooner. Mylah shuddered as she closed his eyes. Leaning down, she kissed his forehead and whispered, "create lovely dreams Pa and tell me…" she choked on the words but forced herself to finish. "Tell me all about them when I see you again." Grief held her there, sobbing over her father's lifeless body.

Mylah had to use the desk as leverage as she pulled herself up from the floor. She had requested the others stay outside but realized she may have to call them to be carried out after she found her mother. She staggered out of the office.

Before venturing any further, Mylah paused to take a deep breath. Her whole body shook, and nausea roiled in her stomach, threatening to spill her guts on the floor. *I can do this*, she told herself, taking the last few steps to her own room, the last place she saw her mother alive.

Vita lay splayed on the floor in Mylah's room. Her eyes were already closed, denying Mylah a final look into the eyes she had inherited and cherished so dearly. Again, Mylah collapsed to the floor, unable to keep her emotions from overtaking her. Her hand flew to her mouth as a sob tore free from her chest, echoing in the silent house.

"Mama," she said through the tears flowing down her cheeks. "I will make things right. I promise." Mylah brushed her mother's hair away from her face. A pool of blood leaked into the floorboards beneath her, but Mylah saw no wound, which meant she had been stabbed in the back. Only a coward would have killed her that way. Rage boiled up inside of Mylah as she hunched over her mother.

"Mylah." Garrick stood in the doorway; his eyes filled with pity. "The collectors are here. It's time to go." The collectors of the dead...word had spread fast. Mylah's heart dropped. She had expected to have more time to say goodbye.

"Okay, I just need one thing." She attempted to stand, but her knees gave out. Garrick reached down and helped her up. She nodded to him in thanks and went to her wardrobe, opening the first drawer. Her sapphire necklace sat on top of her clothes, and she grabbed it. Turning back to her mother, she remembered something else.

"Her ring," Mylah gasped. "She's not wearing it." Mylah half ran, half stumbled to her parents' room and tore through Vita's jewelry. "He took it...the shreeve stole my mother's ring." There were plenty of other possibilities, it could have been lost in the struggle, but Mylah knew in her heart that it was gone.

"Come, Mylah. We don't have time to worry about trinkets," Garrick's voice was soft, but she could tell he grew impatient from the tension in his neck. Mylah glanced around the room one last time and followed him out of her home. She noticed his eyes gleaming and couldn't tell if it was tears or a trick of the light.

Once outside, Mylah doubled over and heaved into the bushes. Garrick and Crane waited for her to finish and said nothing about it while they walked back to their house. Mylah clutched her necklace in her hand so hard the setting of the sapphire cut into her palm and blood dripped between her fingers. She squeezed the necklace tighter, letting the pain center her. In that moment she realized her parents understood the danger they were putting themselves in by having that book in the house. That was why Vita had bought the necklace for Mylah. She had wanted her to have something to remember them by.

"Mama knew..." Mylah murmured, and Garrick turned to her, placing his arm around her shoulders in an attempt to comfort her. She could tell it made him uncomfortable.

"They knew taking on the task of translating the book painted a target on their backs. We had a plan in place in case of this event, but obviously, the shreeve outsmarted us. We'll be ready if they try to come back." Garrick's low voice soothed her, but the words sounded wrong. How could her parents have chosen to put their family at such a high risk? *They wouldn't*...she thought. But they had. *Just a few more days,* her father had said to her mother when she told him it was too dangerous to keep the book in the house... *a few more days.* Too late.

Two days later, Mylah stood beside her parents' graves wearing the necklace. It had left a nice scar on her palm that she hoped would never fade. Everyone else had already left, the funeral long since over. Greyson and Cassia had lingered for a while, but even they were gone now.

The graves lay separate from the rest of the graveyard, under a looming willow tree. It had been Vita's wish to be placed there when she died, and Emil's request had been to be placed wherever Vita wanted. The willow tree had been planted by one of Vita's ancestors, and it had been a favorite spot for her and Emil when they were young and newly in love. The thought of them falling in love under the tree brought a smile to Mylah's face, even though tears still streamed from her eyes.

On the other side of the willow tree, leading back towards the town, was a stretch of forest that separated the dead from the living. At one time, it had been believed that on a full moon, the dead would wander the forest, looking for their loved ones. But, no matter how many times Mylah had snuck out there with Greyson, they never saw any ghosts.

Mylah had officially moved in with the Callisters. Once she turned eighteen, she'd be able to move back into her parents' home, but until then, it would remain empty and untouched.

She knelt between her parents, laying a hand on each of their tombstones, which had yet to be engraved.

"I promise I will find whoever did this, and they will pay." Her vision narrowed as rage welled up inside of her. "They will not get away with this."

"Mylah." King Florian strode into view, two guards trailing him. Mylah stood too fast, and black dots swam in her vision.

"Um, sir, er, I mean King Florian," Mylah floundered as she stood before the king. She had never been alone with him before, let alone been addressed by him directly. In a panic she bowed to him, her hands fluttering at her sides. Every piece of her seemed too awkward and had a mind of its own.

"No need for formalities, it has been a hard day for you." Mylah glanced up at him and saw him attempting to smile, but it came off as more of a sneer. Mylah cringed but tried to cover it up with a cough.

"W-why are you...I mean what do you...I mean..." he stopped her there.

"I'm simply here to offer my condolences," he said, patting her a little too hard on the shoulder. "Though, I did wish to speak with you about your father's work."

"It's all gone," Mylah choked out as the thought of her father brought fresh tears to her eyes.

"Yes, I know. Though you saved the most important piece, the book you brought with you to Garrick's home." A hunger gleamed in the king's eyes causing Mylah to take a step back.

"Y-yes." She glanced around. No one remained in view of the grave besides the king's two guards, and for some reason, that left a hard knot in her chest.

"Whenever you're ready, I'd like for you to continue your father's work on the book," the king said, and Mylah jerked her head up and down in an attempt at a casual nod. "There's no need to be afraid of me, Mylah. I want to keep our people safe, and this book will allow me to do that. Do you understand?"

"I understand."

"Good." The king stepped back among his guards. "If you ever need anything..." he left the sentence open ended as he turned away. Mylah watched him fade into the surrounding trees and fell to her knees once more as relief at his departure overtook her.

Four

At the next council meeting, King Florian declared war on the Elowyns. If any were to step foot into Adair, they would be killed on sight. Though the declaration brought Mylah no sense of retribution, she did breathe a bit easier knowing that border patrols would be increased, and new bases would be set up along the borders. There was originally one outpost on each border of Adair, but they were building three more along the Elowyn border.

Mylah longed for the day she'd be able to join Adair's army and do her part in protecting the kingdom. When Garrick wasn't schooling her and the boys, Mylah spent all her free time training in combat, stealth, and politics. Cassia joined her some days, but she wasn't planning on entering the army as Mylah was. The shreeve book sat untouched in the iron room at Garrick and Elena's house. Mylah couldn't stand to look at it, let alone attempt to continue translating it. Every day she feared the king would show up again to push her to work on the book, but he never did. He kept his word that she could wait until she was ready.

Two years passed at a snail's pace, each day allowing Mylah's rage to boil down deep into her until it was a pinprick compared to what it had been, but any time she needed it, it came rushing back to the surface. The day after the second anniversary of her parents' deaths, there was a council meeting. Mylah had quit sneaking out with Greyson and Cassia after her parents died. She clung to every bit of information thrown her way regarding Elowyn and the shreeve. Someday she would exact her revenge, even if it took her whole life to do it, and she needed all the leverage she could get.

At the council meeting, the king seemed particularly giddy. He didn't show emotion often, so it surprised Mylah when he walked in wearing a grin. Even the queen, who never showed much interest in their meetings, wore a slight smirk.

"What do you think that's about?" she whispered to Greyson on her left.

"Who knows what goes on inside that man's head?" Greyson murmured back.

"Welcome, my council," King Florian opened his arms wide, addressing the entire room. "Today I bring you interesting news," he paused, letting the anticipation build, though Mylah already brimmed with it. "King Haldor of Elowyn is dead." A collective gasp echoed through the chamber. Mylah's face heated as her buried rage simmered to the surface. He had been the one to issue the order to kill her parents.

"There is no word on *how* he died, only that it happened in the Unbound territory," the king continued talking while Mylah considered the information. A mysterious death... she didn't know much about the

Unbound territory, other than from the stories her father used to tell her of his adventures there. There was a whole host of creatures who lived in the Unbound territory who could be responsible for King Haldor's death.

In the weeks following the announcement, King Florian became less enthused by King Haldor's death. The new king, King Castien, the old king's stepson, retaliated against the Unbounds by claiming a portion of their land in the name of the Elowyns. He also recruited or enslaved Unbound creatures to work in his castle. Sprites began being used as lie detectors, making it necessary for all of Adair's council members to be skilled in lying. Hosath forbid any of them were ever apprehended by the Elowyns, they'd be able to keep Adair's secrets. King Florian hired a few sprites of his own to help in the training. Mylah dreaded the training at first because she'd always been a terrible liar. But, with time, it became easier.

Knowing that Elowyn had a new king who seemed to be more despicable than the last renewed Mylah's sense of duty to avenge her parents. She realized the best way to do that would be to translate the shreeve book and find information to help Adair gain an advantage in their war against Elowyn. She attempted to translate the book again with Garrick's help. The king was the only one who knew they still had the book and was pleased to hear that they were working on it.

No matter how long Mylah stared at the strange letters and symbols, nothing made any sense. She and Garrick spent two years trying their best to decipher the language to no avail. They may have had some luck if the shreeve hadn't taken all Mylah and Emil's notes, along with the book Emil had previously translated.

Mylah was near her breaking point when Garrick suggested they take a few weeks off for her birthday month. She was finally turning eighteen and would be able to join Adair's army. With Greyson and Crane already on the border, Mylah had recruited Cassia to help her more with combat training.

"Nice block," Cassia said. Mylah grinned. After years of training, she felt stronger and more powerful than ever. It was only a matter of time before she'd come face to face with a shreeve and be able to avenge her family.

"Thanks for training with me, Cass." Mylah knew it wasn't Cassia's favorite pastime, but she did it for her friend. Cassia had become almost as skilled as Mylah with her sword, but her heart wasn't in it.

"Have you heard from Greyson?" Cassia asked. Mylah smirked and knew who Cassia was *really* interested in hearing about.

"Crane sent word from the border that they're both well and can't wait to come home for my birthday."

"Oh, that's good." Cassia's shoulders relaxed and her eyes brightened. Before the troops were sent to the border, Cassia had spent a lot of time at the Callisters' visiting Mylah. She had grown fond of Crane in that time, but then he'd had to leave to join the border patrols. The border was a six-hour journey, so it was a bit of a hassle to come home too often, and they could only leave with permission from their commander. Greyson hadn't been home since he'd left two months ago.

"Come on, Cass. Let's get lunch."

That afternoon, Mylah worked on perfecting her ability to lie. As she'd learned, the sprites could pick up on the small changes that happened when a person lied. For instance, their heart rate might increase, or they may start to sweat, or have a nervous tick. Some of which anyone may learn to detect, but because of the sprites' size, they'd developed a much stronger sense of hearing than any other creature as a defense mechanism. They could hear a change in breathing, heart rate, or even small movements that were undetectable by sight.

"What is your name?" A sprite flitted at Mylah's shoulder.

"Leylah Farrow," Mylah lied smoothly.

"And where do you come from?" the sprite continued. When they had first started their sessions two years earlier, it was hard not to be distracted by the absurdity of the situation. The sprite, whose name was Bellingham, was about as tall as Mylah's forearm. His voice was deep, but also squeaky at times because of his size. His wings were sheer and beat a small breeze past Mylah's ear.

"The Kingdom of Umbra."

"Not bad," Bellingham said. "Try a more complicated lie. What are King Florian's plans?"

"I don't know, I've never been to Adair."

"And what of King Aeron's plans, will he send troops from Umbra to aid Adair if fighting breaks out?"

"I am not on the council. I know nothing of any plans." Mylah kept her heart rate steady and her facial expressions neutral, as she'd been taught.

"Impressive, Mylah. You've come far. What do you think?"

"I'm not Mylah, I'm Leylah," she corrected, and Bellingham smirked.

"Good girl." They continued to practice for another half hour, until Garrick came into the room. He had become a father figure for Mylah. He could never replace Emil, but he cared about Mylah and had taken her in without hesitation.

"It's time for our meeting with King Florian," he told her. Four years ago, that would have been strange to hear. Now, Mylah was used to it. She was always being called in to report on her progress with translating the book, even though her report was always the same: nothing so far.

"Okay. Let me change out of my training clothes and we can go."

Left alone in the room, Mylah changed into her dark, forest green Adairian uniform. The pants clung to her legs, which was meant to keep them from snagging on branches out in the wild. The top was a button up long sleeve, that also fit snuggly. The boots she had to wear were black and covered half of her calf. Lacing them was a chore. She tucked her necklace under her shirt.

Garrick and Mylah walked side by side towards the castle gardens in their matching uniforms.

"We're wasting our time," Mylah hissed as they entered the gardens.

"We have to respect the king's wishes," Garrick sighed.

"It's been four years." Four years since her parents were killed. Four years since she vowed her revenge. Four years of no progress.

"I know, Mylah." Garrick's face betrayed his frustrations. He would never go against the king, but Mylah knew he understood her annoyance.

King Florian waited for them among the rosebushes. He wore his usual flowing green robes, but he wasn't wearing his crown for once, which surprised Mylah. She'd noticed he liked to use any opportunity to remind those around him of his status, and theirs. Mylah and Garrick bowed in unison as they approached him.

"King Florian," Garrick said.

"Garrick, Mylah." The king inclined his head to them in greeting. "Let's take a walk, and please update me on your progress." As they walked, Mylah noticed armed guards stationed at every exit. They were there to protect the king, but it still sent a shiver through her. In the time since the king declared war on Elowyn, the number of guards in the castle had nearly tripled. Though, Elowyn seemed to have given up on retrieving the book.

"Mylah and I have been working on translating the book every night, sir. We're making little progress," Garrick started.

"As I've said before – my father had a whole translated book of the shreeve language that was stolen the night of..." Mylah gulped. "The night he died. Along with all of his notebooks. If we could find someone to help us with the translation, maybe an Unbound creature..."

The king cut her off. "It's too dangerous. King Castien controls the Unbound territory now. If word reached him about what we're trying to do, I fear we'd face another attack like the first." Mylah knew he was right, but it didn't change the fact that they needed to do *something*. After the attack on her house, they spread the word that the shreeve book had gone missing, even to the advisors. Mylah, the Callisters, and the king were the only ones who knew the truth. But they were never going to make any progress without any help. They were out of options.

"We'll keep trying," Garrick promised, but the king raised his hand to stop him from continuing.

"It's not good enough," the king said, bowing his head, and taking a deep, steadying breath. Mylah clenched her jaw and her hands balled into fists at her sides. "I've devised a new plan."

"What?" Mylah let slip before she could stop herself. Garrick nudged her with his elbow.

"Please elaborate," Garrick said.

"I have received word that the shreeve may be planning to take over all of Adair," the king paused for effect. Mylah and Garrick glanced towards each other, masking their reactions.

"This is something that we have feared for some time. Our best course of action will be to send someone to infiltrate the Elowyn kingdom. We need intelligence on the inside to alert us to any current plans they may have and to help us progress in our task of translating the book." As Mylah listened, she realized the plan would be the perfect opportunity for her to find who had killed her parents and fulfill her promise to avenge their deaths.

"What do you expect of us, your majesty?" Garrick sounded wary, while anticipation built in Mylah.

"I would request that Mylah is sent to infiltrate the kingdom."

"Out of the question," Garrick responded before Mylah could speak for herself.

"I will do it," she spoke loud and clear, talking over Garrick's protestations.

"I understand your concern, Garrick, but Mylah turns eighteen tomorrow, and she can decide for herself." The king turned his gaze to Mylah, speaking directly to her. "I want you to know the risk involved and the preparations required before you agree to this." Mylah didn't need to hear anymore, but she decided to humor him.

"In preparation you will be deprived of your normal luxuries. No training, other than with Bellingham. He will be the one to determine if you will be able to step foot in Elowyn. You will learn to go without food for long stretches so you can learn to adapt your body to be prepared for any circumstances; imprisonment, getting lost in the Unbound territory, or worse."

"We are counting on the Elowyn kingdom to take pity on you for having been cast out into the Unbound territory. That is how you will enter their kingdom. It will be on *you* to fend for yourself and find your way to the Elowyn border to beg for mercy. That is where the real trial begins. There is no guarantee they will take mercy on you – so it must be convincing. If they do accept to help you, you'll most likely be brought to the sprites for questioning, so your lies must be flawless. If you pass that test, we assume you'll then be brought before the king who will make the final decision as to whether you will live or die." Mylah took it all in. "No human who has gone into Elowyn has ever been seen again."

"I understand the risk involved and I am ready for any preparation I need to be sent behind enemy lines," Mylah answered.

"I should be the one to do it," Garrick argued.

"Who do you think they will be more likely to suspect as a spy," the king cocked an eyebrow at Garrick.

"It has to be me," Mylah said.

"You and I know better than anyone why she's perfect for this mission." The king gave Garrick a knowing look. Mylah knew he referred to her knowledge of the shreeve book. No one else in their kingdom knew of it or was as familiar with it as her.

"King Florian, I don't believe Mylah should go. It's far too dangerous. There are so many things that will be left to chance. Is it really worth risking anyone's life for?" Garrick tried one last time to voice his objection.

"I will be sure that every precaution is taken while we plan Mylah's venture. If we determine it poses too great a risk, she won't go. Trust me," the king said. Garrick remained wary, but he sighed with acceptance.

"This is a lot to consider," he said. "Can she have a few days to think about it?"

"Of course."

"I want to do it. I don't need to think about it. I will do it," Mylah said, her voice rising in agitation. All she could think about was her parents, lying six feet down in a grave. This was her best chance to find who had killed them and repay the favor.

"Good. You'll begin preparations the day after tomorrow. Tell no one the details of this mission. Even the rest of the council will be kept on a need-to-know basis. Everyone must believe you are still going to join the outpost at the Unbound border." King Florian rose from his throne. "I will see you both tomorrow." He left them alone in the garden, his guards following him into the castle.

"You don't have to do this, Mylah. There are plenty of others who would be willing..." Garrick began, but Mylah cut him off.

"You know I do. I know the shreeve book backwards and forwards. I know who to talk to about the language, and what to look for," Mylah said.

"This isn't about the book, though. I know you too well." Garrick crossed his arms as he stared her down.

"Fine, you're right. I want to find who killed my parents. But that's a bonus to everything else I'll be doing for our kingdom." Mylah didn't try to hide her true motives from Garrick. If anyone would understand, it would be him.

"I need you to promise me that you will not put yourself or this mission at risk to find that man. Your parents would want you safe above all else."

"Fine, I won't." Lying came too easily to Mylah since she'd started training with Bellingham. She purposefully avoided making a promise. She could not guarantee what she would do when she found her parents' killer. Her response appeased Garrick, though.

"Come. We should get home before Elena begins to worry." Garrick led the way out of the castle.

That night at dinner they ate in a comfortable silence. Mylah's mind still reeled from the king's proposal. Though she had accepted his mission, she had begun to consider whether he also had ulterior motives for sending her. Why now, after all this time? What had changed? The threat of the shreeve attacking had been looming over them since her parent's deaths, that was nothing new.

Garrick's mind seemed equally occupied as he stared off into the corner most of the meal, his face unreadable.

Elena was in a state of bliss knowing that her boys would be home in less than twenty-four hours.

When a knock on the door reverberated through the house, they all jumped. Garrick motioned to Mylah who was already in motion, her heart racing as she headed for the safe room with Elena right on her heels. They kept the book there whenever they weren't studying it. Any time an unannounced visitor showed up, they took every precaution so that the night of her parents' deaths would not be repeated.

Before they made it to the safe room, a voice called through the front door. "It's us!" Elena squealed with delight and ran to the door, beating Garrick there. Mylah followed to the entryway and smiled at the happy reunion. Elena had Crane and Greyson wrapped in a tight embrace and Garrick smiled for once.

"You're early!" Elena said as she finally released them.

"Our replacements showed up early, so the commander gave us the okay to head home," Crane explained.

"Myles," Greyson greeted her as he stepped through the door. He grinned as she threw her arms around him. "I missed you, too," he chuckled.

"I can't believe it's already been two months," she said as she pulled away. She'd missed training with Greyson and sneaking out of the house on warm nights to swim in the lake. Since he'd left, she'd had to endure those long nights alone. Cassia had always been too afraid to sneak out with them.

Crane walked over and pulled Mylah into a hug. Even though he'd left to protect their borders a few months after Mylah had moved in, they'd still become close in that time and during his visits since. She saw Crane and Greyson as brothers.

"Well don't just stand there, come join us for dinner! I made plenty for everyone." Elena ushered them all into the dining room, making plates for Greyson and Crane as they settled in at the table. Mylah leaned against the wall, having already finished her meal and too antsy to sit.

"How was the ride home?" Garrick asked, pride radiating from him as he watched his two boys. Mylah studied them as well. In four years, Greyson had filled out his string bean form with muscle and he'd grown taller. He now had to look down when he talked with Mylah. But since she'd seen him two months ago, he'd changed even more. His gaze was more intense and a little haunted, that innocence that used to sparkle there had extinguished. The thought tugged on Mylah's heart, but she kept a smile plastered on her face.

Greyson and Crane appeared weary from their journey and had mud caked to their pant legs. Otherwise, they seemed well.

"Not so bad," Greyson answered, his eyes flicking to Crane who had covered his mouth to hold in a laugh.

"Not so bad...except for the bats you mean?" Crane said, raising an eyebrow, still trying not to laugh.

"Bats?" Garrick asked, unable to stop himself from smiling along with Crane.

"It was nothing," Greyson muttered, and Crane guffawed.

"Thought they were a hoard of pixies coming to terrorize us," Crane joked. "You should have seen his face as he fell flat on his arse off that horse..." Crane couldn't stop laughing at the memory.

"Come now," Garrick spoke through his own laughter. "I'm sure it's rough being out there so long. Leaves you on edge."

"Thank you," Greyson said as he smacked Crane's arm. "That's what I tried to tell him." Mylah smiled, warmed by the fact that Greyson and Crane's personalities hadn't changed since they left.

It was like old times that night and Mylah basked in the glow of it. Everything felt right again, as if the boys had never left. Elena was in her prime – fussing over Greyson's hair that needed a trim, and Crane's thinner frame. She shoved multiple plates of food at them both and they accepted them with gusto.

"So, have you seen any action on the border yet?" Garrick asked as Greyson and Crane finished eating.

"Not really," Crane said. "There is a constant patrol along the Elowyn border, as there has been since..." his eyes flicked to Mylah, and he didn't finish his sentence. "But the shreeve keep to their side, and we keep to ours. It's like they're holding back for some reason."

"It may have something to do with whatever's in that stupid book," Mylah muttered. "I wish I had my pa's notes so I could finish what we'd started."

"Don't be hard on yourself," Garrick said. "You may be right though about it keeping the shreeve away. So, that's not a bad thing."

"Every once in a while there will be someone who grows bored and strays too far over the border, they don't usually come back," Crane said. "And if they do...well they don't last long," he added.

"That's awful," Elena said, gripping the edge of the table.

"There's nothing we can do about it. If Elowyn wanted to attack, they would demolish us. Whatever's holding them back, be it the book or something else, I'm grateful." Crane sat back and put his hand on his stomach. "That was delicious, Ma. Thank you."

"We could put up a good fight," Greyson chimed in.

"You know what I mean." Crane waved off his words and left the table to do the dishes.

Mylah understood the king's urgency when it came to translating the book. If it was truly the only thing that would save them from being wiped out by the Elowyns, then she had to make sure to do everything in her power to decipher the old language.

The following morning, Mylah trained with Greyson and Crane, surprising them both with her ability to keep up and out parry them with her sword.

"You've been slacking," Mylah joked.

"We'll be lucky to have you joining the border patrols next week," Crane said, sparking a strange look in Greyson's eyes.

"So, you're still planning on joining the king's army?" Greyson asked.

"Obviously," Mylah said, feeling guilty she hadn't told them about the king's plan, but she'd promised to tell no one.

Mylah put her sword back on the weapons rack. She'd practiced with all the weapons there – swords, throwing knives, bow and arrows, axes, and spears.

"I've been training for this for years, I'm ready."

"Most definitely. You're better trained than most of the men out there," Greyson said, rolling his eyes. "You'd think most of them had never held a weapon in their lifetime."

"Most probably haven't, Grey," Crane pointed out. "We got lucky. As children of an advisor, we've had access to this training room anytime we want. Everyone else in the village has to make do with their own weapons and training areas."

"Mylah?" Cassia's voice interrupted their conversation. She appeared in the doorway a moment later, smiling brightly when she saw them all. "There you are!" Mylah watched as a blush crept up Crane's neck. His eyes followed Cassia as she hurried towards Mylah. Cassia glanced his way and nodded to him. The interaction seemed so strange to Mylah, it wasn't like she didn't *know* they had feelings for each other, even though they'd never made it public.

"What is it, Cass?" Mylah reached out to take her hand.

"Our gowns are ready for tomorrow." Mylah had forgotten about the dress she'd had made to wear for her birthday ball at the castle. It was tradition on a council member's eighteenth birthday for a royal ball to be thrown.

"Right. I guess we better head to the dress shop," Mylah said, though she'd rather continue training with the boys. "See you later." She waved to them as she and Cassia left the training room.

At the dress shop, Mylah and Cassia tried on their gowns one last time. Cassia had chosen a powder blue ball gown with sheer, off the shoulder, long sleeves. It complimented her skin tone beautifully.

Mylah's dress was a sapphire blue, strapless gown with silver embroidery decorating the bodice, and a sparkling tulle that covered the skirt. When she moved in the light it made the sparkles look like stars in the night sky. She chose the dress color to match her necklace, so she felt as if her mother had played a role in helping her pick out her gown.

"Oh, Myles, you look stunning!" Cassia had her hands on Mylah's shoulders and gazed into her eyes. Mylah realized tears had formed in her own eyes and wiped them away.

"That gown truly fits you beautifully," Sissany said, appearing from the back room as she held out a shawl to Mylah. "Take this as well, it's bound to be chilly tonight." Mylah took the shawl and hugged Sissany. The days were still warm enough that the shawl seemed unnecessary at the moment, but the nights had begun to cool down as the leaves began to change colors. They hardly ever had to worry about snow, that usually only happened in the mountains, but it could get quite chilly at night in the fall and winter. Mylah would want an extra layer that night.

"Thank you for everything," she murmured in Sissany's ear before breaking their embrace.

"Your mother would be so proud of you," Sissany told her before leaving her alone with Cassia again. Mylah took a deep breath and turned back towards Cassia.

"Tomorrow night will be our last chance for fun before you leave me to join the king's army," Cassia said, wrinkling her nose. "You're sure you want to go?"

"Why does everyone keep asking me that? I've been waiting four years for this. I'm sure." Mylah lifted her skirts as she stepped down from the small platform in front of the mirror.

"I know. I'm being selfish. I'll have to make new friends once you're gone, I guess." Tears glistened in Cassia's eyes.

"Oh, Cass." Mylah pulled her into an embrace. "I'll write every week, and I'll come visit every chance I get." The lie came out too easily and guilt formed a hard knot in Mylah's stomach.

"I know, Myles."

Five

The next morning, Mylah sat in the lower gallery of the council's chambers for the first time. Cassia and Greyson flanked her again, and everything felt right. She could hardly sit still with her excitement that she was eighteen and officially among the council members of the king's court.

"What do you think the king will talk about today?" Cassia asked, sounding bored already. "I hope it doesn't go on too long, I have a lunch date with Crane." Mylah glanced down the row towards Crane who watched the platform that rose above them with anticipation.

"I'm sure there's nothing of great interest to report on today," Mylah said. The king wouldn't be mentioning her mission, since no one else could know about it, unless absolutely necessary.

"There haven't been any big developments on the borders, so he won't have much to say about that," Greyson said as the king strode through the door onto the platform, Queen Aurelia trailing behind him, and took his seat on his throne.

"Thank you for gathering here today," he began as he always did. "As many of you know, there have been some whispers about possible invasions from the Elowyns. I would like to put these whispers to rest and assure you we are doing everything in our power to secure Adair's borders."

"What about the Unbound borders?" someone shouted from the crowd. Mylah scanned the room, noticing Alessia Asmund, Cassia's mother, on the edge of her seat.

"We have resumed our patrols there as well," the king assured them. The patrols along the Unbound border had halted a few weeks back due to a lack of activity. The council had voted to relieve the soldiers there of duty for the time being, giving them time to rest and visit with their families.

"Should we prepare for the worst?" another voice rose from the opposite side of the room.

"There is no need to panic or worry, everything is under control." The authority and confidence the king spoke with had even Mylah believing him. "If anyone has any concerns, or suggestions, feel free to bring them to me privately. However, it is my belief that we are well prepared and have no reason to fear if the shreeve do decide to push in on our borders."

A tension released from the crowd. Mylah gazed around at the faces surrounding her and tried to determine how many of them knew the truth. The shreeve were most likely planning on taking over all of Adair if what the king had told her was true.

"This meeting is adjourned. Anyone who wishes to air any grievances, please remain behind and I will address them." Everyone rose from their seats, no one seeming to have any reason to linger and speak with the king. Mylah and Greyson met up with the rest of the family at their carriage. Cassia waved from beside her parents as she followed them in the opposite direction.

"I think the king is hiding something," Crane said as they waited. Mylah glanced up at him, trying to keep her face neutral.

"Why do you think that?" Greyson asked.

"We've been on the border, there's nothing going on there. I don't know where these *whispers* have been coming from, but it's not us." Mylah pursed her lips, considering Crane's words.

"If the king thinks that there is a threat, then there's a threat," Greyson stated and Crane shrugged, not bothering to argue with his brother. Mylah had to believe that the king was telling the truth, especially since she was about to risk her life to infiltrate the Elowyn kingdom and find out how imminent the supposed threat was.

"Come on, kids." Garrick came up behind them. "Let's go home." He climbed into the carriage, Elena following closely behind him. Crane hopped onto the front of the carriage, taking the reins, as usual. Once Mylah and Greyson were inside, they began rolling down the road towards town.

"What do you think of the threat the king spoke about, father?" Greyson asked. Garrick's eyes flicked to Mylah before he answered.

"I think the king is right to take action, but not to be too concerned yet."

Greyson narrowed his eyes at Garrick.

"You're not telling me something," he said.

"You're too perceptive for your own good," Garrick chuckled. "But you're right. There is something Mylah and I should tell you all, but now is not the time. We will talk at home."

"I knew it!" Greyson shouted, but then he blinked in confusion, furrowing his brows. "Wait, you and *Mylah?*" He turned to her. "*You've* been keeping things from me?"

"I didn't have a choice," she defended herself. "The king made me promise..."

"The king? You have secrets with the king now?" He threw his hands up. "What has happened with this family since I've been gone?"

"Greyson, we will talk at home," Garrick repeated, his tone demanding enough to shut him up. Mylah kept her eyes trained on the floor of the carriage, avoiding Greyson's gaze that burned into her. Garrick stared out the window while Elena attempted to make small talk to fill the awkward silence.

At home, Mylah was bombarded with questions. Garrick fielded most of them, explaining the mission the king had tasked her with and the logistics they knew so far. But the questions from Greyson were less about the mission itself and more about Mylah.

"How could you accept this mission?" If his ears could be steaming, they would have been. "It's too dangerous! You'll be killed on sight!" Mylah clenched her fists at her sides, trying not to yell at him for his nearsightedness.

"I have to do this," she said calmly. "I'm the only one who knows the book and the symbols and can translate it without having it with me."

"That's not a good enough reason," Greyson snapped.

"Greyson," Garrick said in a warning tone. Mylah decided Garrick could handle the rest of Greyson's questions and locked herself in her room to prepare for the ball, allowing Elena in to help her with her hair and makeup. Elena had already finished readying herself while Garrick had been answering Greyson and Crane's questions. Thankfully, Elena didn't ask Mylah anything.

Mylah's mind drifted while Elena brushed through her hair, the rhythmic motions making Mylah feel like she could fall asleep. Every time she thought about living among the shreeve, she panicked. She'd have no familiar faces or places to comfort her. What if they decided not to take mercy on her? What if they imprisoned her? She took a deep breath to calm herself. Her upcoming month in training was meant to prepare her for either of those outcomes. She would not fail; it wasn't an option.

When Elena started putting pins in Mylah's hair, Mylah was wide awake and back in the moment. Pain pricked her scalp from some of the pins. Her hair wound up pulled into a twisty bun, with a few curls left out to frame her face.

Elena lined Mylah's eyes with a kohl liner and put rouge on her cheeks and lips. Then, Elena held out Mylah's dress for her to step into.

"There, you're ready." Elena buttoned the last button on Mylah's dress. "Oh, wait." She grabbed Mylah's necklace from the vanity and clasped it around her neck. "Perfect."

"Thank you, Elena." Mylah gazed up at her in the mirror. "For everything."

"So, you're really going?" Tears welled up in Elena's eyes.

"Yes, I need to."

"I understand, though I wish you wouldn't."

"I'll be okay. I can do it," Mylah was trying to reassure herself as much as Elena.

"I know. You are so much like your father. Though, you have your mother's stubbornness. They'd both be so proud of you, Mylah." Mylah grasped Elena's hand and squeezed it in response, unable to talk over the lump in her throat. "Come on, dear. We should be going. The guest of honor can't be late to her own ball!"

Mylah followed Elena into the sitting room where Garrick, Crane, and Greyson waited. They all stood when Elena and Mylah entered.

"Beautiful girls," Garrick said, giving them one of his rare smiles. "I'll bring the carriage around."

"Stunning, Ma," Crane said. "You too, Myles." Greyson remained silent, but his lips parted, and his eyes slightly widened as he gazed at Mylah. He looked put together and handsome in his uniform. The shocking white of his hair offset his dark uniform brilliantly.

They heard the gravel outside crunching as the carriage pulled up outside and Crane offered his arm to Elena. She took it and let him lead her outside. Mylah was about to follow when Greyson walked over to her and offered her his arm. She took it gratefully.

"I'm sorry about earlier," Mylah said. "I didn't mean to shut you all out. I needed a little time to digest everything." Greyson led her down to the carriage.

"I'm just worried about you, Mylah." He helped her up into the carriage, where Garrick and Elena were already seated. Crane sat in the driver's seat holding the reins.

"Finally talking again?" Garrick raised an eyebrow at Mylah. Elena smacked his arm and said, "Hush, you."

"Yes. I'm ready to answer any questions."

They spent the carriage ride talking over the full plan and all the obstacles Mylah would have to overcome.

"So, what's the story behind why you are going to be cast out of the kingdom?" Greyson asked.

"We haven't come up with that yet," Mylah said.

"I feel like it's an awfully important piece to the whole plan," Greyson pointed out.

"Got any ideas for me?" Mylah nudged his arm.

"Thief, drunk, deserter, take your pick," he teased.

"None of that would result in being cast out," Garrick cut in.

"An attack on the king might," Elena said thoughtfully.

"What?" the rest of them said in unison.

"When I was a young girl, someone plotted an attack on King Lev, King Florian's father. He was cast out into the Unbound territory and anyone who tried to help him would meet the same fate," Elena elaborated.

"But wouldn't an attack on the king warrant someone being put to death?" Greyson asked.

"The council at the time deemed the attacker mentally unwell and saw it as too cruel to put them to death," Elena explained.

"Is it not crueler to cast them out to fend for themselves in the Unbounds?" Mylah pointed out, but Garrick jumped in before Elena could respond.

"That's perfect, Elena!" Garrick surprised them all with his enthusiasm. "We can stage the attack once it's time for Mylah to leave and make sure it's public. That way, word will spread. Crane and Greyson can share the tale with the other soldiers, and eventually word will reach the

Elowyns. It will make her story that much more believable. No one can know your true identity, so we'll be sure no one sees your face."

"Your mind scares me sometimes, dear," Elena said.

"I'll run it by King Florian tonight," Garrick said, ignoring Elena's comment.

"Anything to give me a better chance of being accepted by the Elowyns," Mylah agreed.

As the carriage rolled over the bumpy roads, Mylah gazed out the window. Adair passed by almost too quickly as she tried to memorize every building and person she saw. She would hold onto her memories of home to help get her through the next few months. A peal of laughter caught her attention, and her gaze found a group of children playing tag down a side road. The curtain fluttered closed and Mylah did not reopen it. Tears filled her eyes, but she hid them from everyone else in the carriage, wiping them nonchalantly with the edge of her shawl.

The carriage rolled to a stop. Her nerves started making knots in her stomach. This was her last night of freedom. Tomorrow she would begin preparing for her departure from Adair, and if all went well, she would be in Elowyn in a few short weeks.

Six

Inside the ballroom, people filled every open area. The space had been draped with gauzy tulle and twinkling lights. Mylah gazed around in awe of the view. Tables were placed evenly spaced along the edges of the dance floor. On each table, a large vase of blue dahlias towered over the occupants. Mylah's eyes flicked upwards as a flutter caught her eye. Sprites flitted through the air, some dropping flower petals that danced lazily down to the floor, while others danced around the chandelier.

It seemed half of the village had shown up for Mylah's birthday.

"It's beautiful," she murmured.

"I told them your favorite flower," Greyson said, rubbing the back of his neck. Mylah chuckled and kissed his cheek.

"Thank you." She stepped forward, looking around at all the faces she'd be leaving behind, and fear of the unknown clutched her. She clung onto Greyson's arm trying to calm herself. Even though she wouldn't be leaving Adair for another month, she'd have to remain hidden until then.

Everyone outside of her family had to think she'd left to fight in the war as planned. Cassia hurried over to them, distracting Mylah from her internal panic.

"You both look amazing," Cassia said, but her eyes strayed to Crane who had entered behind them.

"You look amazing yourself, Cass," Mylah said, thankful for Cassia's interruption. Crane dipped his head to Cassia, and she blushed.

"Do you mind if I steal your date for a moment?" Cassia asked Greyson.

He responded, "Not at all" at the same time Mylah said, "I'm not his date." Greyson flushed and stepped away from them, following Crane towards the refreshments table.

"Harsh, Myles," Cassia chided, but she took Mylah's arm and led her away from all the crowds. "I wanted to talk to you before we're too busy because I have a feeling that Greyson is going to finally talk to you tonight...try letting him down easy, would you? He may be all buff and chiseled now, but he's still fragile." Mylah gave her a quizzical stare.

"What do you mean? You're the one he's been pining after since we were twelve," Mylah argued, but Cassia shook her head, causing her loose curls to bounce lightly across her shoulders and back. Mylah noticed Crane watching Cassia and smirked, but then realized something else. Greyson watched *her* with the same lovelorn look Crane wore. Mylah gulped, maybe Cassia was right.

"He may have had a crush on me when we were younger, but he's always loved you, Mylah. I never told you this, but a few days before your parents died, he told me he was going to ask you on a date. He said he tried to at the book shop one day, but you had to leave, and then he didn't see you again until the night your parents died. He didn't think it was a good time to ask you then, and he worried about making you uncomfortable while you were living together. Why do you think he's been so worried about you joining the war?" Cassia sighed. "He can't bear the thought of losing you, Myles."

"I love him too, Cass, but like a brother. I don't know if I could ever see him any other way," Mylah said, her heart breaking for Greyson. She'd always believed it would be Cassia who would have to let him down easy.

"Like I said, be careful, he's fragile."

"He's leaving tomorrow, as long as I'm not alone with him before that, I may not have to let him down at all." Mylah tried to sound hopeful, but if Greyson wanted to talk to her, he would find a way.

"Oh, Mylah, so naïve." Cassia patted her arm. "But I guess you can try to avoid him."

"Don't leave me alone with him, promise?"

"I don't want to see him hurt either. I'll do my best."

"Thanks, Cass."

"Come on, let's rejoin the party." Cassia swept them back through the crowds towards Greyson and Crane.

Mylah was approached by many people, wishing her well and thanking her for joining the king's army. She plastered on a smile, knowing everyone still believed she was simply going to be fighting to defend their borders. Little did they know, she was risking so much more.

She and Cassia were asked to dance on multiple occasions and acquiesced each time. It was actually quite fun for Mylah, getting to know villagers she'd only seen from afar. The final dance was announced, and Crane plucked up the courage to ask Cassia to dance. She agreed without hesitation, breaking her promise to Mylah, and leaving her alone with Greyson.

"Would you like to take a walk?" he asked her once Cassia and Crane started dancing. Mylah was relieved Greyson hadn't asked her to dance but feared a walk may give them a better chance of finding themselves truly alone. But she couldn't refuse him.

He led the way to the gardens they'd always snuck away to during the council meetings. They used to represent freedom for Mylah, but now they seemed desolate and eerie. She paused on the threshold.

"Is everything alright?" he asked.

"I don't want to miss saying goodbye to anyone," she improvised.

"We'll just be a moment; we can head back whenever you want." Mylah took the steps into the garden. As they walked, a static built between them.

Mylah broke the silence. "I can't believe you and Crane are already leaving tomorrow."

"It seems like I was gone for years instead of months," Greyson said. "I missed you."

"I missed you and Crane, too." Mylah took a turn that would lead them back to the ballroom, hoping they could reach it before Greyson said too much more. She was about to take the last step back into the castle when Greyson put his hand on her elbow.

"Mylah, wait. There's something that I've been wanting to tell you." He gazed at her intently. Nausea churned Mylah's stomach. This was it; he was about to tell her that he loved her, and she would have to break his heart.

"Greyson..." she started, and then changed her mind. She couldn't hurt him. "I have to get back inside. We can talk later." She turned away and hurried into the ballroom before he could stop her. Mylah spotted Cassia across the dance floor. The dancing had stopped, and people were beginning to leave. Mylah made it to Cassia and pulled her into an alcove where they wouldn't be overheard.

"So, what happened? I saw you go off with Greyson..." Cassia whispered.

"He was about to say it, and I ran away," Mylah admitted, putting her head in her hands, embarrassed by her cowardice.

"You *ran away?*"

"Well, I told him we could talk later, and then ran away, but yeah."

"Mylah, you can't keep stringing him along like this. He needs to know the truth. He needs to know how you feel so that he can move on," Cassia chided her.

"I'm sorry. I can't do it. Why does it matter anyway? He'll be gone tomorrow and then I'll be leaving shortly after." Even though the thought terrified Mylah, it also brought her a bit of relief, so long as she never had to hurt Greyson.

"But you'll see him on the border, right?" Cassia pointed out, and Mylah remembered that she was still in the dark about Mylah's true destination.

"I've been assigned to a different outpost," Mylah improvised.

"Well, you don't have to tell him, I guess. It may be better he doesn't go back to the frontlines heartbroken," Cassia said, though Mylah could hear the disapproval in her voice.

"Thank you, Cass." Mylah was relieved that she could put off destroying her friendship with Greyson by breaking his heart. Cassia meant well, but Mylah wasn't sure who it would be helping to tell him now.

"I'm staying quiet for Greyson, not you, Mylah. And, if he asks me about you, I'm not going to lie to him." Cassia was upset with her and Mylah understood. She may not be hurting Greyson now, but eventually, he would find out that his feelings were not reciprocated.

That night after the ball, Mylah stayed in her room, avoiding Greyson. She had claimed to be feeling ill every time someone had knocked on her door, and they had left her to rest.

"Mylah! The boys are leaving!" Elena's voice echoed through the house waking Mylah. Mylah made her way to the front door and saw Greyson and Crane each mounted upon their horses. She wished she could change her feelings. Greyson had always been kind, understanding, and fun to be around. He would make a great husband... but not for her. He and Crane had been like brothers to her since she had lost her parents. There was no way she could ever see herself with him as more than friends. Not to mention, she had too much else going on in her life with her formidable task of infiltrating the Elowyn kingdom. Nothing would be the same once she left Adair.

Greyson gazed at Mylah with a question in his eyes. She forced a reassuring smile onto her face and waved as he and Crane left to return to the border.

Seven

Over the next month, Mylah remained hidden away in the castle, practically starving herself, so she could pass off as someone desperate enough to attack a king. She lost about fifteen pounds, making all her features that much sharper. The only visitor she had was Bellingham. The lonely hours wore on her, but she kept her one singular focus of being able to go after her parents' killer in mind and pushed onward.

Bellingham taught Mylah about the creatures she may encounter in the Unbound territory. There were mermaids, sirens, sprites, pixies, kelpies, naga, dryads, and more. He warned her that the sirens would be what she needed to look out for most, since she'd be making her way along the River of Anguish towards Elowyn. He helped her study the maps of the entire continent as well. Bellingham became Mylah's only friend in the castle.

"Tell me, Leylah of Adair, how did you come to be in the Unbound territory?" Bellingham questioned her, again. They had decided her lie would include living in Adair because the best lies were rooted in truth.

"I plotted and executed an attack on King Florian. I failed, but I was cast out," Mylah said.

"Why were you trying to kill the king?"

"Because I am against the war. He is sending our soldiers away to patrol the borders, separating them from their families, and endangering them."

"No. Try again," Bellingham had detected her lie. The hardest things to lie about were topics that she had strong opinions on. For Mylah, it was the war. She completely agreed with the king's decision to start the war because her parents had been murdered by the shreeve.

Mylah took a deep breath. "I am *against* the war." Bellingham shook his head.

"No, again. Use as much truth as you can to power your lie," he instructed. Mylah paused, thinking through her next response before speaking again.

"I attacked the king because he sent my brothers away to fight in a war that should have never been started. Soldiers are suffering for this war, and I wanted to make him pay." Mylah chose her words carefully that time. Being ambiguous where she could and using as much truth as possible.

"Much better. *That* I believed," Bellingham smirked. "Anytime you have to talk about wanting to kill King Florian, pretend you're talking about your parents' killer."

"I *was* thinking about him. I *do* want him to pay," Mylah said, clenching her hands into fists at her sides.

"Good. Now, tell me, Leylah, are you a threat to the kingdom of Elowyn?" Bellingham continued his questioning. Mylah had to backtrack a few more times throughout the lesson, but overall, she was able to lie without detection.

At the end of their lesson, Bellingham requested that the guards bring the king down to see Mylah's progress. They went at once to find him. When he showed up at the door, Bellingham gave him a broad grin.

"King Florian, I present to you, Leylah Farrow of Adair." Bellingham gestured towards Mylah with a flourish of his arms. "She is ready to take on the kingdom of Elowyn."

"That's good to hear. We're having a festival in the village tomorrow, so it will make the perfect spot for her attempted attack," King Florian said. He had agreed to Garrick's plan the night of the ball. It was the best way to ensure that Mylah would be accepted into the Elowyn kingdom. She would be a known outcast for her crimes against the king.

As for how she would be sending information back to Adair once she was in the Elowyn kingdom, Bellingham was working on that. He knew sprites who worked in King Castien's castle. They were never allowed near any meetings or conversations regarding the war, or else they could share what they knew without Mylah having to risk her life. But once Mylah found a way to get the information King Florian wanted, she could tell the sprites and they would relay it to Bellingham, who would pass it on to the king. Bellingham had to figure out which sprites would be willing to help and who could be trusted. He himself could not go to the Elowyn castle, or else Unbound creatures loyal to King Castien may recognize him and alert the king to misdeeds occurring in the kingdom. It was well known among the Unbounds who was loyal to whom.

Mylah was as ready as she'd ever be, though she worried about the fake attack on the king. Nerves filled her, causing her hands to shake uncontrollably and nausea to roil in her stomach. They had practiced the attack multiple times. Mylah had a mask that she needed to wear, and a cloak with a hood. The mask had been left over from a masquerade ball at the castle. It was red with a black trim that had been bejeweled. While dressed in the cumbersome outfit, she had to "sneak" past the guards and attempt to kill King Florian with a spear. They figured a sword would give her away as someone who could afford a weapon that was to be reserved for the soldiers. So, a spear made the most sense, because you could make one yourself if you had to.

The plan would never work in real life, but thankfully it didn't need to work. Once Mylah was cast out as Leylah Farrow, they could claim she had gone mad and blame any inconsistencies on that fact.

"Remember, finding information on the shreeve book is just as important, if not more important, than discovering any attack information," the king told Mylah as he clasped his hands behind his back and paced before her. "Make that your priority."

"But shouldn't knowing whether they plan to attack be a priority?" Mylah asked, thinking that an imminent attack should be the most pressing issue.

"What good is knowing their plans if there's nothing we can do to stop them? No. Translating the book is the priority." He left the room with his guards in tow before Mylah could ask any more questions.

"What are you thinking, Mylah?" Bellingham asked as he rested on the arm of her chair.

"The king lied to me," Mylah stated. There was no denying the fact that there were never any 'whispers of an attack.'

"Yes," Bellingham sighed and Mylah's eyes widened in surprise. She hadn't thought Bellingham would tell her the truth.

"Why?" she asked, hoping he might elaborate.

"Isn't it obvious?" Bellingham gave her a tight-lipped smile. "He has a plan for whatever is in that book." Mylah nodded, knowing that there was nothing she could do to change her course. Whether the king wanted intel or not, she still needed to go to Elowyn. It may be her one chance to find whoever had killed her parents.

"I'm worried about tomorrow," she changed the subject. "What if someone guesses it's me? Or, what if we don't make it convincing enough?" she fretted.

"Calm yourself, Mylah. Everything will be fine. There are going to be so many things happening at the festival and so many people, no one will even notice you until it's too late. All they'll see is you getting caught and hauled off to the castle," he reassured her. It did make her feel slightly better, though not great.

"How long will I be kept in the castle before they cast me out into the Unbound territory?" Mylah hoped to begin her journey as soon as possible. The wait had begun to gnaw at her nerves.

"There will need to be a council meeting before you are cast out, where they will decide what to do with you," Bellingham repeated what Mylah already knew. Her heart still dropped into her stomach as it did the first time she'd been told that. There was a chance the council would try to put her to death, but the king promised her that he had final say, so it couldn't happen. Garrick and Elena would also be there to help sway the other members towards exile.

"But probably no more than two days. The king wants you in the Elowyn kingdom as soon as possible," Bellingham finished.

"Do I get to say goodbye to Garrick and Elena?" Mylah hadn't seen them since entering the castle a month ago. She kept thinking they would show up, but they hadn't yet.

"I'm sorry, Mylah. The king forbade them to visit. He thought their visits would draw suspicion if anyone saw them here." Bellingham spread his wings and lifted himself into the air. "You're going to do great. I'll see you again, someday." He waved as he flew out the door.

Mylah sat alone for a while, unsure what she was supposed to do next. No one came to find her. She was on her own.

The next day, Mylah dressed for the festival. She wore all black, except for her hooded cloak, which was the same forest green as the Adairian uniforms. She pulled her hair into a ponytail, and had the mask hanging around her neck, ready to be put in place once she was out in public. At her throat rested the necklace her mother had given her, and she gripped it tightly. It had been a difficult decision whether to wear it or not. It would surely be taken from her once she reached Elowyn, but it brought her comfort. So, she decided to take the risk and wear it. She looked down at her hand where the scar still marked her palm from the time the necklace had bit into her skin the day her parents died. With that in mind, she took a deep breath, and knew she was ready for her mission.

The king had already left for the festival with all his guards in tow. Mylah was to walk there from the castle, staying hidden all the way. She took a deep breath as she stepped outside. There were few times she was allowed outside the castle in the past month for fear of being seen.

The sun beat down on her and sweat beaded on her forehead, though the air was cool. The leaves on the trees lining the road to the castle had just begun to change from green to a pale orange. The anniversary of her parents' deaths had recently passed, marking the turn of summer into fall for Mylah. The thought left a hollow ache in her chest as she pulled her mask on and yanked her hood up. She grabbed her spear from where it sat against the wall, and it brought back all the memories of practicing her spear and axe throwing with Greyson over the years. He had always been superior with the axe, but he didn't hold a candle to her spear throwing. It made the decision easy when it came to deciding what Mylah would use in her attempted assassination of the king.

Taking one last deep breath, Mylah dashed towards the trees that lined the road leading away from the castle. The castle was empty of everyone except the guards, so Mylah did not have to worry about being seen from that direction. The guards were all on a need-to-know basis, but they at least knew that Mylah was not a threat to them or the king.

The trees lining the sides of the road were dense enough to conceal Mylah, but not by much. If she made one wrong step, she could be seen. She'd practiced this route multiple times at night, so as not to be seen by the villagers. In the daylight it was a little trickier, but she made it to the village without incident.

People filled the streets. There were tents set up all along the sides of the streets packed with yummy foods and homemade goods. Mylah longed to join in the fun, but she didn't have that luxury anymore. She spotted the king's platform right in the center of all the festivities. There was no way that Mylah would be able to sneak up to the platform without anyone spotting her first. Not to mention he had the queen and his two children with him, which meant more obstacles to avoid with her spear.

Trying not to go into a full-on panic, Mylah decided to get a closer look before deeming the task impossible. She kept her head down so no one would notice the strange person wearing a mask. She stuck to the alleyways and shadows and made it within a stone's throw of the king. She had her spear hidden beneath her cloak, but it stuck out at the bottom. She needed to figure out her next move quickly. It was only a matter of time before someone noticed her.

Her chance arose when a large group of villagers started to move from one tent to the next. Merging in behind their group, she walked diagonally until she was within range of the king. She would have to throw her spear and be sure to aim well enough *not* to hit him and his family.

"Excuse me," a man grumbled as he bumped into Mylah, causing her to lose her footing. "What..." the man had seen her mask and spear. He was backing away, and Mylah could tell he was about to shout out to the guards. Panic tried to overwhelm her, but she pushed it down, knowing she would only get one chance.

In one swift motion, Mylah took her aim, shouted "Bring our soldiers home!" and threw the spear. She watched long enough to see that the spear struck the king's robe but did no bodily harm to him. She turned on her heel and began her futile run. Her heart threatened to beat out of her chest. Even though she knew what would happen, she couldn't stop the fear of being caught from setting in and pushing her to move faster.

The guards were upon her within seconds. The ground rushed at her, and the impact left her breathless. Her hands were tied at her back, and she was hauled to her feet by strong hands. She fought to reclaim her sense of calm, but her body reacted on its own, bucking and fighting against the guards. It made the whole scene more believable but left her muscles aching.

Everyone around them was still in shock and silence had fallen. Once the guards started to drag Mylah away, the crowd began to jeer and yell. Some even threw food or rocks at Mylah. The guards did their best to block the projectiles, but many found their target. Tears fell unbidden down Mylah's face as the adrenaline began to wane.

Mylah was thrown into the king's carriage and taken back to the castle. She was covered in food particles and blood from the scratches caused by the rocks thrown at her. The guard sitting in the carriage with her offered a rag for her to clean herself, but she refused it, too proud to show him any weakness. She kept her head held high even as she plucked bits of unknown food from her hair. Her tears had stopped, thankfully, but they had created tracks in the dirt and grime that covered her face thanks to her fall. She would be able to clean up once they arrived back at the castle, or so she thought.

Mylah had forgotten what Bellingham had said about being put into the dungeon after the attack. The servants in the castle had no idea about the plan and couldn't know. So, she had to keep up appearances. She was still given a rag, though, when she entered the dungeon. She wiped herself up as much as she could. Her cuts stung, but there was nothing too deep or troublesome.

The quiet in the dungeon unnerved her. There were other prisoners down there, but none of them so much as whispered. Mylah pulled her cloak tightly around herself, relishing in the small amount of warmth and comfort it brought her. Her eyes locked with the prisoner in the cell across from hers and he sneered. If Mylah had to guess, the man looked to be in his early sixties, and he'd probably been in the dungeon for at least a quarter of that time.

"Pity," the man croaked. Mylah pressed herself back against the wall as far from him as she could get, but his voice still carried to her. "Would have been nice if you could have followed through with your assassination attempt." Mylah didn't respond. It made sense that anyone who had spent time in the dungeon would bear ill will towards the king.

"Do you think that he's the savior? Just like they all do... He's a murderer and a liar. But that should come as no shock to you," the man said as he pulled himself towards the bars of his cell, reaching out to touch them. He cursed as he touched the bars, jerking his hands back against his body. "Every once in a while I forget where I am," he muttered.

Mylah's eyes widened in shock. The man...he was not just a man. He was also *fae*. His pointed ears had been covered by his thick, shaggy, graying hair, but Mylah could see them as he cocked his head to the side and the light from the torches fell on him just so. He grinned, knowing the realization she had come to, and his elongated canines glistened. She knew he was fae rather than shreeve because he bore no blue or green markings, at least, that she could see. But fae were also few and far between on the continent of Olliria. They were plentiful elsewhere, but most had fled Olliria back when the shreeve had first staked their claim. The shreeve were also scattered around the world, but Mylah had no idea how many were actually out there.

"I know what you're thinking," he rasped.

"Leave me alone." Mylah curled into herself.

"So, she speaks!" the man jeered and clapped his hands. "You're thinking, *how is this man a fae, but so old?*" he voiced a thought that had crossed Mylah's mind, though it was not the most pressing issue that had presented itself.

"Maybe..." she muttered.

"After so many years in this cell, I have to find ways to entertain myself somehow." He transformed before Mylah's eyes. His face became less haggard and worn, and the wrinkles smoothed out, while his hair unmatted itself and seemed to regain its bounce and shine, along with its dark brown coloring. The man's body filled out a bit more, though he still appeared lanky and as if he hadn't eaten a proper meal in years. Mylah could almost imagine him being handsome if the expression he wore wasn't one of malice. His dark brown eyes were flat and empty.

"A glamour," Mylah commented. She'd heard of them, anyone with magic could attempt one, but the fae were known to be the strongest as it.

"Hey, you," a guard called out, marching down the aisle towards them. The fae man winked at Mylah and replaced his glamour. "Leave the newbie alone. She doesn't need you filling her head with lies and conspiracies."

"As if I'd have the energy for that," the fae man scoffed and slumped back into his corner, covering himself with his blanket again. He did not attempt to talk with

Mylah again, but his words had left her with a chill she couldn't shake.

Eight

Garrick sat beside Elena in the council chambers as the king and queen entered the room. Normally everyone would quiet down as soon as the king made an appearance, but that day, all the council members were on edge and couldn't stay quiet.

"Everything will be fine," Garrick murmured into Elena's ear. She squeezed his hand in response. Though he knew Elena was a nervous wreck just as he was, they both hid it very well. No one seemed to be paying them any attention.

"Thank you all for coming on such short notice," the king began. All the advisors had been summoned as soon as the king had returned home from the festival. There would be no delaying Mylah's mission, and to everyone else who had no idea of the mission, the attempted assassination certainly warranted an impromptu council meeting.

"As most of you know by now, there was an attempt on my life at the festival today by an Adair citizen," the king spoke again, and everyone fell silent.

"They must be put to death!" Garrick recognized Atticus Calhoun's voice.

"There are some details I would like to provide before a decision is made," the king said, ignoring Atticus. "The girl, claiming her name to be Leylah Farrow, has been questioned thoroughly by Bellingham, my guards, and even myself."

"As if they had time for that," someone murmured to Garrick's left. He turned and saw Cassia's mother, Alessia, whispering to her wife, Caroline.

"It has been concluded that the girl is mentally unstable. None of what she told us led us to believe that she was in any way totally in control of her own mental capacities when she attacked at the festival. Though she seems perfectly capable of taking care of herself, as she has done so for years in our village. For this reason, I propose we exile Leylah Farrow rather than execute her." No one in the room seemed surprised and Garrick let out a breath of relief. "All in favor, please raise your hand." Every hand in the room went up. Elena sagged against Garrick, tension releasing from her features as they stole a quick look at each other.

"It is decided. She will be exiled." The king rose from his throne and dismissed them all. Garrick and Elena chose to linger in hopes that they might be able to visit with Mylah. After the rest of the council members left, they approached the king and queen who remained standing before their thrones.

"King Florian," Garrick said as he reached the stage. "I would like to request a visit with Mylah. You kept us away during her month of training, and I..."

"I will allow it," the king interrupted him. Garrick gaped at the king. "But not until tonight, after more of the less trustworthy help have retired." Garrick narrowed his eyes, assuming the king spoke of the few Unbound creatures who worked within his walls. The king's past spoke volumes on his attitude towards any non-human being.

"Should we return home in the meantime?" Elena asked.

"It would be better if you stayed. Less of a chance someone spots you going back and forth that way," the king said and beckoned for them to follow him as he left the stage and exited through the back door.

"We can have tea," Queen Aurelia said, smiling at Elena. Garrick and Elena glanced at each other, surprised by the invitation. They had never been among the king's favorite advisors and so were hardly ever asked to tea. They climbed the stairs onto the stage and followed the queen out of the room.

They were led down a long hallway that split leading in two directions. They veered to the right and came to a sitting room that had a giant window overlooking the gardens. Beside the window sat an iron table with four chairs. The walls were lined with bookshelves. The king had already occupied one of the chairs and the queen sat beside him, placing her hand over his on the arm of his chair.

"Please, sit," Queen Aurelia said, waving to the two empty chairs. Garrick and Elena joined them. Garrick took steadying breaths, keeping himself calm as he gazed out towards the garden. He had no idea what to expect. The only alone time he'd ever spent with the king had been to discuss the shreeve book.

A servant entered the room with a tea cart. She left it beside the table and retreated out of the room. The queen surprised Garrick by serving the tea herself.

"It's a peppermint tea," she said as she poured the steaming liquid into each of their cups. "I made it myself."

"You make your own tea?" Elena asked, intrigue sparking in her eyes. "I'd love to learn more about that!"

"Of course!" The queen smiled again, and Garrick marveled at it. He had never seen the queen smile at any of their council meetings. "There are many things I have learned over the years within these walls." Garrick had to imagine that living in the castle had to be lonely at times. They received visitors sporadically from the two other human kingdoms, Umbra and Cambri, but they couldn't just have dinner with another couple as Garrick and Elena liked to do. It always had to be a big production, for safety purposes, but also to keep up appearances he assumed.

"I can teach you what I know some time," the queen offered to Elena who nodded vigorously. "Wonderful."

A squeal sounded in the hall followed by the patter of feet running. Two heads of black hair peeked around the corner into the sitting room. Two sets of bright hazel eyes twinkled with mischief as Princess Mina and Prince Ari spied the group at the table.

"Oh." Queen Aurelia stood and practically floated across the room. Her grace had been something that came to her naturally once she became queen, and it suited her well. "Where is Nan? She's supposed to be watching you." Though the king wore a tight expression, his lip slightly curled as he watched his children, there was nothing but love in the queen's eyes. Her voice was stern, but her actions were anything but. She gathered the children into her arms, hugging them as they tried to squirm away, thinking it was all a part of their game.

A frantic, yet exhausted, woman came running into view. She scolded the children, and they took off back the way they had come.

"Sorry, Nan," the queen said before the woman groaned and followed the children. "Sorry about that. Ari just turned six and Mina is eight. They are two bundles of energy and antics. Poor Nan can never quite keep them under control," Queen Aurelia said as she rejoined them at the table.

"We should probably talk about Mylah and the book," the king stated, his composure returning to normal.

"What about her?" Garrick asked, unsure what more they could talk about since she'd be leaving the next day.

"We need to discuss what happens if she fails," the king's words clanged in Garrick's ears. Elena gasped beside him.

"She won't fail. You made sure she was ready for this," Garrick reminded him, his voice rising along with his heart rate.

"Failure is always a possibility," the queen added.

"If she fails..." the king began again, but Garrick cut him off.

"We won't speak of it. She won't fail," Garrick growled. The king's eyes widened, and his nostrils flared.

"You should be careful to remember who you are speaking to, Garrick," King Florian's voice lowered and deepened, sending a shiver through Garrick.

"We're sorry, King Florian," Elena interjected before Garrick could respond. "Garrick is only worried about Mylah and her safety. He means no offense to you, we will

84

of course, be willing to talk about...that," she gulped. "If the time comes. But right now, we'd like to stay positive that Mylah will be successful and come home to us safely."

"Very well." King Florian rose from his seat. "I have something I must attend to, Aurelia. Please, keep our guests entertained in the meantime." Garrick watched the king stride from the room and the tension in the air dissipated as he disappeared around the corner. Garrick trusted his king, but he worried that he may have made a mistake allowing Mylah to carry out the king's mission. There was no turning back now.

Nine

Mylah had lost track of time when she heard shuffling in the hallway. The fae across the way didn't budge as a guard ushered Elena into Mylah's cell, closing the door behind her. Joy surged through Mylah as she grinned at Elena, shocked that she'd been allowed to visit. Elena fell to her knees beside Mylah, throwing her arms around her.

"Mylah...I'm sorry I didn't come sooner," her voice cracked as a sob broke free from her throat. "The king forbade us."

"It's okay, I know," Mylah reassured her as she pulled away. Elena took in the sight of her and gasped. She ran her hands over Mylah's thin face and gripped her arms.

"I think I'll be leaving tomorrow," Mylah said, trying to draw Elena's attention elsewhere. A lump formed in her throat. She hadn't been willing to admit it to anyone, but she was scared.

"If anyone can do this, it's you." Elena reached into her pocket and pulled out a letter. "Cassia wrote you a letter after she thought you left, she still has no idea what's going on. She gave this to me to send to you. I've been holding onto it for you." Mylah took the letter, her hands shaking.

"You've got one minute," the guard said as he opened the cell door again and Garrick hurried inside. Mylah and Elena rose to their feet. Garrick enveloped them both in a hug.

"You came," Mylah gasped out.

"Of course." Garrick pulled away and gave Mylah a once over. The pain in his gaze was evident. Mylah hadn't looked in a mirror for a month and she could imagine how terrible she must look.

"I'm okay," Mylah said.

"Just say the word and we can call this all off," Garrick said and Mylah gaped at him in surprise. Even if she wanted to call it off, she wouldn't. She'd come too far. She'd prove to them all she could do the impossible and infiltrate the Elowyn kingdom.

"Thank you, but I'm doing this," Mylah said, and Garrick nodded in understanding.

"Time's up," the guard snapped, opening the cell door. Garrick and Elena left, waving to Mylah as they went. Mylah collapsed back to the floor once they were out of sight and let her sobs drown out the receding footsteps.

She forced herself to open the envelope, her hands trembling as she did so. She pulled out a letter, and another envelope slipped out.

"What the..." she unfolder the letter, recognizing Cassia's flowing handwriting covering the page. She scanned it, glossing over the parts about how much Cassia would miss her, and read the bottom.

Greyson sent me this letter to give to you, but I didn't have a chance. Sorry, I may have peeked at it.

Mylah glanced at the envelope and noticed it had been opened. She shook her head, her lips twitching as she pictured Cassia attempting to reseal the letter and failing.

I know you're tempted to throw it away and not read it...

Tears pricked Mylah's eyes. Cassia knew her too well.

Don't do that Myles. He loves you and you owe it to him to read his letter.

Cassia signed her name, making it almost illegible with all the swoops and swirls. Mylah gripped Greyson's letter in one hand and Cassia's in the other. Panic overtook her. Whatever words he'd written on that page...she couldn't read them. At least, not yet. No matter what, it wouldn't change everything that had happened and was about to happen.

She shoved both letters into the pocket of her cloak and closed her eyes, leaning back against the cell wall. Guilt swirled in her gut at the thought of ignoring Greyson's letter, but she couldn't bring herself to do it. The words she would surely find would only bring remorse for not talking to him sooner, grief at the fact she'd most likely never see him again, and self-hatred for her inability to love Greyson in the way he deserved. Tears pricked her eyes, and her breathing became rapid and shallow.

"Everything comes to an end..." the fae man across from her muttered so low Mylah almost missed it. Wiping her sleeve across her face in an effort to hide her tears, she peeked over her shoulder towards him.

"What are you talking about now?" she asked, and he chuckled.

"You are so young and naïve. You'll learn soon enough." He hid himself behind his blanket and Mylah assumed that was all he was going to say on the subject. She huffed and closed her eyes again, hoping sleep would take her swiftly.

Ten

The king and his guards retrieved Mylah from the dungeon the following morning. She felt the fae's eyes on her as they led her away from her cell, but he said nothing. They brought her out of the castle in shackles, and with a sack covering her head, so anyone who may witness her being moved would not recognize her. As had been explained to Mylah before the attack, she and the king were put into separate carriages, each with two guards accompanying them.

Once they were moving, the guards removed Mylah's hood. "Thank you," she said, grateful to be able to breathe easier.

"You're welcome."

Mylah did a double take, unable to believe her eyes. Garrick sat across from her. She couldn't stop herself from throwing her arms around him and hugging him tight. He laughed and hugged her back.

"What are you doing here?" she gasped, and realized she was crying. He wiped away her tears.

"I had to see you off. Elena wanted to be here too, but it would be too suspicious if we were somehow spotted," he said. Mylah's muscles relaxed along with her nerves. She didn't feel so alone now that she had Garrick with her.

"You did a great job yesterday. No one suspects anything, and everyone is talking about the attack. Word will spread to the borders fast. Bellingham already let Greyson and Crane know to start spreading the story too." Mylah's heart clenched when he said their names. *Greyson*...she still had his unread letter in her pocket. She should have told him the truth when she'd had the chance. Now it was too late.

"So, they're doing well then?" Mylah asked, hoping her pain and regret didn't show on her face.

"Yes. Crane has been promoted to commander of his outpost, so he's no longer doing the border patrols. Elena was over the moon when she heard that. Having both sons on the patrols, and you heading directly into the fire, Elena has been a wreck. But she'll be better once we hear you've made it safely to the Elowyn castle. Bellingham told me he'd be setting up a network for you with the sprites there." Mylah could listen to Garrick talk all night. His voice soothed her and reminded her of all the nights he would sit up with her when she had nightmares about her parents. He would tell her the stories of when he and Emil used to explore the Unbound territory together.

"Bellingham told me that as well. He also told me about some of the creatures I might come across while in the Unbound territory. I remember your stories from when you and Pa used to explore there." Mylah wished to hear those stories one last time.

"Ahh, yes. The sirens, oh could they sing. They are the ones you need to watch out for. If you hear any beautiful songs, or sounds, stay away. They lure in humans and other creatures for an easy meal." Mylah gulped, and Garrick continued. "There are mermaids too, though. They look remarkably similar, but mermaids don't sing. You can tell by looking in their eyes which ones are the monsters. There's a cold, haunted look in those who have stolen the lives of men. I remember a time your father mistook a siren for a mermaid and nearly got a chunk bitten out of his leg!" Garrick guffawed, making Mylah smile. "He never made that mistake again! The eyes always give away any creature. You can always see the demons swimming there."

"What about the ogres and orcs?" Mylah asked. Those were the creatures she was really worried about.

"Never came across any of them, just our one encounter with a troll. They usually stick closer to the mountain range, so as long as you head straight for Elowyn, you should be fine. There aren't any mountains along the route you will be following," Garrick waved off that concern. Mylah let out a breath of relief. There were a few less monsters to worry about.

"I've seen a kelpie out there," the guard sitting in the carriage with them broke his silence. "Watch out for them."

"Bellingham mentioned them, what exactly are kelpies?" Mylah asked.

"They resemble horses, but they eat humans. They are usually found near bodies of water," the guard said, looking haunted as he talked of the kelpie. Whether he'd witnessed the horrors he spoke of; Mylah didn't want to ask.

"There are sprites out there as well. Most of them are friendly, so if you need help, they are your best bet," Garrick said, moving the conversation away from the horrific side of the Unbound territory. "Be careful not to mistake a pixie for a sprite, they aren't necessarily bad, but they aren't known to be helpful. They'd rather play tricks and get you turned around until you're lost."

"Okay, so how do I distinguish between a pixie and a sprite?" Mylah's nerves began firing again, increasing her heart rate, and making her breaths become more labored.

"A sprite is more human-like in appearance, while pixies usually have pointed ears, long fingers, and some have horns. You'll probably be able to tell if you come across one."

"Good. I wish we'd spent a little more time on this in my training," Mylah groaned. "Bellingham was so worried about me being able to lie, rightfully so, but we didn't have much time for talking about Unbound creatures."

"You'll be fine. Just remember what we've told you, and you'll be fine," Garrick reassured her, though he kept fiddling with the hem of his tunic and looked like he needed some reassurance himself. For the rest of the ride, Garrick told stories of his adventures with Emil. Mylah found herself smiling and laughing along with him even though she'd heard them all before. She missed her father so much that it hurt, but hearing the stories brought her more joy than pain, so she let Garrick keep talking.

"What about mother? You never tell many stories about her..." Mylah wanted a few stories of her mother to hold onto.

"Ah, Vita. You remind me of her every time you smile," Garrick said, making Mylah's heart leap. She had always thought her smile resembled her mother's, but no one had ever said as much. "Your father was in love with her the moment he laid eyes on her, but she was not so easily won over." He told Mylah stories of Emil's attempts at courting Vita.

"Her father was a bit of a hard ass," Garrick repeated what he'd told her in the past.

"Unlike you and Pa?" Mylah said, cocking her eyebrow at him. He laughed and patted her knee.

"He was close with the king before he worked in his family's shop."

"Wait, really?" That was something Mylah had never heard before.

"Before King Florian became king, they did border patrols together. After, though, Vita's father left the king's army and returned to his family's shop, where he remained for the rest of his days." Garrick peeked through the small opening between the curtain and the window of the carriage and Mylah knew he was done talking about her grandfather. She would have to remember to ask him more about it when she returned from Elowyn...*if* she returned.

They ate lunch in the carriage, and Mylah drank her fill of water as they rode. There was no guarantee she would find any drinkable water before she made it to the Elowyn territory.

By the time the carriage stopped moving, darkness had fallen. Mylah pulled the hood up on the cloak she still wore. There was little chance there would be anyone else out there since the king had chosen a time the patrols would be elsewhere, but she couldn't be too careful.

Garrick and the guard climbed out of the carriage first. Garrick helped Mylah out and led her to the border between Adair and the Unbound territory. It didn't look like much; she couldn't even tell where one side began and the other ended.

Large oaks and evergreen trees stood all around them. The forest stretched into the Unbound territory and seemed to go on forever. From maps, though, Mylah knew that there was the River of Anguish that connected to the Lake of Anguish on the other side of the forest, along with the Forsaken Mountains south of the lake. She needed to travel through the forest until she came to the river. If she followed that Northeast, she would come to another forest, and Elowyn lay beyond. She had memorized her route over the last month, which had been easy enough since it was almost a straight shot.

"Leylah Farrow, as punishment for your crimes against the crown, you are hereby cast out of Adair by the order of King Florian. You are to never return to Adair, or else you shall be executed," the guard who had been riding with Mylah and Garrick made the pronouncement. Mylah had heard it before, but this time it hit her differently. This time, it felt real, because she was *leaving*. She could return to Adair, but that didn't mean she would. There was no guarantee that she would survive the journey she was about to set out on.

"Do you understand the punishment you are being served?" King Florian asked.

"Yes. I understand. I can never return," Mylah's voice came out small and scared. She figured it would seem more convincing to anyone listening in, although she hadn't exactly had control over it. She *was* scared.

Garrick stepped up to Mylah to remove her shackles. He bent down close so he could whisper to her.

"I love you, Myles. Be careful, and come home safe," his voice trembled. Tears welled up in Mylah's eyes. He had never told her that he loved her before, but she'd always known. Garrick and Elena loved her like their own, and Mylah had never felt like an outsider in their home.

Mylah gave him a knowing nod and felt a weight drop into her cloak's pocket before the shackles fell from her wrists. Garrick stepped back in line with the rest of the guards.

"Go now," King Florian commanded. Mylah tore her gaze from Garrick and strode into the forest, entering her new reality. As she walked, she felt eyes watching her from every direction.

Eleven

Mylah walked until she reached the end of the trees. Before her lay a vast expanse of land that was edged with the Forsaken Mountains. Night had fallen and she could see the outline of the mountains. According to the map she had studied, the Lake of Anguish and small copses of trees and forests lay somewhere ahead of her. Instead of venturing towards the unknown, she decided to get some sleep.

Mylah reached into her pocket and pulled out a dagger. Garrick must have hidden it up his sleeve and dropped it into her pocket as he took off her shackles. There was a note attached to it. *Stay Safe*, it read. Mylah clutched the note to her chest before placing it back into her cloak pocket alongside the dagger and Greyson's letter.

She settled in against a tree and closed her eyes. Sleep came quickly, and when Mylah woke, the sun had already risen above the treetops. She cursed herself for sleeping so long. It would take her at least three days to reach the Elowyn border and she had no food or water. Every second counted.

She ventured out of the trees and found herself
blinded by the sun. She envied the shreeve in that moment
for their eyes, designed to withstand the harsh light of day.
For those of the shreeve who had magic, sunlight fueled
their power, or so she'd been told, making all their spells and
tricks much stronger in the daylight. She wasn't sure if that
fact was due to the mix of fae and human blood in their
DNA, or if it was something the witch who had created
them planned.

As Mylah stepped forward, something tugged on her
cloak. She turned but saw nothing except for tree roots. She
took another step and felt the tug again. This time she
turned to see the same tree roots gripping her cloak like
fingers and heard tittering filtering through the trees.
Dryads. Mylah gave her cloak a yank and it slipped free of
the roots. She hurried away from the trees before the Dryads
could play any more tricks.

She gazed around in awe. She wasn't sure if her eyes
were playing tricks on her, but all the colors appeared more
vivid, and everything seemed to be *alive.* She ventured
forward in a daze. Wings flitted on the edge of her vision
and whispers filled the air. She was probably among few
humans who had ventured into the Unbound territory since
Elowyn had staked their claim. Before, humans had trekked
through the Unbound territory at least once a month on
their way to the trade isle.

The trade isle was between Hyrdian; the land of the
witches and warlocks, and Amaris; the other shreeve
kingdom. Before King Castien's reign, all the kingdoms of
Olliria had gathered there once a month to trade goods.
Since he'd blocked that route, tensions were even higher
between Adair and Elowyn as resources became scarcer.

Adair had set up a trade agreement with their neighboring continent, Cyprian, in the meantime, but it took much longer for the ships to go back and forth between the continents.

"*Stay with us...*" Mylah heard amongst the whispers. "*Come play...*" Fingers tugged her hair and she whipped around to see what she assumed were pixies scattering. They wore nothing but mischievous smirks as they danced in the air, just out of reach.

"Get lost," Mylah growled. They stuck out their tongues at her but flew away. Mylah trudged onward, warier than before. After two hours, she came to the river that connected to the Lake of Anguish at both ends. She shuddered as she imagined being dragged down to the bottom of the lake by a siren. They were less common in the river, as she'd been told, but she still needed to be on her guard.

The river would lead her toward Elowyn. When it reconnected with the lake, she had to head North to the official Elowyn border. They held claim to all the Unbound land West of the lake. All the Unbound land East of the lake was too overrun with even worse creatures to bother claiming.

Mylah decided to take a quick break and sat on a rock close to the river. She kept her gaze trained on the water, watching for the slightest ripple that may indicate danger. She debated whether the water was safe to drink. She could survive the next few days fine without food, but she'd need water sooner.

"Go ahead, dear."

Mylah leapt off the rock and landed in a heap on the bank. A beautiful woman with bright violet eyes and matching hair giggled at her from the middle of the river. Scales covered her torso and stretched up over her bosom where they faded to glistening, light brown, human-like skin at her chest. "Didn't mean to frighten you."

"Y-y-you're a mermaid?" Mylah asked, searching the woman's eyes, where she saw only genuine intrigue. There was no cold, haunted look as Garrick had warned would be in a siren's eyes.

"A mermaid to you." She flipped her tail up out of the water as she dove under and resurfaced an arm's length away from the riverbank. Mylah resisted the urge to scoot away from her for fear of insulting the woman.

"What's a lovely young woman such as yourself doing so far from home?" She placed her elbows on the bank and rested her chin in her hands, gazing up at Mylah. Her eyes twinkled when the sun hit them.

"I've been exiled from my home." Mylah had to begin living her lie even out there. There were ears everywhere who may report to King Castien.

"My poor, sweet, girl."

"I tried to kill the King," Mylah said, and the woman's eyes widened, as a grin spread across her face.

"My, my, a human with some fight in her. Tell me, dear, what's your name?" Her eyebrow lifted in an elegant arch.

"Leylah Farrow." Mylah had no qualms about giving her full fake name. There was no way it could be used against her as her real name might.

"Ah, Miss Leylah, where do you suppose you will go now?"

"I am heading to the Elowyn border..."

The woman drew back and let out a hissing sound, hatred filling her gaze.

"Murderers and thieves," she snapped.

"I only hope to find refuge there. As an exile, I cannot go to any human kingdom without being killed on sight." That was not entirely true, but Mylah needed an excuse as to why she chose Elowyn.

"What makes you think *King Castien* will be any more merciful?" She said his name with mocking in her tone.

"Hope, because it's my only chance, or else I must fend for myself out here," Mylah said, casting her eyes down to try to evoke pity from the woman.

"As a rule, I scorn any being associated with Elowyn, but since you are not yet a part of their kingdom, I will help you." Mylah wasn't sure whether she should trust a mermaid who could be trying to lure her in, only to betray her.

"You've not yet told me *your* name," Mylah pointed out.

"You don't trust me, I can tell. Understandably, I'm sure you've heard stories of humans lured into their watery graves." The smirk that played at the woman's lips had Mylah taking a step back.

"And you still didn't answer my question."

"Genevieve, at your service." She dipped her head to Mylah. Mylah tried to recall whether her father or Garrick had ever mentioned a Genevieve, but they had always been vague when it came to names as they told her their adventures. "Shall we move along, then?"

"I guess there's no reason to stay," Mylah agreed reluctantly. She stood and began walking along the riverbank. Genevieve drifted lazily down the river alongside her. "Out of curiosity, why are you helping me?" Mylah hazarded to ask.

"I have my reasons," Genevieve disappeared under water and resurfaced clenching a whole fish in her teeth. She took a vicious bite, revealing dagger-like canines, and held it out to Mylah. "Hungry?"

"Um, no thanks." Mylah tried to conceal her disgust.

"Oh, right, I forget you humans have to cook your food. Weak stomachs and all." She took another bite of the fish and then tossed the carcass into the river behind her. "What do you plan on eating until you happen upon the shreeve?"

"I wasn't planning on eating anything."

"Oh, come now. That's preposterous. You'll need all your strength to face those monsters."

"I'll be fine." Mylah had prepared for that very situation. She could fight well enough after going two days without food. Three days wouldn't be much harder. Two days was the longest she went without food in her month of training. It was to show her the effects that deprivation caused and how her body would react. Otherwise, it was too dangerous to push her body to its limits if she didn't need to.

"I'll catch you a fish and you can start a fire to cook it," Genevieve offered.

"What makes you think I know how to start a fire?" She did, but Genevieve didn't need to know everything.

"Hmph." Genevieve disappeared beneath the water again. This time when she resurfaced, she held a silver chalice filled with water. "At least drink some water. This cup is enchanted to purify the water." She held it out to Mylah who eyed it warily.

"I'm not that desperate yet." Mylah ignored the offering and continued walking.

"Let me know when you change your mind."

As they continued, Mylah thought she saw pixies among the flowers. They seemed to be following her. She ignored them for the first few hours, but as the sun began to set, a few dared to come closer.

"Is it her?" one whispered to its companion.

"Of course it's her! Look at the eyes: human!"

"What do you want?" Mylah whirled towards them, and they gaped at her, eyes blinking rapidly.

"S-sorry Miss," one sputtered.

"Who's bothering you, dear?" Genevieve called from the river. She pulled herself halfway onto the bank to get a better look. "Sprites," she realized as she threw her wet hair over her shoulder. "What news have you?"

Mylah turned back to the winged creatures. *Sprites, not pixies.* She should have known. They were wearing clothes and did not have long fingers or pointed ears like pixies.

"Bellingham told us..." at the mention of Bellingham, Mylah panicked. Genevieve could not know the truth.

"Let me speak to you alone, please." Mylah walked out of earshot of Genevieve, much to Genevieve's dismay. "You must not speak openly of whatever Bellingham has told you," Mylah hissed to the sprites who cowered before her.

"We're sorry, Miss."

"Now, what is it he told you?" Mylah asked, glancing back towards Genevieve to ensure she wasn't listening in.

"To help the human girl as much as we can, but we must not tell anyone...oh..." the sprite realized he had already disobeyed the most important part of the order. "S-sorry, Miss. It won't happen again."

"Good."

"What do you need? We can help!" the other sprite, a female, chirped.

"Food a human can eat and clean water," Mylah requested.

"Yoo-hoo! I'm still here!" Genevieve called to them.

"Find us along the river when you have what I need. Do not mention Bellingham again. And," she paused, "thank you. I'm sorry for putting you to work, but it is much appreciated."

"No, thank you. You will free our people if you succeed." The sprites flew away before Mylah could respond. What had Bellingham told them to get them to help? Guilt twisted in her gut like a knife. She had no intention of freeing anyone, but now... she shook her head. Her mission was to gain insight into translating the shreeve book. Nothing more.

"What was that about?" Genevieve asked as Mylah returned to walking along the river.

"They knew a friend of mine from my village. They offered to help me." Mylah stuck to the truth. It was easier than to come up with more lies. She hadn't realized how much it would weigh on her to keep up with all her lies.

"Ahh, how unlike them; those two in particular. They have a special distaste for anyone who enslaves their people. That includes humans."

"We don't enslave sprites," Mylah snapped. "We employ them. There's a big difference."

"As far as you know."

"What do you know about humans? You can't even leave the water." Mylah figured that in the past humans may have been guilty of enslaving Unbound creatures, but it didn't happen anymore. The only Unbound creatures she'd ever seen in Adair were in the castle, and she'd heard that they were all paid livable wages for their labor.

Genevieve remained silent for a while after that, giving Mylah time to think. Her mind played through different scenarios of how she would be received in Elowyn. Whether she would have to find her way to the castle, or if she would be stopped immediately across the border. She couldn't bring herself to think about what would happen if they turned her away at the border...or worse.

"You are very angry for one so young," Genevieve broke the silence. "There is a great amount of resentment and sadness in your heart. I can sense it." Mylah gritted her teeth.

"What are you talking about? Obviously I'm angry, I was exiled!" Mylah yelled, scaring a few pixies who had been hiding in the grass.

"No...this is something else, something deeper." Genevieve seemed to be staring right through her and it made Mylah uncomfortable. She turned away, hiding her face from the mermaid.

"You're being ridiculous. I'm fine," Mylah snapped.

"Whatever you say. Either way, you should know, you won't get far in life if your heart is overcome with negative emotions." Genevieve let her tail slap against the water, making Mylah jump and showering her with tiny droplets of water.

"How do you suggest I overcome all these negative emotions I supposedly harbor?" Mylah glared at her, and Genevieve smirked.

"Love, dear. Love will heal you." As an afterthought she added, "and forgiveness."

Mylah scoffed. "I have more important things to worry about. Besides, what do you know of love?" Genevieve gazed at the sky as she drifted along, apparently thinking of how to respond.

"I've been around for thousands of years, dear. Love has come and gone for me, never staying long." She dipped under the water and reemerged a few feet closer to the bank. "Never let it consume you but enjoy it while it lasts."

"What's that supposed to mean?" Mylah tried not to think about the poor souls who had fallen in love with Genevieve and their fates.

"I mean, live a little, dear. You've been given the lifespan of a human, which means you don't have thousands of years like me to test the waters. Enjoy yourself and allow yourself to love again." Mylah was reminded of what the fae told her in the dungeon, *everything must come to an end* and wondered if he meant life, love, or something else. Whatever he meant, she didn't have time to ponder it any longer.

"I don't want to talk about this anymore," Mylah huffed, hopping over a small boulder. Genevieve flipped onto her back to drift down the river.

They continued for another couple of hours, until the moon began to descend in the sky. Mylah removed her cloak and spread it out away from the riverbank. She still did not trust that Genevieve would not drag her into the water while she slept.

"Still refusing to drink water?" Genevieve held the chalice again.

"Not yet." Mylah was parched, but she was holding out for the sprites. She settled onto her cloak and closed her eyes.

"Sleep well," Genevieve said in a melodic voice. *"Somewhere along the River of Anguish, the Lady of the Lake will grant a wish. She brings sweet dreams and sings of fantastical beings...no one can resist..."* Genevieve's strange song lulled Mylah to sleep and weaved itself into her dreams.

Mylah woke to the sprites poking her side. The sun was rising, and Genevieve appeared to be sleeping. At least, she floated in the river with her eyes closed.

"We brought food and water, Miss." The sprites nudged an apple toward her and...a silver chalice filled with water. Mylah bit back her annoyance. She would have to trust that the chalice did nothing other than purify water.

"Thank you," she said as she sat up and bit into the apple. It made her stomach growl at the first taste of it. The sprites flitted away.

"Good morning, dear." Genevieve splashed in the river behind Mylah.

"I'm guessing I have you to thank for this?" Mylah held up the chalice without turning around.

"Where else did you suppose the sprites would find you water? Sorry, dear, you're going to have to trust me." Genevieve floated on her back with a triumphant grin.

"Not yet," Mylah tossed the chalice to Genevieve, water sloshing out of it.

"You humans are such mistrusting creatures."

"We have reason to be, after centuries of trickery and misguidance." Mylah stood, shaking the dirt from her cloak. Her dagger fell out of the pocket, and she snatched it up.

"Ohh, mysterious." Genevieve swam closer. "An armed exile – that's a first."

"I stole it."

"Sure you did, dear." Silence fell. Mylah realized everything was *too* quiet. The whispers, wing beats, chirps, and titters had all ceased. The only noise came from the flowing river.

"What's happening?" Mylah whispered to Genevieve who looked around, worry creasing her flawless features. She opened her mouth, scenting the air.

"Ogre..." her eyes widened, and she beckoned to Mylah. "Quick, into the water. There's no time to hide."

"I'm not getting in there!" Mylah squealed.

"Sorry, but you don't have much of a choice. Either trust me and come into the river or be discovered by the ogre and be eaten." *Eaten by a mermaid, or an ogre...* at least Genevieve would probably lull her into complacency first.

Mylah debated for another second, and then moved to the river's edge, placing her legs in the water first.

"Hurry!" Genevieve urged. Mylah took a deep breath and before she submerged herself in the river, she heard the deafening roar of the ogre. Genevieve gripped Mylah's arms, and her eyes flew open, water stinging them as they did. Genevieve began towing her down the river underwater. Mylah did not have a great record for holding her breath and wasn't sure how long she'd be able to remain submerged. She couldn't take the sting of the water in her eyes, so she had to close them again.

After twenty seconds, Mylah began panicking. She tugged on Genevieve's arm. Genevieve turned and realized what was happening. She stopped and blew a bubble that encased Mylah's head. Mylah took a deep breath, gulping down the air.

"Sorry, I forgot about the whole *humans can't breathe underwater* thing," Genevieve's voice was garbled, but understandable. "That bubble will last you about five minutes if you stop sucking down the air like that." Mylah forced herself to breathe normally. Genevieve began towing her down the river again. As they moved, Mylah saw the gills on Genevieve's neck that had been concealed by her hair before.

Genevieve refreshed Mylah's air bubble two more times before they resurfaced.

"I think we'll be okay now." Genevieve released Mylah's arm. Mylah swam to the riverbank and hauled herself onto the grass.

"I'll take that drink of water now, if the offer still stands," Mylah gasped out. There was no longer any reason for Mylah to believe Genevieve meant to harm her.

Genevieve pulled the chalice out of the water. Mylah had no idea where she kept it, but she didn't ask questions. She took the chalice and chugged the water. Genevieve watched her, curiosity sparking in her eyes, but she said nothing. After two more refills, Mylah was ready to keep moving.

The sun shone brightly overhead, drying Mylah's soaked cloak, pants, and tunic. She'd been wearing the same outfit since the day she staged her attack on the king. It was probably a good thing they had gotten somewhat of a washing. Mylah reached into her cloak pocket and pulled out a sodden piece of paper...Greyson's letter. She had never read it and now it was destroyed. She sighed as she let the paper fall to the ground in a lump. It was probably better not knowing what had been in the letter as it would only add to her guilt.

They had covered more distance in the water than they could have with Mylah walking. By the end of the day, they would reach the point where the river merged with the lake, and she'd be on her own.

"I didn't think ogres ventured so far from the mountains," Mylah said as she balanced on a log edging the river.

"They usually don't. I've been seeing more and more of them lately. Something must be drawing them out."

"I'll try to find out from the shreeve, maybe they know something about it," Mylah offered.

"You'd have more luck asking a warlock or witch. They live closest to the mountains. Of course, you'd have to get past their impenetrable wall first." Genevieve's eyes sparkled with mischief. "Or cross the Lake of Anguish."

"I don't know if I'll have the opportunity to do that, but if one presents itself, I'll see what I can find out. It's the least I can do after all you've done for me."

"You should know...I withheld a bit of information from you." Genevieve turned her head down, her hair draping over her face. Mylah stopped.

"What didn't you tell me?"

"The chalice you drank from was not only enchanted to purify the water," she admitted. Mylah's heart began to race. What had the mermaid done to her? "It is also enchanted to turn the water to ash in the drinker's mouth if they are not who I know them to be. It reveals shapeshifters and deceivers alike." Mylah's mouth went dry. The water had not turned to ash, yet she had lied about her identity.

"I don't think I understand..."

"I'm sure you do, *Leylah*. You passed the test. You are exactly who I thought you were." She winked and beckoned Mylah closer. Mylah crouched on the riverbank and leaned in close. "Daughter of Emil." Mylah's eyes flew wide open.

"How did you know my father?"

"Shhh...little ears," Genevieve gave her a knowing look and Mylah nodded in understanding. Not all of the Unbound creatures were on their side. "Why don't we take another swim? It's a much faster way of travelling." Mylah hesitated for a moment, unsure whether she should speak with the mermaid about her truth. Emil popped into her mind and his stories of his adventures in the Unbound territory. It was entirely possible Genevieve was a part of one of those stories. Mylah had to learn more. She slipped into the water and let it envelop her again. Genevieve blew an air bubble for her.

"Is it safe?" Mylah asked.

"For now," Genevieve glanced around, not giving Mylah much confidence. "I met your father when he was your age. He cut me free from a fisherman's trap. You look just like him. He was handsome for a human man. He came to visit often, bringing friends sometimes, like Garrick and Wren."

"Garrick told me I could trust mermaids! But not sirens. I'm sorry I wasn't entirely sure which you were until you saved me from the ogre."

"Garrick was half right," Genevieve smirked. "But your father stopped coming four years ago. I knew something was wrong. When word spread of the attack in

Adair, I guessed who had been killed." If they were not underwater, Mylah could tell tears would be flowing down Genevieve's cheeks, as they were her own. "I grieved for them, and for the daughter they left behind. He spoke so fondly of you, Mylah."

"How did you know who I was?"

"I was fairly sure the moment I saw you. You have his strong jaw and sharp cheekbones. Simply beautiful. But, once I sensed the anger and sadness in your heart, I knew beyond a doubt. There are few things that can cause such deep wounds as those."

"But you let me lie to you..." Shame burned hot in Mylah's chest.

"Because I knew you had your reasons. I trusted your father, and that trust extends to you."

"Then please understand I can't explain why I lied." Mylah wished that she could be honest with Genevieve and spill her entire story to her, but it wasn't safe.

"I understand. Now, let's get you out of the water so you can dry off before night falls." Genevieve returned them to the surface.

Back on dry land, Mylah let everything she had learned seep in as she walked. Genevieve drifted along in the river, content with the silence. Mylah's heart warmed at the thought that she had another link to her father through Genevieve. Maybe someday she'd be able to tell her side of the stories to Mylah, but they had no time for that at the moment. As the sun dipped below the horizon, the river began to curve back towards the lake.

"This is where our paths must diverge," Genevieve said, breaking their silence.

"Thank you for all your help." A lump formed in Mylah's throat. "I'll keep my promise about the ogres."

"Thank you, dear. I wish you safety and a whole lot of luck. The shreeve are not known for their kindness. Do not let your guard down." Genevieve swam closer and lowered her voice. "A mutual friend reached out and told me you may be looking for a friend in the castle." She winked and Mylah knew she meant Bellingham. "If you find yourself in need of help, find the sprite named Briar. You can trust her. If you're out here, near the water, simply call my name, Genevieve, Lady of the Lake, and I will find you," she smiled and slipped beneath the surface of the water.

"Lady of the Lake..." Mylah had heard that before. The Lady of the Lake was said to be the most influential and murderous of the sirens. "Wait..." but when Mylah looked back to the river, Genevieve was gone. Mylah stared out over the water, waiting to see if she resurfaced, but she didn't. Her heart raced and her palms began to sweat as she moved away from the riverbank, towards the woods that would lead her to Elowyn.

Twelve

The woods grew darker as Mylah ventured on. She began to think that maybe she should return to the river until the sun came up. She could call Genevieve back and ask her whether she was really the infamous "Lady of the Lake."

A hissing sound caught Mylah's attention. She whipped around and noticed glowing red eyes peering at her from deep in the forest. The eyes blinked and then appeared closer than before when they reopened. Mylah held her breath as she reached into her cloak for her dagger. The hissing grew louder.

"Ssso far from home," the voice was like a caress, and it put Mylah at ease. She watched as a figure began to take shape before her. The upper body of a human, covered in scales, with the lower half curving into a snake form. The being, which Mylah recognized as a naga from her studies with Bellingham, slithered forward, and wrapped themself around her. "My preciousss, what ssshould I do with you?" Mylah found herself incapable of responding. She clutched her dagger in her pocket but could not bring herself to remove it.

"Pretty, young...I could ussse you for ssso many thingsss." The naga pursed their plump, red lips together. Mylah gazed up at the flowing black hair that reached down to where the upper body transitioned to a snake form. It shone like the naga's scales. The muscles of the naga were enough to make Mylah worry that she would not be strong enough to take on the monster. Naga assigned themselves no gender, but the upper half of this one appeared to be a male figure.

"Tell me, human, ssshould I eat you now?" They cocked an eyebrow at Mylah, and she felt a release that allowed her to speak again.

"I am protected by the Lady of the Lake," she tried, but the naga laughed.

"Where isss ssshe now, my sssweet?" They made a show of looking around as if a mermaid would be able to appear on land.

"I'm going to Elowyn to find out what's happening in the mountains," she tried again. This time, the naga seemed a little more interested. Their eyes glittered with curiosity.

"Elowyn you sssay...very interesssting indeed." The naga appeared to be thinking as Mylah maneuvered her dagger out of her pocket. Before they could speak again, Mylah made her move. She swung her dagger towards the naga's abdomen, but the naga caught her arm. "Do not try to ssslay me!" they hissed furiously. "You are no match, *child*."

"I need to get to Elowyn!" Mylah struggled to free herself from the naga's grasp now that she could move again.

"I will let you go, if you will promissse me one favor." The naga tightened their grip on Mylah and she stopped fighting.

"Fine," she sighed, knowing she would not be able to escape on her own. "What do you want from me?"

"In Elowyn, find a witch named Edrisss. In their home, find a necklaccce on which hangsss naga fangsss. Bring thisss to me, and I will ssspare you." The naga stared into Mylah's eyes.

"I will do it," Mylah promised.

"To make sssure you do not forget about my requessst..." The naga grabbed Mylah's left arm and raised it to their lips. They grazed one of their fangs that appeared to have grown, along her forearm. It left a minor scratch, barely breaking the skin. "If you leave that to fessster, you'll be dead in a week."

"W-what?" Mylah gazed down at the seemingly harmless scratch.

"Bring me what I want, and I will provide you with an antidote." The naga loosened their grip on Mylah. She watched as they slithered away, back into the cover of the forest. She had no idea whether she would be able to complete the naga's task within the time frame necessary. If she didn't, though... she shook off that thought. For the moment, Mylah was glad to be free of the naga. She would worry about the rest once she was in Elowyn.

Grabbing her dagger from where it had fallen, Mylah ventured onward. There was no telling what else she may encounter, and when she would happen across the Elowyn border. It should still be at least a few hours' journey, but they may have moved it since claiming the Unbound territory. Now that she had a much more imperative deadline, she moved more swiftly through the trees, being less careful of staying quiet.

By the time the sun rose above the trees the next day, Mylah was sure she must be getting close. She had encountered pixies, dryads, and sprites throughout the night, but they had mostly left her unbothered. As she continued, there were fewer and fewer creatures present. There was an eerie silence that surrounded her, even the trees seemed to be making an effort to remain as still as possible.

"Take a load of this one..." Mylah stiffened as she heard a male voice. She pressed herself against a tree and peered around, trying to figure out where it came from. "What do you think did him in? Kelpie? Banshee?"

"You know banshees don't do the killing..." another voice, this one female, answered. "From what's left of the body, I'd say these wounds are consistent with a kelpie for sure. Though, it is a little far from the lake."

"They've been roaming further and further from the water," the male voice sounded worried. Mylah shuddered. She was thankful that she had come across a naga instead of a kelpie. The kelpie would not have bargained with her for her life, they would have simply devoured her.

As Mylah hid behind the tree, she debated whether she should hold onto her dagger or not. If the shreeve decided to take her to the king, they would search her and find it. It would be suspicious for an exiled woman to have a weapon. On the other hand, if they decided to kill her, she would need *something* to defend herself.

She decided to take a risk and knelt to bury the knife at the base of the tree. She tried to be as quiet as possible. After burying the knife, she smudged dirt onto her face, arms, and legs, and mussed up her hair. She needed to look like she had fought her way through the wilderness to get away from Adair, which she had.

"Do we tell the king?" the male asked. Mylah took a deep breath, turned her cloak askew, and stumbled out into the open. She still couldn't see the shreeve that the voices belonged to, but she stumbled onward.

"What is that?" The woman stepped into view first, sword raised to strike. She had dark ebony skin that made her blue and green markings stand out starkly in contrast. Her eyes appeared to glow; a purple iris with a light green color where, if she were human, would have been white. Mylah fell to her knees and put her hands above her head.

"P-please," she breathed heavily. "I seek refuge." Even though she knew what she was doing was a means to an end, it went against everything she had been taught. Putting herself in such a position of vulnerability made her instincts scream at her to stand up and fight.

"What do we have here?" The man's tone was amused. Mylah snuck a glance at him. He had a lighter skin tone, but the colorful markings were just as noticeable. "A groveling human, what ever should we do with her?"

"King Castien said we're not to bring him anymore refugees," the woman said, and panic gripped Mylah. She'd considered that they may turn her away, but not that the king had already given the order not to take anyone in.

Mylah lifted her head and turned her face to the woman. "I've been exiled from my home for an assassination attempt on my king," she said, figuring maybe they would be more likely to be merciful if they knew she was on their side.

"So, you're a deceitful, traitorous human. The worst kind," the woman sneered.

"N-no. I..." her whole plan began to unravel before her eyes.

"I've heard of you," the man said, surprised. "Just yesterday I heard talk of a young woman who had tried to kill her king. Our spies overheard it on the border. Humans are a gossipy lot."

"If you show me mercy, I may be able to help your king gain an advantage against Adair." Mylah decided to switch her plan. Before it had been imperative that she seem of no use to the shreeve so that she would appear docile and non-threatening. But clearly, that was not going to get her into Elowyn.

"What use do you think you'd be to our king?" The man pointed his sword at Mylah, using it to tilt her chin up towards him. She swallowed, the tip of the sword digging in enough to nick her skin.

"I was friends with someone on the council. They didn't tell me a lot, but I overheard some of the king's plans..." she could give them that much.

"Tell us what you've heard," the man commanded.

"If I tell you now, what's to stop you from killing me and taking the information to the king yourself?" Mylah countered and the man smirked.

"Clever girl." He returned his sword to his side and motioned to the woman. "Help her up, Sabine." Sabine groaned but held her hand out to Mylah. Mylah took it and let Sabine pull her to her feet. "We shall take you to the king and he will decide whether to hear you out or not."

"He's not going to be happy about this..." Sabine sounded wary, but the man did not seem worried. He said nothing as he turned to walk back leading the way deeper into Elowyn territory.

Thirteen

The shreeve brought Mylah back to their horses. They tied her there while they finished their border patrol. Her mouth became parched and her stomach's rumbling unbearable as she waited. Though the air was cool, the sun beat down on her and sweat had soaked through her shirt before the shreeve returned and untied her and the horses. Mylah knew that even by horseback, it would be at least a two-day trip to the king's castle, and she figured they'd be stopping somewhere to rest.

"Time to go…" The man looked her over. "What's your name?"

"Leylah," Mylah lied. She had to tell the lie as if she believed it every time, or else she would be discovered once they questioned her with sprites.

"Broderick and Sabine," the man reciprocated, and Mylah nodded. "You can ride behind Sabine." Sabine took that as her cue and climbed into the saddle of one of the horses. Broderick stepped up behind Mylah and picked her up in a swift motion, placing her on a padded seat behind the saddle.

"Hold tight," Sabine said and Mylah reluctantly put her arms around Sabine's waist. "If you start feeling nauseous, please tell me before you throw up." Mylah furrowed her brow in confusion but said nothing. Broderick climbed into his saddle and took off at a trot before them. Sabine's horse followed. They began to pick up speed, until the trees were rushing past them on either side. Mylah held as tightly as she could to Sabine whose body shook with laughter.

"What is this..." Mylah's voice was carried away by the wind, but Sabine had heard her. Mylah was beginning to understand why Sabine thought Mylah might throw up, and that may have been the case if she'd had anything in her stomach.

"Enchanted horses. Otherwise, it would take us days every time we wanted to do a border patrol. Might as well live out here at that point," Sabine yelled over the wind. Mylah should have guessed. The shreeve had magic, of course they would use it to make traveling faster.

As they rode, they passed a large town. It was bigger than the village in Adair, though not by much. They passed it too quickly for Mylah to take note of any place in particular that may house a witch named Edris.

They arrived at the Elowyn kingdom within hours rather than days. Mylah was grateful for that since she was on a time crunch thanks to the naga. She'd have to find some way to get her hands on one of the enchanted horses when she went back out to deliver the naga's request.

They trotted up to the castle at a normal pace and Mylah turned to see the town laid out in the distance below them. There were so many buildings and houses, so many places to search for Edris. Mylah sighed and turned back towards the castle.

Surrounding the castle was a large wall that probably helped to keep out any unwanted visitors. Mylah was surprised they didn't have a moat as they had in Amaris. She had studied all the maps while confined to King Florian's castle and knew more than she thought she'd ever need to know about every kingdom. Elowyn and Amaris were the two shreeve kingdoms, then there was Hyrdian which was mainly made up of witches and warlocks, though some fae lived there as well. And, of course, the human kingdoms; Adair, Umbra, and Cambri, which were all clumped together on the Northeast side of the island.

Mylah shoved all the maps to the back of her mind as they came to a stop outside of a small door that looked like a servant's entrance. Broderick hopped off his horse with ease and helped Mylah down from Sabine's horse. Sabine leapt down beside her. A younger shreeve came out the door and his eyes widened in surprise when he saw them. He said nothing, though, and took the reins of the horses, leading them away.

"Come, we must make you presentable for the king." Broderick took Mylah's arm and led her into the castle. The door opened into a long, stone, hallway. At the end was a kitchen filled with servants. Some sat at a table, chatting, while others were baking, cooking, or cleaning. They all turned to look as Mylah was led into the room.

"Back so soon?" one of the cooks asked Broderick.

"Had to deliver a package to the king," Broderick joked, and the cook laughed.

"I hope she fares better than the last one," the cook said before turning back to his steaming pot, stirring it once.

Mylah's heart threatened to beat out of her chest as her nerves increased. No one had given her any confidence that the king would be willing to even hear her out.

Broderick led Mylah out of the kitchen into another hallway. Sabine followed behind them. They took a staircase down a flight, entering another hallway, and stopped at a closed door. Just as King Florian's castle had been, the Elowyn castle was entirely made of stone, except for the window and doors, which were wooden.

Sabine knocked on the door three times and stepped back to wait. It took a solid minute before it opened. At first, Mylah saw no one. Then she heard a voice.

"Not another one..." Mylah looked down to see a wrinkled old woman glaring up at her with glowing yellow eyes. Mylah recognized her as a goblin, though she had only seen a few in King Florian's castle. Most of his servants had been human. "Bring her in."

"Thank you, Petra. I owe you." Broderick pulled Mylah into the room and Sabine shut the door behind them. The goblin woman, Petra, hobbled over to a bath and began running the water.

"I don't know when you will learn..." Petra grumbled. "I hope she's a lucky one." Mylah watched as Petra pulled her own scraggly hair into a bun with her knobbed fingers and secured it there with a tie. "Now, shoo you two. I'll make her presentable." Mylah was hesitant to be left alone with the woman, but she had no say in the matter. Broderick and Sabine retreated through the door and Mylah turned back to the bath.

"What do you need me to do?" Mylah asked, her voice shaking. She hadn't meant to do it, but it was a nice touch.

"Nothing, girl. You're about to be put through enough," Petra said. There was pity in her eyes, and Mylah gulped.

"Is it going to be that bad?" she nearly whispered. Petra didn't reply, but she beckoned Mylah forward.

"Strip down and climb into the tub. I'll bring you new clothes." Petra walked away, allowing Mylah to undress in private. There was soap on the edge of the tub, and Mylah used it to scrub all the dirt from her skin. When Petra returned, she held out a towel to Mylah, who took it as she climbed out of the tub.

"How many humans has Broderick brought to you?" Mylah asked, not sure if she even wanted to know the answer.

"You're the fourth." Petra motioned for Mylah to follow her. They walked through a narrow passageway that opened into a bigger room. There was a small bed made of straw in one corner, and a wardrobe stuffed full of gowns and dresses in the other. Mylah could tell that none of the clothes belonged to Petra, who wore a simple tunic with matching fitted pants. Her bony feet were bare and Mylah shuddered at the sight of them.

"Put this on. I haven't tried this one yet." Petra held up a sleek gray gown with long sleeves, a deep v-neck, and a jewel studded belt at the waist. Mylah pulled it on, but before she could pull on the left sleeve, Petra grabbed her arm and traced the scratch left from the naga's fang. It appeared redder than the night before.

"This is not good, girl." Petra dropped her arm and let Mylah pull it into the sleeve. "What are we supposed to do with you once that poison has spread through your system? You won't last the week even if you get lucky with

Castien..." Petra's eyes widened in panic, and she stuttered, "K-King Castien."

"Don't be proper on my account," Mylah smirked, and Petra's shoulders drooped as she let out a breath of relief. "As for the naga's venom, don't worry about that either. I have a deal with them."

"Tsk, tsk. Deals with the naga are dangerous. But that's *your* problem. If you survive the night, you can deal with that another day." Petra took Mylah's arm and hauled her over to a chair. Mylah sat as Petra took her hair and began pulling it tightly against her head. Mylah tried not to cry out in pain.

"No, no..." Petra released all Mylah's hair, and it brushed against her back that the dress had left mostly bare. "I did that last time..." Petra spoke to herself.

"Does my appearance correlate with whether the king will let me live?" Mylah asked, wincing as Petra gripped her hair again.

"Not sure," Petra grunted, twisting the hair into a new formation. "But it can't hurt." Petra sighed and released Mylah's hair again. This time, she grabbed half of it and braided it into a crown on Mylah's head, leaving the bottom half to curl down her back. She smeared red onto Mylah's lips, and some deep purple shadow onto her eyelids.

"Is there anything you can tell me to help me survive the king?" Mylah asked.

Petra was silent for a few minutes as she outlined Mylah's eyes with a charcoal color. Petra sighed as she finished her masterpiece.

"Don't talk unless spoken to, don't make eye contact, shower the king with compliments, and don't lie. The sprites will catch you on all your lies. That's the fastest way to get yourself killed."

"Thank you," Mylah was not only referring to the advice, but to her whole new appearance. Looking in the cracked oval mirror on the wall, she barely recognized herself, and not just because of the makeover Petra had done. Mylah's cheekbones, collarbones, and jaw line were more pronounced from all the weight she had lost during her month in King Florian's castle. Her muscles were more defined on her arms and legs, which she worried would give away her extensive training, but so long as she didn't flex, they weren't obvious.

Mylah had to turn away from the mirror when she noticed the hollowness of her eyes and Genevieve popped into her mind. *There is a great amount of resentment and sadness in your heart. I can sense it.* It hadn't just been a sixth sense that had given that away to Genevieve, Mylah now realized.

Petra placed a crooked finger under the necklace hanging at the base of Mylah's throat.

"Where'd you get this?" she asked. Mylah grasped it protectively and Petra smirked.

"My mother gave it to me." Mylah had forgotten she had it on.

"Pretty. Don't let the king know where it came from if you can get around it. He doesn't care much for sentiment."

Mylah stood from the chair and followed Petra back into the room with the tub. Petra opened the door revealing Broderick and Sabine still waiting outside. Sabine gave Mylah a once over and nodded her approval to Petra. Broderick immediately pointed to the necklace, drawn to it as Petra had been.

"That's not from here," he stated. "It's dangerous for her to wear it in front of the king."

"Shush, Broderick. She'll do fine." Petra squeezed Mylah's arm, directly on the naga's scratch. Pain flared along the wound and Mylah gasped. She attempted a smile to cover up for the pain, but Sabine and Broderick seemed suspicious.

"Let's get this over with," Sabine said, striding down the hall. Broderick took Mylah's arm, and they followed. This time, they went up a flight of stairs, passing countless chambers and mysterious rooms. There were a set of huge double doors that Mylah assumed led to a ballroom.

Finally, they came to a large opening, but stopped short of it. Mylah could hear voices but couldn't make out what they were saying. Broderick held Mylah back as Sabine stepped into view of the room beyond.

"King Castien," she said, bowing deeply. She did not rise until another voice spoke. She walked further into the room, out of sight. "You have ordered us to bring you no more human refugees." A harsh voice followed. "Yes, I understand. However, Broderick and I..."

"I SAID NO MORE." Mylah heard that loud and clear.

"King Castien, please, she has news from the human king. She said she knows of their plans in the war." Silence followed. Sabine stepped back into view and motioned to Broderick to bring Mylah forward. He took a deep breath and led her in.

Mylah kept her eyes on the floor, trying to follow Petra's advice and not make eye contact. She glanced at the surrounding guards, though. There were four on each side of the room, standing completely still. None of them wore armor, but similar outfits to what Petra had been wearing. Tunics with matching pants. The tunics were sleeveless so Mylah could see the blue and green markings along their arms.

Before her, without looking up, she could see the base of the throne and King Castien's lower body. It was hard to make out his face without making eye contact, so she avoided it. Beside him was another, smaller, vacant throne.

"What makes you think you are worthy of my time and mercy?" King Castien spat the words out.

"I have inside information from King Florian's war council," Mylah said. The sprites fluttering around the room had not escaped her notice. There were about twenty in total. She would have to stick as close to the truth as possible. Lying to one sprite was difficult enough, but with twenty around, it was much more likely for one of them to pick up on a lie.

"*Inside information.* And what makes you think I want to hear it?"

"I've heard of your prowess, King Castien." *Shower him with compliments,* Petra had said. Mylah would do just that. "Your ferociousness, ambition, and guile have not gone unnoticed." These were all facts, not that Mylah believed them, but they *had* been noticed by her.

"Flattery will only get you so far. Tell me your name," the king demanded.

"Leylah Farrow," Mylah said as if it were second nature. She had been going by the name for the last month, so it felt true enough. None of the sprites had made a move, meaning they must have believed it as well.

"Leylah...interesting." King Castien mulled it over. He snapped his fingers and two guards, one from each side of the room, began moving towards Mylah.

"King Castien, if I'm not being too forward, you've barely given her a chance," Broderick said, and Mylah realized what he was afraid of. The king had already decided she was not worthy of his mercy.

"Step back, Broderick, and stop fretting. I have a few tests I want her to pass before I make my final decision," King Castien said as he stood from his throne. Broderick stepped away from Mylah as the two guards reached her side and each took an arm. They began pulling her forward, towards the king. They stopped before the throne. King Castien placed a finger under Mylah's chin and lifted her head so that she was forced to make eye contact with him.

What she saw turned her blood to ice and made her heart skip a beat. Not only was he cruelly beautiful, with his pointed ears and blue and green markings giving him away as purely shreeve, but she recognized his eyes. Sunset orange surrounding a gray iris. For a moment she was transported back to the night her parents died and she saw him standing at her bedroom window as she hid behind a tree. It took every ounce of resolve for Mylah not to rip herself free from the guards and strangle their king right then and there.

"You remind me of someone," the king said, but Mylah could barely hear him over the roaring in her ears. He gave her a wicked grin and sat back on his throne. "Begin the questioning." The guards shifted and threw Mylah down onto her back forcing all the air out of her lungs. At least one of them had the foresight to stop her head from cracking against the stone floor. The sprites swarmed in around her and shooed the guards away. There was no need for them.

Mylah tried to move her limbs, but they felt tethered to the floor. *Magic,* she assumed.

"What is your name?" a sprite, that Mylah guessed to be the leader of the rest, asked. He had long, red hair and wore only pants for clothing. All the others seemed to be fully clothed.

"Leylah Farrow," Mylah gasped out. She was still winded from being thrown to the floor.

"Which kingdom are you from?"

"Adair."

"Who is your king?"

"King Florian."

"How do you come to be in Elowyn?"

"I tried to kill King Florian and was exiled. I came to Elowyn to seek refuge." Mylah was grateful she hadn't had to tell a real lie yet, other than her name. That was the easiest one.

"Why did you try to kill your king?" The sprites closed in around her.

Mylah took a deep breath and recited the lines she had practiced with Bellingham. "I tried to kill the king because he sent my brothers away to patrol our borders for a war that should have never been started. Families are suffering, and I wanted to make the king pay."

"Do you pose a threat to King Castien?" That was the question Mylah dreaded, especially since learning exactly who the king was.

"I am no threat to the king," she purposefully did not speak his name, but the sprites did not let that one slide.

"Tell us that you will not harm King Castien," the sprite demanded. Mylah cleared her mind of all thoughts. She had told Garrick she would stick to her mission of gaining intel. Focusing on that, and forcing herself to believe it, she spoke with as much conviction as she could muster.

"I will not harm King Castien."

The sprites tittered around her, but they seemed to have believed her.

"Enough, Taz," the king commanded, and the leading sprite backed down. The rest followed suit. "Guards, take her and administer the tests." The same two guards stepped forward again and lifted her from the floor. They carried her out through the back of the throne room, and down deep into the castle. Where her screams wouldn't be heard, Mylah assumed.

In what Mylah could only guess was the dungeon, the guards threw her to the floor again. There were shackles bolted to the floor and wall, but they didn't bother to put her in them. She figured they assumed she wouldn't try to escape since she had been the one to seek out the king for asylum.

The guard on her left, who stood at least two heads taller than her, withdrew a dagger the length of his forearm from his belt and approached Mylah. She had prepared for this. She could endure, and she *would*. He pushed up her right sleeve and ran the dagger across her arm in a swift motion. The pain was quick and bearable.

The guard took a vial from his pocket and collected the blood dripping from Mylah's arm.

"Alec, take this to Madame Edris so she can test it." Bells sounded in Mylah's head at the name. *Edrisss*, the naga had said was the name of the person who Mylah had to find. These guards had made her life that much easier, as long as she survived whatever the next tests were.

"What was that for?" Mylah asked, feigning disinterest.

"Testing your blood for magic and potions. Making sure there's nothing in your system to help you deceive the king," the guard explained, cleaning his dagger, and replacing it in his belt. Mylah had no idea what kind of potions she could have used to help her lie, but she was sure some existed.

"You should know that I've been poisoned by a naga, then. I'm sure it will come up and I don't want it to be construed as anything else." Mylah rolled up her left sleeve, revealing her wound which somehow appeared worse than earlier. It was still bright red, but now it was becoming puffy. The guard grabbed her arm and sighed.

"It will likely come up...but I have to follow orders." He pulled his dagger back out. "This is going to hurt..." he sounded apologetic, but that did not stop him from sticking the point of his dagger into the base of the wound and dragging it along the entire span of it. Mylah could not hold back her scream. Blood poured from her arm, stemmed only when the guard waved his hand over the laceration. Mylah's vision blurred and the only thing holding her up was the guard. Otherwise, she'd be passed out on the floor.

Her arm still bled, but it had slowed considerably. Instead of wrapping the wound, the guard massaged the area around it, causing Mylah to scream out again. That time, she did pass out. When she came to, she was up against the wall of the dungeon with bandages wrapped around her arm. Both guards stood before her.

"What was that for?" Mylah managed to gasp out. They turned to her, realizing she was awake.

"I had to be sure there was nothing hidden in your arm," the guard explained. Mylah's blood still covered his hands, and the sight made her dizzy.

"*Something in my arm?*" Mylah tried to lift her arm, but it remained limp at her side.

"You'd be surprised what people have done to themselves in order to get close enough to the king to kill him."

"Okay. What's next?" Mylah's breaths came out in short gasps. She wasn't sure she would be able to handle whatever came next, but she had to try. The guards appeared surprised.

"Most humans give up after that test," the guard named Alec commented. "What do you think, Nic?" He turned to the other guard. "Should we keep going?"

Nic nodded solemnly. "Let's get it over with."

"Do you want me to do it this time?" Alec offered, but Nic shook his head. Mylah closed her eyes, preparing for whatever was coming her way. Instead of anything physical, she felt a tug on her heart instead. It surprised her, but with it came a wave of grief. Memories of her parents flashed in her mind. Their last moments and walking into their home to find them dead stuck out the most. Nic gasped and Mylah worried that he could see her memories. They would give her away as a liar.

"What's happening?" she whispered, trying to hold back her tears.

"Nic is triggering your worst memories, but he is also feeling what you were in those memories. It's a side effect," Alec explained. Thankfully, he said nothing about Nic actually knowing what the memories were, only the feelings associated with them. The grief mounted and forced the tears down Mylah's cheeks. Nausea roiled in her stomach, and she teetered on the edge of losing herself, but she forced her mind to the moments *after* her worst memories.

Garrick was there, Elena, Crane, and Greyson. Happiness sparked inside her and began to wash away the grief. Before it completely dissipated, Nic excused himself and Mylah heard him throwing up in the hallway. Her mind went back to its normal state of careful consideration.

"Is he going to be alright?" Mylah asked, wiping away the remaining tears. Alec seemed worried, but he said nothing. Nic returned a minute later.

"That's the first time anyone's been able to find their way out of their grief while I performed the manipulation." Nic appeared pale but intrigued. "How did you do it?" Mylah would not reveal her secrets to these strangers.

"I don't know," she lied. If she had to die to protect her family, she would.

"Well, it doesn't matter. I talked to Madame Edris, and your blood is clean, other than the naga poison, which she claims will kill you within the week."

"I know," Mylah said. Nic and Alec exchanged a disconcerting look. She knew that she was not what they had expected.

"I guess you've passed the tests then," Nic said, and he and Alec helped Mylah to her feet. "Time to return to King Castien so he can make his final decision."

"That's it?" Mylah asked, shocked there weren't any more vigorous tests.

"What were you expecting? Each test we administered had a purpose. We don't torture humans for fun, only out of necessity," Alec said, and relief washed over Mylah. She had done it; she had passed their tests. Now, she had to make one last good impression on the king, and she could find Madame Edris and complete her quest for the naga. Everything seemed to be going smoothly. Other than the fact that her arm throbbed, and the pain was ten times worse than before.

"Out of curiosity, what is the purpose of making someone relive their worst memories?" Mylah asked as they led her from the dungeon.

"The worse the grief, the more you've been through. Any exile, or someone claiming to have attempted an assassination on their king wouldn't be without trauma," Alec explained.

When they returned to the throne room, King Castien still sat on his throne, waiting for them.

"I was beginning to wonder if you'd be back," he grinned at Mylah who shuddered. She couldn't forget that he was the cause of her worst memories, and she would find a way to make him pay. "How did it go?" He looked at the guards who brought Mylah to a halt before him.

"Unexpectedly well," Alec spoke first.

"She did struggle with the second test, but otherwise, she surprised us." Nic gazed down at Mylah, obviously still questioning how she had overcome her own grief.

"Interesting. She doesn't look like much. I hadn't expected her to be back," the king said. He stood from his throne and approached her, his eyes locked onto hers, until he stood right in front of her. He glanced down and lifted the pendant on her necklace slightly. Mylah remembered what the others had said about him not caring much for sentiment, and kept her mouth shut.

"Did anyone inspect this? It could be a charm..."

"Petra inspected it," Broderick spoke, causing Mylah to turn. She had not noticed him standing amongst the guards at the edge of the room. "I suggested we confiscate it, but Petra said not to."

"So, Petra is now the expert in charms and trinkets? I'll be sure to remember that next time." The king yanked on the necklace, breaking the clasp and jerking Mylah's head forward. She gasped. Anger welled up inside her. "Take this to Madame Edris." He dropped the necklace into Alec's palm.

"Will I get it back?" Mylah dared to ask.

"What does it matter to you?" King Castien returned to his throne.

"I-I just like it," she said, but King Castien did not respond to her.

"If the necklace checks out, she can stay. If not, dispose of it and her." King Castien waved his hand and Alec went one way to bring the necklace to Madame Edris, while Nic steered Mylah the other way.

Fourteen

Nic led Mylah out of the throne room. As they walked, he loosened his grip on her arm.

"What are you planning on doing about that arm?" He gestured to her naga bite. It throbbed from the wound that Nic had inflicted.

"I'll worry about that once I find out if the king accepts me," Mylah said. It was not entirely untrue, though she knew exactly what she planned to do. She was going to steal the necklace of teeth from Madame Edris somehow and get it to the naga. Thankfully Nic asked no more questions.

They came to a small sitting room with bright red couches lining the three walls. There was a large, low table in the center of the room littered with books and other trinkets.

"Wait here. Someone will retrieve you once the final decision has been made." Nic nodded to Mylah as he left. She sat down on the nearest couch and allowed herself to fall back against the cushions. Her body immediately relaxed. Her aches and pains seemed to seep away into the couch and her eyes became heavy.

She studied the paintings on the walls. The first she observed appeared to be a portrait of King Castien, while the next was of someone who looked completely different. While King Castien's skin was of a tanner complexion and his features sharp and strong, the next portrait was of a man with fair skin and softer features. His eyes were narrower and his nose crooked. He was not as naturally beautiful as King Castien. Her best guess was that it was a portrait of King Haldor. Mylah had heard about King Haldor, King Castien's predecessor and his stepfather. There were more portraits lined up on the walls, but Mylah's eyes drifted closed. She curled up on the couch and fell asleep.

When Mylah felt someone shaking her shoulder to wake her, she jumped to her feet, startling them. Sabine stood there holding Mylah's necklace.

"You did it," she said as her eyes lit up. "I don't know how, but you convinced the king to let you stay." Sabine handed her the necklace and Mylah put it in her pocket, hoping she'd be able to fix the clasp later. "Congratulations, you are now a prisoner of the Elowyn kingdom."

"Oh, stop it," Broderick chided as he walked into the room. "She's not a prisoner."

"What else would you call someone who is held captive in a castle?" Sabine raised her brow, turning her gaze on Broderick.

"Alive," Broderick answered, and Sabine guffawed. Mylah found nothing to laugh about, though she was grateful she had made it that far. But, if she were not allowed to leave the castle, it would make keeping her promise to the naga that much more challenging.

"Would you be able to take me to Madame Edris?" Mylah figured scouting out Madame Edris' room was a good place to start when it came to finding the necklace.

"Not sure you want to go there. She's a nasty witch," Sabine said, glancing at Broderick who nodded in agreement.

"Unfortunately," Mylah lifted her sleeve to reveal her now purple forearm. The worst of the damage was still covered with a bandage. "I don't have much of a choice if I want to stay alive any longer." Sabine gasped and Broderick grabbed Mylah's arm, inspecting it.

"Damn it. We had such high hopes for you," Sabine said, sighing.

"No. We're not giving up that easily. We'll take her to Madame Edris. She'll have something to help." Broderick's eyes gave away the fact that he believed the opposite to be true. "Come on." He pulled Mylah along behind him, seeming to forget her injury and causing her arm to burn.

He led her down towards the dungeon with Sabine following them. Madame Edris' room was a few doors down from the dungeon where Mylah had been *tested*. Broderick knocked on the door. A clanking sound came from within, and the door was thrown open. Behind it stood a tall, beautiful woman with bright green hair and matching eyes. A wildfire burned in her eyes as she took in the sight before her.

"What do you want?" her voice came out as a screech and made Mylah cringe. The woman's looks began to fade and she shrunk down into a hunched back old woman, as Mylah had originally pictured. Her eyes glazed over, and her skin stretched to become leathery and sagging.

"Trying out a new glamour?" Broderick joked, but his laugh came out strained and nervous. The witch waved her hand in the air and let out a hiss.

"I'll turn you into a pile of cock-a-roaches if you don't get on with it," she threatened.

"Right, sorry, Madame. Our new guest is in need of some healing." Broderick pulled Mylah to the front and pushed her towards Madame Edris.

"Ah, yes. The naga bite. I found the poison in her system when I tested her blood." Madame Edris gripped Mylah's arm with her talon like fingers, letting the sharp nails dig into Mylah's skin. Mylah flinched but did not pull away. "I have nothing for that, but I can numb the pain." She kept hold of Mylah's arm as she led her deeper into the room. Shelves lined the walls and were filled with all sorts of horrors. From what Mylah could see, there were jars of all different body parts, swirling liquids, live creatures, dead creatures, and many more that she couldn't even guess at.

"Sit," Madame Edris commanded, shoving Mylah down into a chair by her shoulder. She started rummaging through a drawer in an old wooden desk. In the middle of the room there were multiple cauldrons of different sizes, some steaming, others bubbling. Hanging from the ceiling Mylah noticed some hides, herbs, and what appeared to be laundry. "Ah, here." She held a vial filled with a dark green poultice. She pulled out the stopper and began to unwrap Mylah's bandage. Underneath, the wound from Nic had mostly healed, which didn't surprise Mylah because she was sure he had used magic on it. The naga's bite festered, though, and it looked darker, and deeper. Madame Edris poured the contents of her vial over the wound and spread it

Holly Huntress

out. It stung at first, but then the pain lessened. After a minute, the pain was completely gone.

"There, now you shall die a painless death," the witch sneered and revealed her perfect teeth. They didn't quite fit with the rest of her image and Mylah wondered how she managed to keep them that way. There was no way she was asking, though. Instead, she took another look around the room, spotting what it was she had come for: the necklace of naga teeth. Madame Edris noticed her staring at it.

"The very cause of your ailment," she commented, hobbling over to the wall on which the necklace was so prominently displayed. "It's taken me hundreds of years to collect all of these. Yet, I still have not developed an antidote for their poison." She held the necklace lovingly in her hands before replacing it on its perch jutting out from the wall.

"Do you mind if I take a closer look?" Mylah asked, knowing it was going to be impossible to take it now, but she needed to try. Madame Edris hissed at her in answer and Mylah put her hands up in surrender. "Sorry, I'll stay away."

"Good. Now get out, the lot of you." She shooed them from her room.

"That went well," Sabine groaned. "So much for this one..."

"Don't worry about me, I'll be fine," Mylah said, smiling. Broderick and Sabine looked at her like she was crazy, but she didn't care, because she knew exactly where to find the necklace that was going to save her life.

"She's high off whatever that salve was. Great." Sabine rolled her eyes and stalked off down the hall.

141

"Do I have a room or anything?" Mylah asked Broderick, who appeared crestfallen.

"Maybe Petra knows of something that can help..." Broderick was too busy talking with himself to hear Mylah. She sighed and realized that maybe she could use his strange need to keep her alive to her advantage. She took hold of Broderick's shoulder and made him look at her.

"Would it make you feel better if I told you I have a plan to save myself?"

"You do?" His eyes lit up. "What is it?"

"I can't tell you here." Mylah inclined her head towards Madame Edris' door and Broderick nodded in understanding, though his eyebrows furrowed in worry.

"Come on. I'll take you to your room."

Fifteen

Broderick showed Mylah to a room on the same floor as the throne room where Sabine rejoined them. There were so many hallways and turns, Mylah was sure she would get lost if she ever had to walk around alone. The room was small, holding only a twin-size bed, armoire, and vanity.

"It's nothing fancy, but better than the dungeon I'm sure," Broderick commented, closing the door behind him. "We should be safe to talk in here."

"Good. Do you mind me asking *why* you wanted the king to accept me so badly? Why not let me die as I assume all the others who have passed through here have?"

"Broderick has some sense that he can restore the king's humanity or some nonsense," Sabine said, rolling her eyes.

"Well, I have no idea how that will happen," Mylah said, doubting she would have any effect on the king. She was there to find someone who could help her learn some of a forgotten shreeve language. She had enough on her plate without worrying about helping the Elowyns.

"So, what is your plan for that bite?" Sabine asked.

"I made a deal with the naga."

"Those never end well," Broderick groaned.

"Well, let's hope this one is different. I promised the naga that I would bring them the necklace of naga teeth that Madame Edris has." Mylah stopped as Broderick threw his hands in the air.

"That's impossible! She never leaves that room! This is hopeless...you're going to die Leylah." Broderick sunk onto the bed with his head in his hands. Mylah paused at the sound of her fake name.

"That's why I need your help. If you can distract her long enough for me to grab the necklace and get out, I can save myself."

"You are forgetting that not only will you have to accomplish stealing the necklace," Sabine started. "But we also have to get you out of the castle unnoticed, back to the Unbound territory, find the naga, get back before anyone notices you're gone, and then pray that somehow Madame Edris never finds out you stole her most prized possession."

"So, are you in?" Mylah grinned and Broderick groaned in frustration but nodded his head.

"It will certainly liven things up around here." He looked up at Mylah and smirked.

"Are you crazy?" Sabine asked, her gaze darting between Mylah and Broderick.

"You'll help, won't you?" Mylah hoped Sabine wouldn't ruin everything by revealing her plan to Madame Edris, but she couldn't pull off her theft alone. Mylah's life depended on the plan going off without a hitch.

Sabine sighed and her shoulders drooped. "Yes," she groaned. "I'll help."

"Thank you!" Mylah yelled and then brought her voice back down, realizing someone may overhear them. "Really, thank you, Sabine. I've come so far I really don't want this scratch to be the death of me." She traced the black veins spreading out from the wound on her arm. She pulled down her sleeve to cover it.

"You should change and get some rest. I'll send up food and water. We need to do this tonight. I don't think you have as long as you think. Whatever they did in the dungeon sped up the spread of the poison." Broderick stood from the bed and opened the door. Sabine marched out in front of him.

"Thank you," Mylah said.

"Don't make us regret helping you." Broderick closed the door behind him. A whisper of guilt nagged at Mylah, but she pushed it away. She could not feel guilty lying to these people, she had to stay focused. Staying alive meant the chance at repaying King Castien for the murder of her parents. She could do nothing that would risk exposure, though, until she had completed her mission for King Florian. Then, it wouldn't matter whether she lived or died.

Mylah stripped off the dress and found a pair of black trousers and a black tunic in the armoire to wear. After devouring the meal Broderick had sent for her, she crawled into bed and fell asleep almost instantly.

King Castien haunted her even in her dreams. His eyes swam before her, watching her as she hid in the woods, clutching the shreeve book to her chest. He always found her no matter how long she hid, or how far she ran. His laugh echoed through her head and pulled her from her sleep.

When she woke, Broderick stood over her with Sabine at his side. Mylah stifled a scream.

"I told you we should have knocked," Sabine whispered, but Broderick brushed her off.

"Come on, we have to go now."

Mylah climbed out of bed and slipped on a pair of boots. She was still dressed in the pants and tunic, ready to attempt their daunting task. Broderick led the way through the corridors, ducking into rooms when guards approached. Mylah worried about what would happen to them if they were discovered.

They made their way towards Madame Edris' room. In the final stretch, Broderick stopped. He turned to Mylah and took her arm. He pulled up her sleeve to reveal her wound.

"Sorry about this..." he said, but before Mylah could respond, he dug his nails into the still healing knife wound while Sabine covered Mylah's mouth to stifle her scream. Her arm immediately began to burn and ooze. Whatever salve the witch had put on it earlier took over again and wiped away the pain.

Mylah gasped once Sabine removed her hand from her mouth.

"We needed a reason to be down here," Broderick said. He knocked on Madame Edris' door and they waited. After a few seconds they heard shuffling on the other side of the door. This time when the door opened, Madame Edris wore no glamour, and she did not look happy.

"This had better be important, or else I'll rip your pretty little eyes out of your head and cook them in my stew," she growled, her eyes roving over the group of them.

"It is Madame. Here, take a look." Broderick grabbed Mylah's arm and thrust it towards the witch who clucked her tongue. She took hold of Mylah and pulled her into the room once more. Sabine and Broderick shuffled in behind them. Mylah noticed Sabine gazing around at all the shelves. Broderick inclined his head towards the necklace on the wall, and Sabine gave an almost imperceptible nod.

"This is not looking good for you, girl." Mylah sat down in the chair and waited as Madame Edris rummaged through her desk again. Mylah knew she needed to stall.

"I'm sorry to interrupt your sleep," she said, drawing the witch's attention away from the drawer. "It started oozing and I was worried."

"Rightfully so," Madame Edris grunted. "You'll be dead in a few days, though, so I don't see much point in slowing down the inevitable."

"Well, hopefully I'll be able to find someone to help me before then." Mylah knew if their plan worked, and the naga cured her, Madame Edris would be suspicious. She would have to come up with a good story as to how she cured herself.

"If I can't save you, no one can," she cackled and Mylah cringed. Madame Edris pulled a small box out of the drawer and placed it on the desk. Across the room, Sabine took great care not to make a sound as she removed the necklace of naga teeth from its perch on the wall and folded it into her pouch at her side.

"This should stop the oozing." Madame Edris placed leaves over Mylah's arm and pressed them down, covering them with a bandage. "Now please leave my sight and don't come back unless you're actually dead. Then I could use what's left of you for some of my tonics and salves."

Mylah shuddered. "Will do," she said as she stood and followed Sabine and Broderick out of the room. As soon as the door shut behind them, they broke out into a run.

"It won't be long before she notices the necklace is missing. We need to be gone when she does," Broderick said as they ran. He led the way to the kitchens where they had entered the castle earlier that day. Now it was empty. "Come on, I had the stable boy bring the horses round for us."

Outside, two horses grazed by the door. Broderick helped Mylah up onto the first one, swinging himself up behind her. Sabine climbed onto the other and they took off. Mylah could not believe her luck that they had made it so far without being stopped.

They had almost made it to the edge of the forest when another horse bolted in front of them, causing the horse Broderick and Mylah sat upon to jerk to a stop. The sudden motion would have sent Mylah flying, had Broderick not had a strong grip on her. The figure on the horse blocking them was cloaked and unrecognizable until he threw his hood back.

His beauty was striking, as King Castien's was, but his features weren't as sharp, and he didn't have pointed ears. While the king had blonde hair that was cropped on the sides and longer on top, the man before her had shaggier, dark brown hair. His eyes were similar to Mylah's own, a dark grayish blue, but surrounded with a light green where hers were white. Based on the portrait Mylah had seen of King Haldor earlier, the features of the man before her, specifically his crooked nose, gave him away as King Haldor's biological son.

"Prince Elias," Broderick gasped. Sabine inclined her head to him in a bow. Dread crept up on Mylah as she realized it was most likely the end of their mission.

"May I inquire as to what you are doing out here? And who is *she*?" Prince Elias took in the three of them.

"Sir, the girl has been accepted by the king into the court, but she is dying," Broderick began to explain.

"What do you mean?"

"She was bitten by a naga while seeking refuge, and we are simply helping her to fulfill a deal with the naga so that she can be cured and returned safely to the castle."

"Does Castien know of all this?" The prince eyed Mylah, his brows furrowed, and lips pursed in suspicion. "How do you know it's not a trick of some kind..." As if on cue, dizziness washed over Mylah, and she slumped to the side. Broderick barely caught her. Prince Elias leapt from his horse to help lower her to the ground.

"It's the...poison..." Mylah gulped past a lump in her throat. "I think...whatever the witch did..." she closed her eyes, unable to speak anymore, though she remained conscious.

"It's the leaves. They are probably meant to help her rest," Broderick said as he pulled up Mylah's sleeve to show the prince. They both gasped at what they saw. Mylah could only imagine how much worse it had become since leaving the castle. Having no pain helped her in a sense, but it also made her unaware of the severity of the wound.

"We need to get her to the naga now," Sabine urged.

"But Castien..." the prince began to protest.

"We can worry about him later," Broderick hissed. "She needs help *now*."

"Fine, but I am coming with you." Prince Elias helped lift Mylah back onto the horse where Broderick secured her in his arms. The warmth radiating from him helped ease the tension building in her chest. She wondered if the poison was reaching her heart.

Mylah could feel that they were moving, but she still couldn't open her eyes, or help Broderick support her weight. The wind whipped her hair around her face, and she knew it also plagued Broderick. She thought that she slipped in and out of consciousness but couldn't be sure. It may have all been a dream.

Eventually, they stopped and Mylah was taken from the horse. She gained a second wind and opened her eyes to see the forest surrounding them. Prince Elias crouched before her, concern in his eyes. Broderick and Sabine were gone, probably looking for the naga.

"I thought we'd lost you for a second." The prince breathed a sigh of relief. Mylah managed a grimace and pushed herself up to a sitting position.

"I wasn't so sure myself..." she tried to get to her feet, but her body wouldn't support her.

"Careful, don't push yourself. I think the poison is working its way through you much quicker than normal."

"Great. Something else I can add to my list of achievements: fastest poison absorber," Mylah joked, and Prince Elias chuckled.

"A sense of humor at a time like this? I think you'll fit in nicely in the court. Though I have no idea how you got so lucky to have my brother accept you." He shook his head.

"Must be..." Mylah winced as pain bloomed in her head. "Ugh." She closed her eyes.

"Stay with me." Prince Elias gripped her hand in his.

"The charm," Mylah gasped out.

"What?"

"I was saying...your brother...the king..." Mylah tried to explain, but it hurt too much to talk.

"Oh right, your charm, yes, that must be what made him decide to let you stay," Prince Elias filled in the gaps. A rustling sound came from behind Mylah, and she forced her eyes open.

"I sssee you've found your way back to me. But do you have what I asssked after?" The naga slithered past Mylah to stand in front of her and the prince. "What a pity to sssee sssuch a beautiful and ssshort-lived life dwindling away."

"I...have...the necklace..." Mylah forced the words out.

"Well where isss it?" The naga looked at her expectantly. Mylah gripped Prince Elias' hand and looked up at him.

"Sabine," she choked out. He nodded in understanding and took off into the woods to find Sabine.

"It seemsss you have acccelerated the processs of dying. My poissson doesss not normally work that quickly." The naga observed Mylah with interest. "Could be the Belladonna leavesss." They smirked and Mylah turned her head to her arm, brushing the leaves from it with great difficulty. Sabine and Prince Elias came crashing back through the woods towards them.

"Here! I have the necklace!" Sabine yelled as she pulled the necklace from her pouch.

"Thank you." The naga took the necklace and hung it around their neck. "Now you ssshall have the antidote. But it will not help with the Belladonna'sss poissson now coursssing through her veinsss."

"What are you talking about?" Sabine rushed to Mylah's side, grabbing the vial that the naga held out to her. "Belladonna." Sabine noticed the leaves that Mylah had brushed off her arm and realization dawned on her. "Madame Edris," she groaned. "She was thinking to speed up your death because she knew it was inevitable...that accursed witch. The leaves wouldn't have been enough, she probably had it in the salve too."

"Bessst wissshesss." The naga slithered back into the woods as Broderick ran into view.

"What's happening, did you get the antidote?" he asked as Sabine tipped the antidote into Mylah's mouth. It immediately eased the tightness in her chest and the pain in her head.

"I'm no longer dying from the naga's poison," Mylah said as Broderick knelt beside her.

"That's great!"

"But," Mylah couldn't stop herself from laughing and Broderick's eyes widened in confusion.

"But what?" he asked, looking at Sabine and Prince Elias for help.

"The witch poisoned me too. Nightshade..." Mylah gestured to the leaves beside her.

"You've got to be kidding me..."

"I wish I was, but fate apparently doesn't want me to survive this night." Mylah could not believe her terrible luck.

"That's why the poison seemed to be affecting you so much faster than we expected," Sabine said.

"We need to get you back..." Broderick began, but Prince Elias stopped him.

"There's no time. She'll be dead before we get there, it's a miracle she's lasted this long," the prince said.

"We can't just let her die!" Broderick cried out. Mylah stood shakily and reached out to him. He let her take his hand.

"It's okay," she smiled at him, but he shook his head. She'd at least be able to see her parents again. A wave of calm washed over her at that thought.

"I'm not going to let her die," Prince Elias said, taking hold of Mylah's injured arm. "This might feel weird, bear with me." He closed his eyes and gripped Mylah's arm tightly. A tugging sensation began in her arm, and it started to ooze again, though this time what came out was black and viscous. Mylah's stomach turned at the sight.

"Prince Elias, you shouldn't risk it." Sabine stepped forward, but the prince waved her back, never opening his eyes or losing his focus. After a few more minutes, the liquid coming from Mylah's arm turned to blood. He had pulled all the poison from her veins.

"There," he gasped as he released Mylah's arm. "We should still have you checked when we get back, but you'll survive." He appeared exhausted and his eyes were bloodshot. A small trickle of blood dripped from his nose, but he swiped it away before Sabine or Broderick saw.

"Thank you," Mylah was exhausted herself, but she no longer felt near death.

"We should get moving." Prince Elias turned away and climbed onto his horse, not waiting for the others to follow. Mylah watched him in awe. He had used magic to save her, just as Broderick and Sabine had risked themselves to help her. Maybe the shreeve weren't as horrible as King Florian thought them to be.

Sixteen

When they returned to the castle, everything was quiet. No one had noticed Mylah's absence, and Madame Edris had not noticed her missing necklace. They entered through the kitchens again, which struck Mylah as odd, since they now had the prince with them, but he did not seem fazed by it.

"I can't go back to see Madame Edris, she's the one who tried to kill me," Mylah reminded them as they discussed their next move.

"Only because she thought you were already dying," Sabine countered. "She probably figured she was doing you a favor."

"Still..." Mylah gave her a knowing look. They had not told the prince that the necklace they had given the naga was stolen from Madame Edris.

"She did say not to come back unless you were dead," Broderick added. "Petra may be able to help."

"Madame Edris will see her. I will make sure that she doesn't try anything else to harm the girl," Prince Elias' voice overpowered them all and his words were a command.

"It's Leylah," Mylah corrected him. He couldn't be much older than her, and it made her uncomfortable to be referred to as 'the girl.' He didn't respond but led the way to Madame Edris' room. Mylah loathed to be going back there for the third time. Madame Edris would know immediately something was off when she saw Mylah still alive, and then it was a short leap to her realizing her necklace was missing.

Before knocking, Prince Elias turned to Broderick and Sabine. "You two should return to your posts. I can deal with Madame Edris." Neither of them protested, though Broderick hesitated before turning and leaving with Sabine. Prince Elias knocked on the door, and Madame Edris actually smiled when she saw him standing in her doorway.

"To what do I owe this pleasure, Prince Elias?" Her voice sounded higher and more girlish. Mylah noticed her features beginning to change as well to resemble that beautiful woman she had embodied when Mylah first met her. Mylah could still see the old witch underneath the glamour though.

"I need you to make sure there is no lingering poison in Leylah's blood." The prince pulled Mylah forward and a scowl immediately replaced the smile on the witch's face as the glamour faded.

"You again...you're supposed to be dead," the witch didn't sound surprised, but annoyed.

"No thanks to you and your nightshade," Mylah pointed out and the witch shrugged.

"You seem to have overcome it, I'd say, no harm done." Madame Edris took a step back and waved them into her room. "Let's get this over with so I can get some peace. Girl, come, sit." She pointed to a chair and Mylah sat. Mylah couldn't help glancing towards where the necklace should have been on the wall and prayed that Madame Edris would not notice its absence while they were there.

Madame Edris took a vial of Mylah's blood, from her hand rather than her already wounded arm. She took it to one of her cauldrons and poured it in. She remained silent as she stirred other liquids into the pot. After a few minutes she raised her eyebrows in surprise.

"Poison free. I'm curious how you managed..." she turned to the wall where her precious necklace of naga teeth had once been displayed and let out a terrible screech. Mylah clamped her hands over her ears. Madame Edris' eyes landed on Mylah, and rage burned there. Before Mylah knew what was happening, Madame Edris was on top of her with her hands around her throat. "You wretched, little..."

"MADAME EDRIS," Prince Elias' voice boomed across the room making the witch loosen her grip on Mylah, though her hands were still at her throat. "Release her at once. She is a guest of the king, and you will be sure to remember your place." Madame Edris slowly released her hold of Mylah and took a step away, never taking her eyes from her.

"She stole my most prized possession. Surely the king does not look kindly upon thievery in his castle," her words came out like daggers pointed straight at Mylah who shuddered.

"Where is your proof? The king will not condemn someone for thievery if there is no evidence."

"She gave it to the naga, there will be no evidence left," her voice shook with rage.

"Leylah was with me all night. I healed her, there was no naga," Prince Elias lied, and Mylah gaped at him. What reason did he have to lie for her?

"Are you willing to declare that before the sprites?" Madame Edris turned on him and stalked across the room.

"Are you questioning my authority and my allegiance to my kingdom? That could be considered *treason*, Madame. I would watch your tongue before you spread any sort of rumors regarding your crowned prince." The way he spoke struck fear into Mylah, even though she knew he was bluffing. He had lied and Madame Edris knew it, but there was nothing she could do.

"I will not forget this. Leave, the both of you. Do not seek my help again." Madame Edris snapped her fingers and the door to the room flew open, slamming against the wall. Mylah didn't hesitate. She leapt from the chair and ran from the room. Prince Elias took his time, breezing across the room with authority enveloping him like a cloak. Mylah watched from the hallway, captivated by the way he moved with such grace. As soon as he cleared the doorway, the door crashed shut behind him. Without looking at Mylah, the prince turned to the left and continued walking. She had to jog to keep up with him.

"Thank you," Mylah said as she caught up to him.

He whirled on her. "You cost me my credibility and Madame Edris' trust. Don't talk to me right now." He turned and kept walking, forcing Mylah to run again.

"I didn't ask for you to lie for me," she said, and he laughed.

"I didn't do it for you." He stopped again, not turning to Mylah, but glancing back. "You will never tell King Castien about anything that happened tonight. I'll bring you to your room and we will pretend tonight never occurred." He didn't wait for Mylah's response.

The next morning, a soft knock on Mylah's door woke her. She rolled out of bed, stretching as she dragged her feet to the door. Petra stood outside waiting patiently.

"Good morning, Leylah." Petra brushed past her into the room. "Oy, you'd think they would have at least given you the room with the bath," she commented. "Oh well. Follow me." Petra left and Mylah trailed behind her out of the room. A few doors down, they came to a washroom. Petra ran the water to fill the tub and motioned for Mylah to undress.

Once Mylah was in the tub, Petra handed her a cloth to wash herself, pulled a partition closed to conceal Mylah, and left the room. When she returned, she held a gown and shoes. She draped the gown over a chair that sat against the wall. She grabbed a towel off a shelf and held it out to Mylah, who took it gratefully, wrapping it around herself.

Petra took hold of Mylah's arm, making her jump.

"I see you were able to keep your deal with the naga," Petra said, tracing her jagged nail along the wound that had already faded to a pink line. "It'll scar, but at least you survived." She dropped Mylah's arm and began to help dress her. That day's dress was a simple peach gown. It was much less revealing and more comfortable than the previous day's gown.

"Petra," Mylah began.

"Yes?"

"Only some shreeve have magic," she paused, watching for Petra's reaction.

"Indeed. As they are a hybrid of both fae and human, it would only make sense that some of them did not inherit the magic of the fae," she said matter-of-factly.

"Do either the king or the prince have magic?" She had to pretend not to know about the prince yet. As for the king, she truly had no idea.

"The king has never revealed whether or not he has magic," Petra said, leaving out any information regarding the prince.

"How is that possible?" Mylah shifted as Petra finished the braid with her hair and placed it over her shoulder.

"Do not ask such questions," Petra snapped. "You'll get yourself in trouble with inquiries such as these."

"I'm sorry," Mylah said, her eyes widening in surprise. She hadn't realized how sensitive of a topic magic would be. "I won't ask again."

"Come, we mustn't keep them waiting." Petra turned, letting Mylah slip on her shoes, and started towards the door.

"Who must we not keep waiting exactly?" Mylah asked.

"Why, the king of course, and the prince. I'm sure you've been anticipating this meeting, given your declaration that you know of certain war plans from Adair."

"Oh, yes." Mylah's nerves began flipping in her stomach. She still had no idea what she was planning on telling King Castien about Adair's plans. But she couldn't let herself panic. If the sprites were present at the meeting, she would have to be ready to expertly craft her lies.

Seventeen

Elias sat staring at his brother across the long, oak table. There were two empty chairs on the opposing sides of the table, one would be occupied by Leylah shortly.

"You seem like you have something on your mind," Castien drawled and took a sip of his tea. "Spit it out, brother." Elias sighed. He could never hide anything from Castien.

"I'm only wondering why you brought that girl into the castle," Elias admitted. Castien had never shown mercy to a human in the past and wasn't sure why he would start now.

"She's hardly a *girl*, if that's what you're worried about," Castien teased, and Elias groaned. His brother was constantly pestering him about taking his pick of women from the revels and galas he held. It wasn't as if he'd never been with a woman, but he hated that they all were only using him to get closer to the king.

"I'm not worried, only curious," Elias lied. Of course he was worried. Every human who had been brought before his brother had been killed, either by Castien or one of his guards.

"You may understand once you meet her why I chose to let her live unlike the others." Castien's eyes dropped down to the placemat in front of him and he rolled his shoulders. "Or maybe I'm just bored and wanted to liven things up around here." Castien forced a smile onto his face and Elias didn't point out that Castien needn't put on airs before him, though he wanted to. Elias *had* noticed a certain familiarity when he'd first seen Leylah, but he couldn't admit that to Castien who thought they hadn't met yet. As much as he wanted to tell his brother what had happened the previous night, he didn't want to condemn the poor girl to death if Castien reacted violently to the news that she'd caused Elias to make an enemy of Madame Edris.

Footsteps sounded in the hall and Elias recognized Petra's stride and assumed the unfamiliar steps were Leylah.

"I guess we shall see," Elias commented as Petra rounded the corner with Leylah at her heels.

"Please, sit," Castien gestured to the chair closest to him on the right.

"Curtsy," Petra murmured to Leylah who did as she was told and took a seat at the table. Elias noticed Leylah's lips pinch together, and her posture stiffened in unease.

"Thank you for joining us on such short notice. I'd like you to meet my brother, Prince Elias." Castien inclined his head towards Elias.

"It's a pleasure to meet you, Prince Elias." Leylah bowed her head to him. His nerves grated at the use of his title, but he said nothing. He was just grateful she was keeping their secret.

"Now, as for the real reason you are here," Castien spoke as a servant brought out a tray with three plates of food. The servant placed a plate in front of each of them and then retreated into the kitchen. Castien took a bite of his food, but Elias had no appetite that morning. They both turned their heads to Leylah as Castien said, "your supposed knowledge from the courts of Adair."

"Yes," Leylah paused, and Elias noticed a twinge in her jaw. "The plan King Florian has to..." she took a sip of water from her goblet. "Sorry, what was I saying? Oh right, the plan...to use the book." Elias' heart dropped and he found Castien's eyes across the table. His fear was reflected there.

"So, he's done it then? He's found someone to translate it. Last I heard he'd lost it after an attack some years ago," Castien said. Elias cocked his eyebrow as Leylah nearly choked on her water. "Something wrong?" Castien asked, clearly also noticing her change in disposition.

"No, nothing, sorry. Wrong tube." Leylah breathed deeply and Elias studied her, wondering what had caused such a reaction. "It was believed to be lost, yes. As was revealed right before I was exiled, he's had someone working on the translation ever since that night. I guess they must have made some headway with it."

"Well, do you have any *useful* information? Like how much of the book has been translated? Or whether he even understands what the book reveals?" Castien's irritation was clear in his tone and Elias understood. His brother had been fixated on retrieving that book for years.

"I can only guess that he does since he plans on using it," Leylah pointed out.

"Brother, we should warn the knights," Elias said.

"No, not yet. We must find out how much he knows first. I won't take the word of his traitorous exile." Castien was calm again. He continued eating his breakfast in deep thought. Elias and Leylah followed suit, eating in silence.

Once they'd all finished eating, Castien left without a word. Elias groaned inwardly realizing he was meant to deal with Leylah. He cleared his throat, trying to think of something to say as she sat picking at her nails.

"Do you...need anything?" he tried. Her head lifted and her eyes met his.

"Like what?" she asked, and Elias racked his brain for what she may be in need of but came up short.

"I don't know," he admitted, making her smile.

"I think I'm quite alright, thank you." She glanced around the room, seeming to be as lost as Elias when it came to what they should be discussing or doing. She straightened suddenly and turned back to him. "Actually, there is something."

"Oh?" Relief flooded Elias at the thought that he wouldn't have to keep grasping at straws.

"Your brother, King Castien," she began, biting her lip as she paused. "He broke my necklace, and I was hoping maybe you'd have some tools I could use to fix it." Elias cocked his head to the side.

"He broke your necklace?" Elias couldn't imagine what Castien could have been doing that would have resulted in that, but maybe it wasn't his place to ask.

"Yes. It's in my room, I can go get it..." she trailed off. "Sorry, you probably have more important tasks you should be working on."

"As a matter of fact, I don't. Come on, let's go take a look at this necklace." He rose from his seat and let Leylah lead the way to her room.

Eighteen

Mylah opened her door and stopped before her desk, grabbing her necklace. Elias entered behind her, glancing once around the room, his cheeks reddening slightly. Mylah smiled to herself before handing him the necklace.

"The clasp is broken," she said. Elias turned the necklace over in his hands, pursing his lips as he considered the damage.

"This should be an easy fix." He placed one hand over the other, covering her necklace, and closed his eyes. Mylah took a step back as a warmth spread out around Elias.

"I guess that's one way to do it," she murmured. Elias opened his eyes and handed her back the necklace.

"Good as new," he said. Mylah studied it in awe. He was right, it looked brand new again.

"T-thank you," she stuttered. "Petra told me it was okay to wear it even though King Castien doesn't like sentimental items," Mylah let slip and slapped her hand over her mouth as she realized what she'd said. Petra could get in trouble for speaking ill of the king in that way. Elias' brows furrowed.

"My brother does tend to resent sentimental items, but only because he himself was denied the ability to keep anything from his loved ones who had died. Our father, well, his stepfather, King Haldor, was harsh and felt that holding onto someone after they were gone was a sign of weakness. So, he made us destroy anything we had left of our mothers," Elias explained, and Mylah didn't know how to respond. Thankfully he broke the silence.

"Do you want me to..." he gestured to the necklace, and she heated as the thought of him helping her put it on, but she nodded, nonetheless. He took it back from her and she turned around, lifting her hair. His fingers grazed the back of her neck sending a tingling sensation through her. The warmth that seeped into her seemed to chase away a chill that she hadn't been able to shake since she'd arrived at the Elowyn castle.

"There," he said, his voice low and gruff. Mylah turned back to him and noticed he was already leaving her room.

"Thank you," she said again. He turned his head back to her slightly and offered her a half smile before disappearing out the door.

Mylah sat down at her vanity, staring at her own reflection in the mirror. Elias had left her feeling breathless and dizzy. Taking a deep breath, she closed her eyes, remembering his touch against the back of her neck.

She shook her head. It was of no use to think about such things. Though his comment about King Castien not being allowed to keep anything from his mother or father made her pause. It didn't line up with everything else she'd heard about the king. She had looked into his eyes at breakfast, trying to read them. Garrick had warned her that a

Holly Huntress

monster could be identified by the haunted look in their eyes, and she hadn't been able to sense anything amiss with King Castien. There seemed to be some resentment there, but nothing as cold as Garrick had explained.

Mylah couldn't let those thoughts get to her, either. No matter who these people were, she had one mission and that was to learn how to translate the shreeve book.

The next few days, Mylah saw only Petra and the guards they passed in the halls. She had trouble finding moments to snoop around or find the sprites who were supposed to be helping her communicate with Adair. Someone seemed to always be around.

On her fifth day in the castle, Petra came to her in the morning as usual, but this time, she carried with her an invitation.

"Leylah Farrow, you are cordially invited to attend a gala this evening in honor of the King of Elowyn," she read the letter aloud. Petra busied herself laying out Mylah's outfit for the day. "Very interesting. The king ignores me for days and now invites me to his gala?"

"He likes to keep everyone guessing," Petra commented. "But this is a good chance for you to get to know some more people, branch out a bit."

"Are you tiring of my company, Petra?" Mylah quipped. Petra gave her a rare smirk. "Have you seen Broderick or Sabine lately?" Mylah hadn't seen them since the night they'd helped her steal Madame Edris' necklace.

"They don't usually work within the castle. But they will be at the gala tonight."

"Good, it will be nice to see some familiar faces."

Mylah spent the day in her room practicing her story about being exiled in case someone asked about it at the gala. She could only assume there would be sprites present, so she could not be caught off guard.

Petra returned in the late afternoon to help Mylah prepare for the gala. She brought with her a brilliant green gown, much like the gray dress Mylah had worn the first day. When the gown was on, any movement made it ripple as if it were made of liquid emeralds. Mylah was stunned by the beauty of it.

"Where did you get this dress?" she asked Petra who watched her in the mirror. Mylah could have sworn she saw tears in her eyes, but she blinked, and they were gone.

"It was made by a fae witch who specializes in the art of dressmaking. The king himself had it specially ordered for someone who was never able to wear it," her voice cracked, but she maintained her composure. "I thought it would be nice if it finally had the chance to be worn." Mylah turned to Petra and grasped her hands.

"It's absolutely stunning. Thank you, I don't think I deserve the honor of wearing it, though." Guilt found its way creeping back into Mylah's mind. She was lying to these people; Petra, Broderick, Sabine, and Prince Elias, after they had shown her only kindness.

"Nonsense. You will wear it and that's that." Petra set to work finishing Mylah's hair, leaving it loose, but taming her curls a bit. A knock resonated through the room causing them both to startle. "Oh! The time!" Petra scurried to the door and flung it open. "She's ready. Sorry, I lost track of time." Sabine stood in the hallway looking radiant in an off the shoulder, shimmering gold gown. It made her dark skin glow under the pale light.

"Don't worry, Petra. The later, the better. We want everyone to notice our arrival," Sabine gave her a wink.

"I don't think anyone could miss you," Broderick's voice echoed down the hall. Mylah hurried to the doorway so she could see him. He wore his usual uniform, minus the protective armor, but he had his hair slicked back. He grinned at Mylah, and a sense of ease seeped into her body, chasing away the tension from her nerves.

"Ready to go, Leylah?" He looped his arm through Sabine's and offered the other to Mylah. She took it and waved to Petra as she was led away.

"Petra did a number on you tonight." Sabine craned her head forward so she could look at Mylah.

"Is that a good thing?" Mylah asked, and Sabine laughed.

"Of course!"

As soon as they neared the ballroom, their ears were assaulted with loud chatter, music, and laughter.

"Before you go in, Leylah," Broderick released her arm and turned to look at her. "Be careful. Not everyone in there is fond of humans and they won't behave kindly towards you. Try to stick close to someone you know when we aren't around."

"Where will you be?" Mylah had been hoping to stay with them all night.

"We may look the part of guests, but we're on duty. We'll be patrolling the grounds and the halls. You'll see us around, though," Broderick tried to reassure her.

"You have to go in alone." Sabine squeezed her hand. "We've already broken protocol by escorting you here. Best of luck and keep a sharp eye out."

Mylah took a deep breath and broke away from the safety net that was her new friends. She approached the double doors that would open to the ballroom and glanced back one last time. Broderick and Sabine had already disappeared.

The doors opened before Mylah, and she was temporarily stunned. The noise poured out of the room, overwhelming her ears. A massive chandelier hung overhead lit with an unnatural blue firelight that cast shadows all around the room. There were four pillars spaced out at the edges of the room, and on each pillar hung a torch lit with the same blue firelight. It gave the room a dreamy, sultry tone.

Bodies moved all around her as some people writhed to the music, their movements fluid and graceful. Others gossiped along the outskirts, not hiding who it was they talked about. Longing, envious, and judgmental stares were cast about freely. She took note that not everyone was as tall as she'd been led to believe all shreeve were. She assumed that had to do with their human genes. Some, though, reached at least a foot over her head.

Everyone turned to look when the doors opened, and their eyes fell on Mylah. Whispers filled the room, and she knew she had become the topic of every conversation. She took a step forward and multiple shreeve descended upon her.

"What's a human like you doing in a dress like that?" A woman prodded her in the side and Mylah tried to find the culprit.

"Care to dance, sweetheart?" A man took her hand, making Mylah whip around and rip her hand from his grasp. His smirk turned feral.

"Pretty, little, plaything, aren't you?" Someone tugged on Mylah's hair, and she closed her eyes, wishing for everyone to disappear. Above all the cacophony, Mylah heard someone clear their throat, her eyes flew open, and the crowd parted to reveal King Castien.

"Sorry, King Castien..."

"We didn't realize..."

"My apologies..."

"Be gone," the king commanded, and the group scattered. His gaze ravished Mylah, making her insides squirm from discomfort. A blush crept up her neck and into her cheeks. "It looks as I always thought it would..." he spoke so softly Mylah almost missed his comment.

"Umm, thank you?" She wasn't sure how to take the statement. She noticed he had two ear piercings, one in each ear. The gold jewelry glinted in the dim lighting.

"Would you care to dance?" He held his arm out to her and she looped her own through it.

"How could I refuse a king?" She forced a smile onto her face. His touch made her skin crawl. This was the man who killed her parents and every fiber of her being screamed at her to take her revenge. But she couldn't. Not yet.

He led her to the center of the dance floor where he pulled her in close. Now that they stood facing each other, she realized how tall he was. Her head barely reached his chin. His hand went to the small of her back and Mylah turned her head to the side trying not to breathe in his intoxicating aroma. It was a mixture of gardenia and a fresh rain fall. She hated that she felt drawn towards him.

"You've caused quite the stir in my castle since you've arrived," his voice was low and rough. Mylah knew anyone trying to listen in would not be able to hear their conversation over the noise in the room.

"Have I?" she asked, feigning innocence while focusing on not tripping as he moved her around the dance floor.

"My servants and guards have a great interest in your well-being. Even Madame Edris who hasn't cared about a single soul since being bound to these grounds has inquired about you."

"Other than my first day here, I've only seen Petra since I've arrived. I've been mostly confined to my room." Mylah prayed there were no sprites listening in. So far, she had spoken truths, but it was only a matter of time before she would have to lie.

"Well, we will have to fix that going forward, won't we? We don't want our guest growing bored." King Castien spun her around, pulling her back hard against him. "I may have saved you from certain death, but don't think I can't change my mind." He ran a finger down her cheek and gave her a devilish grin, making her heart skip a beat. Anyone watching would think that he was flirting with her.

"I guess I will have to make sure not to get on your bad side then." Mylah gave him her own deceiving smile and the king threw his head back and laughed. Everyone around them turned to stare enviously at the human who had made the king laugh so jovially. While the crowd watched, King Castien took Mylah's chin in his hand, tilting her face up to his and for a horrifying moment she thought he was going to kiss her. Instead, he leaned in close and whispered in her ear.

"There is nothing that you can hide from me in my own castle. Whatever secrets you are keeping will be found out, and I look forward to destroying you if you ever attempt to deceive me." His lips left a burning sensation on her cheek as they grazed it, and the playful smile left her mouth. Panic flooded in as Mylah thought he may already know exactly who she was. Though, she figured he would have thrown her out or had her killed if that were the case. She would have to take care to be extra discreet as she attempted to find someone or something to help her translate the book.

The king released Mylah from his grip and turned to walk away when she noticed a peculiar marking on his neck in the shape of a bird...

"Wait," Mylah breathed her hand lingering on the king's arm. He looked at her with a question in his eyes.

"Are you meaning to waste more of my time?" he asked and Mylah realized it was not the time to be asking him about family.

"No, sorry. It was nothing." She curtsied to him and strode towards a table against the wall that held massive platters of food. Her mind whirled. Her father had told her of a man who had helped him with translating a shreeve book, a man with a bird tattoo named Wren. Could the king be related to him? How could someone her father talked so fondly of be in any way related to such a monster?

"What is he like?" Mylah heard a lighthearted voice behind her and felt a tap on her shoulder. She turned to see a shreeve girl, who looked to be about her age, with bright green eyes surrounded by a light pink. Her eyes reminded Mylah of watermelon.

"I'm sorry?" she questioned the girl who laughed at her.

"What is King Castien like? I've only heard stories, this is my first gala I've been able to attend," she clarified.

"Um, he's kingly I guess," Mylah said, grasping at straws. The girl scoffed.

"I've heard he's a real ass, but don't tell anyone you heard it from me." She laughed at first, but her face fell when Mylah didn't react. "Oh, crap, you're not like, friends or something, right? I assumed from the grimace on your face after dancing with him that you didn't like him. I'm so sorry if I overstepped..."

"No, no. It's okay," Mylah cut her off, smiling. "I'm not friends with him, or anything close. I was exiled from my home, and he allowed me to find sanctuary here."

"Oh, wow. Maybe he's not as bad as everyone says," she shrugged. "I'm Anastasia, but you can call me Ana, everyone else does."

"It's nice to meet you, Ana. I'm Leylah."

"I should say you're lucky. People can come to these galas, revels, and debauches all their lives and never dance with the king. I'm assuming this is your first one, and you were his only dance so far tonight," Ana rambled. Mylah listened while she ate a plateful of delectable sweets. "Do you want to take a walk? I could use a break from all the chaos." Mylah nodded, setting her plate down, and followed Ana out of the ballroom. They each grabbed a champagne flute on their way out.

"We can take a walk through the gardens; I heard that the king is constantly changing them," Ana offered.

"That sounds nice. I haven't been outside the castle in days."

"Wow. Sounds a little like you're more of a prisoner than a guest." Ana began to lead the way towards the gardens. "Maybe the king will let you leave now that you've had some experience with other Elowyns. They can be a bit pretentious, but once you befriend them, you'll never have to worry about them turning on you. We make friends for life. Friendship and trust are everything to Elowyns."

"Really? Because it seemed like a lot of gossip was happening at the gala tonight." Mylah couldn't forget those stares so soon.

"Well, I never said that everyone is friends with everyone," Ana pointed out with a grin. They were approaching a door guarded by two knights. "Hello, sirs, just passing through to the gardens, please." Mylah was taken aback by the ease with which Ana spoke to the knights of the castle, and they didn't even hesitate. They opened the doors and let them pass without question.

"That seemed too easy," Mylah said, looking back as the knights closed the doors behind them.

"It's a gift," Ana smirked. "I've always been able to put people at ease with just a look. I inherited it from my mother's side. She used to work in the castle before I was born. They used her to help make prisoners so comfortable that they would spill all their secrets." Mylah stopped dead in her tracks. *Spill their secrets...*

"Is that what you're doing with me?" She couldn't help the panic that edged her voice. "Are you trying to get me to reveal my secrets to you? Did the king put you up to this?"

Ana stepped back looking stricken. "N-no, I thought we might be friends..." Guilt made a knot in Mylah's stomach as tears sprung into Ana's eyes. "This always happens. People are scared to be around me, but I swear, I've never used my abilities to hurt anyone!"

"I'm sorry, Ana. I'm just paranoid, I swear I didn't mean anything by it. If you still want to be friends, I want that too." Mylah couldn't afford to alienate anyone else. She needed as many allies as she could get while she was in Elowyn.

Ana took a deep breath. "Okay, and I promise to never use my ability on you, unless you want me to."

"Thank you."

"Leylah!" They both turned to see Broderick hurrying towards them. "What are you doing out here? You should be inside."

"What does it matter? The king doesn't want me there." Mylah figured it was best to stay far away from the king until she found a way to make him spill his war plans to her or help her learn the old shreeve language. Otherwise, she risked upsetting him and having him throw her out.

"Then why is he asking about your whereabouts? You need to get back in the ballroom and stay there." Broderick had never been so demanding with Mylah, it scared her a little. But he only wanted to keep her safe.

"Seems like someone wants to keep an eye on his prisoner," Ana commented, giving Mylah a knowing look.

"She's not a prisoner, but even if she were, it's better than being dead," Broderick repeated the phrase he'd said to Sabine on the first day after Mylah had been accepted into the king's court. She was beginning to wonder if he was right and hoped she would never have to seriously weigh those options.

"It's fine. I'll go." Mylah gave one last look around at the gardens. They reminded her of home and the gardens she used to sneak away to with Cassia and Greyson. She hadn't thought of her friends since she'd arrived in Elowyn. It brought tears to her eyes that she quickly swept away.

Without another word to either Broderick or Ana, Mylah made her way back inside.

As she walked, Greyson stayed in her thoughts. The last time she had been in those gardens in Adair with him, she should have let him talk. She should have told him she didn't feel the same way...she should have read his letter. That damned letter. What could it have said? Approaching the doors to the ballroom, Mylah braced herself for the onslaught of comments she would likely receive.

The doors opened before her and this time she was met with cold shoulders and indifference. No one wanted anything to do with her now that they knew she belonged to the king. Ana came up behind her and put a hand on her shoulder.

"They're all jealous because the king never pays them any attention," she reassured Mylah, though that wasn't what bothered her. "Speak of the devil," Ana cocked her head to the right, indicating the king who made his way around the room. He had a woman on each arm, both beautiful and elegant.

"What do they see in him?" Mylah asked Ana.

"Opportunity. Every woman goes to bed with him thinking she will be the next queen, but he has yet to place that crown on anyone," Ana spoke with disdain. Mylah wondered if Ana yearned for the opportunity to gain such status and power, or if she was happy with her life as it was. "Those two are his favorites. Maybe someday one of them will finally convince him to marry."

"Why doesn't he marry? If something happens to him, he has no heir." Mylah knew Prince Elias would be the next in line, but most kings wanted their own children to succeed them.

"It's a mystery to me, but any sane person should know better than to marry into that family." Ana looked around as if to make sure no one was listening and lowered her voice as she continued. "King Haldor had many wives and all of them died of mysterious illnesses after not being able to bear children for him. It's suspected he had his witch poison them all." Mylah gaped at Ana. "Both King Castien and Prince Elias' mothers were casualties of that reign. If King Castien is anything like Haldor, which in cruelness he seems to be, I wouldn't risk marrying him for fear I would not be able to bear children in a timely manner and meet the same fate as those poor women."

"That's insane, and horrible." Mylah watched the king move about the room with his lovers. His own mother had been murdered and yet he'd still found it within himself to take someone else's parents away from them in the same fashion. It made it so much worse knowing that he understood the pain he was causing when he killed Mylah's parents. Rage boiled deep inside of her, and it took every ounce of restraint for her not to unleash her aggression on King Castien. She needed to find a way to hurt him in the worst way possible.

"Excuse me," Mylah dipped her head to Ana and made her way across the floor towards the king. It was time for her to start using every weapon in her arsenal to get the information she needed so she could exact her revenge sooner rather than later.

On her way across the room, Mylah grabbed a goblet of wine and took a sip. A bittersweet flavor of peaches and grapes danced through her mouth, sending a buzz into her mind. Whatever was in the wine, it was potent.

Mylah approached her target, the woman slung on the king's right arm. Mylah began to sway and feigned tripping over herself as she passed the woman. Her wine dumped expertly down the side of the exquisite satin dress the woman wore. She let out a startled cry and turned her enraged gaze upon Mylah. The misty gray color surrounding the woman's vivid sapphire-colored irises seemed to darken as she took in Mylah standing there.

"Oh, I am so sorry!" Mylah dropped her goblet which exploded as it hit the floor. "Let me get you..." she turned to look for napkins but saw nothing nearby. Turning back to the woman, she gave her a pathetic apologetic smile.

"You filthy, little..." The woman reared back, clearly about to slap Mylah across the face, but King Castien caught her hand. "Didn't you see what she did to me?" the woman screeched.

"Yes, Davina, and it was clearly an *accident*. Now, you should be going. We can't have you prancing about in a soiled gown." He gave her a small push towards the door, and she gaped at him, aghast.

"You can't treat me like this! I'm...I'm..." she fumbled over her words.

"You're what, exactly?" the king sneered, and Davina did not respond. "That's what I thought. Now, run along." She stormed off, her honey blonde hair began to escape her bun as she moved, and it swung down across her exposed back. Mylah almost felt bad for causing her such humiliation, but it was necessary.

"I feel terrible." Mylah bit her lip and furrowed her brow. "It's the wine, it goes straight to my head," she giggled for effect.

"What would my people think if I didn't replace Davina with someone equally as beautiful and ruthless?" King Castien gave Mylah a conspiratorial wink. He knew the spill had been no accident, so Mylah fluttered her eyes and played up her flirtatious behavior. He had to believe she was truly interested in him, which wouldn't be hard for someone as gorgeous and self-absorbed as himself.

"I may have heard you were looking for me earlier, and it made me wonder..." she left her comment open ended, hoping he would fill in the blanks for her.

"Things became boring once you disappeared..." The woman on his other arm snorted in derision. "Now, Aleese, I don't want to have to replace you as well." That shut the woman up, but it did nothing to help the sour look on her face.

"I was quite surprised to hear I was missed, after your threats earlier, I was sure you wouldn't want me around," Mylah dared to say. He raised a brow.

"Quite the contrary, Leylah Farrow of Adair." He eyed her necklace again and reached out his hand to grasp it. Mylah grabbed it first on instinct. She dropped her hand once she realized what she had done, and he took the pendant in his hand, while stroking the base of her throat with his thumb.

"I still wonder about this...it seems familiar somehow, like I saw it in a dream." He gazed at it in question. Mylah realized that he may have seen it if he had gone through her wardrobe after killing her parents.

"I found it," she said, her voice coming out too strained, but King Castien didn't seem to notice.

"Interesting." He dropped the pendant, letting it fall back against Mylah's throat. "A story for another time.

Come, Aleese. I tire of this gala and the charade. Leylah, I will make sure you are thoroughly entertained for all the days you remain in my castle." He moved away from her with Aleese clinging to him. They disappeared behind a door that Mylah assumed led towards the king's bed chamber. She was relieved to not have to continue pretending to like the king, but also disappointed that he had chosen Aleese over her. She needed him to choose *her* and to trust her with all his secrets.

"What was that about?" Ana appeared at Mylah's side. "I thought you didn't like him."

"It's complicated." Mylah didn't trust Ana with any more information than that.

Nineteen

Petra came to help Mylah get ready in the morning as she always did. She dressed her in riding gear which tipped Mylah off that something was different that day.

"I actually get to leave the castle?" Mylah asked as Petra braided her hair.

"With the supervision of the prince and two of his finest knights. But, yes, you get to leave the castle today." Petra tied off Mylah's braid.

"The prince? Doesn't he have more important duties to attend to?" Mylah yawned, tired from the festivities the night before.

"Since Prince Elias returned from the border, King Castien has been keeping his workload light. Now, come. We must get you fed before you leave." Petra led Mylah to the sitting room where she usually had her meals. Elias already waited there for them. Petra bowed to him.

"I'm sorry, Prince Elias, I didn't realize you were waiting, or we would have arrived earlier." Petra remained in her bowed position.

"Don't worry about it, I just arrived myself," he tried to reassure her, but she still seemed on edge.

"I'll take my leave." She backed out of the room and hustled away.

"Please, sit and eat. I figured we'd get going early so we'd have plenty of time to tour the kingdom." The prince sat on one of the plush couches and Mylah sat opposite him in a stiff armchair. She grabbed a bowl of fruit from the table in front of her and popped a strawberry into her mouth.

"Where were you last night?" Mylah asked once she'd finished eating.

"At the gala, just as you were." He appeared amused by Mylah's confusion.

"I didn't see you." She mentally scanned her memories and had no recollection of the prince being anywhere in the ballroom.

"My brother tends to garner all the attention at most gatherings. From what I saw last night, he seems to have already got you under his spell."

"What? No, I..." Mylah stopped herself. If she wanted the king to believe she liked him, she needed *everyone* to believe it. "He surprised me."

"He enjoys doing that. Anyway, shall we be going?" He stood and Mylah joined him. Together they left the castle, this time through the front gates.

"So, did you enjoy yourself last night?" Mylah asked. She still had no idea how she had missed him.

"As much as I could, under the circumstances," he said, veering their path towards the stables.

"What circumstances? If you don't mind me asking."

"Nothing you need concern yourself with," the prince said, remaining vague, which annoyed Mylah.

"Your Highness!" A stable boy appeared from behind the stables. "I've readied the horses for you." He bowed as Prince Elias approached him.

"Thank you, Stav. No need to bow." The boy righted himself and blushed. Prince Elias and Mylah mounted their horses and began trotting towards the village at a lazy pace.

"I thought there were supposed to be knights accompanying us?" Mylah glanced around, thinking she would see them lurking in the shadows.

"Ah, well, I may not have informed them of our early departure."

Mylah gasped in mock horror. "Prince Elias, should I be worried?"

"No," he chuckled. "They are just bothersome. And, please, call me Elias. I'm not particularly fond of the 'prince' title."

Mylah turned to him in surprise. "What's wrong with being a prince?"

"It's not that there's anything wrong with being a prince, it's only that I've done nothing to deserve the title." He ducked his head, appearing shameful.

"I'm sure you're being modest. Petra told me you just returned from the Adair border," Mylah pointed out.

"Ah, yes. My heroic two-week journey where they had me sit safely behind the line marking the entrance to what is considered the 'war zone.' Castien would never let me near a potential threat. Even though he fought in the border skirmishes and along the Unbound border for eight years before becoming king." Mylah expected bitterness, but she only heard envy and admiration in Elias' voice for his brother.

"So, I take it you two aren't close then, if he was gone for so long while you grew up."

"Quite the opposite, actually. We've grown apart a bit since he's become king, but we've always been close," Elias said, surprising Mylah yet again.

"Oh." She didn't think King Castien had it within him to bond with anyone, even his brother. "Well, doesn't he think that your magic would be of use to the other soldiers?"

"My magic..." he scoffed. "I've barely learned how to control it, let alone utilize it."

"But you used it on me, and at night," Mylah pointed out. Elias stayed quiet for a moment and Mylah stole a glance at him. His brows were furrowed, and his head dipped down as he stared at the saddle.

"I'm lucky it didn't kill me. Without the sun to fuel my magic, it's even more shaky and uncontrollable," his words came out a near whisper.

"Why would you risk your own life to save mine? Someone you've only just met." Mylah wanted to keep him talking and hopefully find out more about his power and King Castien's potential magic.

"If I can save someone, I'm going to do it, regardless of who they are. I wasn't going to stand by, knowing I had the power to save you and watch you die."

"Thanks, I guess." Mylah's cheeks reddened. "How long have you been using your magic?"

"My whole life. It used to explode out of me randomly, and anyone nearby...well a lot of people got hurt." The shame on Elias' face made Mylah's sympathy for him grow, and she resented that. She didn't want to feel sorry for Elias, or King Castien. "Over time, I learned to repress it so

185

I wouldn't hurt anyone anymore. But then," he paused. "Never mind," he said too fast. Mylah watched as his face went from slack, to tight and closed off. He had been about to reveal something to her.

"But what?" she tried, but Elias' horse trotted ahead, and he didn't answer her.

They passed through a copse of trees and stood at the edge of a cliff. Splayed out below them was a bustling town. "Wow," Mylah gasped.

"We can go down if you'd like," Elias offered.

"I'd like that."

They steered the horses along the cliff until they came to a passageway that led them down a winding trail. At the bottom, they tied the horses to a rail off the road, tipping a boy to keep watch over them, and began their walk through the town.

Everyone recognized Elias and bowed to him as they passed. Some villagers offered him goods or their services, but he politely declined each time. He even had a few women approach him with offers that left him blushing and Mylah with stitches in her side from laughing. By the time they stopped for lunch, Mylah felt as if she could enjoy Elowyn, if she weren't planning to betray it.

They stopped at a café, which was new to Mylah. The closest thing they had to a café in Adair was a table set up outside the butcher shop where people sat to wait for their orders to be ready. But they didn't eat there. There were also a few bars in Adair, but Mylah had never been to any of them.

"Take a seat anywhere, your Highness," a woman called from behind the counter. Elias chose a vacant table near the window. Mylah knew that he could have chosen an occupied table and they would have happily given the table up to him.

A young man walked over to them and asked what they'd like to eat. Mylah looked to Elias for help. He turned to the man and said, "Two of your best cuts of beef and a side of greens for the both of us."

"Thank you," Mylah said after the server walked away. "I'd have no idea what to say."

"They have a list somewhere, but I figured it would be less overwhelming for you this way." He rubbed his neck nervously.

"You were right," Mylah reassured him. "So, is this what it's always like when you come into town?"

"Mostly, although, the lewd offers are new..." he blushed, and Mylah couldn't help but laugh.

"You could have your pick of any of them, as your brother does, so why don't you?"

"Who says I don't?" He cocked an eyebrow, but then broke out in laughter. "Kidding. It's different for me. They're only after me to get close to him."

"You don't know that for sure," Mylah said, though she figured he was probably right.

"Sure I do. Isn't that why you're here with me? Impress the prince to gain favor with the king. It's not my first time around, Leylah," he sighed.

"Do you think so low of me?" Mylah asked, pursing her lips. She may have been trying to get information out of him, but she wasn't using him to get to the king. "Am I not allowed to spend a day with you without you thinking I'm scheming? It's impossible I was actually enjoying your company..." she pushed her chair away from the table.

"Leylah, please, I didn't mean anything by it. I just thought..."

She cut him off. "What? That I would throw myself at you in an attempt to...I don't even know. I need some air." She stormed out of the café.

She had no right to be upset. She *was* using the prince, only not in the way he thought. But she had been enjoying herself for the first time since leaving Adair and he had to go and ruin it. She wasn't sure who she disliked more at that moment; herself for getting too comfortable, or Elias. She should go back into the café and apologize, but her pride stopped her. He was the one who should be apologizing.

"Leylah!" Mylah whipped around at the sound of Ana's voice. "You're here! They let you out of the castle!"

"Ana, it's good to see you. How are you?" Mylah smiled a genuine smile. It was nice to have a friendly face in an unfamiliar place.

"Still lagging a bit from last night, but I had to get to the shop this morning. Are you here alone?" Ana asked, turning her head from side to side, looking for a guard.

"Not exactly." Mylah tilted her head to indicate Elias still sitting at the table by the window watching them.

"First a dance with the king and now lunch with the prince! Your life is so exciting!" Ana exclaimed. Mylah couldn't help thinking *If you only knew...*

"Why don't you join us? I'm sure the prince won't mind." The least she could do was share some of the excitement with Ana who clearly deserved it more than Mylah ever would.

"Okay!" Ana required no convincing and practically bounded into the café behind Mylah. Elias appeared wary as they approached the table.

"*Prince* Elias," Mylah put extra emphasis on the title he disliked so much. "This is Anastasia."

"Ana," Ana corrected her quickly. "Call me Ana, or Anastasia, or whatever," she babbled.

"Please, sit." Elias waved to the chair beside him. Ana sat with a smile as wide as her face would allow. Mylah thought that Ana may burst from her excitement.

"You looked handsome at the gala," Ana commented. "If it's okay I say that...is it okay?" She looked to Mylah nervously.

"It's fine," Elias laughed and gave Mylah a pointed look that said *See, I was there,* but she ignored it. Their food came out and their server appeared confused by the addition to the table. Ana waved him away claiming she'd already eaten. She prattled on about her daily life while Elias and Mylah ate.

When they finished and left the cafe, Ana stayed with them until they reached their horses, saving them from having to converse with each other.

"Well, I need to be getting back. We should do this again sometime!" She hugged Mylah and turned back to the town. Mylah and Elias began the awkward ride back to the castle. Neither of them spoke until they were walking towards the castle gates.

"I'm sorry about what I said," Elias caved. "I'm used to everyone around me thinking I'm only a pawn. Before people were using me to get to Castien, it was my father."

"I may have overreacted a little. I'm sorry, too," Mylah hated to admit she was wrong, but Elias had opened up to her and she felt the need to reciprocate. "I know a little bit about having brothers...girls used to try to befriend me to get close to them. Though, my brothers were never interested in any of them. You remind me of them a bit." A smile crept onto her face as she thought of Greyson and Crane. She missed them so much it hurt.

"Did you leave them behind when you were exiled?" Elias gazed at her with pity in his eyes and Mylah hated it.

"I made my choice knowing what it would cost me," she said over the lump that had formed in her throat.

"I don't know that I'd be able to do the same. Castien practically raised me; I owe him too much to ever leave his side."

"Yeah, well, I didn't have the luxury of thinking that way. My brothers are on the front lines of this war, protecting Adair from *your* people." Mylah's blood pressure shot up and she clenched her fists. She was giving away too much, she needed to reel herself in. "Sorry," she mumbled.

"Don't be. I think this war is pointless as well. It is hardly worth the number of lives that have been uprooted to guard the borders on both sides," Elias stopped as they came to the gate. Mylah cocked her head to the side, trying to gauge whether Elias realized that the war was because of his own brother's actions. The gate opened before them and on the other side, two knights stood with their arms crossed.

"Prince Elias, we were under strict orders to accompany you to the village," one of them growled.

"Sorry, fellas. I needed to take a breather. Your presence can be so stifling." Elias breezed past them. They stood aside and Mylah heard them grumbling to each other as she walked by.

Once inside, she caught up to Elias and he led the way to yet another sitting room she had not seen yet, though it was much like the other she had been to the first day. Couches surrounded a coffee table and portraits of past kings were hung on the walls. These couches were a light beige color, though. Elias collapsed onto one of the couches, draping his arm over his eyes. Mylah lounged on the couch opposite him.

"You mentioned that you don't agree with the war..." Mylah couldn't help but pry a little. He lifted his arm to reveal his eyes as he gazed at her.

"I did," he said.

"Well, I also don't agree with the war because it has been going on way too long..." Mylah lied. She wanted the Elowyns to pay for what had been done to her family, but she had to keep up appearances. "King Florian began the war after your people committed an atrocity against the king's council." That grabbed Elias' attention. He sat up, his eyes widening with intrigue. What she was saying was clearly something he had not been informed of.

"Up until King Florian declared war, there were only border skirmishes. Our people had nothing to do with any atrocities done to the council of the king," Elias disputed, but Mylah shook her head.

"Maybe it wasn't a sanctioned attack, but Emil and Vita," she nearly choked on their names, but she forced herself to continue. "The Orson's were murdered in their home over a book they had been given to translate." Comprehension dawned on Elias' face. This was not something he had been blind to after all, he had just not considered the murdering of Mylah's parents an atrocity.

"King Florian *stole* that book from our stronghold. He is to blame for every event that came after."

"Okay, well don't you think it was a little out of line to *murder* the man assigned to translate the book and his wife who had nothing to do with it? Would simply retrieving the book have not been enough?" Tears threatened to spill down Mylah's cheeks, but she forced them back. She could not give herself over to her emotions.

"I wasn't there that night, so I don't know what events transpired that led to the killing of those people," Elias remained on guard.

"But you do know who killed them, so why not ask *him* what happened?" Mylah suggested, attempting to bring her tone back to normal and slow down her breathing. "I'd be curious to hear his side of the story."

"It's too bad he was one of the first casualties of the war. I'm sure it would be an interesting story to hear." Elias stood from the couch. "I need to take a walk." He left Mylah stewing in her shock and confusion. Did he not know that it was his brother who had killed Emil and Vita? Or was he trying to lead Mylah astray? She had gone too far today and risked outing herself by letting her emotions get the better of her. It was for the best that Elias didn't realize who she was talking about or else he may guess at the resentment she held towards the king. She needed to be more careful. He could be going to King Castien to warn him. The thought made Mylah panic. She needed to get to him first.

Twenty

Mylah left the sitting room and turned right. She had no idea where the king may be, but she would do her best to find him. She wandered down the hall, passing empty rooms and closed doors. A few of them she poked her head into to find closets, another sitting room, and a library. The library piqued her interest and she lingered there. If she were going to find any information on a forgotten shreeve language, the castle library would be a great place to start looking.

Inside there was a massive oak desk covered in open books. That was where she went first. The books were nothing like anything Mylah had ever seen. She had not been much of a reader after her parents died and her entire life had been upended. All her time had been dedicated to training and attempting to translate the shreeve book.

Mylah left the books on the desk behind and ventured further into the library where there were rows and rows of books that seemed to stretch on for the whole length of the castle. It would take ages to look through them all. She ran her hand along the spines as she walked down the first row of books. She stopped as the title *Shreeve Magic: The Basics* piqued her curiosity.

Mylah slid the book out from where it had been nuzzled between *A Book of Poultices and Salves* and an unmarked book. The magic book fell open in her arms to a page titled: *How to know if your child has magic.* Mylah skimmed the page, noting words like *shapeshifting, setting fires, healing wounds, stronger aversion to iron, weaker at night...* nothing she hadn't already learned. She flipped to another page and began reading.

As products of a magical union, shreeve bear qualities from both of their predecessors. Over the years, some have inherited more fae attributes, while others have become more human-like. The more fae blood a shreeve has within them, the longer their lifespan, and the more likely they are to be able to use magic. All shreeve bear the blue and green markings that signify a being created by magic.

Mylah sighed and put the book back on the shelf. Her fingers brushed the unmarked book beside it, and she pulled it out. Opening it to the first page, she realized it was a journal.

Jacinda gave me this journal and I promised her I'd use it. I have never had any desire to write in a journal before, I don't know why she thinks I'd use it now. But I'll keep my promise to her.

I thought I could forget about her and move on. She proved me wrong. Maybe she'll be right about this journaling, too. Maybe it will help keep me from going crazy that we can't be together. There's no telling what her husband would do if he found out.

Mylah let out a gasp and covered her mouth as she realized what she was reading. Whoever wrote this journal had been seeing a married woman named Jacinda. That name seemed familiar to Mylah, but she couldn't remember why. Either way, the journal's writer had hooked her into their story, and she had to finish it.

"I know what you were trying to do last night..." Mylah stiffened at the sound of King Castien's voice. She looked around but saw no one.

"Forgive me, it was not my intention to upset you," Mylah recognized Petra's voice. *What is she doing in the library with the king?* she thought.

"I know what your intentions were," the king growled. "If I think you are trying to manipulate me again, I will have you thrown out of the castle and stripped of your merits."

"I-I'm s-sorry your majesty. You can be sure it won't happen again." Mylah could picture Petra cowering before the king and her hatred for him bubbled in her gut. A long silence followed and Mylah assumed they had both left the library, so she continued onward, placing the journal underneath her arm. When she reached the end of the row, the room opened to a sitting area.

"What are you doing here?" King Castien snapped. Mylah's heart leapt in her chest and her hand flew to her throat as she turned to find the king sitting in an armchair beside an empty fireplace.

"Elias and I returned from the town, and he left me alone. I got lost finding my way back to my room. I can leave if I'm not allowed in here." Mylah watched as he visibly relaxed, sinking back into the chair he occupied.

"No, you may stay." He returned his gaze to the book in his hands. It bore similar symbols to the shreeve book Mylah had back home.

"May I ask what you're reading?" Mylah took a seat in the armchair on the other side of the fireplace. "I've never seen anything like it before."

"It's nothing of great interest. It was something my father left to me." He closed it and set it down on the side table beside his chair.

"Your real father?" Mylah figured this was as good a time as any to ask him about Wren. King Castien nodded solemnly. "Do you mind me asking what happened to him?"

"He committed treason and was dealt with as a traitor should be," his voice was cold, but his eyes betrayed the hurt that he held deep down. "King Haldor was a harsh man, but he kept order in the kingdom by upholding the laws."

"I'm sorry for your loss." Mylah dipped her head to him.

"I'm not, it made me into who I am today." The king sat up straighter and his gaze became steely. Mylah wondered if he knew how his kingdom talked of him. Ana had mentioned that most people thought of him as a monster.

"Well, either way, it takes a toll on a person, losing their parents. I'm sorry you had to go through that." Mylah wanted to try to get some sort of response from him that was more than what she expected from a monster.

"My parents were weak and spineless. Had King Haldor not raised me, I may have turned out like them. I have lost nothing." He stood from his chair and grabbed his book. "Enjoy the library, feel free to use it whenever you like." With that, he left the room and stalked off down the hall. There were too many books in the library for Mylah to keep blindly searching for one that may help her, so she decided to give up on that avenue for the time being.

Mylah found her way back to her room with the journal still tucked under her arm. She was surprised to find Petra waiting for her.

"We need to get you ready," Petra announced, ushering Mylah into the room. Mylah shoved the journal under her pillow, she'd find time to read it later.

"What for?" Mylah asked, wincing as Petra pinched her side, indicating she needed to undress.

"The king is throwing a revel tonight." She pulled a dress from the armoire that was nothing like the stunning emerald gown. It was knee-length and strapless. The pink color did nothing for Mylah's light skin tone and washed her out.

"Why another gathering so soon?" Mylah let Petra dress her like a doll, and then sat in her chair so she could have her hair done.

"He is the king; he can do what he wants." Petra pulled Mylah's hair away from her face and twisted it up into a bun. She clipped long earrings onto her ears that grazed Mylah's shoulders and bounced the light around the room every time she moved.

"What happens if I don't attend?"

"We won't be finding out," Petra snapped, smearing a dark rouge color onto Mylah's lips.

"Isn't it a little early for a party?"

"I have to run an errand, so I won't be here to help you later," Petra was being cryptic. Mylah wondered if it had anything to do with the conversation she'd overheard in the library earlier.

"Well, thank you for helping me, but I think I can take it from here." Petra nodded and hurried out of the room. Whatever her errand was, it must be important. As soon as Petra was out of sight, Mylah closed her door and stripped off the terrible pink dress. She dug around in the armoire and found a much better sky-blue colored dress that brought out the slight blue in her eyes.

Mylah wiped the rouge from her lips and pulled her hair from the bun, doing a half up half down look instead. She felt much better about the change. There was no way she would impress anyone, let alone a king, in that horrible pink fabric.

She waited in her room for a while to see if anyone would come to retrieve her, but eventually gave up. It had to be time for the revel to begin, so she left her room behind and made her way towards the ballroom. The guards she passed along the way nodded to her in greeting but said nothing.

This time, the doors to the ballroom were propped open and there were much fewer guests. The ones who had attended appeared to all be of the younger generation. Everyone else must have work or other obligations. It was a lot to expect people to come to gatherings in the castle every night, Mylah assumed. She hoped Ana would be there.

Someone grazed Mylah's upper arm and she turned, looking up into the face of the shreeve who had bumped her. He wore a patch over his right eye, but the other blazed a deep red color surrounded by a much paler orange. It reminded Mylah of the way her father had described Wren's eyes, but that was the only similarity between the two men.

The first thing she noticed after his astounding eyes was the burn that swept across his right cheek and brow. His shocking white hair contrasted his dark brown skin, which also made the blue markings stand out that much more. He was one of the most beautiful people Mylah had ever seen, even with the burn that marred his face.

"Oh, sorry," he smiled and Mylah felt a blush creep up her neck.

"Oh, uh, fine. I mean, it's fine," she fumbled over her words.

"You must be the human King Castien pardoned," his voice was silky smooth, and it made Mylah want to melt.

"Uh, yes. Leylah. My name," Mylah pinched herself and groaned inwardly. "Sorry, I'm not usually so brain missing. My name's Leylah."

He chuckled. "I'm Torin." He stuck his hand out and Mylah shook it, holding it a moment longer than she should. "I noticed you last night, but you seemed a little preoccupied. Though, I enjoyed watching Davina getting knocked down a peg. She could do with a little more of that on a regular basis."

"Oh, yeah, that was an accident." Mylah twirled her hair nervously.

"Sure, and me bumping into you now was also an accident," he winked, and Mylah let out an obnoxious giggle, covering her mouth to try to minimize the embarrassment.

"You got me there," Mylah said, biting her lip as she looked away. She spotted the king on his throne watching the crowd before him. This time she looked around for Elias and found him alone, leaning against the wall in a corner with his hands in his pockets, watching her. At least he couldn't accuse her of using Torin to get to King Castien.

When he noticed her looking his way, he pushed himself away from the wall and stalked towards the drinks table.

"If you'd excuse me, I need a drink," Mylah told Torin. He stepped out of her way as she strolled towards the wine.

"Watch yourself," Elias said as she stepped up beside him. He grabbed a goblet and chugged the contents.

"Excuse me?" She took her own goblet and sipped from it.

"Torin has a reputation almost as bad as my brother. Just be careful," Elias explained, and Mylah glanced back over her shoulder to where Torin was already talking with two other women.

"Hmm does the prince of Elowyn actually care about *me*?" Mylah mocked and nudged Elias with her elbow. "I think I'll be okay but thank you for the warning." Elias strolled away without another word and Mylah watched as he approached his brother. It was strange to see King Castien genuinely smile at Elias when she had only seen sneers, or calculated grins. She turned away from them and scanned the room, seeing no one else she recognized.

Figuring tonight would not be the night she would be discovering any important information, she decided to have a little fun. She walked back over to Torin and joined in his conversation with the other women.

"So, Torin, I heard that Davina left you for King Castien. Better him than someone else I guess," one of the women said, while the other tittered. Mylah understood why he had enjoyed her spilling her drink on Davina the night before.

"She was a place holder anyway," Torin smirked and glanced at Mylah who suddenly felt uncomfortable in the conversation. She had no experience with relationships or men in general. All she knew of flirting she had learned from watching Cassia interact with Crane. She'd been too busy after her parents died with training to worry much about relationships.

"Speak of the devil." One of the women subtly gestured across the room to where Davina draped herself over the arm of the king's throne.

"I can spill a drink on her again, just say the word," Mylah joked and was surprised when they all laughed.

"I think I'd rather if you honor me with a dance." Torin did a half bow, offering his hand to Mylah. The other two women had looks of slight shock and horror, but Mylah ignored them and took his hand. He twirled her into his arms and led her in a dance towards the center of the room. They were the only one's dancing.

Mylah couldn't stop herself from laughing, and she tilted her head back to let her hair swing around behind her. Torin laughed, the sound like music to Mylah's ears. Eyes were burning holes in Mylah from all around, but she ignored them. They danced from one song to the next, never breaking stride. Eventually, the dance floor filled with more couples.

"This is fun," Mylah said. "I can't remember the last time I had *fun*." Torin grinned and leaned closer so she could hear him.

"Would you be opposed to me kissing you now?" he asked as he continued to swirl them around the floor. Mylah found herself laughing again, but she shook her head and leaned in closer to Torin. She figured maybe it would make King Castien jealous and help her win him over.

Torin bent his head down and when his lips met hers, it seemed as if everything in the room had stopped. All noises dropped away as if they were the only ones in the room.

When Mylah opened her eyes, they were still dancing. Before they could go one more round, though, King Castien appeared on the dance floor, halting their movements.

"Torin, I'll be cutting in now," he said it as a command, but Torin hesitated, keeping his arms around Mylah. Mylah noticed Davina glaring at her from the corner of her eye. "Now, Torin." Torin lifted his hands in surrender and stepped away from Mylah. The king took Torin's place and began moving Mylah around the dance floor at a much slower pace.

"Did Petra dress you in that?" King Castien asked, and Mylah shook her head.

"She had me in a different dress, but I changed after she left. I liked this one better," Mylah's skin burned in all the places where her body touched the king's. "Is there something wrong with this dress?"

"Nothing." King Castien spun her out and back in, pulling her close against his chest. "You should stay away from Torin."

"So I've been warned, and as I already told Prince Elias, I can handle myself." Mylah was frustrated that no one trusted her to be able to make her own decisions.

"I'm not worried about Torin, but who is associated with him," the king said, which left Mylah confused, but he didn't elaborate. "I think you should turn in for the night."

"I just got here!" Mylah protested. King Castien had danced her closer to the door and he spun her out of his arms and towards the exit.

"Goodnight, Leylah," there was an edge to his voice that made goosebumps rise on Mylah's arms. She turned and hurried out of the ballroom. The halls were devoid of people, including guards. As Mylah turned a corner she ran headlong into a solid mass. She opened her eyes to see Davina sneering at her.

"You are truly pitiful," she snarled, grabbing Mylah by the throat, and shoving her up against the wall. Mylah gasped and clawed at Davina's arms, but Davina only laughed. "Squirm all you want, no one's here to save you now." Mylah tried to scream but it came out as a garbled choking sound. She tried to focus her thoughts on her training with Greyson and Crane. Her legs were free, she needed to use them.

Using all the strength she could muster, Mylah thrust herself away from the wall and kneed Davina's hip hard. Davina cursed and lost her grip on Mylah, who slipped down to the floor and started to crawl away.

"You bitch, where do you think you're going?" Davina grabbed Mylah's ankle and dragged her backwards. Mylah attempted to scream again, but her throat was raw, and it came out as a moan instead. She rolled onto her back and curled her knees into her chest, yanking her leg free of Davina's grip. If she could get on her feet, she'd be able to fend off Davina's attacks better.

Davina lunged for Mylah again, but this time Mylah struck out. Davina caught Mylah's fist in her hand and pulled her forward, letting her nails dig into Mylah's skin.

"Go near Torin again, and I will rip your pretty little hair from your scalp," Davina hissed into Mylah's ear. "This is far from over, *human*," she spit out the last word like a curse. As she walked past Mylah she kicked out with her heel, slicing the side of Mylah's thigh. Blood trickled out and dripped onto the floor.

Mylah mopped up the drops of blood with her dress and stood shakily. Davina was much stronger than her usual opponents, she hadn't been nearly prepared enough for that fight. She would have to make it a point to start working out again and maybe find someone to spar with. Broderick would probably be up to the task.

Mylah passed a few guards on her way back to her room, but she skillfully hid her wounds. Back in the safety of her own room, Mylah stripped out of the bloodied dress. Petra had left a wash bucket in the room, as usual, but this was the first time Mylah had needed it. She took the cloth and wiped down her leg. The cut wasn't bad, and it had only bled for a few seconds, but it was long. Mylah would have to remember to wear bigger heels to any event from now on since they proved to be a useful weapon.

In the mirror, Mylah could already see bruises blooming on her neck. It would be impossible to hide the evidence in the morning, but she would cross that bridge when she came to it.

Twenty One

Petra came in the morning to help Mylah get ready. She seemed distracted and didn't notice the bruises on Mylah's neck until she was brushing her hair. When she saw them, she gasped and stroked them lightly.

"Where did these come from?" she demanded.

"I may have gotten into a little scrape last night..." Mylah's cheeks reddened, embarrassed that she had let her guard down even after all the warnings.

"A little scrape," Petra scoffed. "You look like someone trampled you with their horse!" She gestured to the cut on Mylah's leg revealed by the slit in her gown.

"I'd say I did pretty well, considering," Mylah joked.

"How can you joke about this? You could have been killed! We must tell King Castien. He will want to know someone tried to harm his guest," Petra sighed, as if that was the exact opposite of what she wanted to do.

"No, it's fine. Really. Let's cover it up, and it will be gone in a few days. No one has to know." Mylah would rather no one know of her fight with Davina. She had a feeling Davina would not look too kindly on her if she tattled to the king.

"But if it happens again," Petra tried to argue but Mylah shook her head.

"No. It won't happen again," she said, hoping that she was right, but if it did, she would be ready.

"Hmph." Petra dug into the armoire and pulled back with a scarf in her hand. "This will do the trick." She wound the scarf around Mylah's neck and tied it into a fashionable bow to make it look purposeful.

"Thank you," Mylah grasped Petra's hand.

"Come, the king requests your presence at breakfast this morning." Petra pulled her hand from Mylah's grasp and beckoned for Mylah to follow her.

"Did you see the king this morning, did he seem upset?" She worried that he was about to tell her off again.

"He always seems upset, girl. Never anticipate anything *good* when he requests your presence." Petra gave her a pitying look and left the room. Mylah followed her and tried to prepare herself for whatever was coming.

They arrived at the dining room and Mylah realized there was a third person at the table; Torin. She immediately grew hot and was grateful she had the scarf to cover the blush creeping up her neck, though her cheeks had to be red as well.

"How good of you to join us this morning," King Castien drawled. "Take a seat." Mylah took the only unoccupied seat.

"What's that?" Elias spoke with concern in his voice, causing Mylah to look his way. She realized his gaze was fixed on her exposed leg and she groaned inwardly. Petra should have had her change into a different dress.

"I slipped and scraped it on something." Mylah pulled her dress together to cover the mark.

"It wasn't there yesterday," Elias pointed out, and Mylah shot him a frustrated look.

"No, it wasn't, because I fell after I left the revel last night, on my way back to my room." Mylah wished he would drop it, but instead, King Castien joined in.

"This is the first day you haven't worn your necklace..." He stood from his chair and strolled towards her. Mylah stiffened as he ran his hand along the scarf around her neck.

"What does it matter to you what I wear?" she snapped.

"It doesn't, but it does concern me that you're *lying to me*." He tightened his grip on the scarf and Mylah yelped as it strained against her bruises. In a flurry she unwound the scarf from her neck and lurched out of the chair to face the king head on.

"There, are you happy? Your precious consort cornered me in the hall last night and tried to kill me," she spat the words like venom. "Forgive me for wishing to hide the evidence of my humiliation." She watched in satisfaction as the king's expression changed from victorious to taken aback. She moved to walk past him and out of the dining room, but he blocked her way.

"Come with me," he ordered and took her hand to lead her from the room. Mylah glanced back at Torin and Elias who both stared at her neck with fury in their eyes. King Castien took her a few doors down to the library and closed the door behind them. He let go of her hand and turned to face her.

"If anyone so much as *breathes* on you, I want to hear about it immediately, I don't care who it is. Do you understand?" His eyes blazed, and heat poured from him in waves.

"Y-yes," Mylah stuttered.

"Good. As for Davina, I will deal with her." He turned away and began pacing. "To have escaped her with your life you are either extraordinarily lucky, or you've been hiding something else from me..."

"I don't know what you mean." Mylah tugged on her hair, playing with the ends of it as she tried her best to appear innocent.

"I mean, Davina doesn't usually let her victims walk away from a fight." King Castien eyed her suspiciously.

"I mean, I technically crawled away," Mylah admitted, but it did not sway him, he still awaited an explanation. "Fine, I have some fighting experience."

"Good," he smirked. "I think I may have use for you after all."

They returned to breakfast after that. Mylah's mind whirled as she ate and considered what possible use the king could have for her. She was grateful once everyone finished eating and King Castien requested them all to follow him to his study. Her curiosity was about to be satisfied. There were already two other people in the study who Mylah had never seen before.

"Leylah, this is Korriane, my strategist." King Castien nodded to the woman lounging in the chair against the wall. "And Killian, my advisor." He gestured to the man hovering over a large round table in the center of the room. Korriane and Killian appeared to be siblings, if not twins. They had similar markings and almost identical faces, though their hair was different. Korriane's was a bright purple with white tips, and Killian's was a blazing fire red. "You've already met Torin, my war general." Mylah peeked over her shoulder at Torin who winked at her and turned her head away from him quickly.

Maps were scattered across the table and Mylah tried to peer closer, but King Castien stepped in front of her.

"You're probably wondering why I brought you here." He turned and strode to Killian's side, beckoning Mylah forward. She blinked in surprise as she realized that the map on top of the others was of Adair. She should have guessed since they were the ones who the Elowyns were at war with. What surprised her though was that the focus was not on the border, but on the castle. They had drawn what appeared to be a map of the inside of the castle, and to Mylah's dismay, it was very accurate.

"Since you told me the king is planning on using the book, we have been discussing the best course of action to thwart his efforts," King Castien began to explain. "Since you are human, it will be less suspicious for you to be seen in Adair."

"And now that you know I can fight," Mylah added, sighing as she realized what it was that they wanted her to do. An overwhelming sense of déjà vu came over her.

"Now that I know you can fight, I think you'll be able to help us retrieve the book from the king." King Castien grinned and leaned over the table. "We've mapped out the castle and we've pinpointed the most likely places he would keep the book hidden."

"You're sure he has the book hidden in the castle?" Mylah didn't want to give away its true location, but she also resented the idea of breaking into the castle to steal something that wasn't even there. Although, she'd have someone else to blame when she inevitably failed her mission. And, while she was in the castle she could check in with the king and tell him anything she'd learned.

"It's the only logical place to keep it," Korriane said, joining them at the table.

"I'll do it," Mylah said, hoping she didn't sound too eager. "But I'll need more training first. If someone recognizes me, they'll know I've been exiled. I'm to be put to death if I reenter Adair. I need as much training as possible to be able to fight my way out." She wouldn't have to do any fighting, but she wanted the training in case Davina tried to attack her again.

"You'll receive training, but you won't be going in alone. Korriane, Killian, and Torin will accompany you," King Castien said, and Mylah's heart dropped. She wouldn't be able to talk to anyone without the others knowing something was up. Instead, she'd have to send word ahead of time. "We will wait for the final word from my inside man as to the location of the book in the castle, and then you will go. The longer we wait, the more likely the king will be ready to use the book. We have to hope that he doesn't have all the means to complete the spell."

Spell. That was what was in the book. Finally, a useful piece of information. Now to discover what the spell did.

"I'd like to accompany them on the mission," Elias said, stepping forward and joining the circle that surrounded the table. Everyone turned to him in surprise, clearly having forgotten he was in the room.

"No, out of the question," King Castien brushed him off. "Now, Torin will be training Leylah..."

"I am going, whether you want me to or not. I'm one of our best fighters and you know it," Elias spoke again, but King Castien ignored him. "And I should be the one to train Leylah, I've trained most of our knights." Elias' features tightened and his fists clenched at his sides.

"Fine, train her. But you're not going on the mission!" The king whirled on Elias and slammed his hand onto the table making the maps flutter, some of them slipping off the surface to the floor. Silence filled the room as King Castien and Elias seemed to be having a stare down. Korriane rolled her eyes and flopped back into her chair while Killian picked up the maps and organized them.

"We can start training now," Elias said as he turned away from King Castien first. King Castien seemed smug in his victory.

"I'll tag along to make sure you're teaching her everything she needs to learn," Torin offered, but Mylah figured he just wanted to be clear of the king's temper.

"Unnecessary, but do what you want," Elias commented as he led the way out of the study.

Twenty Two

Elias took Mylah to her room first, where she changed into suitable clothing for training. Afterwards, they walked down to the same floor as the dungeon and Madame Edris' room. Mylah had nearly forgotten about her down there and realized that was one more reason for her to brush up on her training.

Beside the dungeon, there was a training room. It reminded Mylah of the training room she'd used in Adair; a big empty space with a training mat on the floor and a wall filled with weapons to choose from. Torin waited for them in the center of the room. Elias went to the wall and took down two swords, but Mylah shook her head and took down the daggers instead.

"We're going in undercover right?" she pointed out. "I won't be able to conceal a sword easily, but daggers..." She threw one at the target on the wall and it sunk into the bullseye. Mylah couldn't help but smile. Being able to hold weapons again had her heart soaring, especially since she was still as skilled as she'd been when she stopped training. Elias and Torin both gaped at her.

"Apparently you've had more than a little practice..." Elias muttered. "But you're right. We should practice with the weapons you will actually be using on the mission." In one swift motion, Elias knocked Mylah's hand aside, taking the dagger she still held, and with the other arm, he pulled her against him, holding the dagger against her throat.

"I guess I still have a lot to learn," Mylah gasped out, glaring up at Elias who smirked.

"Alright, break it up. My turn." Torin grabbed a sword from the wall. Elias released Mylah and stepped back to watch. "Just because we won't have swords, doesn't mean the people we are fighting won't. Try to disarm me." He took his stance and Mylah took two knives from the wall. These were about three times the size of the daggers, but still small enough to conceal beneath a cloak without sticking out.

Mylah approached Torin, watching him to see if he would reveal any weaknesses. She edged around him, making an arc, and he pivoted to follow her movements. Mylah noticed he favored his left leg, and in her next motion she lunged forward, dodging his sword, and slid into his leg, sending him sprawling. In another moment, she sat atop him, trying to steady her breathing from the sudden movements, as he lay on his back with the sword out of his reach. She held one of her knives to his throat to prove that she had won.

"You're lucky you caught me on a bad day." He pushed himself up onto his elbows, making himself come face to face with Mylah. She realized she had lingered too long on top of him and blushed. Before she could stand, he caught her by the waist and lifted her swiftly to her feet as he stood. Mylah noticed where his pant leg had bunched up that his right leg was also scored with burns, just as his face was.

"I'm sorry, I didn't realize..." she looked away, ashamed and embarrassed.

"Don't be. When you're fighting someone larger than you, it's easiest to take advantage of their weaknesses and bring them down that way. Otherwise, I could overcome you with brute strength. You did perfectly." Elias cleared his throat from beside the weapons wall.

"This is my training session, Torin. Perhaps you'd do better to return to my brother's side." Elias swept forward, picking up Torin's sword from the floor.

"You've been trained, and well for sure, Prince Elias, but you haven't fought in *real* combat. You need my help, and you know it," Torin countered. Mylah had to agree that Torin would give a valuable perspective, but it was not her place to speak up.

"You don't know what I've done or who I've fought," Elias spoke calmly enough, but his eyes gave away his true resentment at Torin's words. "If you'll please see yourself out, I will call you back if necessary." Torin said nothing, but he bowed to Elias and left the room. "Now," Elias stepped up to Mylah, taking a fighting stance as Torin had done. "You do realize that Torin *let* you take him down, right?" Elias said, as Mylah began circling him. She paused.

"I found his weakness and took him down, fair and square," she objected, and Elias laughed.

"Torin doesn't *have* a weakness, or, at least, if he does, it's not his leg. That burn hasn't caused him any issues since it finished healing," Elias explained. "He is a war general, Leylah. Did you really think he'd be taken down that easily?"

"It did seem a little too easy..." Mylah admitted. "But why would he do that?"

"Is it not obvious that he likes you? I thought your kiss last night would have been some indication." Elias dodged as Mylah made her first move. "That's why I asked him to leave." He evaded her next attack. "It will do you no good to have someone who's not pushing you," he dodged again, "to your limits." Mylah feigned an attack to the right and at the last second spun to strike Elias' in the ribs, but he side-stepped her attack, anticipating her every move.

"It does me no good to keep attempting attacks only to have you thwart them and not tell me how to do it better next time," Mylah huffed. Elias knocked away her knives and twisted her right arm behind her back.

"Move faster, smarter, and more deliberate." His breath was hot against her ear and sent a shiver down her spine. He released her. "Take up the sword. This time you will defend. Watch my moves and take notes." Elias picked up the knives and handed Mylah the sword. He did not begin by circling Mylah as she had done him. Instead, he went in for an attack right away to Mylah's exposed side. She barely swung her sword in time to block his knife from hitting its target.

"Attack before your opponent has time to react," Elias instructed as he struck her other side with his knife, pulling back at the last second so as not to do her any real harm. "When you're fighting someone stronger, time is not on your side."

"It's not exactly fair," Mylah said, lowering her weapon. "You can inherently move faster than me."

"That's not true. Sure, my fae side makes it easier for me, but you can learn how to keep up. Come on, show me what you can do."

Mylah lunged forward with her sword, but Elias trapped it between his knives, disarming her. For the most part, she'd fought against opponents wielding the same weapon as herself. She'd had little practice fighting as she was with Elias.

"Can I show you what I know, sword versus sword? And then we can go from there." Mylah picked her sword back up and Elias retrieved another from the wall.

"Impress me," he said. Mylah took a deep breath and began. She parried with Elias, as she had done hundreds of times before with Greyson and Crane. She used the time to determine his patterns and weak points. He tended to favor protecting his torso and head while leaving his legs and feet unprotected. It would not be an incapacitating blow, but it may give her an advantage.

She continued as usual for another minute, to keep Elias thinking this was all she would do, and then swept low with her sword, making sure to hit him with the flat side of the blade. The force knocked him sideways, and in the seconds it took him to regain his balance, Mylah was able to disarm him. She stuck her sword out towards his chest and grinned in triumph.

"Don't tell me you let me win, I won't believe you this time." She lowered her sword.

"Now we're getting somewhere. Let me show you how you can transfer some of those moves and tactics over to the knives." Elias fetched the knives, and they spent the next few hours practicing with them. By the time they decided to call it a day, Mylah was able to at least hold her own against Elias.

Mylah could barely lift her arms as they left the training room. They started down the hall, but Elias stopped and ran back to the training room. When he returned, he gripped a dagger in his hand.

"Here." He held it out to her. Mylah hesitated, not sure if it was a trap of some kind. "In case Davina tries to hurt you again." Mylah took the dagger.

"Thank you. Am I supposed to be armed though?" King Castien had proven that he was still wary of her, for good reason. He would not approve of her carrying around a weapon.

"I trust you," Elias shrugged. "If anyone asks you about it, tell them to come talk to me."

"Okay." Mylah smiled and gripped the dagger tight. It brought her comfort to have a weapon at her disposal again. If Davina, or anyone else, came at her, she would be ready. Then as an afterthought, Mylah realized she could kill the king if she were alone with him again...but first she needed to get more information from him about the book. If he were dead, it may solve all their problems and end the war, but it could also make it worse.

"*My prince*," the voice like nails on a chalkboard came from Madame Edris' doorway. Elias and Mylah paused and turned back to see Madame Edris slink out into the hallway. She wore her strange glamour that did not quite transform her from old, crippled self, to what Mylah assumed was her younger self.

"Madame Edris." Elias inclined his head toward her. "What do you need?"

"A favor, for a favor," she snarled. "You owe me, and I am in need of some supplies." Her lips curled up into a vicious smile.

"What is it that you need?" Elias responded, sounding annoyed. Mylah knew that the only reason he owed the witch anything was because of her. *She* should be the one to retrieve whatever the witch requested.

"I have a list here..." Madame Edris disappeared back into her room and reappeared holding a folded-up slip of paper. "I expect it all in my doorway by tomorrow morning." She handed the paper to Elias and retreated to her room, closing the door behind her.

Elias unfolded the paper and groaned. "I should have guessed."

Mylah peered over his shoulder. "That shouldn't be too bad, it's just three things."

"Yeah, three items that can only be found in the Unbound territory." He crumpled up the paper and shoved it into his pocket. "Belladonna, probably because she used her store on *you,* hair from a kelpie, and water from the Lake of Anguish."

"I can help you," Mylah offered. "I owe you."

"You don't owe me anything." Elias veered towards the kitchen. "Go back to your room, Petra will fetch you once dinner is ready." For a moment, Mylah debated letting him go alone, but instead, she ran after him.

"I'm coming with you, whether you want my help or not," she said. They entered the kitchen and the servants looked surprised to see the prince there. Each of them bowed as he passed them.

"You're just going to be a burden," Elias said as they stepped outside. "I will get this done much faster if I don't have you with me."

"Rude, but I'm still coming." Mylah followed him to the stables.

"I need a horse, Stav," Elias told the stable boy, and then he turned back to Mylah. "I need you to stay here. We don't need another incident like what happened with the naga."

Mylah groaned. "That was different. I was alone, weakened from being on the run, and it was nighttime."

"It will be nighttime by the time we leave the forest," Elias pointed out.

"I'm coming. Stav, another horse please," Mylah said as the stable boy led a horse out of the stable.

"Sorry, miss. All the horses are already out," Stav said, avoiding making eye contact with either of them.

"That makes this easier. Stay." Elias took the reins of the horse from Stav, but Mylah grabbed them too.

"No. Take me with you. The only reason you're doing this is because you had to help me. Now let me help you, then we can be square," Mylah demanded, and Elias sighed.

"Fine. Stav, change the saddle, this one won't allow for two people." He handed the reins back to the boy, who nodded and led the horse back into the stables. "Don't make me regret letting you come with me." Mylah grinned in triumph.

Once they were both seated in the saddle of the horse, they took off at full speed. Mylah sat in the front with Elias' arms on either side of her as he gripped the reins. She had ridden that way with Broderick and Sabine, but with

Elias it felt more intimate, even though he had never even shown interest in her.

"You're trembling, are you okay?" Elias yelled over the wind and Mylah snapped out of her thoughts, blushing as she realized what was happening. She was developing feelings for the brother of the man who had killed her parents.

"I'm fine," it came out harsher than she had anticipated. The rest of the ride to the forest Mylah tried everything to keep her thoughts from going back to Elias, even though he was pressed up against her. She thought about Greyson, Crane, Garrick, Elena, her parents...

"We should be able to find the belladonna here," Elias said as the horse slowed to a trot. "I found a patch of it out here last time Madame Edris sent me to fetch her ingredients." The horse continued through the woods until Elias pulled up on the reins and forced them to a stop.

"Is it here?" Mylah asked.

"There," Elias jumped down from the horse. Mylah shivered as she was hit with a cool breeze where Elias' body had previously pressed against hers. She watched as he pulled on gloves and began gathering the belladonna plants into a sack. Once it was full, he returned to the horse and tied the sack to the saddle. He stayed on the ground, leading the horse with the reins on foot. Mylah remained in the saddle, keeping watch for any signs of trouble.

"Where will we be able to find hair from a kelpie?" Mylah asked.

"Probably nearer to the lake," Elias said. He led them into a small clearing and then hefted himself back onto the horse behind Mylah. It was almost a relief to feel him behind her again. She tried to shake the feeling as the horse began trotting faster through the woods. They reached the lake and Elias slipped from the saddle again. This time Mylah joined him on the ground. The sun had begun to set and howls sounded from the forest making Mylah shudder.

"We can at least get this now." Elias pulled out a jar and dipped it into the lake, collecting water. He topped the jar off and replaced the lid before slipping it into one of the saddle bags. "Now for the kelpie hair..."

"I might be able to help with that!" Excitement jolted through Mylah at the prospect of being useful on their mission. "Genevieve, Lady of the..." Elias slapped a hand over her mouth and hissed.

"What are you doing?" He looked around wildly and Mylah ripped his hand away from her mouth. "Are you trying to get us killed?"

"What are you talking about? Genevieve will help us!" Mylah urged. "She promised me if I ever needed her, she would come."

"You can't be serious? Why would a siren ever help a human?" Elias confirmed Mylah's suspicion that Genevieve was no ordinary mermaid, but it did not change the fact that she had saved Mylah's life.

"You said that you trust me, is that still true?" Mylah crossed her arms over her chest and cocked her eyebrow at Elias.

"Fine. Yes, I still trust you, though I'm worrying that I may already regret the decision."

"Good. Now, Genevieve, Lady of the Lake, I need your help," Mylah finished her request. She had no idea how long it would take for Genevieve to appear, but she had to imagine it wouldn't be too long.

"And what if she doesn't show?" Elias asked, keeping his eyes on the water.

"She'll show," Mylah said. As they watched, ripples appeared on the surface of the lake and a head emerged. It was not Genevieve, though, who stared up at them.

"Beautiful creatures...come swim with me, dance with me underwater..." Her voice was enticing and made Mylah want to approach the edge of the lake. *"Come to me, stay with me..."* Before Mylah realized what she was doing, she stood at the edge of the lake, her toes in the water. Elias waded into the water beside her, his eyes glued to the mermaid, and he wore a giddy grin. Mylah felt a flash of jealousy that broke whatever spell the siren had her under.

"STOP!" She covered her ears and glared at the siren. "Genevieve, Lady of the Lake!" As soon as the final word left her mouth, another ripple formed, and Genevieve rose from the water.

"Fiona, leave the poor shreeve boy," Genevieve commanded, and the other siren shrugged, disappearing back under the water and breaking Elias' reverie. "How wonderful to see my sweet Leylah again," Genevieve crooned, winking at Mylah. "As for you," she hissed as she looked upon Elias.

"I told you this was a bad idea." Elias turned to Mylah who ignored him.

"I have a favor to ask," Mylah said as she took another step into the water. "We need hair from a kelpie. I thought that you may know where we could find one." Genevieve eyed Elias with suspicion and turned back to Mylah.

"Why should I help him?" She drifted on her back, placing her arms behind her head like a pillow, her hair billowing out in the water around her like a halo. "His people have done nothing but harm here."

"King Castien does not represent all shreeve, and Elias is nothing like his brother. He is kind, and good. He is worthy of your assistance." Mylah hated to compliment Elias right in front of him, but they needed Genevieve's help. Mylah kept herself from looking at him, but she could feel his eyes on her.

"I trust your judgement." Genevieve nodded to her and disappeared beneath the water's surface.

"Who's the liar now?" Elias joked as he walked closer to Mylah. She turned to him and shook her head.

"I wasn't lying. I can't lie to Genevieve; she would know if I did." She strolled past Elias towards the horse to wait for Genevieve's return.

"I thought you liked my brother." Elias continued to watch the water.

"Your brother and I have an understanding..." Mylah said, realizing that even if King Castien didn't know it, they were both using each other as a means to an end. They each wanted the shreeve book, him to keep King Florian from using it, and her to translate it and *help* King Florian.

"How were you able to break free of the siren's song?" Elias asked and Mylah blushed again. "We would have both been dead if you hadn't been able to break through."

"I'm sure Genevieve would have come and saved us, or at least me," Mylah smirked.

"Maybe, but that doesn't answer my question," Elias said. Genevieve popped out of the water at that moment and Mylah let out a rush of air, relieved at her timing.

"Take this." She held a single hair out towards Elias. He reached for it, and she grabbed his wrist with her free hand pulling him further into the water. "If you deceive or hurt that girl, I will be sure to feed you to Fiona," she growled and then placed the hair into his hand, releasing him from her clutches.

"You must have left some impression on her." Elias splashed out of the lake and joined Mylah beside the horse. He sealed the kelpie hair into a jar and put it in the saddle bag.

"She's a family friend," Mylah said, smirking at Genevieve who waved her over. Mylah glanced at Elias who still adjusted the saddle and approached Genevieve.

"I see you've taken my advice about healing your heart," Genevieve said, winking.

"No, no. We're just friends," Mylah said, backing away from Genevieve.

"Don't worry, I'll keep your secret. Safe travels," she said before she disappeared.

"Well, come on," Elias called to Mylah. She made her way over to him. "And don't think I forgot you never answered my question. How did you break free of the siren's song?"

"Um, not really sure. I guess I got distracted so I was able to break free." Mylah knelt down to tie the laces of her boot which had come undone, avoiding Elias' gaze.

"What distracted you?" he pushed.

"I guess *you* did," Mylah admitted, and she noticed Elias stiffen in surprise. He relaxed after a moment and turned to the horse to tighten the saddle.

"Leylah, I..."

"Don't," she snapped, knowing what would come next; some explanation for why he didn't feel the same way. "Couldn't you have used your magic to protect you from falling into a trance?"

"I told you, it's not that simple." He flexed his hands at his sides and Mylah turned her head up as she stood so she could look into his eyes.

"No, you didn't tell me, not really," she pressed.

"I just..." He turned away from her and started pacing. "I can't control my magic well enough yet."

"Have you tried? It seems to me you spend more time worrying about everyone else's problems. Maybe you should focus more on your own." Mylah wanted to understand Elias better, and out there, away from the castle, was the best opportunity she would get to find out more of his story.

"You don't understand," he said, pausing his pacing to turn back to her.

"What's not to understand? It's like combat training. You practice until you get it right, and then you practice some more."

"Magic is different," Elias tried to say, but Mylah shook her head. "Why are you pressing the issue? What does it matter to you?"

Mylah finally looked away from him and glared at her feet. "I guess it doesn't matter. I'm just trying to understand you," she admitted.

"Well, stop trying." Elias made to climb into the saddle.

"Real nice," Mylah said, and Elias turned back to her, eyes narrowed.

"You're infuriating," he grumbled.

"Because I actually care, when no one else seems to?" Mylah raised one brow and crossed her arms over her chest.

"You are *not* the first person who has tried to help me," Elias growled.

Mylah threw her hands up in the air. "I don't know why I even bothered. I guess I thought you were different." She closed her eyes, wishing she could disappear.

"Different than who? Please, tell me who you think I am."

Mylah's eyes flew open at his mocking tone. "A prince! Someone who cares about his people and their well-being. Someone who puts his family first, and someone who saw something in me that was worth saving..." she trailed off at the end, tears building in her eyes. She nearly choked trying to hold them back.

"That's ridiculous," he scoffed.

"You're ridiculous! You have the power to help people and change lives, yet you hide it away and cower from it."

"You have no idea what I am capable of!" Elias broke and yelled back.

"Tell me then!"

"My magic killed my father!" As soon as the words left his mouth, his face slackened, and his shoulders began trembling. Mylah regretted pushing him to his limit, and stepped forward, meaning to apologize, though she had no idea how.

"Shit, shit, shit." Elias fisted his hands into his hair and bowed his head. "We need to get back to the castle." He turned to the horse.

"I-I'm sorry," Mylah stuttered in a whisper. "I won't tell anyone, I swear. I didn't realize..." she stopped. Of course she hadn't realized, no one had. Everyone assumed King Haldor had been killed by an Unbound creature, which was what had sparked King Castien to take over the territory.

"We can talk about it later, but not here," Elias said, his voice low and brimming with anger. Mylah wasn't sure if that anger was at himself or her, and she didn't want to find out.

He helped her onto the horse and climbed up behind her again. They started towards the forest at a slow trot. They couldn't go full speed through the forest, but they cleared it fast enough. Once they were out in the open, the horse moved faster than Mylah had ever seen it go.

They didn't talk the whole ride back to the castle. When they reached the stables, Elias handed the reins over to Stav and led Mylah silently into the castle, using the side kitchen door again. Dinner would have been hours ago, but Mylah was starving. She hadn't eaten since breakfast.

"Castien will be having another revel," Elias said more to himself than to Mylah. "He'll have noticed we were missing."

"Another revel? It's probably winding down by now, right?" Mylah couldn't imagine people being able to stay out late, night after night, and still keep the party going.

"Doubtful. Petra should be able to help you get ready, come on."

"I can get ready myself," Mylah said. There was no need for anyone to help dress her, she'd done it herself since she was four.

"Fine, go get ready. I'll be outside your door in fifteen minutes." Elias left before Mylah could respond.

Twenty Three

Mylah hurried to her room, still shaken by all that had been revealed. She used her wash bucket to clean up and rummaged through her armoire, pulling out the first dress she came across. It was like her dress from the night before, but a dark green color. She swept her hair up into a high ponytail and brushed some rouge onto her cheeks. As she slipped on her heels, with a heel that could do some damage as she'd learned from Davina, Elias knocked on her door.

"Ready!" Mylah opened the door and Elias stood waiting for her. She looped her arm through his and he rushed them down the hall. "Do you think King Castien is going to be upset that we're late?"

"I don't know." Elias slowed as they neared the ballroom. "Do you still have your dagger?" Mylah nodded. She had remembered to strap it to her thigh beneath her dress. Its weight brought her comfort. "Good."

The doors were open again, as they had been the night before. Elias took his arm from Mylah's before they walked into the room, stepping away from her and entering a step ahead. All eyes in the room went to them. Mylah glanced across the room to see the king on his throne with Davina and Aleese draped on either side of him. He watched his brother with curiosity in his gaze, and then his eyes found Mylah's. Before she could take another step, Torin was at her side.

"There you are," he said as he took her hand. "I've been waiting for the perfect dance partner." Mylah was only half paying attention to him. She watched Elias who strolled across the room towards his brother.

"Sorry, I don't feel much like dancing tonight." Mylah shrugged him off.

"Leylah! I was worried I wouldn't see you tonight!" Ana came bounding over to her. "I snuck out to have a little fun, but I couldn't find you!"

"Ana, I'm a little busy," Mylah said, immediately regretting her words. Ana winced and backed away. "Sorry, I didn't mean that. It's been a long day." She grabbed Ana's hand. "Have you met Torin? He's the war general," Mylah introduced them and left them to entertain themselves. She crossed the floor towards the king and Elias.

"Leylah, how good of you to grace us with your presence," King Castien's words were slow and deliberate. He was drunk. "My brother tells me you did well with your training today. That does not excuse your absence at lunch and dinner."

"I was helping..."

"She was with me," Elias interrupted. "I took her into town, and we lost track of time."

"You know I hate when you go out without guards," King Castien scolded Elias. "Anything could happen."

"But nothing did. We both came back in one piece."

"Fair enough. Don't do it again." The king rose from his throne. He stumbled but caught himself. Aleese and Davina flanked him, but he shooed them away. "Leylah, a dance please." She let him lead her away from the throne. He leaned on her heavily as they danced.

"Why don't you ever dance with Aleese, or Davina?" Mylah asked him.

"Because they may forget their place otherwise," he said, and Mylah realized what he meant. They were playthings for him, nothing else.

"So why dance with me, then?"

"Because I know you will never mistake it for anything more than a chance to speak privately," he stated. Mylah wondered if he was only being so honest with her because he was drunk, or because he had begun to trust her as Elias had. "Elias seems different tonight."

"I don't know what you mean." Mylah glanced over at Elias who still stood by the throne. His face was tight and revealed none of his emotions to her. She hoped he would forgive her for forcing his confession earlier, but she would also understand if he refused to ever speak to her again.

"I don't know either." King Castien straightened up and halted their dancing. "Elias," he called to his brother. "Please, take my place, I am having trouble keeping up." The king stumbled off the dance floor, leaving Mylah to stand and wait for Elias to take his place. Thankfully, there were other people on the dance floor, so no one appeared to have noticed she had been abandoned mid-dance by the king.

"You don't have to dance with me," Mylah said as Elias stood before her.

"Yes, I do." He took her hand in his and placed his other hand on her waist. "Let's get this over with," he mumbled and began moving Mylah around the dance floor. She was stung by his words. Clearly, he did not wish to be dancing with her, which meant he did not feel the same way that she was beginning to feel about him, not that she blamed him after their day together.

"You clearly don't want to be dancing with me," Mylah said, trying to pull away as tears pricked her eyes.

"Finish this dance and then we can be done." Elias kept hold of her and continued moving, but Mylah stopped following his lead. The interruption caused another couple to bump into them, but Mylah didn't care. She pulled her hand out of Elias' grasp.

"I don't want to dance anymore." She turned on her heel and left the dance floor. She noticed Torin and Ana still talking by the front door and made her way towards them. As she approached, they started towards the dance floor, and she veered aside so as not to interrupt them. She found the refreshments table and shoved her face full of food. She had nearly forgotten her hunger in the whirlwind of King Castien and Elias.

"Classy," a voice jeered. Mylah turned to see Davina there, watching her.

"What do you want?" Mylah was itching to take her frustration and anger out on someone, and Davina was the perfect target.

"Nothing from you," she sneered as she grabbed two drinks from the table and stalked back towards the king, leaving Mylah alone again.

Mylah turned to watch Torin and Ana on the dance floor. They looked like they were enjoying themselves, and she felt envious. That could have been her, but Ana deserved a little fun. Besides, as much fun as Torin was, that's all he represented for Mylah. Elias had made her feel different, less like a fling, which embarrassed her to think. Not that it mattered anymore. He had made it clear that he did not feel the same way.

Mylah chugged the contents of one of the goblets and was granted with an immediate sense of euphoria. The edges of the world became fuzzy, and all the colors appeared brighter. She understood why the king had decided to drink so much of it. It took all her worries away and left her giddy.

Someone asked Mylah to dance, and she agreed. After spending hours on the dance floor, passing from one partner to another, Mylah felt as if her feet were numb. Most everyone had gone by the time she left the dance floor, even Elias. All that remained were King Castien, Davina, Aleese, Torin, and a few knights who had joined in the revel. Torin bid Mylah a goodnight and disappeared to wherever he spent his nights, and the knights returned to their stations. Most of the effects of the drink had worn off for Mylah, but she still wasn't ready to go to bed. She feared the direction her thoughts would take her once left alone with them.

She stumbled into the hall, each step excruciating. Once she was out of sight of the others, she slipped out of her heels and her feet screamed in delight. She let herself slump down to the floor for a few precious moments off her feet.

From where she sat, she watched as Davina fled from the ballroom, tears streaming down her face. Aleese followed her, trying to calm her down. They were out of sight after a few moments, and then King Castien strolled into the hall. He had not slowed his drinking all night and could barely hold himself up.

He made his way towards Mylah, and she hoped he would pass her by without noticing her sitting on the floor. Instead, he looked right at her and laughed.

"Don't make fun, you've never had to wear heels while you danced all night!" She tried to stand up, but her legs protested and fought against her. King Castien stumbled over and slumped down beside her.

"Maybe not, but on more than one occasion I *have* drunk so much that I couldn't make it back to my bedroom," he stretched his legs out in front of him and leaned his head against the wall.

"Why did you drink so much tonight? The last few nights you barely drank at all," Mylah asked, hoping she wasn't crossing a line.

"It was the only way I could break the news to Davina...if I were sober, I probably wouldn't have been able to get rid of her. She's hard to refuse," he smirked. "I'll have to find someone to replace her tomorrow night, but I have all day to think about it."

"Wait, you mean you got rid of her, like no longer a consort?" Mylah wasn't even sure that's what he called them, but she had no other word for it that wouldn't offend him.

"I told you I'd deal with her, and I did," he shrugged, sliding sideways down the wall. His head landed on Mylah's shoulder, and his eyes closed.

"Oh, no. We are not staying here," Mylah protested, waking him. "Come on." She forced herself to her feet and pulled up King Castien beside her. She slung one of his arms over her shoulders and supported most of his weight. "Where is your room?"

"At the top of the tallest tower." He pointed in an arbitrary direction. "I can't go there tonight."

"What do you mean?" Mylah stumbled under his weight.

"Aleese...I can't face her."

"I saw her leave with Davina," Mylah pointed out.

"No, she'll be back. They always come back." He shook his head. "Sometimes I wish they wouldn't."

"You're the king, just tell them to leave." Mylah didn't understand most of what King Castien did, she wasn't sure why she thought this would be any different.

"I can't, just...take me to your room." He sounded pitiful.

"Fine." Mylah groaned and started walking towards her room, practically dragging the king. "Where do all the guards go at night?" It would be useful if his guards could carry him, but the one time she needed them, none appeared.

"Outside. Once all the guests leave, they make sure no one lingers," King Castien explained. "Except the ones outside my bedroom. They stay there all the time." That would be helpful if Mylah had any idea where that was.

After a long, painful walk, they made it to Mylah's room. She fumbled with the door but was able to open it and get King Castien inside. She flopped him onto the bed and collapsed onto the floor beside it.

"Won't people worry when you can't be found in your bed?" Mylah asked as she let out painful gasps.

"No one will notice I'm missing..." he mumbled as he turned his head into the pillow.

"This is crazy..." Mylah murmured to herself as she pulled a blanket from the bed and curled up on the floor. It was still comfier than the dungeon she'd slept in while in

Adair. Though, that could be from the lingering effects of the wine.

When Mylah woke in the morning, every muscle in her body ached. Sleeping on the floor had done nothing for her already weary limbs. It took every ounce of her strength to push herself to her feet. She jumped in surprise when she saw the king on her bed, and then remembered that was the whole reason for her sleeping on the floor.

He looked so peaceful and...innocent. Mylah almost couldn't be convinced he was the same monster who had murdered her parents. Her hand went to the dagger still strapped to her thigh and her fingers twitched with anticipation. *No. I need him alive...for now.*

As she turned away, she realized Petra had not come to her room yet. Mylah double checked that the king was still asleep and stripped off her dress from the night before, pulling on trousers and a tunic in a few swift motions. She sat in front of her mirror and twisted her hair into a bun.

There was a knock on the door. Mylah opened it and slipped into the hall, coming face to face with Elias.

"I wanted to apologize about last night..." he began, and Mylah realized she'd forgotten about leaving him on the dance floor.

"I should be the one apologizing," she said, her cheeks growing hot.

"I'm s-" he stopped as Mylah's door opened and King Castien appeared in the doorway, disheveled and yawning.

"Good morning, brother," he greeted Elias and breezed past them both, turning back to say, "thanks for last night, Leylah. I owe you," before continuing down the hall. Elias returned his attention to Mylah.

"I guess you didn't need me to get to him after all," he said as he turned to walk away. Mylah knew what Elias thought, but it changed nothing. It wasn't as if he cared for her anyway, he'd made that clear.

She turned on her heel and stalked in the opposite direction. Even though she had little to report, it was high time she found the sprite who was supposed to be helping her communicate with King Florian. She hadn't seen a trace of the sprites, though, since the day of her arrival.

Mylah wandered the halls, passing a few guards doing their rounds. She ignored them for the most part, until one deliberately stepped into her path and nearly bowled her over. As she focused, she realized it was Broderick and he was laughing at her.

"Stay alert, Ley," he chided her.

"Sorry, I've just been thinking..."

"Well, that's no good," he joked, then straightened up. "What are you thinking about?"

"I've been here for over a week now and I haven't seen any sprites since day one. After all of King Castien's threats, I assumed I'd have a whole horde of them following me around every day."

"The sprites tend to stay near the front gates to question visitors or passersby," Broderick explained. "They don't come inside unless summoned by the king."

"Well, that's comforting to know." Mylah wasn't sure she'd be able to inconspicuously find the sprite she needed, but she would try. "Where's Sabine?"

"She's on border patrol today."

"Without you? I'd started to think you two were inseparable." Until that day, she had never seen one without the other.

"We work well together, but no. We change partners often."

"Do you miss her when you do?" Mylah waggled her eyebrows at him, and he laughed.

"I know what you're implying, and you are quite mistaken. Sabine is wonderful, for sure, but she's not exactly my type," as he said this, the guard, Nic, walked around the corner.

"Broderick, back to your station," he commanded. Broderick gave Mylah a wink and left her behind. As she watched, Broderick grazed Nic's arm while he walked by, and a faint smile tugged at Nic's lips. Mylah understood what Broderick had been trying to tell her and she smiled.

Mylah found her way to the front gates and stepped outside. The guards watched her, but they let her wander the grounds. After all, she had proven to be no threat. A few sprites fluttered in the air above a small garden to her left and she approached them, pretending to be admiring the flowers.

"Oh, I'm sorry. I hope I'm not intruding," Mylah said. "These dahlias are so beautiful."

"They're the king's favorite," one of the sprites said.

"Don't engage, Briar, she's not worth your time," another sprite snapped before the other sprites all moved away. Mylah's heart leapt. Briar was the sprite that Genevieve told her would be helpful within the castle.

"Briar, that sounds familiar," Mylah said before Briar could leave to join her comrades. "Do you perhaps know Genevieve?"

"Oh yes! We were great friends! Before..." sadness washed over Briar's features.

"She told me you may be able to help me," Mylah lowered her voice to be sure no one else would overhear.

"I'm not sure..." Briar glanced to where the other sprites had joined the guards at the gate. "It's dangerous to do anything outside of the orders of the king."

"I understand...another friend of mine, Bellingham, thought there may be some friends to be found among the sprites here." It was dangerous to drop his name, but Mylah was running out of options.

"Bellingham? Another old friend..." She seemed to be going back and forth for a few seconds. "I will help you," she decided with conviction. "Meet me in the gardens tonight, once the revel is in full swing." Briar flitted away before Mylah could respond.

Mylah spent the afternoon curled up in bed, with her nose in the mysterious journal.

As I suspected, I keep forgetting to write in this thing. Jacinda will flay me for it when I return it to her, and she finds it empty. I'm supposed to be logging all the important memories I want to share with her so that being apart won't seem so...lonely.

Since I know you'll read this, Cind, I'm doing my best. It doesn't exactly come naturally to me.

Anyway, I'll get to see Jacinda soon.

I'm needed back on the border. There are more of our men turning up dead just inside the border. This is the second time in a month that we've found a body; tortured and battered, before being dumped in our territory. It had to be the Adairian men, but we've yet to catch them in the act. King Haldor has promised that if we catch whoever is committing these atrocities, me and my men will be the ones who can carry out their justice.

Mylah paused and leaned her head back against the wall. For someone to be killing shreeve in that way, for no reason, she'd think she would have heard stories of it at some point. Unless the killer was never caught...she continued reading on the next page. The mystery man wrote of adventures in the Unbounds, like the ones her father had. It made her smile as she pretended that Emil may have encountered whoever had written the journal.

She fantasized that Wren may be the one who wrote the journal, but he died before ever entering the castle, so there'd be no reason for his journal to wind up there.

After a lengthy entry about a night spent hunting with King Haldor, which had almost put Mylah to sleep, she came across a few blank pages in a row. She flipped past them and found the next entry.

Jacinda...I don't know if she'll ever read this journal now. I don't even know why I'm writing in it again. She turned me away when I tried to see her last. Without explanation, she told me to never return. I don't want to admit that she broke my heart...but she did just that. I knew it was all too good to be true, and it could never last. If the king ever found out, I'd be dead. It's for the best.

Mylah closed the journal, grief creeping into her chest for a man she never knew. There were more pages to read, but she needed to take a break, and she had to get ready for the revel that night.

Twenty Four

Mylah wore a black dress that night. Something to help keep her concealed in the darkness of the gardens when she went to meet Briar. Petra had still not seen to her that day and Mylah was beginning to worry about her, but she would have to deal with that later. She braided her hair, clipped on a pair of diamond earrings, and strapped her dagger to her thigh. If Davina came that night, Mylah would be ready.

She strode down the hall with purpose. No one was around because they were all either already at the revel or manning their stations. The ballroom ended up being filled with people that night. Mylah could barely make her way through the crowd to the king's throne. She needed to make sure her presence was known so he would not send anyone looking for her. The crowd would help to conceal the fact that she was missing long enough that she could talk with Briar.

"You look...different tonight," King Castien commented as she approached. "Black suits you." Mylah smirked. She had liked the looks of it as well, it made her feel more like herself and reminded her why she'd come to Elowyn.

"Thank you," she said, bowing to the king. "I'm going to get a drink; would you like one?" Aleese glared at her from the king's side. If eyes could shoot daggers, Mylah would be dead.

"That's kind of you to offer, but I must decline." King Castien placed his hand on Aleese's knee, and she smirked as if she had stolen a prize from Mylah.

"I shall take my leave then." Mylah bowed once more and made her way towards the refreshments table. When she was sure that she was hidden by the crowd, she changed direction and headed for the exit. At the door, she a sense of relief washed over her that she'd made it, until a hand clamped onto her upper arm.

"Human filth," a man growled, and she turned to face a burly shreeve wearing a scowl. His brown and gray eyes burned with a deep-seeded hatred.

"Excuse me." Mylah tried to wrench her arm free from his grasp, but he held tight.

"You have no right to be here, to be *honored* by the king," the man spat with each word he uttered. His grip tightened to the point where Mylah knew she would bruise from his fingers.

"Let. Me. Go. Now," she made her voice as menacing as possible while moving to grab her dagger from its sheath with her free hand. He only moved closer to her and made to grab her other arm. Mylah pulled her dagger out and pressed it up against his throat.

"Oh, the beast has some fight in her," the man sniggered and while he was distracted, she used the moment to overpower him and break free of his grasp. He hissed and lunged for her, but she danced out of his reach, and slipped back into the crowd. She watched from afar as he seethed, scanning the room for her. She should go to King Castien and tell him right away, but Briar was waiting on her.

Mylah pushed her way through the crowd, careful to avoid her attacker's gaze. He had retreated to the refreshment table, and she took her chance to run out the door. She didn't stop until she came to the door that led to the gardens.

"I need some fresh air," she told the guards at the door, and they allowed her to pass. Outside, she hurried through the rows of flowers. "Briar!" she hissed.

"Here!" Briar fluttered up from a bed of roses. "I worried you had changed your mind."

"No, I got waylaid, but we need to hurry. King Castien will notice if I'm gone too long." Mylah was still out of breath from her scuffle.

"I told you I would help you, and I will, I promise," Briar placed her hand over her heart. "What do you need?"

"I need you to get a message to Bellingham," Mylah said, and Briar's eyes widened, but she did not protest. "I need you to tell him that I'm okay, and I am in the castle. Let him know that the book holds a spell, and that the king is planning a mission to steal the book back."

"Giving away that information would be treasonous..." Briar squeaked.

"I know, Briar. That's why you don't have to do this if you don't want to, but I am trying to help end the war that is happening," Mylah tried to reason with her.

"Okay, I will do it. But I do need to know, what is your name?" Briar asked, and Mylah realized she hadn't even told her that much and Briar was still willing to help her. Guilt tried to force its way into her gut, but she reminded herself she was doing this to save Adair.

"Leylah. Bellingham will know me," Mylah glanced around to be sure they were still alone. "Thank you for doing this. I know the risk you are taking, and I will be sure to repay you."

"There is no need." Briar shook her head, her short, brown, bobbed hair swishing around her face. "I must go now; I know where to find someone who is not a part of the castle who can run the message safely. They are only active at night though, so I must bid you farewell." Briar turned and flew over the garden wall. Mylah watched her until the darkness swallowed her.

As Mylah reentered the ballroom, she remained on guard in case someone tried to attack her again. She was on a high though, she had accomplished a feat; finding a sprite to help her communicate with Adair. It made her homesick thinking about the king and Garrick receiving her message from Bellingham.

"Leylah," Ana came up behind her, making her jump, and took her hand. "Are you doing better today?" Mylah looked at her, confused for a moment, and then remembered she had brushed her off the night before.

"Oh, yes. Much. I was having an off day yesterday. How about you? Did you have fun with Torin last night?"

Ana's cheeks turned bright red. "Yes, he's charming," she laughed nervously. "Do you think he's here tonight?" She scanned the room, hopeful.

"I *know* he's here. He's the war general, he practically lives here. Or maybe he *actually* lives here, I don't know," Mylah pulled Ana deeper into the crowd. "I can help you find him."

"I think I'd like to stay with you, if that's okay." Ana pulled back on her hand.

"Oh," Mylah looked at her in surprise. "Yeah, that's fine."

"You probably think I'm weird, or annoying or something, but you've made my life more...fun." Ana turned bright red again.

"I don't think you're weird, Ana! Or annoying," Mylah laughed as she pulled Ana over to the refreshments table. "Here, let's have some more fun tonight!" She handed a goblet to Ana and took one for herself, drinking half of the contents. She could not let her guard down entirely that night; she'd already been attacked once.

"I've never drank this stuff before," Ana said, gazing into her cup, and then she shrugged, chugging the drink. "Oh!" She began laughing and Mylah knew what she was experiencing: the colors becoming more vibrant, the noises more pronounced, and the overall sense of giddiness. Mylah sensed it all too.

"Come on!" Mylah pulled her out to where people danced. With all the people in the room, there was no way to know where the dance floor ended, and the casual crowd began. At least Mylah could expect not to dance with the king. There was no room for that kind of dancing.

Ana spun in circles while Mylah kept an eye on the crowd. There were a few scowling faces, but none that she recognized. The crowd began to thin out as people left. Once Ana started to come down from her drink, Mylah led her off the dance floor. She glanced at King Castien, and he waved her over to him.

"Come on, Ana, I'm going to introduce you to the king," Mylah said, breathless from dancing. Ana squealed in delight. "Just, don't do that in front of him." They both laughed. Mylah took Ana by the hand and walked with her to the throne. They both bowed before the king.

"And who is this?" King Castien asked as they straightened.

"This is Anastasia, Ana," Mylah introduced her.

"And I should care, why?" He picked at his nails idly. *That* was the King Castien that Mylah had expected and despised. She seethed as she thought of the man who had been sleeping in her bed that morning and wondered what happened to turn him so cruel. Mylah sensed Ana shrinking beside her.

"You should care because she is one of your loyal subjects," Mylah said.

"Are not all of the people here the same? I can't pay one more consideration than the next, or else they will all desire to be blessed with my attention. I would never find peace." He snapped his fingers and Aleese sashayed over. "Take a round with me." He stood from his throne and began moving about the room with Aleese on his arm. They stopped at the first group of people and when they moved on, he had found a new piece of arm candy to replace Davina.

"I'm sorry, Ana," Mylah said.

"Don't be. I knew he was a jerk, now it's been confirmed." Ana played it off like she was fine, but Mylah could tell she was hurt. "I should be getting home anyway."

"Do you have someone to accompany you?" Mylah worried that someone may try to harm Ana as they had done to her. Though, the man who had attacked Mylah had only done so because she was human. Ana would not need to fear that kind of attack.

"The knights are usually kind enough to send me with an escort," Ana reassured Mylah. "Goodnight, Leylah. I don't think I'll be back for any more revels...but if you are in the village again, I'd love to do lunch!" She kissed Mylah's cheek.

"I'll be sure to come visit," Mylah promised.

Once Ana was gone, all Mylah wanted to do was go to bed, but she couldn't leave until King Castien dismissed her. She realized that neither Elias nor Torin were present, and she wondered what they were up to.

Her attention went to what looked like a fight breaking out at the back of the room near the exit. Mylah hurried over to find out what was happening. It appeared that two men were fighting over Davina. She leaned against the wall, smirking at the sight before her.

"Please, you can take turns," Mylah heard Davina saying as Mylah pushed her way to the front of the crowd. Mylah lunged for the man closest to her and pulled him away from the fight.

"What the," the man protested at first but stopped when he saw Mylah. "Ah I see, there's plenty of me to go around, darling," he smirked, and Mylah rolled her eyes.

"Get a hold of yourself," she said, looking over his shoulder to see the other man clinging to Davina's side while she glared at Mylah.

"You shouldn't have done that," Davina hissed and strutted over to Mylah and leaned in close. "Let's finish this outside," she whispered into Mylah's ear so no one else could hear. Both men watched as Davina left the room and turned their loathsome eyes to Mylah, blaming her for their loss. Mylah ignored them and followed Davina out of the room. As soon as Mylah stepped into the hall, Davina grabbed her arm, pulling her out of view of the ballroom and threw her to the floor.

"You cost me *everything*," she spat at Mylah who rolled to the side as Davina slammed her heel down. "My dignity, my crown..."

"You would have never gotten the crown," Mylah growled as she jumped back to her feet and grabbed her dagger. "King Castien never planned on marrying you, or Aleese for that matter."

"Shut up. You know nothing of Elowyn or its king." Davina lunged towards her, sloppy in her anger. Mylah swiped out and sliced Davina's arm with the dagger. Davina screeched and whirled around, swinging her arm to knock the dagger from Mylah's hand.

"I know enough. Like how you were always only going to be a plaything for him." Mylah ducked as Davina threw a punch aimed for her nose. She stayed low and ran at Davina, taking her down to the floor.

"Maybe you're right," Davina's response caused Mylah to falter. She sounded dejected and drained. Mylah pulled back and Davina took that moment to lash out with her cat-like nails and scratched Mylah across the face. "At least I'm not *you*. I'm not a pathetic, little human." Mylah grabbed her dagger from the floor and held it against Davina's throat.

"Better that than a used-up toy for the king..." Mylah hissed and pressed down on the dagger. Blood dribbled down Davina's neck and she coughed, pushing the dagger in a little deeper.

"Do it. Kill me," Davina dared, fire burning in her eyes.

"Stop," Mylah heard the command, but she did not move. "Leylah, let her go." King Castien strode up beside Mylah and grabbed her arm, pulling her from Davina. "And *you*, I told you to never return to this castle. If I find you here again, you will be convicted of treason and punished in accordance with the laws."

Davina wiped blood from her neck with her sleeve and stood. "You two deserve each other," she growled as she left. Neither King Castien nor Mylah spoke until Davina was out of sight.

"Where did you get this?" He took the dagger from Mylah.

"The training room." Mylah left Elias out of it. "I knew I would need it, and I was right. I was attacked *twice* tonight."

"Davina and who else?" King Castien's eyes flew wide, and his nostrils flared.

"I don't know who the other was. He attacked me in the ballroom," Mylah said, and King Castien strode away. She assumed he meant for her to follow, so she did. In the ballroom, there were only a few stragglers left. Aleese and King Castien's newest consort stood by his throne.

The king swept through the ballroom, his cape flowing out behind him. Those who remained seemed to sense the change in the room and began making their way to the exit.

"Aleese, and you," he pointed to his newest consort.

"It's Rem-" he cut her off before she could finish.

"I don't care. Leave, both of you," he commanded, and they gaped at him.

"King Castien, this will be the second night in a row..." Aleese tried to protest.

"Leave. Now." The malice in his voice was enough to scare them both into motion. "Where is Torin?" King Castien roared. The two guards at the back of the room glanced at each other before responding that neither of them knew. "And what of Elias?" Again, the guards knew nothing. "What good are you? Find them." King Castien collapsed onto his throne and began playing with the dagger that still had Davina's blood on it.

"Would you like me to leave?" Mylah asked.

"No." He seemed to have cooled down. "You won't be going to your room tonight. I can't sleep alone."

Mylah sputtered. "Why did you send away your consorts then?"

"Do you have a problem with spending the night with me? If I remember correctly, you were the one throwing yourself at *me* the night of the gala."

"I figured you'd decided I wasn't good enough for you," Mylah countered. It was true, and even though she hated him, it had still stung a bit.

"Trust me, that wasn't the issue." Before Mylah could respond, Torin and Elias entered the room followed by the guards who had been sent to fetch them. As they approached, they took in Mylah's disheveled appearance and the scratches on her face that leaked blood.

"What happened?" Torin spoke first.

"What happened is that neither of you were around to keep an eye on Leylah and make sure no one tried to kill her, *again*," the king's tone was light, but his rigid posture and clenched fists gave away his simmering anger.

"We were training and lost track of time," Elias said.

"Where have I heard that excuse before...oh yeah." King Castien tossed the dagger and it clattered at Elias' feet.

"You're hiding things from me, brother, and I won't have it." Elias picked up the dagger.

"Whose blood is this?" he asked.

"Davina's," Mylah smirked.

"Very nice," Torin said, raising his brows at her, but Elias shook his head in disapproval.

"I'll be sure to keep her unarmed, but under close watch from now on," Elias promised.

"Good. As for tonight, no need to stand guard, I think my knights will suffice." King Castien stood and beckoned to Mylah. She walked to his side and let him put his arm around her waist. "Goodnight." No one spoke as he led her from the room.

As soon as they were out of sight of the others, King Castien removed his arm from Mylah and strode on ahead. They came to a door with two guards stationed outside it. The guards opened the door as the king approached, allowing him and Mylah through to a spiral staircase leading up to King Castien's room.

At the top of the stairs, Mylah gazed around the room. There was a bed three times the size of her own with billowy curtains framing it at the back of the room. There was also a tub partially concealed behind a screen and a wardrobe overflowing with clothes. Before that, separated by a gaping archway, was a sitting area. The sitting area had a couch, a table with chairs, and a large plush rug beneath it all.

"You can choose a couch to sleep on. They're probably more comfortable than your bed anyway." King Castien marched through the archway and behind the screen. When he emerged, he wore nothing but a gold chain around his neck. Mylah turned away, but not before the image of him had been burned into her brain. She fought the blush that bloomed on her cheeks.

"You're too modest," he laughed. "Here," he threw a shirt at her. "Don't worry, you can look now." She turned hesitantly and saw that he was in bed under his blankets.

"I guess this isn't what I expected," Mylah admitted, making her way behind the screen. She stripped off her dress and put on King Castien's shirt, which covered her almost to her knees.

"What were you expecting? Me to have my way with you?" Mylah's blush deepened at his words. "I know your true affections lie elsewhere. I wouldn't want to be with someone who would be dreaming of someone else the whole time."

"Torin and I..." Mylah began, but the king cut her off.

"I'm not speaking of Torin," he disputed. Mylah emerged from behind the screen.

"Why am I here?" she asked.

"I told you, I can't sleep alone."

"No, why am I *here*, in your castle. Why show me mercy?" King Castien sucked in a breath and turned his head away from her.

"Goodnight, Leylah," he said.

"Fine, don't tell me." She stomped to one of the couches and flopped onto it. King Castien was right, it was comfier than her bed.

"You remind me of someone," he said so quietly Mylah almost missed it. She decided not to push him anymore. She pulled a throw over herself and attempted to fall asleep.

At breakfast the next morning, the awkward silence was stifling. Elias took Mylah to the training room after and still refused to talk.

"Can we please talk about this?" she asked once she'd had enough of the silence.

"What is there to talk about?" He tried to hand her a sword, but she stepped away.

"You said we could talk more about what happened by the lake once we were back at the castle, and well, we've been back for quite some time now." Mylah didn't want to push him again, but she couldn't stand the tension between them.

He sighed but put the sword back on the wall. Before he spoke again, he walked to the door, checked that it was shut and locked, and then returned to stand before Mylah.

"You are now the only person who knows about my father, besides Castien and Petra," he began.

"Petra? Why Petra?"

"Someone had to make sure the body had the right wounds for it to be believable as a death by kelpie. Petra was the only one we could trust to help us with that." Mylah's stomach turned at the thought of them marring King Haldor's corpse.

"What exactly happened to make you, or your magic, kill him?"

"As I told you before, I used to try controlling my magic by repressing it. After so many years of that, eventually I lost my hold on it."

"And King Haldor was the cost?" Mylah asked, knowing the answer.

"The two of us were out hunting alone. Normally we'd have knights accompanying us, but this time he'd asked them to stay behind. He wanted to talk to me about something he didn't want anyone overhearing..." Elias paused, and an unexpected rage simmered in his eyes. Mylah reached out and put her hand on his arm.

"You don't have to tell me if you don't want to," she said, but he continued.

"He began by saying he knew that I wasn't fit to be his heir or to rule the kingdom," he scoffed. "All my life I'd looked up to this man, thinking he loved me and cared about me. Only to find that he'd been attempting to replace me, the first chance he got. Unfortunately for him, and his wives, he had no luck with bearing any more children after me."

"That's horrible," Mylah murmured.

"Yeah. At least he didn't dispose of me as he did my mother, and Castien's mother, and all the other women who failed to produce another heir for him."

"Ana mentioned something about that..."

"That he killed them all because they were barren, even though he was the one who couldn't reproduce?"

"But he had you," Mylah said, and Elias raised a brow, tilting his head.

"Did he?"

"You have his nose," Mylah tried again, but Elias laughed.

"He did that. He broke it when I was six so that it resembled his and people would stop questioning my legitimacy. He couldn't have people thinking there was anything wrong with the high and mighty king." Mylah cringed at the thought of a father breaking his own son's nose for so petty a reason.

"But you still thought he was your father?"

"Up until the day he died, when he revealed to me that I was more likely the offspring of a warlock my mother had met while she spent a few months in Hyrdian. She was being aided by the healers to try to enhance her likelihood of conceiving with King Haldor. Clearly, they figured out the problem while she was there, and came up with a new solution."

"He also told me that's likely the reason my magic is so unpredictable, because it's source is both fae and warlock in nature," Elias stopped and took a deep breath. Mylah couldn't believe all that he had revealed to her, and yet she had no desire to ever inform King Florian of anything she'd learned from Elias. It confused her, because the information that he had been the one who killed his father would send Elowyn into chaos, which would benefit Adair and the other kingdoms. She should *want* to share that with King Florian...but she had no desire to.

"Is that when you lost control?" Mylah asked.

"No. I lost control when he informed me that he had killed all his wives *knowing* that he was the cause of them being barren. I lost control when he told me that my mother was worthless and simple minded, just like me." He flopped down onto the training mat and let out a huff of air. Mylah sat beside him.

"I'm sorry," she said.

"Don't be sorry. He deserved it. But now, I have to live with the fact that I killed my own father, or whatever he was to me." Elias glanced over at Mylah. "And now, you know my biggest secret. You could potentially destroy me with this secret, and for some reason, I don't care."

"I wouldn't do that. I won't tell anyone, I promise." Mylah clenched her jaw as she fought the urge to reciprocate with her biggest secret, but she wasn't ready to reveal that bit of information yet. There was no telling how Elias would react, and she couldn't betray Adair. "Can we go back to being normal friends now?"

"You think we're friends?" Elias eyed her skeptically.

"I mean," Mylah hadn't realized the words that had come out of her mouth. But she had meant it. "I guess. Unless you don't want to be..."

"No, we're friends." Elias grinned. "It'd be strange if we weren't after everything I've told you."

"Well, as your friend, maybe I can convince your brother to let you go to Adair for our mission," Mylah offered.

"You can try, I doubt he'll change his mind." Mylah stood and took the sword from the wall.

"Glad to have you talking again," she smirked.

Mylah fell flat on her back, a grunt escaping her as the air left her lungs. Elias pinned her to the floor, his dagger pressed against her throat. His eyes met hers and a smirk played at his lips.

"Just say when," his breath grazed her ear and sent a shiver through her. Breathing heavily, she shifted beneath him, trying to gain any kind of foothold so she could use the floor as leverage.

"Not so fast," she said, distracting him as she gripped his arm and bucked her hips up at the same time, using all her strength to knock him off her. He rolled gracefully, regaining his balance, but it gave Mylah enough time to get out of his reach.

"Good one," he huffed, rising to his full height. Mylah grabbed her sword from the floor and pushed herself to her feet, still trying to catch her breath.

"You're going easy on me," she accused. "How will I ever become strong enough to fight a Shreeve, or a fae, if you keep letting me win?"

"If I never gave you a chance to practice your own techniques and tactics, you'd never learn," Elias pointed out. "And I'm not going easy on you, trust me."

"I don't believe you." Mylah stepped towards him, pivoting as he circled her. She backed away as she watched him, trying to find a weak spot. Their last scuffle had left them closer to the wall than she realized, and she hit it, cursing herself for the stupid mistake. Elias didn't hesitate to take advantage of her lapse in judgment, striding up to her. She didn't bother lifting her sword as he stood toe to toe with her.

"Rookie mistake," he said, lifting a brow. Mylah rolled her eyes.

"I know, I miscalculated the distance to the wall." Her face heated as his eyes remained locked on hers. She found her gaze being drawn to his lips, mere inches from her own. "It won't happen again," she said, her voice coming out breathy and betraying her rising heart rate. Elias' eyes flicked to her mouth and his lips slightly parted. Mylah leaned forward.

"Soups on!" Torin's voice boomed in the echoey room. Elias jerked away from Mylah, leaving her stunned, her mouth agape and chest tight with anticipation. "What's got you all wound up?" Torin's gaze flicked over Mylah to Elias.

Mylah cleared her throat, releasing the tension she'd been holding onto. "Nothing," she snapped, striding over to the weapons rack, and placing her sword back in its holder.

"I was talking to the one as rigid as an orc over here, but now that you mention it…" Torin winked at Mylah, and she rolled her eyes. "I'll see you at lunch." He backed out of the room and turned on his heel in the hall, striding towards the stairs.

Mylah bent down, stretching her back, in order to avoid making eye contact with Elias. Her muscles ached again. They still hadn't fully recovered from her first day of training.

"I'm glad I gave you the dagger. I'm sorry you had to use it, though," Elias said, breaking the awkward silence.

"It was like putting your training to use." Mylah finished stretching and met Elias' gaze. "I didn't tell your brother you gave it to me, the dagger I mean. He thinks I took it on my own."

"Oh," Elias blinked in surprise. "Well, thank you. You didn't need to do that."

Twenty Five

Unable to fall asleep that night, Mylah pulled the journal out from under her pillow. The next entry only took up two lines.

Jacinda sent me a message this morning. I don't know whether to be elated or terrified. She's pregnant.

Mylah gasped and flipped to the next page, relieved to find that he hadn't stopped writing.

I haven't heard from Jacinda in months. I don't know when the baby is due, or if it's already come. I have no idea how far along she was when she sent the last message. I'm going crazy.

Mylah had to flip to the next page again, his entries were too short to satisfy her curiosity.

Jacinda wrote to me again...I'm meeting her on the border tonight. Her husband rejected the baby, our baby girl. She was born with the shreeve markings, and he knew immediately he wasn't the father. He threatened to drown the baby...I could kill him. But instead, I will bring the baby here, to the castle. Petra has promised to keep my secret and look after her for me.

Mylah's heart warmed at the thought that Petra had taken in a baby who no one else wanted. But then another realization came to her. If the baby was brought to the border, that meant Jacinda lived in another kingdom. And, since the father was shocked by shreeve markings, that meant they were humans, which meant they likely lived in Adair since it was the closest human kingdom to Elowyn. She tried to remember if she'd ever heard the name Jacinda before, but it barely registered, as if in a very distant memory, or maybe she'd read it in a book.

The entries stopped after that. Mylah flipped through the rest of the journal, hoping for some glimpse into what happened next, but there was nothing. She flipped through once more and almost missed a small entry towards the back.

I don't know why I'm writing this...they're dead. They're both dead. I couldn't stop it. But I've finally found a way to repay the king for killing the only two people in this world I ever loved. It's taken years, but I found it. The Book of Creation...I have it and I'm giving it to the only person I know who hates Elowyn as much as I now do. King Florian. I'm doing this for you, Jacinda.

Tears streamed down Mylah's cheeks, and she wiped them away. She had no idea who these people were, but she couldn't stop the ache in her heart. The child couldn't have made it out of their teen years if they had died years before King Florian received the Book of Creation. And whomever

Jacinda was...Mylah wondered if Garrick knew her. She would have to remember to ask if she saw him again. At least she had learned something in regards to her mission from the journal. The shreeve book she and her father had been translating was called the Book of Creation.

Petra came to Mylah's room early the next morning.

"Where have you been?" Mylah asked, relief clear in her voice.

"I was taking care of a special errand for the king," Petra explained, remaining vague.

"What special errand?" Mylah pressed.

"None of your business," Petra said, and Mylah dropped it. "Now, go clean yourself up. The king would like you to join him in his study after breakfast." Mylah raised her eyebrows at Petra, but she did not elaborate. Instead, Petra went digging through Mylah's closet to pick out her outfit for the day.

Mylah went to bathe and when she returned to her room, Petra was gone. She had laid out a long, simple, dress for Mylah to wear. It was beige with a dark green belt at the waist. She pulled it on, and it fit snugly. As she pulled her hair into a high ponytail, she began making her way to her dining room.

"Oomph..." Mylah dropped her hands to her side at the noise. She looked around and realized she had elbowed Briar in her efforts to fasten her hair.

"Sorry!" She reached out, thinking to steady the sprite in the air, but Briar had already righted herself.

"No worries, miss," Briar looked around before continuing. "I have a message."

"Come with me." Mylah hurried back to her room as Briar flitted along behind her. She closed her door so they would not be interrupted. "Were you able to deliver my message?"

Briar nodded. "Yes, miss. I made contact with my friend, and he promised to pass on the message," Briar said. "But it may be a while before he can get back to me with a response. It's too risky for him to come to the castle, and I won't be able to sneak away again so soon."

"That's fine, Briar. As long as Bellingham receives my message, that's all that matters. Thank you so much for your help." Briar left and Mylah forgot about eating breakfast. She went straight to the king's study.

As she approached the door to the study, she heard muffled voices filtering into the hall.

"Why are you doing this?" Mylah recognized Elias' voice and he sounded frustrated.

"It's for your own good." That was King Castien, sounding flippant as usual. Mylah assumed they were talking about the mission to retrieve the book from King Florian. Sighing, she knocked on the door and entered the room.

"Why don't you let him join the mission already?" Mylah drawled as she flopped into one of the armchairs along the wall. "Save us all the trouble of having to hear him complain about it." She winked at Elias.

"What –" King Castien began, but he shook his head instead of finishing. "Where's Torin?" he asked the room but neither Mylah nor Elias answered. She hadn't seen him since the last revel. The doors opened again and Korriane and Killian entered.

"Sorry we're late, there was a brawl in the courtyard and Korriane insisted on staying to watch," Killian said, smirking at his sister's back. Korriane joined Mylah along the wall, sitting in the other open armchair.

"What can I say, I like to study the techniques of the fighters in hopes of learning something new. Unfortunately, Killian dragged me away before I saw any fun moves." Korriane gave Mylah a smile before turning her face back to the king.

"Who was fighting in the courtyard?" Elias asked while King Castien remained unfazed by the announcement.

"Torin and some poor guard," Killian said. "It looked more like a sparring match, but it was hard to tell with all the men surrounding them."

Mylah stood from her chair. "I'll go fetch him," she offered at the same time Elias said, "I should retrieve him." Their eyes locked and Mylah didn't turn her gaze away. Elias broke first and motioned for her to leave the room. She hurried out and down the hall towards the entrance to the castle. As she neared the door, she could hear shouts and laughter coming from the other side. There were no guards to open the door for her as there usually were, so she shouldered it open herself.

A handful of guards stood to the side as Torin, and a guard Mylah didn't recognize sparred. The loudest of the laughter came from Torin as he sidestepped the guard easily over and over. He wasn't even trying at that point, and it seemed cruel to let him continue.

"Torin," she called out to him, and he turned his head lazily to find her. He gave her a grin as he continued to effortlessly deflect the guard's attacks. After another few seconds he bowed out of his match and left the guard panting in his wake.

"Let's do this again sometime," Torin said as he passed the watching guards. "You all need to do some brushing up on your training if we are to continue trusting you to protect our king."

"Why bother when you seem to be skillful enough for the lot of them?" Mylah joked as he approached her. She turned back into the castle as he joined her, and they strode through the hall together.

"Did the king send you?" Torin asked.

"Not exactly." Mylah wasn't sure what had been going through the king's mind in the study. He certainly didn't seem fazed by the fact that his war general was sparring with his guards while they should be manning their posts and protecting the castle.

In the study, Mylah returned to her chair against the wall while Torin joined the king at the table filled with maps.

"Done roughing up my guards?" King Castien asked, a smile pulling at the corners of his mouth.

"Not quite, but Leylah over there was pretty insistent on me being here." Torin rolled his shoulders as if loosening up his muscles. "Now, tell me you aren't wasting my time?"

The king scoffed. "If you don't want to be a part of this, you are free to leave. No one is holding you here."

"Touchy today, huh?" Torin grinned and put his hands up in surrender. "I promise to play nice from now on." King Castien ignored him and went into his reasoning for gathering them.

"I've received word from my inside man that the Book of Creation is not in the castle as we once believed.

This changes everything and we will need to come up with a whole new strategy." King Castien wiped his brow with his sleeve. His whole body tensed as he gripped the edge of the table.

"What exactly is in the book?" Mylah asked. "I feel like if I'm putting my life on the line for it, I should at least know what I'm risking everything for."

"As if I'd tell you," King Castien began, but Elias put his hand up to stop his brother.

"You think she doesn't deserve to know? After all the time she's spent here, you still don't trust her. Why bring her in on this at all if that's the case?" he argued.

The king turned to glare at his brother. "*You* tell her, then. If you have so much faith in this human, tell her all your secrets," King Castien hissed.

Elias's cheeks reddened and his eyes grew dark. He turned to Mylah. "The book holds the key to undoing all shreeve," Elias said, glancing at his brother who was visibly shaking. "If King Florian were to decipher the words in the book, he could potentially reverse the spell that created shreeve all those years ago and return us all to our most basic state; fae or human. Anyone in range when the spell is used would be affected. For those whose blood is too mixed to clearly define as one species, it would mean an agonizing death," Elias let it all out in a rush. Mylah gaped at him as she realized what exactly was at stake for them if she were to reveal this information to her people. If she didn't though, she would be a traitor to her kingdom and exiled...for real.

"I see," was all she could say. A roaring filled her ears. The war raging in her mind was all consuming. Revealing the information to King Florian was her duty and the whole reason she came to Elowyn in the first place. But murdering innocent shreeve because their bloodlines were too diluted...it was all too much.

"See, she can't even handle the truth," Korriane clucked. "Poor thing practically has steam coming out of her ears." She brushed a strand of Mylah's hair away from her face, revealing her ear beneath.

Mylah whipped her head to the side. "I do not. I'm fine," she snapped. "I'm just processing."

"Well, take your time. This raid may not be happening for a while now," the king groaned. "Unless you happen to know where else they may keep such an item in the kingdom?" He eyed Mylah as she shook her head slowly. "I thought not."

"I'll do some recon," Torin offered. "I can go back to the border and try to force some answers out of the soldiers there."

"No!" Mylah forgot herself in the turmoil of it all and realized her mistake. Everyone turned to stare at her. "I mean," she gulped. "I need to step outside for a moment, excuse me." She stood from the chair and practically ran from the room. She hurried to the gardens to clear her head and think through the options weighing on her mind.

On the one hand, she could send the information along to King Florian and he probably wouldn't be able to decipher the book anyway. Even if he did, there were specific ingredients needed for spells, he'd need those before he could do anything.

On the other hand, she could keep the information to herself, and help King Castien and the others retrieve the book to ensure that no innocent lives were ever lost because of it.

Or she could continue as if she still knew nothing about the contents of the book. She had already tipped off King Florian to the imminent attempt to retrieve the book, so she had kept up her end of the deal so far. And now that King Castien didn't know where the book was being held, who knew how long it would be before they attempted their mission.

"Psst," a soft voice whispered in Mylah's ear. She turned to find Briar flitting at her shoulder. It had barely been an hour since Mylah had last seen the sprite.

"Briar, there's something I need you to do for me…" Mylah paused, unsure of what she was about to do, but she continued anyway. "I know you just delivered a message for me, but I have another one if you're up for it."

"I may not be able to get away from the castle right away, miss, but I can do my best."

"Thank you. I need you to deliver another message to Bellingham…" Mylah waited as Briar nodded. "Please tell him that I was misinformed before." Mylah closed her eyes, on the verge of tears. "The king is hoping to retrieve the book, but there is no plan to at this time. They have no clues as to where the book is, and until they do, they won't make any moves. I will send another message if I find out they have made any solid plans."

"Okay, I will remember, miss," Briar said, clenching her fist over her heart.

"Thank you, Briar." Mylah watched the sprite join the rest of her comrades along the wall. Her heart clenched in her chest. She wasn't finished yet.

Twenty Six

Mylah took a deep breath as she stood outside of the king's study. She could hear everyone inside and considered turning around and walking away. She still had the option to change her mind, but she reached for the doorknob and pushed open the door.

Instead of everyone ceasing their conversations and turning to stare as Mylah expected, they continued as if she wasn't even there.

"I don't know, Torin," King Castien said as he leaned on the table. "I think King Florian would take offense to you torturing his soldiers, one by one." Mylah cringed imagining what Torin could do to Greyson or Crane. They didn't stand a chance. That made what she was about to do a tad more bearable. She could convince herself she was betraying her people to protect them, and not because she was weak.

Kindness is not weakness... her father's voice rang in her ears. Mylah shook her head to clear it.

"I need to speak with King Castien alone," she declared, making everyone stop and stare at her. Korriane shrugged and exited the room with Killian on her heels.

"Call us when you need us," Killian said as they left.

Torin crossed his arms over his chest. "I'm sure whatever it is you need to tell him, Elias and I –"

"Leave, Torin," King Castien cut him off. "You too, Elias." They left without further complaint, though Elias lingered at the door a moment longer than necessary.

"Well, we're alone now. What is it you need to tell me?" King Castien sat on the edge of the table and clasped his hands in his lap. Mylah opened her mouth to speak, but nothing came out. The king rolled his head and cracked his neck, clearly annoyed that Mylah was taking her time.

"I'm sorry, I- there's something I need to tell you."

"As has been stated," King Castien said with a yawn.

"It's about the book, and its possible location," Mylah clarified, and the king perked up. "I may actually have an idea of where it is."

"You have an idea, or you know *exactly* where it is?" King Castien seemed to read her mind. Mylah stood her ground as he stared her down.

"A house on the outskirts of town. There is a safe room there made completely of iron, the only other place the king would keep such a valuable item." Mylah felt as if a knife pierced her heart as she divulged her secret. She could be putting Elena and Garrick in danger, but there was so much more at stake. She tried to convince herself that they would understand.

"And I presume you know which house it is that has this room?" the king said, eyeing her suspiciously.

"Yes."

"And if you're wrong?" King Castien stood from the table and stepped closer to Mylah, towering over her, close enough that she could wrap her hands around his throat and... No, she thought. *I can't take my revenge yet.* Though, that desire for revenge receded every day she spent in Elowyn.

"I'm not wrong. There is nowhere else in the kingdom he would keep it." Mylah held his gaze until he stepped away from her.

"Good. You will lead the mission in three days. Go retrieve the others, we will create a new plan." Mylah agreed and hurried out of the room to find everyone. It took her much longer to find Elias than anyone else. She came across him sitting on a bench in the garden.

"Elias, there you are." She forced a smile as she sat beside him. "Your brother wants us all back in the study. We are going to retrieve the book in three days." For some reason, being near him calmed her nerves. Her actions stung less like a betrayal, and warmth spread through her at the thought of helping save the lives of everyone in Elowyn.

"What changed his mind?" he asked, though his eyes gave away his suspicion of Mylah.

"I helped him pinpoint the only other location they would keep the book."

"That seems risky," he pointed out. "If we don't know for sure..."

"Thank you for trusting me," Mylah cut him off, changing the subject. "You didn't have to tell me what was in the book."

Elias averted his eyes. "Don't thank me, you've proven yourself to be trustworthy." Mylah's chest tightened. She hadn't proven herself at all, but she had fooled Elias into thinking she had. He stood from the bench. "Come on, we shouldn't keep Castien waiting."

That night, Mylah tossed and turned in her bed. Her head kept screaming at her that she was betraying Adair, but her heart reminded her of those she was saving. And there was that murmur playing over and over in her ear in her father's voice, *Kindness is not weakness.*

"Gah!" she sat up. "This is useless! It is done..." she threw off her covers and pulled on her silk robe. "Pa would have done the same..." she told herself, though she only half believed it. "He was friends with Wren..." a shiver went down her spine. "Wren," she said the name again and the shiver intensified. "Okay," she shuddered, but took it as a sign from Emil. "I'll find out what happened to him." He'd been hung for treason, but Mylah had never asked *why*. At the very least, she owed it to her father to find out Wren's story.

Even though it was well after midnight, Mylah crept out of her room and found her way to King Castien's tower. The guards at the base of the stairs gave her a sly grin but did not stop her from ascending the tower. She knew what they assumed, and she didn't care. *Piss poor defense around here,* she thought. If she ever decided to exact her revenge, it would be easy to do so.

At the top of the stairs, Mylah peered into the room. There was another guard inside. That was why the others had let her pass without a fuss. So maybe it wouldn't be so easy to attack the king, but that was an issue for another time.

"What is your business here?" the guard demanded in a low tone. "The king is asleep, as is everyone else in the castle."

"I need to speak with him. It's urgent," Mylah lied. What she wanted to ask him could wait until morning, but she didn't want to wait. This was something she needed to find out for herself and for her father.

"Fine, but he doesn't take kindly to rude awakenings," the guard said. He turned and made his way to the king's bedside, hesitating before he leaned down and shook the king's shoulder lightly. "King Castien," he spoke clearly, but Mylah could hear the uncertainty. "Wake up."

"Agh," King Castien groaned, rolling to the side. "What is..." he yawned and opened his eyes. "What is going on?" He forced himself into a sitting position and stretched his arms over his head, showing off the muscles of his bare chest. Mylah maintained her composure, this was not a man she could be attracted to, even if it was just a physical attraction.

"Miss Leylah Farrow is here to speak with you, she says it's urgent," the guard said as he pointed to Mylah standing in the entryway. The king eyed her curiously, but waved her in.

"Thank you, Gerard. You may take your leave until further notice." King Castien shooed the guard away from his bedside. Mylah couldn't help wondering if he was sleeping naked again, but she willed away those thoughts.

"I'm sorry to wake you, King Castien," Mylah began.

"Please. You're in my bedroom, again, while everyone else sleeps. Call me Castien. There is no need for formalities here," he smirked and stretched again, letting out another yawn. "Why are you here?"

Mylah heard the door close behind the guard and walked further into Castien's room.

"You're going to think I'm crazy..." she sighed.

"That ship has sailed," he said, but the gleam in his eyes told Mylah he was joking.

"I know we've talked about him before, but I have to know...what exactly happened to your father?" Mylah watched as a range of emotions passed over Castien's face. First anger, then sadness, then disbelief.

"My father? That's what you woke me in the middle of the night to ask me about?" His voice took on a low, gruff tone. Mylah nodded in response. "What in the world possessed you to think that he was of any importance?"

"My father," she paused; she couldn't reveal the whole truth. "My father was friends with someone who knew him."

"And so, you feel you have a right to know all of his secrets? Because your father heard his name? Most people have heard my father's name, and none of them deserve that." Castien threw his covers off and Mylah turned away as she realized he was in fact naked again. "Shying away again?" he scoffed. Mylah's cheeks burned. "Never seen a naked man?" His voice passed her by as he walked to his dressing screen and when he reemerged, he wore a robe. "Better?" He tilted his head to the side and Mylah rolled her eyes.

"It makes no difference to me," she lied.

"Come, take a seat." He led the way to the couches and Mylah sat as far from him as she could manage. "So, you want to know more about Wren." He chewed on his bottom lip, which made him appear more uncertain and younger. Pity welled up inside Mylah.

"If you don't mind," Mylah clenched her hands in her lap.

"He died when I was five years old, so most of what I have left of him are stories," Castien paused, gazing at the portrait of King Haldor looking down on them. He scowled and continued. "I've been told he was a good man, but his actions proved otherwise. My mother was devastated when he died."

"Why did King Haldor sentence him to death?" Mylah asked and Castien laughed.

"I'd think that after all he did for your people, you'd at least know the story of his demise." Castien leaned his head back against the couch. "He was hanged for committing acts of treason. Those treasonous acts were helping a human learn a forgotten shreeve language. Considering that most of our books that are written in that language contain information that can harm our race, you can understand why he was executed."

"Not unless those humans planned to use the information maliciously," Mylah said, furrowing her brow. "I'm sure whoever he taught the language would have been trustworthy with the information. He would have known when to share and when to withhold certain things." Deep in her heart, Mylah knew what she said was true. It brought her some peace to think that her father would have made the same decisions regarding the shreeve book that she had made.

"We'll never know," Castien sighed. "Twenty years later and I killed the man who my father taught the forgotten language." Mylah's heart stopped and jumped into her throat. She had never expected Castien to admit to what he had done, especially after finding out that Elias had no knowledge that his brother had killed Emil and Vita.

"Y-you," she stammered, trying to form a sentence.

"Don't sound so surprised, Leylah. I know what people told you about me, even in my own castle. I'm terrible, cruel, *wicked*."

"No one..."

He cut her off. "Don't lie to me. I have to choke down Elias' lies every day; I don't need yours too."

"Elias loves you," Mylah said.

"I've no doubt about that. His lies are meant to protect me, as if it would help at this point. I'm the one who has been protecting him his whole life." Castien stretched his legs out and crossed them at the ankles. "Killing those humans in place of him isn't even the worst of what I've done," he laughed, but it was a hollow, broken sound. Once again, Mylah's heart skipped a beat and felt as if it had lodged itself back into her throat.

"K-killed them for him? Elias was meant to..." she trailed off, staring at Elias' portrait on the wall. Castien's eyes had been burned into her memory that night, but had things been different, it could have just as easily been Elias'.

"He doesn't know, and he can never know," Castien warned.

"Why tell me, then?" Mylah asked, still in shock.

"You remind me of someone I used to know. She was easy to talk to, too." He smiled a genuine smile.

"So, you've told me..." Mylah remembered how he had told her the same thing the last time she was in his room. "Mind telling me about her?"

"There are many things I will be open about with you, but she is not one of them. Ask me something else," he commanded.

"If she was so important to you, don't you think she deserves to be talked about, and remembered?" Mylah pointed out.

Castien let out a long sigh and leaned his head back against the couch. "Her name was Sascha," Castien said, surprising Mylah. She had expected him to refuse her again. "She was born half human, and half shreeve, which isn't uncommon, at least in Elowyn and Amaris. For her parents, or her father anyway, it was a shock, because both he and her mother were human."

"I see," Mylah cringed. "Aren't all shreeve half human already though?"

"Yes...and no. The original shreeve who were created by the witch Ailsa were all fifty percent fae, fifty percent human. Any children they bore would also have exactly fifty percent of each species. But, over the years, since shreeve began spreading out, they started to reproduce with fae and humans. Now, there are hardly, if any, shreeve left who are exactly fifty, fifty. So, a lot of people consider shreeve to be their own race, which we are," Castien explained. "But there are some who take it a step further and curse those who kept us bound for so many years to servitude."

"I understand why they may feel that way..." Mylah murmured.

"As for Sascha, she was abandoned on the edge of the Unbound territory. She could have died, and would have, if Petra hadn't found her." Castien smiled. Mylah felt a tug in her chest as she thought about her kindhearted handmaid.

"Petra has been helpful to me while I've been here," Mylah said.

"That's how she is. She took Sascha in and raised her here, in the castle. For the most part, she was human. She looked human, acted human, and everyone assumed that's what she was. Except, she had the blue markings on her back that indicated her heritage as a shreeve. Obviously, no one would know unless she revealed that to them."

"Wait," Mylah interrupted him. Her mind drifted to the journal she had read and the baby who had been brought from Adair to the mystery man and given to Petra to raise. "I think I found a journal that belonged to Sascha's father."

Castien's head whipped towards her, and his nostrils flared. "What? Where is it?"

"In my room, under my pillow," Mylah said a bit sheepishly. She wasn't sure if she would be reprimanded for reading someone's private journal.

"Guards!" Castien yelled and two came running up the stairs. They both scanned the room as if expecting a threat.

"Yes, your majesty?" one of them asked.

"Please go to Mylah's room and fetch a journal that is under her pillow," Castien demanded and the guard who had spoken nodded and disappeared back down the stairs. "You are dismissed," he said to the other guard who followed the first one. Castien stared into space for a moment and then started talking again.

"Where did you find the journal?" he asked.

"In your library. It doesn't have the person's name, only his love, Jacinda, Sascha's mother," Mylah explained.

"I don't know who that is," he said, furrowing his brow and leaning forward with his elbows on his knees.

They sat in silence as they waited for the guard to return with the journal. When he did, Castien flipped through it and threw it down when he'd finished.

"I recognize this handwriting...that explains why father had him killed," he broke the silence. "General Ansel was Sacha's father, and he gave up the Book of Creation to King Florian." He shook his head in disbelief.

"I know because of the journal that she died, but what exactly happened to her?" Mylah asked, hoping that Castien wouldn't change his mind about sharing Sascha's story.

Castien closed his eyes and pinched the bridge of his nose as if in distress, but he continued his tale.

"Sascha grew up here. I came here when I was seven years old, and she was six. We played together as children, and eventually we fell in love. I told her I loved her on her seventeenth birthday." The look in his eyes told Mylah exactly how much he had loved Sascha, and her heart broke knowing the ending of that story.

"What happened?" Mylah pressed, her curiosity getting the better of her.

"We kept it hidden from everyone in the castle, besides Petra, for three years. Somehow, someone found out about us and told the king. He was furious that I had fallen in love with a human, and one of his servants, which was even more humiliating for him." He gazed down at his hands, a sad smile transforming his face.

"On Sascha's twentieth birthday she was brought forth before the entire kingdom to be executed. She was accused of treason and tricking a prince to fall in love with her," he gulped. "The king used his own magic to tie her down and set her body ablaze." The pain on Castien's face made Mylah cringe.

"I'm so sorry," was all she could think to say. "You must have been devastated." It made sense why he hadn't chosen a queen yet.

"Yes..." Tears glistened in his eyes. "I remember standing in the crowd. King Haldor had his men restrain me and force me to watch."

"And yet you stayed here, in the castle, with that monster?" Mylah cried out.

"I had Elias to think of as well. Elias worshipped his father, and I didn't want to ruin his childhood."

"It seems like you did a lot for Elias, and still do," Mylah said.

"I think that's enough talk of Elias and Sascha for tonight." He stretched and yawned. "Why don't you finish your sleep on the couch? No point going back to your bed tonight." He stood from the couch and strolled back to his bed, taking the journal with him. He dropped his robe before climbing back under the sheets and tucking the journal into his side table.

"I can't seem to figure you out," Mylah said.

"For your own sanity, I'd say that's a good thing. Don't dwell on me too much, I'm not worth the trouble." He blew out the candle on his bedside table and disappeared into darkness. Mylah blew out the candle in front of her and laid down. Somehow, she fell asleep.

Twenty Seven

Mylah woke to Castien's voice, but through the haze of transitioning from dream world to the real world, she couldn't make sense of what he was saying.

"She's awake," was the first thing she understood. Her eyes fluttered open, and she sat up, her robe fluttering open to reveal her less than modest nightgown. After Castien's talk of her being too prudish, she didn't bother fixing it.

"Good morning," she said, stretching her arms out in front of her and rolling her shoulders. Her voice was still husky from sleep.

"Good morning," Elias responded, and Mylah's eyes opened fully to take him in, standing with Castien in the archway between the sitting room and the bedroom.

"What time is it?" she asked, looking around as if there would be some indication of the time somewhere.

"Nearly noon. Long night?" Elias had an accusatory look on his face.

"Ah, yes. Your brother and I made love all night, and then he made me sleep on the couch," she snapped, making

Castien burst out laughing. "Oh, wait, no that was someone else."

"Point taken," Elias said, trying to hide his smirk.

"Why are you here anyway?" Mylah stood from the couch, adjusting her robe to cover herself again.

"My brother was supposed to be meeting with an advisor from Amaris this morning. Thankfully, Sylas is running late, but Castien needs to get moving if he wants to make his meeting on time."

"It's a good thing you're here to keep me in line, brother. Otherwise, who knows what would happen," Castien mocked him. "You've delivered your message; now let Mylah and I finish our rendezvous in peace." He winked at Mylah who rolled her eyes.

"Pass," she said, waving as she left the tower. Elias caught up with her at the bottom of the stairs. The guards ignored them as they left.

"I used to find myself sleeping on those couches often," Elias said, and Mylah cocked an eyebrow at him. "I mean, my brother is harsh, but he's also comforting. I understand why you're so drawn to him, is what I'm saying..."

"I'm not drawn to him," Mylah clarified. "I think there's a lot more to him than I first thought, but I was only there to talk with him last night."

"I know, he told me." He smirked and Mylah smacked his arm.

"Why were you pestering me then?" she said a little too loud. Her voice echoed down the hall. Elias just laughed. "You and your brother are cruel," she smiled as she said it, and then caught herself. This was how it happened...this was how she betrayed Adair. Her smile turned to a grimace.

Elias seemed to sense the change in Mylah's composure. "Is everything alright?"

"Yes, I just," she gritted her teeth. "I need to get dressed." She veered down the hallway that led to her room, leaving Elias behind.

Once she was safely in her room, she broke down. Her whole body shook from her sobs, forcing her to collapse on the floor, unable to keep herself standing. *I betrayed them all*, she thought. *What would my parents think? What would Garrick think? Greyson and Crane...they would never forgive me.*

"I'm a traitor," she whispered the words, her voice cracking. No matter how many times she told herself her father would have acted in the same way, it never convinced her. Her father was a kind, loving, and loyal man. He would never have betrayed Adair. Mylah couldn't help but feel as if she may as well consider herself an Unbound now that she'd betrayed both Elowyn and Adair. Tears welled in her eyes, and she gritted her teeth. *Maybe Genevieve will take me in once everyone shuns me for my lies...*she thought.

"Shit," she cursed, slamming her fists against the floor. Pain radiated up her arms from the impact. *Kindness is not weakness;* her father's words repeated in her mind. "Shut up!" she screamed into the room. No one responded. "Shut up," she repeated, shaking her head. "Leave me alone..." She curled herself into a ball and began rocking back and forth as sobs wracked her body.

"You lied, Pa. Kindness breeds weakness," she whispered to herself. *Why shouldn't I betray the shreeve?* she thought. *They are the reason my parents are dead. King Haldor ordered them to be killed and Castien carried out those orders. Why do I feel the need to protect them now? Why do I feel my hatred of Castien slipping away by the second...why...?*

Mylah sat up, wiping the tears from her face. "You would have helped them, too," she said, realizing the truth in her statement. Her father told her to show kindness to the shreeve because the action of one was not to be blamed on the entire race. King Haldor was to be blamed for her parents' deaths, and though Castien could also share in that blame, Mylah refused to hold it against him. Her father was the forgiving type, and so she would find it in herself to be more like him. She took a deep breath, gathered her resolve, and picked herself up off the floor.

Mylah spent the rest of the day in Castien's study helping to make plans for the mission she would lead into Adair. Korriane and Killian lounged in the chairs against the wall while Torin and Castien hovered over the table as usual. Elias and Mylah sat cross legged on the floor in front of the chairs, playing out the mission with little figurines.

"Torin will be here," Elias said, putting the figure that represented Torin into a makeshift bush.

"Do you think he should be there?" Korriane asked, teasing. "The bush might be on fire when you arrive." They'd been over this so many times already that day, they were all starting to go a bit crazy.

"I'm honestly loving that look for him," Killian chimed in, plucking the figure from Elias' grasp, and turning it over in his hand. "Just needs a little eye patch." They all chuckled.

"This isn't going to work..." Mylah groaned. "Look, that letter opener will beat any weapon I carry with me," she smirked, and the others added more critiques of the makeshift town.

"Enough fun and games," Castien's voice broke through their laughter. "What happens if your plan goes south?"

"Backup plan?" Mylah offered.

"And what is that exactly?" Torin asked, strolling towards them. "We need to make a backup plan, assuming that everything goes wrong." Mylah sighed and laid back onto the plush rug beneath her.

"I know. I've been considering that," she admitted. "There is always a chance Garrick and Elena will have guests when we arrive."

"That late at night?" Elias asked.

"Sometimes. Not often, but it happens." Mylah could remember a few nights when her parents were alive that their visits with the Callisters had extended past midnight.

"And what happens if you and Torin are captured?" Korriane whispered, almost as if saying the words would make it a reality.

"Then we need a plan to escape..." Mylah couldn't admit that she already had a plan for that. It involved using the fact that she'd never *actually* been exiled in her favor. She'd convince the king she was still on Adair's side. Breaking Torin out of the dungeon would be the hard part.

A lightbulb seemed to go off in Mylah's mind as she remembered Ana and what she'd revealed to Mylah. *I've always been able to put people at ease with just a look...*Mylah had an idea.

"I think I may know someone who could help if things do take a turn," Mylah said. "I need to talk to them first, though."

"Who?" Elias asked.

"I'd rather not say." Mylah didn't want to drag Ana into this unless she agreed to help on her own. "But I'll need to go into town to talk with them."

Castien narrowed his eyes at her. "Korriane will accompany you," he commanded. "But you must go now. We have no time to waste."

Korriane hopped out of her seat and held her hand out to Mylah. Mylah took it and let Korriane help her up. "Don't have any fun without us," Korriane warned the others, a hint of a smile on her lips. They hurried out of the room and made their way to the stables. The stable boy brought out two horses for them, saddled and ready to ride.

As they rode, Mylah thought about what she would say to Ana to convince her to help. There was no reason Ana should want to put herself in harm's way, and Mylah hated asking her to do so. If they were captured in Adair, though, Ana would be a great asset in the escape. She could convince the guards not to sound the alarm or calm down any other people who witnessed them escaping.

"Thank you for helping us with this mission," Korriane's voice jolted Mylah from her thoughts.

"Oh, it's nothing," Mylah mumbled.

"It's not nothing. Even if Adair cast you out, it was still your home once. It means a lot that you are willing to go against them to help our people."

Mylah turned to look at Korriane. "I would never stand aside and let countless people be murdered, no matter who they were. But I appreciate you acknowledging that it's difficult for me to go against Adair."

"Killian and I haven't always lived in Elowyn, so I understand having mixed allegiances," Korriane's voice softened. "We came here from Cyprian as children when our mother was murdered by a fae. There are prejudices everywhere you go, but at least in Elowyn, we don't have to fear for our lives anymore." Mylah's heart ached for Korriane.

"I lost my mother, too. And my father. I understand that pain," Mylah's voice cracked, but she held back her tears.

"I'm sorry for your loss, but I have an idea that you wouldn't be here if not for that loss. I can't help but be grateful for the path you were placed on that brought you to us. Without you, this mission wouldn't be happening." Korriane pursed her lips and shrugged. "Without you, I'd be losing a lot more than just my mother."

"I guess you're right..." Mylah couldn't help but wonder why she had been chosen to walk the path she was now on. Why it hadn't been someone else who'd been pushed into a life of grief, lies, and betrayal. But, at the same time, a little voice in her head reminded her of Genevieve, Elias, Ana, and all the others she would have never met if she hadn't started down that path.

Korriane led them to Ana's house. They had to stop to ask for directions a few times, because neither of them knew where Ana lived, but they made good time getting there.

Mylah hopped down from her horse and approached the front door. Korriane flanked her and gave her an encouraging smile when she hesitated to knock on the door.

An older woman with graying hair who resembled Ana opened the door.

"We're looking for Ana," Mylah told her. "I'm a friend of hers."

"I know who you are," the woman grimaced. "Ana told me all about the human who had been welcomed into the castle...well she's not home." Mylah was about to ask where she could be found when another voice spoke from inside the house.

"Don't be silly, mama!" Ana skipped into view. "I'm home." She nudged her mother out of the way. "Leylah is a friend, I told you that." Her mother harrumphed and stalked back into the house.

"It's good to see you," Mylah said, smiling as Ana turned back to her.

"Sorry about mama, she's always skeptical of anyone or anything having to do with the castle," Ana explained. Mylah understood, seeing as the old king had used Ana's mother to help extract information from prisoners in the past. "What are you doing here?" Her eyes flicked to Korriane.

"I need to ask you something," Mylah cringed as she thought about the gravity of that something. "Do you mind taking a walk with us?" Ana glanced back in the house before joining them outside and closing the door.

"I'm Korriane, by the way," Korriane introduced herself and Ana grinned at her.

"I'm Ana. It's nice to meet another friend of Leylah's."

Mylah began walking and the other two caught up with her.

"You better speed this up," Korriane warned. "Castien is waiting on us."

"Like, King Castien?" Ana's eyes widened and she perked up even more than her usual perkiness. "Leylah, please tell me what's happening."

"Okay." She let out a long breath. "I'm leading a mission for the king to retrieve the Book of Creation from Adair."

"Oh my," Ana covered her mouth. "That sounds dangerous."

"It is. And I hate to ask you this, but I wondered whether you might be able to come with us." Mylah closed her eyes for a moment and assumed from Ana's sharp intake of breath that she was about to tell Mylah *no*.

"The Book of Creation... Mama told me about that. You need my help to retrieve it?" Without waiting for an answer, she continued. "I'll do it." All her perkiness had dissipated, and Mylah gazed at her in wonder.

"Why?" Mylah practically spit out the word in her astonishment.

"Because I know what it means if it falls into the wrong hands. If I can help save our people, I'm going to do it." Ana's voice was strong and clear, but Mylah noticed her wringing her hands against her tunic.

"You should know, we'll only need you if we're captured. So, this involves spending time in the dungeon of King Florian's castle." Though the thought of being back in the dungeon scared even Mylah, she knew that Ana would not back down. She'd proven her loyalty to her people and her bravery simply by accepting the proposition.

"I understand and I'm willing to help."

Mylah and Korriane waited outside Ana's house while she packed to move into the castle for the few days that remained before they left for Adair. She'd need to be trained in basic combat and be briefed on the mission details. Korriane offered to let her ride with her on her horse, which

Ana gratefully accepted. Her bags were attached to Mylah's saddle to help spread out the weight.

Back at the castle, they took Ana straight to Castien's study. Killian and Elias were sparring while Torin and Castien gave them pointers from the chairs. Though, the pointers were more of jeers and distractions. They all stopped and turned to see who Mylah had brought to help with their mission.

"No," Castien said as soon as he recognized Ana. "Not her." He rose from his seat and strode across the room to stand before them.

"You have no idea what she's capable of," Mylah snapped. "She's helping and that's final."

"I know *exactly* what she is capable of. I had the pleasure of being questioned by her mother on multiple occasions," his words took the steam from Mylah. She hadn't even thought about the fact that Castien had been in the castle at the same time Ana's mother had and so he may know her. "She happened to be the nail in Sascha's coffin, pun intended." He stared down his nose at Ana who stood her ground.

"My mother was forced into her contract with King Haldor. They threatened her with *my life* if she didn't agree," Ana ground out. "Any death that came of her questioning anyone in this castle, is to be blamed on *him*."

Castien ground his teeth but said nothing more. He stepped back and turned to Mylah. "You're responsible for her," he snapped and stalked back to his chair.

"Great, now I need one more thing." Mylah had been thinking long and hard about what their course of action would be if they were caught, and she knew of someone else who could be of use in an escape. "I need to send a message to someone in the Unbound territory."

"Very well," Castien said, shooing her with a wave of his hand. "Find a sprite to carry your message to them." Mylah bowed her head and left the room in search of Briar.

Twenty Eight

The following day Mylah and Ana trained with Elias. Castien still hadn't agreed to let Elias join them and Torin on their mission. Korriane and Killian would be going with them, but only as far as Snake Head Lake which lay before the village in Adair. They would wait there in case something went wrong before Mylah, Torin, and Ana reached the Callisters' house, otherwise, they were on their own.

The less people involved the better. Mylah wanted to ensure Garrick and Elena's safety, so she made sure she would be the one to go into the house. Torin and Ana would wait for her signal outside. If all went well, they'd leave with the book that night. If anything went wrong, they had a plan for that too.

"Are you attending the revel tonight?" Elias asked as he sparred with Mylah. Ana was taking a break, studying the weapons on the wall.

"I hadn't realized there was anything happening tonight," Mylah huffed, making sure not to take her focus from his sword.

"Oh, well, there is."

"As you've now informed me," she smirked and got in a hit to his side.

"So, you'll be attending then?" he asked again.

"What's it to you?" Mylah asked, wiping the sweat from her brow. "Hoping I can convince your brother to let you join the mission at the last minute?"

"The last minute would be tomorrow night," Elias pointed out and Mylah shook her head, sheathing her knives in the belt Elias had given her.

"Are you asking me to go to the revel with you?" she asked, taking a swig from her water.

"No." He fumbled with his sword and Mylah stifled her laugh. "I just..."

"Leylah," Petra interrupted them, and Elias appeared relieved. "Come girl, I have something to show you." She beckoned from the doorway for Mylah to follow her.

"I guess I'll see you tonight. Go easy on Ana, please," Mylah warned. "Will I see you tonight, Ana?"

"No, revels aren't really my thing. Besides, I need to rest up for tomorrow," Ana said, grabbing her sword again and joining Elias on the mat. "But you'll tell me all about it in the morning, right?"

"Of course! See you then!" Mylah waved to Elias and Ana as she left. In the hall, Petra had already disappeared. Mylah headed to her room where Petra waited impatiently inside. "What's the rush?"

"Ah, foolish girl," Petra pulled Mylah into her room.

"What was that?" Mylah couldn't help but laugh.

"Don't worry about it." She closed the door and motioned for Mylah to sit on the bed. That was when Mylah noticed the large box sitting on the floor in front of her wardrobe.

"What's that?" She started to stand, but Petra gave her a glare that rooted her to her spot.

"A gift from the king. This is why I've been running all over the kingdom the past week," Petra said, pulling the box open. "It had better fit, the seamstress was not exactly thrilled to be making it after the last dress he commissioned went unseen for years. Thankfully she still lives in town, I half thought she'd have moved on by now."

"A dress?" Mylah craned her neck to see into the box.

"A dress," Petra confirmed, grinning. The smile transformed her face and made Mylah realize she had never seen Petra truly *happy* before. "A dress fit for a queen, if I do say so myself."

Mylah blanched at those words. "No. That's crazy." She wrapped her arms around herself. "I could never be a queen." She left the unspoken words, *I could never be with King Castien,* hanging.

"He wasn't always so cruel, you know...he's had his moments, but I knew a kinder version of him at one time," Petra said.

"I never said he was cruel." Mylah noticed Petra's brow rise infinitesimally. "He told me about Sascha. I'm sorry, you lost her too." She reached out and took Petra's hand, surprised when Petra didn't pull away.

"I'm glad he's finally talking about her again," Petra's voice remained steady and strong, but tears glistened in her eyes. "You reminded me so much of her when you first came."

"That's why you thought the king would let me stay." Mylah squeezed her hand. "What King Haldor did to her was horrible and I wish there was something I could do..."

"There is nothing you can do to help her now. But you can help the king heal. Sascha would like that very much." Petra took her hand out of Mylah's and lifted the dress from the box. Mylah gasped. The fabric moved as if it was liquid. The deep red color caused Mylah to flash back to the moment she found her father in his study, and then her mother... she closed her eyes.

"Why red?" she asked. Her eyes remained closed as her throat tightened.

"It's what King Castien requested." Petra draped the gown over the vanity chair. "To the baths." Petra ushered Mylah out of her room into the bathing room. Mylah breathed a sigh of relief as they left the gown behind. The sight of it made her stomach turn.

Mylah took her time in the bath, hoping Petra would forget about her. But, as always, Petra returned to help her prepare for the revel. She made Mylah sit at the vanity, moving the gown to the bed, and braided one side of her hair. The other she left loose and wavy, tucking the braid underneath.

After applying color to Mylah's eyelids, cheeks, and lips, she lifted the dress from the bed. Tears pricked at the back of Mylah's eyes, but she couldn't ruin all of Petra's hard work. She stepped into the gown and marveled at the craftsmanship. It felt like satin against her skin. The long sleeves had loops that held firm around her middle fingers. It gave the gown an elegance that Mylah had never pictured for herself before. The neck sloped down, revealing her cleavage where her sapphire pendant rested. The skirt belled out, and her back was completely bare. When she looked in the mirror, she understood why Petra had said the dress was fit for a queen. Mylah barely recognized herself.

As much as she loathed the color because of the memories it stirred up, she had to admit it was beautiful. Petra helped her into her strappy red heels that matched the gown.

"You should be going. The revel starts early tonight," Petra said, ushering Mylah out the door again.

"If I didn't know any better, I'd think you were trying to be rid of me," Mylah joked.

"Just go, girl." Petra waved her hands at Mylah and Mylah gave her a small curtsy before turning down the hall. As she walked, she couldn't help but admire her dress. It had to be magic that made it move like waves across the shore, cresting but never breaking.

"Watch where you're going," a voice startled her, and she looked up to find Broderick striding towards her. She grinned and threw her arms around his neck.

"Where have you been?" she squealed.

"Around, but you've been too busy for us common folk," he joked. He pulled away from her and spun her in a circle, admiring her gown. "Has anyone told you how spectacular that dress is? And it fits you beautifully."

"Why, thank you." She swished her skirts from side to side.

"Sabine would be jealous, I'm sure."

"Where is she?" Mylah looked around.

"She's on gate duty tonight. If you can sneak away, you could find her and say hi."

"Oh, I will!" Mylah smiled as she continued to the ballroom. At the doors, she paused, searching the crowd within for any familiar faces. Torin stood up by Castien's throne which was vacant. Other than that, the faces were vaguely familiar from past revels. She stepped forward only to be rushed backwards again. Two guards had appeared on either side of her.

"You must wait for the king to arrive," they told her, and she gaped at them for a moment before smoothing her ruffled skirts.

"No need to tackle me," she muttered. "Where is the king?"

"Present," Castien's voice came from behind her. She turned to see him striding towards her in a gorgeous, midnight blue outfit. His crimson cape flowed out behind him and matched her dress perfectly. He stopped a few feet away from her, taking in the sight of her in the dress he had ordered.

"Is it everything you imagined it would be?" she asked, fluttering her eyelashes in a dramatic and joking manner. He grinned and held his arm out to her.

"Better." He took one step and then stopped again, reaching into his pocket. "Oh, before I forget." He pulled a ring box out and held it before her. "It will match beautifully." Mylah took the box, her hand shaking visibly. Her thoughts raced as she considered what the gift meant.

"Why are you giving this to me?" she asked, her voice as shaky as her hands.

"A thank you for your inside information." He gazed at her as she opened the box, waiting for her reaction. Nuzzled inside was a ring with a brilliant oval shaped ruby surrounded by tiny diamonds. Mylah gasped, and Castien smirked.

"Where," Mylah began, but then snapped her mouth shut along with the lid of the ring box.

"What's wrong?" Castien asked. Tears lined Mylah's eyes, but she could not let the king know what was going through her mind...*Her mother's ring.*

"It's too beautiful. I shouldn't wear it," she made up a lie to cover for her reaction.

"Nonsense." He took the box from her, pulled out the ring, and grabbed her hand. He lifted the ring to her ring finger and slid it on. It fit perfectly. "It suits you."

"I guess it does," her voice wavered. She was taken back to the moment she realized her mother's ring had been taken...her parents lay dead on the floor of her home, and blood spattered the walls. Blood the same color as her dress and the ruby that sat on her finger. Her throat constricted and it took every ounce of resolve for her not to turn and run or crumple onto the floor.

"Come." Castien's voice snapped Mylah back to her senses. He led her into the ballroom and all eyes turned to watch their entrance. Mylah felt as if she were in a trance. She knew everything around her was real, but it seemed as if she were watching it through a veil. It was noisy in the ballroom, so she didn't need to speak, thankfully. Castien brought her with him to his throne where he sat and released her arm.

"You look exceptionally beautiful tonight, Leylah," Torin commented, and Mylah gave him a stiff nod. Every time she looked down at her hand, she flinched. The ring was like a beacon, drawing her in. Her mind raced with thoughts, worries, and speculations. *Why did Castien give me the ring? Does he know who I am? Is this a threat? Did I give myself away?*

"Leylah." Torin waved his hand in front of her face, and she tore her gaze away from the ring.

"Sorry, what?"

"Are you ready for tomorrow?" he repeated his question.

"Yes," she lied. If they waited for her to be ready for the mission, it would never happen. She would be betraying her king, committing treason, helping the enemy...

"Good." Torin smirked. Mylah tried to feign a smile, but she couldn't.

"I need...I'll be right back." She lifted her skirts and fled from the ballroom to the gardens. None of the guards tried to stop her. Outside, she thought the fresh air would help her breathe, instead she began hyperventilating as sobs threatened to break free from her chest. Tears spilled down her cheeks, and she brushed them away, not worrying about the makeup Petra had applied.

Mylah ripped the ring from her finger and went to throw it when someone caught her hand. She screamed and whipped around to find Elias standing behind her.

"You don't want to do that," he said, taking the ring from her. "A gift from my brother, I presume?" He studied the ring and twirled it between his fingers.

"Yes," Mylah said, breathless. "I don't know why he gave it to me." She stood up straight and forced back her remaining tears.

"You're risking your life to help us retrieve the Book of Creation. This ring is the *least* he could give you in return." Elias handed the ring back to her and she clenched it in her fist.

"It's not a risk if I don't fear death," she whispered into the night.

"What? Leylah, that doesn't mean you should risk your life if it isn't something you think is worth fighting for." Elias stepped in front of her, forcing her to look at him.

"That's not..." she almost admitted her truth. She was tired of people calling her *Leylah*...thinking her trustworthy and self-sacrificing. "I thought I had the strength to do this." She closed her eyes and another tear leaked out. Elias wiped it away gently, his thumb brushing her cheek and lingering a second too long. Mylah grasped his hand and held it there, laughing through her tears.

"If you don't want to go tomorrow," Elias began, but she cut him off. She opened her eyes to find him staring into them.

"That's not it. I'm going tomorrow. I said I would, and I will." She stepped closer to him, and his hand dropped from her cheek.

"We should get inside. Castien will be looking for us," he said, turning away. Mylah threw her hands up in defeat and placed the ring back on her finger.

"I can't with you," Mylah grumbled as she caught up with Elias and stalked past him.

"What are you talking about?" Mylah whirled around to face him.

"You! I can't figure out what you want!" She released her frustration on him. "You don't want me sleeping with your brother or kissing Torin, but you won't so much as dance with me of your own accord."

"You don't understand," he tried, but Mylah put her hand up to stop him.

"I understand fine. I'm human, I'm not good enough."

"Don't be stupid," Elias snapped closing the gap between them and placing one hand beneath her chin. "You're *too good*. We're the ones who are not worthy." He pressed his forehead against hers and his words caused her body to tremble.

"Do it," she rasped, nearly breathless from his proximity. He crushed her lips with his own and butterflies exploded in Mylah's stomach and chest. She kissed him back, grasping at his shirt, trying to pull him closer, *deeper* into the kiss. His hands wound into her hair, and she felt a few pieces break free of her braid, falling to frame her face.

"*Leylah...*" that false name against her lips brought everything to a halt. Mylah came back to her senses and disentangled herself from Elias, her breath coming in ragged gasps.

"We... should go inside." She turned away before he could see the tears in her eyes. She wiped them quickly. More than ever, she wished she could reveal her secrets to Elias, but she needed to keep them for at least one more night. She just had to get through the mission, and then she could reveal everything.

Elias stepped up beside her and when she was sure the tears were gone, she smiled at him, a genuine smile. He took her hand and squeezed it, releasing it before they reentered the castle.

Twenty Nine

The guests had begun dancing in the ballroom. Elias took Mylah's hand once more to help navigate their way through the crowd. Castien still sat on his throne looking bored. Aleese and his latest consort had joined him.

"There you are," Castien said, as Mylah and Elias approached him. "Not getting cold feet, are we?" He eyed Mylah suspiciously.

"Not at all. I'm ready for tomorrow," she reassured him.

"Good." He stood from his throne and held his hand out to her. "May I have this dance? Then you may depart and rest up for tomorrow." Mylah took his hand and let him lead her to the dance floor. The crowds parted for the king as he approached them.

"Have you decided whether you'll let Elias accompany us tomorrow?" Mylah asked as they moved across the floor.

"No. It was never up for discussion," Castien clarified, his tone severe and final.

"He is a great fighter, and he'd..."

"I said no," Castien snapped. His grip on her tightened. "He is all I have left; I won't risk losing him."

Mylah turned her head to meet Castien's stare. "I'm sorry, I shouldn't have pressed the issue." Mylah let it go. At least she could tell Elias she'd tried.

Once they finished their dance, Castien returned to his throne and Mylah decided to follow his advice and head back to her room for some sleep. It took her much longer to fight her way through the crowd without the king or prince with her. She stopped for a drink before continuing to the door.

"Leylah," Elias stepped up beside her. "May I walk with you?"

"So long as you don't mind us making a quick stop to visit with Sabine," Mylah said. She hadn't forgotten her conversation with Broderick earlier, and she wanted to see her friend.

"Of course not." With Elias on her arm, leaving the ballroom was a breeze. The crowds parted, though not as wide as when the king walked through. In the hall, they were finally alone again. Elias stopped. "Now that we can breathe again, would you do me the honor of dancing with me?"

"In the hallway?" Mylah glanced around, but there was no one else to see them. Elias held his hand out to her, and she took it. She let him pull her in close, press his chest against hers and place his hand on the small of her back. A smile crept onto her face.

"I was devastated when you left me on the dance floor that night," he said and Mylah tossed her head back, laughing.

"Devastated?" she mocked. "Then why were you acting as if it was a burden to dance with me?"

"The thought of being so close to you while not knowing how you felt about me...I was still under the impression you were in love with my brother," he admitted.

"I'm glad you don't have to worry about that anymore," she said, resting her head against his chest. "I'm sorry we didn't get to dance that night."

"As am I." In that moment, Mylah knew what she had to do. She had resigned herself to wait until after the mission to reveal her secret to Elias, but she couldn't keep it from him any longer.

"There's something I need to tell you," she began, and Elias pulled away enough to gaze down at her. In that moment, a force knocked Mylah into Elias. Her back screamed in agony and warmth spread from the point of impact. She staggered out of Elias' arms as she tried to reach around to find the source of the pain. Instead, when she looked at her hands, they were coated in her own blood. Her eyes sluggishly found Elias' before she crumpled to the ground.

"Leylah! Stay with me!" Elias' voice sounded as if he were under water. "Guards! Someone, help!" Feet pounded towards them.

"M-my name..." Mylah tried to say, but she sputtered and coughed up blood.

"What?" Elias brushed the stray hairs away from her face. "Don't try to talk." He held her in his lap and a prickling sensation began in her back where the pain originated from. She wasn't sure whether she was facing the ceiling or the floor, but she felt safe and warm.

"M-m-m," a cough wracked her body. "Mylah," her name finally came out as she lost consciousness.

Mylah woke up in bed with a pounding headache. She forced herself to sit up and realized she wasn't in her own bed. Swinging her legs over the side of the king's bed, an ache radiated out from the center of her back.

"Ah," she gasped as she hunched over.

"You're awake," the voice came from the couches in the sitting area. Petra appeared in the archway; her face scrunched with worry. "Don't move too much," she said as she hurried to the bedside. "Let me look at you first." Mylah remained seated on the edge of the bed and Petra lifted her nightgown to look at her back.

"Well, how does it look?" Mylah craned her neck to try and see her back but all she could see was the bunched-up fabric of her nightgown.

"Stupid boy..." Petra tsked. "Well, you'll be fine." She dropped the nightgown and motioned for Mylah to stand. "But the prince nearly killed himself," she murmured, and Mylah gasped.

"What do you mean? Was there another attack?" she asked, standing from the bed.

"Keep your feet still and twist your torso for me," Petra instructed, and Mylah did as she was told, feeling a slight twinge in her back. "The sole target of the attack seems to have been you. The king has been up all night working with Madame Edris to try and find the culprit. It seems to have been an enchanted dagger that stabbed you."

Mylah took that all in. She was the target, but why? *Davina*...another attempt to kill Mylah would not be out of the question for her, or the man who had tried to harm her the night she'd met with Briar.

"You said Elias was hurt?" Mylah asked, remembering the most important information Petra had mentioned.

"Not exactly," Petra ran the water in the tub behind the wall screen. "Come here, girl." Mylah walked over and stripped down, stepping into the warm water of the tub.

"Then what happened to him? Where is he?" Mylah couldn't help but be a little disappointed that he wasn't at her bedside when she woke after what happened the previous night.

"He nearly drained himself healing you," Petra explained as she helped Mylah wash herself. She obviously didn't believe Mylah was healed enough to do it alone. "If your wounds had been any more extensive, he would have died healing you."

"Why would he do that?" Mylah leaned forward, hugging her knees to her chest as Petra washed her back.

"Why does any man do the things he does?" Petra chuckled softly. "I think you know the answer to that, Miss Leylah." *Leylah*...Mylah remembered correcting Elias last night before she passed out. Had he heard her, or understood what she was trying to tell him?

"Where is he now?"

"Resting. He will probably sleep all day. Recovering from magic depletion is a difficult task." Petra held a towel up for Mylah and she stood, wrapping it around herself. "You may visit him once you're dressed. I will alert the guards so they may accompany you."

"Why? I've never needed guards before."

"An attempt on your life this severe has never been made before, and no, Davina doesn't count. This was the work of someone far more powerful." The words sent a chill down Mylah's spine.

"Is that why I'm in the king's chambers instead of my own?" she asked, and Petra bobbed her head.

"Yes. This tower, and the tower in which Elias' room is located are both warded against magic. And they are easily guarded." Petra laid out a dress on the bed for Mylah that she must have retrieved from her room. "Put this on, I shall return in a moment." Petra descended the stairs to talk with the guards. When she returned, Mylah was dressed.

"Am I free to leave?" Mylah asked and Petra responded with a wave of her hand. Mylah followed Petra down the stairs and cried out in excitement when she saw who guarded the door, Sabine and Broderick. They both turned and smiled when they beheld her. Sabine wrapped her arms around Mylah, squeezing her tight.

"I'm so glad you're okay. When we saw you lying in the prince's arms, I thought..." She pulled away and tears rimmed her eyes. "Well, it doesn't matter. You're okay."

"Yes, I am very okay." Mylah smiled and turned to Broderick who took her in his arms next.

"Don't ever do that again," he joked. "Come on, we will take you to the prince's room." He waved to Petra as he started down a hall Mylah had never ventured down. She followed and Sabine lagged behind to watch her back.

"This is crazy," Mylah commented as they walked. "I can't believe anyone would try to kill me."

"Really?" Broderick turned his head back and cocked a brow. "You've become a favorite of the king and have been drawing the prince's eye as well. Anyone in the kingdom could be to blame for the attempted assassination. You have come closer to being our next queen than any other lover of the king."

"That's ridiculous. The king and I aren't lovers..." Mylah trailed off. Even if she and Castien had never actually done anything, he had certainly made it look as if they were lovers to everyone else.

"Tell that to the host of women he has turned away since you arrived in the castle," Broderick said.

"You think someone tried to kill me out of *jealousy?*" Mylah would understand if that were the case. Being queen was most definitely a highly coveted position for the power that came along with it. The people of Elowyn deserved someone who would help rule their kingdom in their best interests, and they probably saw her as an outsider. A human taking the position from another more deserving Elowyn woman.

"Don't worry, Leylah. We will make sure no one ever gets close enough to harm you again," Sabine promised. They were approaching the next tower. There were guards stationed outside the door leading to the staircase beyond.

"Good morning," Broderick greeted them. Mylah noticed Nic among the guards before them and was surprised how professional he and Broderick acted towards each other. If it were her, she would for sure make a snarky remark, or at least give him a wink. "Leylah would like to see Prince Elias."

"Alec, check and see if the prince is well enough for guests," Nic commanded and Alec ducked through the doorway, disappearing into the stairwell. Once he was gone, Nic turned to Broderick and smiled.

"Is all going well?" he asked.

"Better than that," he gestured to Mylah. "You would never guess she'd been assaulted with an enchanted dagger."

"Good. I'm glad the prince's efforts were not in vain."

Alec returned and reported that the prince was awake and would like to see Mylah. They allowed her to pass, and Broderick and Sabine announced they would wait at the base of the stairs so Mylah could have some privacy with the prince.

Mylah took her time on the stairs. She was about to find out if Elias had heard her revelation, and if he had, what he thought about it. Her heart raced and her palms were sweating as she reached the top of the stairs. She peeked around the corner and saw Elias' room was set up almost identical to Castien's room.

"Elias?" Mylah said as she entered the room. He did not respond, but she could see him sitting up in bed as she walked past the couches. He smiled weakly when he saw her. He looked pale and dark circles shone under his eyes. Mylah rushed to his bedside.

"You came," his words sounded strangled. He coughed and the words came more clearly. "I was worried you would still be bedridden, but you look well."

"Yes," Mylah said, wiping her eyes as they filled with tears. "I'm fine, thanks to you." He reached up and cupped her cheek in his hand.

"They'll find who did this," he said, and Mylah shook her head.

"That's not what I'm worried about right now." She knelt so she could be on his level and leaned forward with her elbows resting on the edge of the bed. "You could have died saving me."

"And I'd do it again."

"You can't...you're the prince. You can't go around risking your life for me anytime I'm on death's doorstep," Mylah protested.

"If I had let you die from the naga's poison, I would have never been able to dance with you," he smirked. "And if I hadn't saved you last night, I would have died of heartache alongside you."

Mylah laughed. "You barely know me. We've had one kiss..."

Elias interrupted her. "And what a kiss it was," he said. "It proved to me what I already suspected; I care for you more than anyone I've ever known."

"You're being ridiculous. You've lost your mind from exhaustion," Mylah joked, casting her eyes down to look at her hands folded before her on the bed.

"I hope so," he said. "If losing my mind means feeling so spectacularly happy anytime you enter the room, or say my name, or look my way, then I'm losing my mind."

"You don't mean that..." Mylah sighed. "You don't know me, Elias."

"Of course I do. If not you, then who have I been spending four hours a day training with?" His eyes closed for a moment and Mylah thought he had fallen asleep, but he opened them again. "*Mylah*," the sound of her real name on his lips made her heart soar.

"Yes," she gasped.

"A beautiful name..." He closed his eyes again. "Who is Mylah? You mentioned her last night..." his voice faded as he lost his energy. Her heart dropped.

"No one important. We can talk about it later." Mylah squeezed his hand. "Get some rest." She stood and left the room with tears in her eyes.

Thirty

Mylah stood in Castien's study. Torin sat beside her, and Killian leaned against the wall on her other side. Korriane and Ana sat on the plush rug in front of the chairs. Ana leaned against Mylah, offering her support. She'd been a wreck when Mylah first saw her, worrying over Mylah and her injury, but she had finally calmed down.

"You're absolutely sure you are still up for tonight?" Castien asked Mylah again and she sighed. She'd already told him that she felt fine, but he refused to believe her.

"Yes, I can do this." There was no turning back, though Mylah would never truly be ready to betray the kingdom that had raised her.

"Good. You leave in two hours. Go prepare yourselves," Castien dismissed them. Mylah made her way back to her room with Broderick and Sabine still at her front and back and found Petra waiting for her. Sabine and Broderick stayed outside Mylah's room while she went inside with Petra.

There were black pants, a black tunic, and black boots waiting for her, laid out on her bed.

"I think I can ready myself," Mylah said and Petra tsked.

"I need to be sure you are fit for your mission," Petra rebuked. "Don't try to shoo me away so fast." Mylah let Petra check her back again. Nothing had changed.

When Mylah was alone, she finished dressing. The pants and tunic were tight, but at least they wouldn't catch on anything. It reminded her of the Adairian uniform. She yearned to return home, but not as a traitor. A traitor to Elowyn, and soon to Adair.

"Leylah?" Broderick called through the door. "You have a visitor; may I permit them to enter?"

"Yes," she called back. The door opened and Castien strode in. Mylah blinked in surprise. "I told you, I'm fine, I can do this," she said, assuming he was there to check on her, *again*.

"I understand, that's not why I'm here." He paced between her armoire and the opposite wall. "Elias is not well," he paused and flicked his gaze to Mylah.

"I saw him earlier, he seemed to be recovering," she said, worry needling its way back into her mind.

"Yes, he will recover. That's not what has me concerned." He stopped pacing and turned to face Mylah. "He told me you mentioned a name before you were rendered unconscious from blood loss." Mylah gulped and sweat began to prick her forehead.

"And," Mylah prompted.

"And I recognized the name. Oddly it sounds quite similar to your name, *Leylah*." He laughed dryly. "I knew from the moment I saw you." He took another step towards her, and she stumbled backwards.

"I didn't...I shouldn't have...I don't..." Mylah's brain raced at a mile a minute and she couldn't get a coherent sentence out.

"I *murdered* your family, Mylah," her name came out as a whisper on his lips. He closed his eyes. "You slept in my room; you could have had your revenge. Yet you restrained yourself. I want to know why."

"What do you mean, why?" Mylah sat down on her bed. "King Florian sent me here to gain intelligence. If I killed you, I would never get that."

"You've gained plenty of intelligence. You know what information the Book of Creation contains. You could end our race. Why not send your information along, because I know you have an inside helper, and then kill me?"

"Do you want me to kill you? Because I would be happy to oblige," Mylah gritted her teeth.

"If I thought you would do that, I wouldn't be here right now, and you'd already be dead," he sighed and sat beside her on the bed. "Tell me everything." And so, she did. From the beginning, including her plan to kill him after she had accomplished King Florian's task.

"That doesn't mean I won't still kill you," she warned, only half joking.

"I'd deserve it," Castien shrugged. "But I trust you, for now."

"Even after all the lies?"

"You betrayed your own kingdom by telling me where the Book of Creation is located. I have to give you a little credit, don't I?" he smirked.

"I guess...though I could still be lying," she pointed out, but he didn't flinch. "Why did you give me this?" She lifted her hand to show him the ring. "Did you know when you gave it to me?"

"I had a suspicion and your reaction helped to confirm it, though I didn't truly know until Elias mentioned the name...*Mylah*." Hearing her real name brought a relief so great, she almost started crying.

"It's weird hearing you say my real name," she admitted. "It was starting to drive me a little crazy having to respond to Leylah."

"It never felt right calling you that, now I know why."

"Why didn't you have me executed the moment you realized I was a traitor?" Mylah asked. "Why give me the benefit of the doubt?"

"Because. After I killed your parents, I promised myself if I ever met you, I would spare you any more grief." The cruel king...admitting he had a heart.

"That's stupid," Mylah murmured. "Kindness is weakness..." she trailed off and Castien took her hand.

"What was that?" he asked.

"My father once said, *kindness is not weakness*." She shook her head. "But I think he may have had it backwards. Kindness *is* weakness, isn't it?"

"I guess it depends on how you look at it."

"Yet you are known for your cruelty, so how can you even consider it true?" Mylah had been dying to know what his people had seen that had pegged Castien as the cruel king in their minds, but she'd never had the courage to ask.

Castien chuckled, throwing Mylah off. "I've never said that I am proud of who I used to be, or even who I've become. You can ask anyone, and they'll have stories for you of my past and those I hurt. You know that better than anyone, I guess." He stopped and clasped his hands in his lap, his knuckles turning white. "Maybe someday I'll be able to drop the façade and prove to everyone I'm not who I once was." Mylah could sense he wanted to drop the topic, so she did, though curiosity still ate away at her.

"So, what do we do now?" she asked, positive that Castien would cancel the mission and have her removed from the castle now that he knew her truth.

"We keep this to ourselves until after your mission," he said, and Mylah gaped at him.

"But I'm a traitor and a liar," she reminded him.

"Even so, I believe your intentions to help us retrieve the Book of Creation are pure. I don't think you would do anything to jeopardize the mission." Mylah was astounded by the confidence he had in her. If the situation were reversed, she would have had him thrown in a dungeon and interrogated by sprites.

"And what will happen to me when we return?"

"We'll worry about that when the time comes. In the meantime, you'll remain Leylah Farrow. I don't want anyone else to doubt your loyalty and question your command tonight."

"Right. Makes sense. I have to admit, the whole time I've been here, I was under the impression if you found out my identity I'd be headed to the gallows."

"We don't have gallows," Castien said, smirking.

"You know what I mean," Mylah returned his smirk.

"Had I learned you were lying the first day you came to me, that may have been true. Maybe even the next couple of days. Since then, though, you've proven yourself useful, and I quite enjoy your company," he shrugged. "It would be a shame to kill you now."

"Ha, a shame. If only my parents had the chance to prove themselves worthy of your pity," Mylah's tone changed to a more venomous nature. The rage boiled up in her stomach and she felt as if she might vomit.

Castien stood from the bed, sensing the change in her. "I didn't have a choice, Mylah. My father ordered me to kill them, if I didn't do it, he would have sent Elias. Elias was too young to take on that burden." He didn't plead with her, and she wasn't sure if it would have changed anything.

"Sorry, old habits," she murmured.

"Don't be sorry, you *should* be upset. I'd be worried if you weren't...but if this is going to cause a problem when you return to Adair, then we should talk about it."

"It won't. I feel like it should," Mylah admitted. "I hate that I've forgiven you for what you did. I hate that I feel this sense of obligation to Elowyn and all shreeve everywhere, and I hate that I now have to betray my own kingdom." Mylah clenched her hands in her lap and let her head hang down.

"You don't *have* to do anything. I mean, I'd be pretty annoyed if you changed your mind now, but I'd figure something else out." He sat beside her again. "Tell me now if that's the case, because I don't want to be putting my people in your hands if you think you might waver."

"I won't. I promise." Mylah lifted her head and met his gaze. "I will do this because it's the right thing to do, and it's what my pa would do...I think."

"Thank you. I'm sure he would be proud of who you've become," Castien said, taking her hand in his.

"I'm not ready for you to talk about him like that." Mylah took her hand from his. "I may have forgiven you for murdering my parents, but that doesn't give you the right to speak to me about them as if you didn't." Her nerves had her leg bouncing up and down.

"That's not what I was trying to do." Castien sighed and stood from the bed.

Mylah put her head into her hands. Her brain was a muddled mess, and she couldn't make heads or tails of her own thoughts. "Just leave me alone."

"Mylah," he tried, but Mylah shot up from the bed.

"Get out!" she screamed it at him, surprising herself with the ferocity of it. Castien hesitated but when Broderick opened the door, investigating the sound, Castien left the room. Broderick and Sabine blocked him from Mylah. Even if they were meant to be protecting her, they still worked for him.

"See to it that she is brought to the stables in an hour," Castien told Broderick, glancing back at Mylah before he left. His eyes were filled with concern, but her rage was all consuming.

"What was that about?" Broderick asked once the king was out of sight.

"Nothing...I just need a moment alone please," Mylah said, and they shut the door for her, respecting her wishes.

She had been pardoned by the king for treason. An act that had been met with execution in the past. Yet, she had lashed out and jeopardized her safety by practically threatening him. She couldn't explain why she had lost control of her anger after all this time, but it was a relief to finally let some of it out.

A while later, a knock jolted Mylah from her bed. Petra came carrying her weapons. She handed Mylah a belt with four knife holsters, two leg holsters to hold one dagger each, and a short sword to strap to her back.

"Thank you, Petra," Mylah hugged her, but Petra pulled away, confusion on her face. "Thank you for everything."

"What's gotten into you, girl?" Petra swatted her with one of the holsters. "Put these on and get moving. The others are already waiting by the stables." Petra hurried from the room.

Broderick and Sabine escorted Mylah to the stables. They would ride as far as the Adair border and wait there until Mylah and the others returned. Torin, Korriane, Killian, and Ana waited for them, already mounted on their horses. Castien was nowhere to be seen, and Mylah figured that was for the best. She still needed time to cool down before talking with him again.

"Ready?" Torin grinned at Mylah as she approached.

"As I'll ever be." She forced a smile as she mounted her horse. Broderick and Sabine followed suit. They took off at full speed.

Thirty One

It took half the time to get to the Adair border than it did to reach the Unbound territory. The sun had set when they reached it. They all slowed down, stopping completely where a rock wall had been built to signify the border line. Killian had scouted ahead to ensure Adair had no border patrols going through at that moment, but they had less than ten minutes before the next one showed up.

"This is where we say goodbye," Sabine announced. "There are more guards who will be meeting us nearby shortly. If anything goes wrong before you reach the village, Killian will signal us. After that, you're on your own." Mylah nodded. They had discussed this during preparations. Killian was the only one of them who had magic, so he would use it to send a signal to the others on the border if anything went wrong.

It would take Mylah's group another two hours before they reached the edge of the village. They would be able to travel full speed to Snake Head Lake, but beyond that, they would have to be much stealthier and slower.

"Stay safe," Broderick said, as Mylah and the others turned their horses back to the border and began making their way into the forest beyond. None of them spoke the entire ride to the Lake.

"This is it," Korriane's voice came out as a whisper. They were too close to Adair to make any unnecessary noise. There was no telling who may be out and about on such a clear night. "Killian will be able to sense if anything goes wrong from here. If it does, you know the plan." Mylah was envious of them being able to stay behind while she, Ana, and Torin walked into the heart of Adair.

Mylah, Ana, and Torin dismounted their horses and tied them to a nearby tree.

"Are you sure you're ready for this?" Torin asked them one more time and both Mylah and Ana nodded. "Good. Let's go." They picked their way carefully through the woods. Garrick's house was a thirty-minute walk from Snake Head Lake. Mylah, Greyson, and Cassia had frequented it as kids.

Every step they took closer to the town brought more anxiety and nerves to Mylah's gut. She took deep breaths, trying not to be too noisy. The first house they came to was her parents' old house. She bypassed it, trying not to dwell too much on the irony of what she was doing. Her parents had died to protect the book she was about to steal.

When Garrick and Elena's house came into view, Mylah stopped dead in her tracks. Torin paused and glanced back at her, waving her on. Ana hesitated beside Mylah, placing her hand on her arm in comfort.

"That's it," Mylah breathed, and Torin returned to her side. "The book is in there." She jerked her head towards the house. "I have to go alone from here." Torin found a spot for him and Ana to hide while Mylah tried to steel herself for what she was about to do. "You know the code," she said as she left them behind.

Torin would be listening intently to what was going on in the house. As a shreeve, his hearing was far superior to Mylah's. The code was that if she said the words 'the book is secure', the other two ran. If she said that, then the plan was to leave her behind and get back to Elowyn. Before they got the book, everyone escaping was the main goal so they could try again another day.

Mylah crept forward, sweeping the area ahead of her with her gaze. No one was out and about, but the lights were on inside the house, which meant Garrick and Elena were home, as she assumed they would be. She hurried to their front door and knocked as loud as she dared.

At first, no one answered. Mylah could hear movement inside, and she assumed they must be eating dinner. The door creaked open a crack and Garrick appeared.

"Mylah?" he said, looking from side to side to ensure she was alone. "What are you doing here?" Mylah couldn't help but smile when she saw him. She hadn't realized how much she missed her adopted family.

"Garrick, I need to talk to you," she said, as was planned. "May I come in?"

"Of course," Garrick said, but he hesitated before stepping aside and opening the door wide for her to enter. As he did, Mylah stepped over the threshold into the house. The door shut behind her, and Garrick led her into the sitting room. Mylah's heart stuttered as she rounded the corner and was met with King Florian, smiling at her from one of the armchairs. A group of his guards stood behind him.

"K-king..." he raised a finger to his lips to silence her, then motioned for her to sit beside him in the other chair. She did as instructed and then clasped her hands tightly in her lap. *We planned for this...we planned for this...* she recited in her mind as her heart threatened to beat out of her chest.

"I know," he said it so quietly, she knew he was aware they were being surveilled. Mylah gulped. "Talk only to Garrick," he spoke in the same hushed tone.

"Garrick, how are you?" Mylah asked.

"Well," he answered. He wore a grave expression and Mylah couldn't tell if he was upset with her, or with the situation. "I must admit I'm surprised you showed up here tonight."

"Yes, I understand," she glanced sideways at the king. "I needed to check with you about..." she paused and cleared her throat. "The book is secure, is it not?" she said a little too loudly, no one in the room seemed to notice her change in pitch. She prayed Torin had heard her so he and Ana could escape, otherwise they'd enact plan C.

"You know it is," Garrick said. "The king had it moved to a more secure location." Mylah dug her nails into her palms. She had suspected that might be the case. Her communications would have tipped him off that something was wrong, even though she had tried to cover up for her blunder.

"I'm glad," she feigned a smile. "I take it you interpreted my messages as intended," she said.

"I believe so." The guards began to move, and Mylah tensed.

"Should I be worried?" Mylah asked, turning a pleading gaze on Garrick, the only one in the room who may hold sympathy for her.

"My dear, whatever do you have to be worried about?" King Florian spoke. "You've done as you were told, you have uncovered the secret of the book and have come to deliver it to us. You will be recognized as a hero." He made no attempt to be quiet and Mylah wondered what had changed. "Guards," he waved them forward and they began a march out the door.

"Yes, yes," Mylah said and loosened her fists.

"And you have brought with you a war criminal." King Florian's eyes blazed and the grin on his face turned feral as the guards marched back into the house, Torin held aloft between three men. He was out cold. Mylah made no move. *We planned for this,* she repeated as Ana was carried in next, also unconscious. Mylah had no idea what had been done to them, but she prayed they were alright.

"I thought we deserved a little justice, after all of the evils the shreeve have committed," she changed her tone to match the king's, and firmly planted a mask of indifference on her face.

"Lovely, Mylah dear. The council will be thrilled to know you have returned safely, though I had on good authority that you were otherwise incapacitated." Something close to disappointment or anger flickered in King Florian's eyes and Mylah's blood ran cold. *He sent the assassin,* she realized. Her breathing became shallow, and her vision blurred. "Oh, and I almost forgot." He turned back to her, and two guards moved away from the rest to flank her. Her thoughts turned from the fact that her own king had tried to have her killed for a moment. "You're under arrest for attempting to steal an Adairian artifact."

Mylah held her mask of calm in place, but just barely. "That's ridiculous. I have the information I promised, and I delivered Elowyn's war general to you," her words came out slightly breathless. She stood and the guards each grabbed an arm, holding her back. "I'm not threatening the king, I'm telling him the facts," Mylah hissed at them. "Unhand me."

"Please, King Florian, has she not proven herself trustworthy to our kingdom?" Garrick stepped in, and Mylah shot him a look of gratitude, but he avoided her gaze.

"I will have her questioned by Bellingham. He will let me know whether she is to be trusted. Until then, she will remain in the castle's dungeon for safe keeping." The king strode out of the house, his guards following behind him, dragging Torin, Ana, and Mylah along with them.

The dungeons were just as horrible as Mylah remembered. She couldn't see Ana from where she was, but Torin stirred in the cell beside hers. Mylah inched closer to the bars that separated them but stayed far enough away not to provoke suspicion. She couldn't be caught talking with him. This was all a test from the king to prove she had betrayed them. No matter that the king had tried to have her killed, she had to get on his better side in order to break Torin and Ana out and returned safely to Elowyn. She tried to focus solely on that task.

"L-Leylah?" Torin croaked, rubbing his head as he opened his eyes. "Where are we?" Mylah closed her eyes and took a deep breath. She was about to make Torin hate her, and he may never forgive her. *It's all part of the plan*, she told herself. His true reactions to her reveal would make her lies for the king all the more believable.

"Shut it, general," she snapped.

"What?" Torin's eyes opened fully, and the look of confusion told Mylah he would be easily duped.

"*What?*" she mimicked. "It's over, my mission is over, and I have no use for you anymore."

"Leylah, what are you talking about?" Torin crawled over to the bars between them and lowered his voice. "Is this a part of the plan?" he whispered. Mylah could take no chances, there could be anyone hidden in the area, listening to them.

"My name's not Leylah," she growled. "And I want nothing more to do with you or any shreeve." She scooted away and crossed her arms over her chest.

"Okay, then what *is* your name?"

"As if I'd tell you my real name," she scoffed. "Leave me alone so I can spend my remaining time here in peace."

"I don't know what's going on, but I demand an explanation!" Torin bellowed. "I followed you across enemy lines, and if you're telling me that all along you've been playing me, and my king, I will *end you.*" Torin gripped the bars between them, and Mylah cringed. The bars were made of iron, so as a shreeve with fae blood in his system, they were probably causing Torin pain, but his anger was stronger.

"Then you're going to have to end me I guess." Mylah moved against the far wall as Torin hissed and unleashed his full strength on the bars separating them. They groaned but didn't break or bend. The dungeon had been built with the shreeve and fae in mind.

"Hey!" a guard shouted and ran down to their cells. "He's awake," he hollered back to the other guards. "Let the king know."

"What does the king have planned for the general?" Mylah asked the guard, but he gave her a scathing look and walked away.

"It seems you're equally as despised here as I am. It's fitting that you've become a traitor to both kingdoms now." The malice in Torin's voice had Mylah cringing, and she understood why he had been chosen to lead Castien's armies.

"I'm only here until I prove to the king that I'm still on his side, then I get to go home," Mylah sneered. "You, on the other hand, will be left here to rot."

"That's enough, Mylah," King Florian approached them, grinning from ear to ear. "Bellingham will question you now." A guard unlocked Mylah's cell and pulled her to her feet, gripping her hands behind her back as he pushed her forward.

"What will become of the general?" she asked as she walked by the king.

"You'll find out alongside the rest of the council, that is, if you are cleared by Bellingham. There is a meeting in the morning where the general's fate shall be determined."

"Good. I can't wait." Mylah leered into Torin's cell as she left. They led her past the fae she had met her first round in the dungeon, and he smirked at her. Beside him, Ana lay curled up on the floor, but she shared a wink with Mylah as she passed. Mylah's eyes widened in surprise, but she schooled her expression back to neutrality. She'd expected Ana to be mad at her, having overheard her conversation with Torin, but she didn't show that.

Bellingham flitted by Mylah's shoulder, peppering her with questions. So far, they had all been validation questions: her name, place of birth, parents' names, and a few others. He had a couple of sprites with him to ensure they would catch her lies, since he had trained her so well to hide them.

"Did you infiltrate the Elowyn castle?" he asked.

"Yes," Mylah answered.

"Did you meet King Castien?"

"Yes."

"Did you tell King Castien your true identity?" Mylah crafted her response quickly in her mind before answering to ensure she would not be caught in a lie.

"I did not reveal my identity to him," she stated. Elias had been the one who had revealed her identity, so it was not a lie.

"Did King Castien know you were not Leylah Farrow?" Bellingham was onto her.

"The king-"

"King Castien," Bellingham interrupted.

"King Castien suspected I was not who I claimed to be at first, but I gained his trust and convinced him he was wrong." For a while, anyway.

"Did you come to Adair to steal the shreeve book?"

"I agreed to come on a mission to retrieve the book, but I never planned to leave Garrick's house with it," she said, and Bellingham landed on the arm of the chair.

"Are you a traitor to this kingdom? Are you a traitor to Adair?" he stared intently into her eyes, trying to catch any hint of uneasiness.

"I am not a traitor," she outright lied as she stared back into Bellingham's eyes. "Everything I have done was for the good of the kingdom, and all of its inhabitants." Bellingham continued to stare at her, holding her gaze captive, until finally, he blinked and lifted himself from the arm of the chair.

"Everyone out. I need a moment alone with the girl." He never took his eyes from Mylah as the rest of the sprites left the room. He smiled at her once the room was clear and Mylah breathed a sigh of relief. "Something seems different about you, but I can't quite put my finger on it," he said. "Glad to have you back."

"It's good to be back," she smiled and realized she wasn't lying.

Thirty Two

Mylah was released from the confines of the castle but ordered to return the following morning for the council meeting. In the meantime, she could do whatever she pleased. While it was hard leaving the castle behind knowing that Ana and Torin were still in the dungeon, she looked forward to meeting Garrick again without the king's watchful eye.

A carriage was spared for Mylah to take her into town. It dropped her off at Garrick and Elena's house and she could hardly believe she was back there again, this time, as a renewed member of Adair's society. When she knocked on the door, Elena answered it.

"Mylah," she said, her eyes widening in surprise. "What are you doing here?" She glanced behind herself and kept the door half closed.

"I was cleared!" Mylah smiled and took a step forward, anticipating Elena opening the door.

"That's wonderful dear, but..." She turned her eyes away again. "I can't let you in, I'm sorry." Mylah gaped at her. The only consolation was that Elena did sound *truly* sorry.

"Elena, please, I have nowhere else to go," Mylah pleaded, but Elena shook her head.

"I'm so sorry, Mylah," she said, and tears glistened in her eyes. "If I'm seen..." she trailed off gazing pointedly into the surrounding trees. Mylah understood that they were being watched. Elena closed the door and Mylah heard the lock click into place. This had not been a part of her plan.

Mylah approached her parents' house reluctantly. She hadn't been inside since the night they were murdered. *Since the night Castien murdered them,* she thought. The door had been fixed and closed tightly, but it was unlocked. She pushed it open and watched as her familiar entryway and kitchen were revealed. The ache in her heart nearly brought her to her knees as she stepped inside and shut the door behind her.

It was dark. Someone had drawn all the curtains closed, but some light leaked in through them. Mylah set to opening all the curtains in the kitchen first. Then she went into the living room and opened those curtains. As she entered her father's study, she nearly threw up when she saw the bloodstains on the floor.

Her hand flew to her mouth as she closed her eyes and backed out of the room before racing out of the house. She settled on the front steps, reserved to sleep out there if she had to. The crunch of footsteps drew her eyes to the left, and she jumped up when she realized who emerged from the path. "Cassia!" she squealed.

"Mylah, you *are* here!" She ran to Mylah and threw her arms around her. "Thank the stars you're okay," she murmured against Mylah's shoulder.

"At least someone is happy I'm back," Mylah said as she pulled away from Cassia. "Elena turned me away at the door."

"Come, we shouldn't talk out here." Cassia tugged on Mylah's hand and led her back into her parents' home. Mylah could almost stand it since she wasn't alone.

"What's going on, Cass?" Mylah asked once they were safely inside.

"Things have gotten a little crazy around here since you left." Cassia sat at the dining room table with Mylah beside her.

"I've only been gone a few weeks," Mylah pointed out.

"Yeah, I know, and it's been awful." Cassia gave her a weak smile. "Someone on the council leaked that you were the attacker who was exiled," Cassia revealed.

"Oh no," Mylah put her head in her hands. "I can never show my face again."

"The entire council is convinced that you did it of your own accord and the king and Garrick could say nothing to the contrary for fear of exposing your mission, which they only just told us all about in a memo this morning! People thought you did it because of your traumatic past, and you wanted some kind of retribution," Cassia explained.

Mylah threw her hands up. "That's ridiculous!" Mylah groaned and leaned her head back.

"Trust me, I know! I may have squeezed all the details of your mission from Garrick while you were gone." She wrinkled her nose and raised her brows. "But now that the king has told everyone the truth, hopefully they will come around. But...there is something else." Cassia bit her lip.

"What, Cass, just tell me...please."

"That you were seen with the crown prince of Elowyn, and that you saved him," Cassia said.

"What do you mean? When was I seen with the prince?" Mylah wracked her brain. The only times she'd been alone with the prince outside of Elowyn was when they'd gone into the Unbound territory to find the naga and then to retrieve the items for Madame Edris.

"Greyson told the king and Garrick, who told me, that he saw you with the prince and you saved him from a siren."

"Of course I saved him! What was I supposed to do, let him get eaten?" Mylah scoffed. "And why was Greyson out there to begin with?" Cassia cast her eyes downward.

"He said he was on a scouting mission, but I know the truth, and you should too!" Cassia swatted Mylah's arm. "You didn't read the letter, did you?"

"It got ruined before I could, I swear, I planned on reading it." She wasn't sure if that was exactly true, but she hoped she would have mustered up the courage to do so.

"Well, if you had read it, you would have known Greyson had planned to meet you at the place where the River of Anguish turns towards the lake before you went off to Elowyn. He must have been visiting that spot as often as he could in case you showed up."

Mylah groaned. "He should have never done that..."

"Well, he did. He told the king that he feared you would not complete your mission, and the suspicion and undermining began. Garrick did everything he could to convince the king you were still on our side, but there was only so much he could do and say." Cassia let out a long sigh.

"Greyson is the cause of all this?" Mylah couldn't believe her oldest friend was the one who had turned their king against her.

"Don't blame him, Myles. He thought he was doing what was best. He came to me and told me everything he saw that day, and everything he heard. It was pretty convincing that you may have changed your allegiance." Cassia shrugged. "But, clearly you haven't, since here you are!" Mylah feigned a smile, hating that she couldn't be honest with her best friend.

"At least that means he's probably over me, right?" Mylah tried to find the silver lining.

"You'll have to talk to him about that to know for sure. Once he knows that he was wrong, he may fall for you all over again, if he ever fell out of love." Cassia glanced around at the house and a look of realization came over her. "This is the first time..."

"Yes. The...the blood stains are still in the floorboards." The air grew thick as she said it and her lungs labored to keep her breathing.

"Myles." Cassia pulled her into a hug. "Come stay with me. I can sneak you in through the window."

"No, I don't want to put you or your parents in that position. I'll be fine here. Besides, maybe after the council meeting, things can go back to normal. Once everyone knows that I'm not a traitor, and the king realizes Elias was wrong."

"Elias? Isn't that the prince of Elowyn?"

"Yes! I meant Greyson!" Mylah couldn't believe she had made that mistake. "Sorry, there's a lot on my mind." Elias in particular... she hoped he had recovered from using his magic.

"Can you tell me about Elowyn? What was it like? What were the royals like?" Cassia's eyes glowed with curiosity.

"It was beautiful," Mylah told her. "And you would die if you saw the gowns I wore while there," she laughed, and Cassia sighed in admiration. "The last one I wore would have been stunning on you." She thought of that blood red dress and how it would have complimented Cassia's skin tone magnificently.

"I'm sure you pulled it off fine," Cassia winked. "So, I'm assuming you attended parties there, if you were wearing all these amazing gowns?"

"Multiple. I even danced with the king." Mylah watched as Cassia's eyes widened.

"Isn't he a tyrannical asshole?"

"Not exactly," Mylah wasn't sure how much she should say, and she had to keep the secret of who killed her parents to herself. She was having enough difficulty dealing with that on her own, she didn't need anyone else's opinion.

"Come on, tell me everything," Cassia pressed.

"He is...different than I expected," Mylah tried to explain, but she didn't want Cassia to think she had grown to like any of the shreeve, especially the king.

"And the prince?"

"I don't think we should be talking about this anymore," Mylah said. "It doesn't matter much anyway, I'm home now." She forced a smile onto her face and Cassia smiled back.

"You're right." Cassia took Mylah's hands and squeezed them in her own. "I'm so excited the gang will be back together again tomorrow! We can spend the whole day together after the meeting."

"Wait, Greyson will be here tomorrow?"

"Yes, for the meeting. The king called him back to be present for the final decision about your status," Cassia said.

"I thought that decision was already made when they let me leave the castle?" Mylah realized that the king had never said she was free forever, just until the meeting. Her palms began to sweat, and her breaths became more rapid as panic set in.

"Don't worry Myles! You'll be cleared at the meeting, and everything will be fine!" Cassia tried to reassure her.

"Yeah, for sure," Mylah said. "Do you mind bringing a message to Garrick for me? I need to try to talk with him before the meeting." Cassia nodded. Mylah grabbed a pen and paper from Emil's study. She avoided looking at the floor and hurried out of the room as soon as she got what she needed. She scribbled a note for Garrick on the paper.

Garrick –

I have some important news about the book. I need to share it with you before I talk to the council tomorrow. Please meet me at my parents' house at your earliest convenience. I'll be here all night.

I hope you can forgive me and understand that I would never do anything to hurt you or your family – you are my family as well.

-Mylah

She handed the note to Cassia who stuffed it into the pocket of her dress.

"I'll go now, I have to be getting home before my parents notice I'm gone." Cassia stood and Mylah walked her to the door. "If you need anything, you know where to find me." She gave Mylah one last hug before she set out.

Mylah turned back to the empty house. She grabbed a bucket and a sponge from the kitchen closet and set to work on the blood stain in the study. She scrubbed it until the skin on her fingers was raw, and she swore the stain looked no different than when she started. She sat back on her heels, wiping the sweat from her brow.

"This is hopeless," she groaned and threw her sponge into the bucket. It splattered bubbles onto the floor, making the blood stain glisten as if it were fresh. Mylah's stomach roiled. She still hadn't stepped foot into her own room. She knew what she would find there, and she couldn't bear it. One blood stain was all she could handle for the day.

Darkness fell and Mylah realized she had no food for dinner. She couldn't go into town, or else she risked being driven out with pitchforks. The best she could do was hope that they had food at the council meeting in the morning.

A knock on the door sent shivers down Mylah's spine and caused goosebumps to raise on her arms and legs. She straightened up and stood tall as she opened the door and sagged in relief when she beheld Garrick standing on her doorstep.

"You came," she breathed. She stepped aside, allowing him to enter the house. He wore a stoic expression, not revealing any emotions. "I'm sorry for the intrusion last night."

"Let's not talk about that. What is it you wanted to tell me?" Garrick gazed around the room, looking at anything but Mylah.

"It's about the book, which is called the Book of Creation by the way," Mylah began, and Garrick finally looked at her. His eyes held sadness and she wondered if it was for her or because he was thinking about her parents.

"So, you were able to extract the information we needed?" he asked, glancing away again.

"Garrick, what is going on?" Mylah had had enough. Garrick was her family, her stand-in dad, and the only person she trusted in Adair. He sighed and beckoned for her to follow him to the living room where they sat on the couch.

"It's Greyson," he began. "What he told us about you and that shreeve. I didn't want to believe it, but he's my son. Please tell me that you aren't involved with the prince of Elowyn?"

"I can't," Mylah's voice was strained. Garrick was the one person she couldn't, *wouldn't*, lie to. He closed his eyes and pinched between his brows with his thumb and forefinger. "But that doesn't change the fact that I still care about you, Elena, Greyson, and Crane. I would never do anything that would bring any of you harm."

"That's not my concern, Mylah," Garrick sighed. "I'm worried about *you*. You can't trust the prince. You can't trust any of them. You certainly can't tell anyone else about this or they will condemn you tomorrow for sure."

"I won't, I promise," Mylah said, and she meant it. "You have to understand, though, they aren't nearly as bad as everyone thinks. King Castien is standoffish and rude, but he also cares deeply for his brother, and he spared me. He figured out who I was, and he didn't kill me, Garrick. He trusted me to come here and help his people retrieve the Book of Creation."

"I guess I should be thankful to him for that, but I cannot dismiss all of the horrible things he has done as king of Elowyn." An image of Mylah's parents flashed in her mind, and she pushed it away.

"I understand, I do. But all the rest of the kingdom has nothing to do with his acts. They are kind, decent people. They dislike him about as much as you do," Mylah told him.

"Is this why you asked me here?" Garrick's brows furrowed.

"No. I asked you here because I wanted you to be the first I told about the Book of Creation. You and my father were close, and I know that if anyone knew what he would advise me to do with the information I have, it would be you," Mylah said, gazing down at her hands, afraid to see Garrick's reaction.

"I will do my best."

"The Book of Creation contains a spell that could undo the original spell that created the shreeve. It could be used to destroy their entire race," Mylah explained, stroking the scar on her palm.

Garrick let out a low whistle. "Mylah," he paused and reached out to take her hand. "That is too big of a burden for you to carry. You don't need to place the fate of an entire race on your shoulders."

"Easier said than done." A smile tugged on her lips even as tears pricked her eyes.

"You want me to tell you whether to reveal this information at the meeting tomorrow," Garrick stated, and

Mylah bobbed her head. "Tell me more about your time in Elowyn." Mylah lifted her head, her eyes widening in surprise.

She recounted her entire trip, starting with Genevieve. Garrick asked a lot of questions about Genevieve, interested to hear about his old friend. The rest of the time, he remained quiet, nodding his head from time to time.

When she finished her story, Garrick appeared thoughtful as he took it all in. Mylah didn't dare speak as she waited for his response.

"It sounds like you made a new life for yourself," he smirked, and Mylah shook her head.

"No! No, I could never leave you all behind," she protested but Garrick put up his hand to stop her.

"Mylah, I'm happy for you. You were so consumed with vengeance and grief while you were here, but it seems like Elowyn brought you back to your true self." Garrick's words made something spark in Mylah and she realized he was right. As much as she was worried about being discovered, or exacting her revenge on Castien, she had enjoyed herself for the first time in a long time. She'd made new friends, found a man she may be able to fall in love with, and given her life a new purpose: helping the Elowyns instead of ending a life.

"So, what do you think I should do?" Mylah asked the question she was dreading hearing the answer to.

"As Emil's stand in, which I am honored to be, I would suggest withholding your information from the council." He put an arm around her shoulders. "From your tale, I can tell that we may not be as informed about the shreeve as we thought. The information in that book could be lethal in the wrong hands." Garrick seemed to be contemplating something and Mylah pulled away from him slightly to take in his full expression.

"What is it?" she asked.

"The Book of Creation, it was never moved," Garrick said, and Mylah's eyes widened as she realized what he was saying. "I should be going. Elena and I are heading out early tomorrow for the meeting, the king wants to talk to me privately." He winked at Mylah before leaving the room. "I'll see you at the meeting."

"Yes!" Mylah said, a little too excited. "Yes, I will see you tomorrow."

Thirty Three

Mylah waited, hunched behind a bush outside Garrick and Elena's house. She'd made sure no one was watching her that morning before heading to their house. The carriage had already been pulled around for Garrick and Elena. Mylah watched as they left the house together. Garrick ushered Elena to the carriage as he shut the front door behind him. It bounced slightly and Mylah realized he had left it open a crack. She smirked.

Once the carriage was out of sight, Mylah dashed to the front door and pushed it open. She shut it behind her and ran to the safe room. There was a lock securing the door, but she found the key easily. It had been moved since she'd lived there, but not far. Before, the family portrait had been used to conceal it, but this time it had been hidden behind the portrait of Garrick and Elena.

The lock thunked as it fell to the floor and Mylah cursed herself. She needed to be quiet, anyone could be lurking around, especially if the king still suspected she may try to steal the book. She pulled the door open and found the book inside, as Garrick had said it would be. She slid it up under her shirt. She had chosen an oversized tunic for this mission so it would be easier to conceal the book in case she ran into anyone on her way back to her parents' house.

As fast as she was in, she was back out of the house. She did a sweep of the area before stepping outside, and then casually strolled back home. Thankfully, the only people who lived on the outskirts of town were the council members, and their houses were well spread out. Mylah didn't come across anyone as she made her way home.

Once inside, she hurried to her room, turning a blind eye to the blood stains on the floor, and pried up the floorboard beside her bed. It had always been loose, but she'd never had use for a hiding place before. Now, she placed the Book of Creation inside and replaced the floorboard. She let out a breath of relief once the book was concealed. *Phase one complete*, she thought. Now, she just had to attend the meeting to keep up appearances before she rescued Torin and Ana and left Adair.

A knock on the door had Mylah in a panic. She swore no one saw her coming back from Garrick's, but then again, she had been in a hurry and could have missed a spy. She swapped out her tunic for a more fitted one and headed to the front door, careful to school her expression into casual indifference.

She opened the door and gasped as she took in the sight of Greyson on her doorstep. For a moment she flashed back to when they were fourteen and he would come to her door with Cassia, picking her up on their way to the lake, or into town.

"Hi," she said. It came out as a whisper and Mylah cursed herself for being so affected by his familiar presence. He had betrayed her and turned the king against her. No doubt it was soon after his revelation that the king decided to send an assassin to Elowyn.

"Hi," he responded, casting his eyes downward and running his hand through his shaggy hair. "Dad mentioned you might need a ride to the castle." He stepped back, revealing the horse waiting outside.

"Why are you here, Greyson?" Mylah asked, fiddling with her mother's ring that still sat on her finger. She hadn't had the heart to take it off.

He furrowed his brows. "I told you; to take you to the castle."

"I understand that. You know what I mean. Cass told me what you did." Mylah crossed her arms over her chest and stared him down until he threw his arms up in surrender.

"I'm sorry, Myles. You have to know I didn't mean to turn the king against you. I was just reporting what I saw. I sent you that letter," he trailed off and his eyes went to the ring on her hand. She turned the stone inward and clenched her fist.

"I never read your stupid letter!" Mylah burst out. "I couldn't do it and then it got ruined in the river, and..." she shrugged. "And that was that."

The hurt was clear in Greyson's eyes. "Why couldn't you read it?" Confusion creased his brow.

"I was scared," Mylah admitted. "I was worried you were professing your love for me, and I couldn't bear it knowing I didn't feel the same way." It was finally out, and she felt a weight lift off her chest, but it was shortly replaced by grief that their friendship was probably coming to an end.

"Oh," he let out a huff of air and stepped back, clutching the railing on the steps. "I-I don't know what to say."

"Tell me I'm wrong. Tell me you didn't tattle on me to the king because you were jealous of Elias. Tell me I've created a whole story in my head and that you don't love me," Mylah's voice had an edge, as she almost pleaded with Greyson.

"I can't tell you any of those things." He took another step back. "I love you, Mylah, and I *was* jealous of the prince, but that's not why I told the king what I saw. I was doing my duty as a soldier of Adair."

"You were doing your duty," Mylah scoffed, shaking her head. "You could have trusted me, Greyson." Even though he had been right about her feelings for Elias, his betrayal stung. And now...now she prayed she was still doing the right thing.

"We need to get to the meeting," Greyson tried to change the subject.

"Go on ahead. I'll find my own way there," Mylah said. Greyson looked at her incredulously but turned away when she didn't budge. It was for the best, ending her friendship with Greyson now would spare him some of the heartache when she betrayed them all later.

"Take my horse," Greyson said as he patted the horse's side. "It will be easier for me to find a ride elsewhere." *Thanks to you,* Mylah thought, but she said nothing as he strode away.

Mylah handed the reins of Greyson's horse to the castle's stable boy. He avoided her gaze and she assumed he knew who she was. Everyone she had passed on her way there had either balked at her or cast their eyes away. She marched inside; her head held high.

The council chamber was already filled with all the members when she walked through the doors. All eyes turned to her as if she had interrupted something, but no one said a word. She strode down the aisle to find an empty seat away from everyone else. She wasn't going to give them the satisfaction of thinking she was nervous.

King Florian strode to his throne shortly after and everyone turned away from Mylah to look towards him. Mylah gripped the arms of her chair as she awaited the start of the meeting.

"As you all know by now, Mylah Orson has returned from Elowyn. And, you know that she was sent there, not exiled." He gazed out towards the faces of his council. "So, our first order of business will be to determine whether we believe her to be fit to return to Adairian society."

"How do we know she can be trusted?" someone called out from the right side of the room. Mylah craned her neck, trying to see who it was. *Probably Leandre, she's always been a pot-stirrer*, Mylah thought.

"Very good question," the king beckoned with his hand and Bellingham flew up beside him. "Bellingham has questioned her extensively. I will allow him to present his findings."

"After a thorough questioning, with myself and some of my best lie detectors, we have determined," he paused, and Mylah wondered if it was for dramatic effect. "Everything she told us was the truth. She is still loyal to Adair and its citizens." It seemed like one collective breath of relief echoed throughout the room. "And we will be keeping a close watch on her for a few weeks, to ensure nothing changes." Anger bubbled in Mylah's stomach. That would make it difficult for her to carry out her escape plan, but she was determined to find a way.

"She also delivered to us Elowyn's war general," the king added. "And has valuable information from behind enemy lines." A few oohs and ahhs floated around the room. "So, now you will determine her fate. All those in favor of reinstating Mylah as a citizen of Adair," he waited as almost everyone in the room raised their hands. "All those opposed," a few council members raised their hands and Mylah noted their faces, so she'd know who to avoid later. "Then, it's decided. Mylah Orson is once again a citizen of Adair." He clapped his hands together with finality.

A few grumbles were heard, but most people seemed unaffected by the decision.

"Onto our next order of business." The king waved to his guards who disappeared behind the door and reappeared with Torin struggling between them. He had iron shackles on his ankles, wrists, and around his waist. Iron chains connected them all together. Mylah had no doubt that were Torin not shackled and weakened by the iron, he could take on everyone in the room and get out unscathed.

"The war general," she heard someone whisper nearby.

"Elowyn's war general. The man behind most of the atrocities that have occurred along our border with Elowyn," the king's voice boomed through the chamber.

"*Atrocities*," Torin scoffed, spitting onto the ground.

"Do not speak unless spoken to," King Florian snarled. "Our council will decide what your punishment will be." The only punishments Mylah could think of were either spending the rest of his days in the dungeon, or execution. She prayed for the former because that would give her more time to adjust her plans.

"Send him to the gallows!" Mylah heard someone roar.

"To the dungeons!" another member hollered.

"Torture him like he's done our soldiers!"

"It seems we have some options here," King Florian smirked and Mylah's stomach roiled. "All those in favor of sending him to the gallows." A handful of members raised their hands. "And those in favor of the dungeons." Mylah couldn't tell if there were more or less people with their hands raised. "As for the torture," a few people raised their hands before he finished speaking. "We don't lower ourselves to that level."

"Not openly, anyway," someone to Mylah's left muttered. She turned to see one of the council members, Magdalena Fable, sneering as she gazed up at Torin.

"It seems as if we have a tie. In that case, we will send him back to the dungeons until our next meeting and we will vote again then," the king said, shooing the guards off the stage. "Now, there is one more thing we must decide. Guards, please bring the next one out." Mylah turned stone cold when King Florian's eyes found hers and he gave her a wicked grin. This was not the king she remembered.

The guards hauled Torin away to the dungeon and returned, dragging someone else between them. Mylah assumed they would bring out Ana next, but she couldn't tell who it was until the guards brought them up on stage and lifted their head for all to see.

Her heart clenched and she forgot how to breathe.

"Elias," she let slip and a few heads turned to her. Every muscle in her body screamed at her to go to him, to save him, but she couldn't. If she made one wrong move, they would all know she was a liar and a traitor.

"Please welcome, the *prince* of Elowyn, Prince Elias." The king opened his arms wide, and laughter filled the room. "Found attempting to steal from us alongside his war general."

Mylah closed her eyes, trying to pretend that none of it was real.

"His fate will be determined at our next meeting as well, we have some questions we want to ask him before we make any final decisions," King Florian said, and Mylah relaxed a little. Whatever plans she had before, they all went out the window. Rescuing Torin and Ana was one thing but rescuing the prince...he was bound to be much more heavily guarded.

Mylah watched as King Florian whispered something in Elias' ear making Elias' eyes flare wide as he tried to wrench himself free of the guards. The king laughed and signaled the guards to haul Elias away. The rest of the meeting, she was too distracted to pay any attention. Her mind whirled as she tried to think of how she would get to Elias. She didn't even notice when the council members began filing out of the chamber.

"Mylah," Garrick's voice broke through to her. She whipped her head up. "Come, we're taking you home." He put his arm around her, holding her steady as she used all her focus and energy to stay calm.

Once they were in the safety of Garrick's carriage, Elena wrapped Mylah in a hug.

"I'm so sorry about yesterday," she said through her tears. "The king ordered all of the council members to stay away from you until after the meeting. He didn't want any of us to be swayed by you."

"I understand," Mylah said, hugging her back.

"Elena, let the girl breathe," Garrick chuckled. "Besides, we need to talk fast before we reach the house. Greyson will be there, and I don't trust him with what we are about to discuss." Mylah was taken aback. Elena was also in shock, but she said nothing. "I gather that was the prince you told me about last night," Garrick said and Mylah bowed her head, her cheeks blazing. "So, I assume you are going to need my help."

"I would never ask that of you," Mylah protested. She had planned on acting alone.

"It's a good thing I'm not waiting for you to ask then. The next council meeting is in four days."

"So, we only have three days," Mylah stated. "I already have a plan."

"What are you two..." Elena trailed off. "Hosath help us all," she shook her head, but Mylah noticed the smile tugging at her lips.

"I was thinking of asking Bellingham for help," Mylah suggested. "I know it seems crazy, but I think he'd be willing to do it."

"We can't trust anyone else, Myles," Garrick pursed his lips.

"I lied to him, and he didn't tell the king. It's possible I'm a good enough liar to fool him, but I don't think so. He trained me and he knows all my tells. I think we can trust him."

"I don't think we should risk it..." Garrick narrowed his eyes and shook his head.

"Please, we need all the help we can get."

Thirty Four

Elias flickered in and out of consciousness. When he was awake, he was aware of a fire burning in his veins, as if every nerve were being torched by an unseen force. So, he sought out unconsciousness to save himself from the agony. Whatever he had been given to cause the excruciating pain made it easy for him to dissociate from his waking self. But every time he found that peace, he was bombarded with memories that brought him a different kind of pain.

Elias rolled out of bed to find that Mylah had gone. It seemed as if she had been there only moments before, but he had no idea how long he had been unconscious. Though he still didn't feel at his best, most of his strength had returned. He started towards the stairs that would lead him out of his tower when he heard Castien approaching. He would always recognize Castien's footsteps.

"You're awake," Castien commented as he entered the room, giving Elias a once over. "You look better."

"Well enough to join the mission, I'd say," Elias tried, even though Castien had been set against him going from the start.

"Out of the question." Castien waved his hand in the air, dismissing the suggestion. "Even if you weren't still recovering."

"Why won't you let me go? I could be of use!" Elias yelled, frustration building as he thought of all the times Castien had denied him helping his kingdom for fear of him getting hurt.

"I can't, I can't." Castien shook his head, his face turning red.

"You can't or you won't? I'm not a child, I'm twenty years old, I've trained since I was eight...I can handle myself." Elias had been primed since the day he was born to be a soldier. He should have known that his father never meant for him to have the crown.

"I can't lose you! I've already lost everyone else," Castien's voice broke.

"Why...why do you care so much about me...I'm not even your real brother." Elias had never said the words aloud. Neither of them had, and Castien's head whipped towards him.

"Don't say that. I've always considered you a brother, no matter what blood runs through our veins. I will always protect you and fight for you." Castien placed his hands on Elias' shoulders.

"I don't deserve that!" Elias yelled, shaking Castien off.

"What do you mean?"

Elias tried to calm himself, lowering his voice and taking a deep breath. "I don't deserve your protection or your concern."

"If anything, I don't deserve yours! I abandoned you! If I hadn't left you alone with our father..."

Elias cut him off. "He wasn't our father."

"If I hadn't left you alone with him, none of this would have happened! He'd probably still be alive and well, murdering innocent women who fail to produce him an acceptable heir. Because everyone knows neither of us were a top choice for him." Castien threw his hands in the air as he paced across Elias' room.

"You didn't abandon me," Elias' voice lowered to a whisper. "You needed to get away from this place. Because of..."

"Because of Sascha," Castien finished. "Yeah," he dragged his hands through his hair. "I was selfish."

"No! You've never been selfish...dammit! You're not listening to me!" Elias ran his hands over his face. "I don't deserve your pity or concern or whatever it is that's made you so concerned for my well-being."

"Don't be ridiculous, I don't pity you. I care about you!"

"Well, you shouldn't! I'm the reason Sascha is dead." Those words stopped Castien. Elias knew they would. Castien's face grew slack, and confusion replaced his determination

"King Haldor killed Sascha. I watched him do it," he ground out.

"But the reason he knew that you two were together, was because I told him," Elias admitted, a weight lifting off his chest as he said the words aloud. "I saw how happy you were, and I didn't know what he would do..." Elias thought back to that moment, when he was eight years old, hopping from foot to foot, so excited to be sharing what he thought to be good news with his supposed father. He shook his head, trying to forget the memory.

"You told him? You were the one..." Castien's head tilted to the side and his shoulders drooped as tears filled his eyes. "I thought it had been one of the servants, or maybe someone in town who had seen us..." Elias could almost feel Castien's heart breaking all over again. His own chest ached, and the pain stole his breath.

"It was me. I wanted you to be happy. I thought our father, the king, whatever he was...I thought he'd want that too. I was young, and stupid..." Elias had done many stupid things when he was young, but this was the one that haunted him the most.

"He never would have let us be together..." Castien murmured.

"I know that now." Elias wished more than anything that he could go back in time and change what had happened, but there was nothing he could do. Sascha had been the love of Castien's life, and Elias had stolen her from him by revealing their love to King Haldor.

"Just go..." Castien whispered. Elias didn't wait around for him to change his mind. He fled the room, heading straight for the armory. He would have stayed, would have comforted his brother, promised to make up for all his wrongdoings and stupidity...if Leylah weren't in danger. He'd never had something he wanted to live and fight for so badly, and she had given him that. Her words rang in his ears, You barely know me, and it brought a smile to his face. How wrong she was. After a few short weeks with Leylah, he felt he knew her better than almost anyone else, other than Castien. Maybe he was crazy to already feel as if he were falling for her, but he didn't care. The exhilaration of that fall brought him more joy than he'd ever felt. If he had to risk his life and journey into enemy territory to ensure she returned to Elowyn safely, that was what he would do.

He took one of the fastest horses they had and took off towards Adair. He knew where Sabine and Broderick would be on the border and he avoided them, along with Korriane and Killian at the lake. Leaving his horse untied to wander back towards Elowyn, he ventured in the general direction Leylah had told them they would find the book.

Before the house even came into view, he'd been apprehended. A dart of some sort had hit him square in the chest and the effects of it were almost immediate. His magic had been quelled and his strength sapped. Exhaustion overcame him, but someone caught him before he hit the ground. Voices filtered through his haze.

"Don't move or we will kill him," the man holding Elias declared. Elias tried his best to access any part of his magic or strength, but he failed.

"Carry them in," he heard someone else say and then a ringing filled his ears.

His eyes flew open, and he was back in the present. The pain had lessened, but it still raged through his body. The memory of Leylah...*Mylah*...caused fury to pulse beneath his skin, overriding the fire that burned away his magic.

King Florian knew his secret. A secret he had only ever told one person outside of Elowyn. Mylah had betrayed him in the worst way possible. He would be sure to repay the favor if he ever saw her again.

Thirty Five

Garrick had to meet with the king the following day, so he agreed to arrange a meeting for Mylah with Bellingham. In the meantime, Mylah did her best to avoid Greyson, which was easy enough since he had accompanied Garrick to his meeting.

Mylah spent the day in her parents' house, studying the Book of Creation.

That night, Elena called everyone to a family dinner. Once they were all seated around the table, silence and tension filled the room. Mylah kept her eyes trained on her plate and spared a glance at Garrick as he passed her the salt.

"This is unbearable," Elena broke the silence. "Can we just agree that Greyson made a mistake and let everything go back to normal?" she pleaded. For her sake, Mylah lifted her head and smiled at Greyson across the table. He grimaced and Elena sighed.

"How did your meeting with the king go?" Elena asked Garrick, giving up on the other two.

"Fine, nothing new to report," Garrick informed them.

"And, Greyson, did you speak with the king as well?" Elena asked.

"Actually, I did. While dad spoke with Bellingham about something, the king asked me to join the royal guard." Mylah's head shot up and Garrick coughed as he choked on the water he'd been drinking.

"That's great honey!" Elena grinned, not realizing what Mylah and Garrick had already figured out.

"Yeah. He wants me to guard the prince of Elowyn while he's in the castle."

"You told him no," Mylah said, and Greyson furrowed his brow.

"Why would I do that? I would never turn down a request from the king." Greyson stared her down and Mylah refused to blink first.

"If the king asked you to jump off a cliff, would you?" Mylah challenged and Greyson scoffed.

"If it would help our kingdom, I'd consider it."

"Son!" Garrick slammed his fist on the table, making both Greyson and Mylah blink. "I didn't raise you to blindly follow anyone, even the king. Do not let his position cloud your judgement."

"So, you're saying I *shouldn't* accept the position on the royal guard?" Greyson turned on his father.

"Not at all! I'm just saying that you need to make decisions for yourself. Don't let the king, or anyone else for that matter, decide what's best for you or what's right." Garrick unclenched his fist, relaxing.

"Why do I feel like you're hiding something from me?" Greyson glanced between Garrick and Elena. Mylah shrank in her seat, hoping he wouldn't fix his gaze back on her.

"Greyson, darling." Elena reached out and covered his hand with her own. "Your father and I only want what's best for you. We are proud of you and will support you whether you choose to join the royal guard or not." Greyson accepted the explanation and returned to eating.

"I guess it would make life easier, following the king's demands like a lost puppy," Mylah said, smirking. Greyson's head whipped up and she met his gaze.

"At least I'm not a traitorous bitch," as soon as the words left his mouth, his eyes widened in acknowledgement of his mistake. "Mylah, I'm-"

"No," she stood from the table. "I don't want to hear anything else you have to say." She left the room and the house in a calm manner, but once outside, she broke out into a run. She heard Garrick calling her name, but she kept moving. She ran home, throwing the front door open and hurtling herself into her parents' bedroom, the one place she hadn't allowed herself to enter yet. She curled up in a ball in their bed and sobbed.

It was her fault; she'd egged Greyson on. She didn't even know why she did it, maybe spite. It didn't matter, though. It was the final straw for her. Losing Greyson, losing his trust, his friendship, his love... it hurt more than she could have imagined. Nothing would ever be the same between them.

"You left the front door open," Garrick's voice echoed through the house as he entered and shut the door behind him. Mylah heard his footsteps as he approached the bed and felt his weight on the edge as he laid a hand on her shuddering shoulder. "You know Greyson didn't mean what he said," Garrick tried, but Mylah's whole body continued to shake from sobs.

"H-he may n-not mean it *yet*," she managed to get out.

"He'll understand someday. Maybe not right away, but someday. Trust me."

"I feel awful." Mylah sat up, pulling her knees to her chest, and wiped her tears away as they continued to fall. "I'm lying to everyone. I lied to Torin to make him believe I'd betrayed him. I lied to the council to make them believe I *hadn't* betrayed them."

"You are doing what's necessary to save lives. Not everyone would have the courage to take the risks you're taking," Garrick praised her.

"You do realize that we're going to have to fight Greyson to get to Elias," Mylah said what they had both been thinking when Greyson made his announcement. "You can't choose between your son and a prince you've never met."

"We'll cross that bridge if we come to it. I won't hurt my son, but that doesn't mean he can't be reasoned with," Garrick suggested. "I fear his allegiance to the king is too solid to break in a few days' time. Hopefully, the heat of the moment will force him to remember family should come first."

"I hope you're right," Mylah murmured.

"Come on, let's take a walk." Garrick stood and held his arm out to Mylah. She slipped her arm through his and let him support her as they left the house. "It's a beautiful night for a walk to the lake," he said a little too loudly and Mylah realized they were being watched.

"Pa and I used to take this walk all the time," Mylah responded. They hadn't, but she wanted whoever was watching to think Garrick was just consoling Mylah in a weak moment.

"Yes, I remember him telling me that."

"I miss him terribly." Mylah didn't have to fake the tears that welled in her eyes.

"As do I," Garrick said, patting her arm. They fell into a comfortable silence and Mylah could sense that whoever was watching them wasn't continuing to follow. They must have been bored with the prospect of taking a walk down memory lane. After a few more minutes, Garrick relaxed.

"I believe we're safe now, but we should still be cautious," he spoke quietly. "Bellingham is waiting nearer the lake."

"I knew he'd agree to help." A smile spread across her face. At least one thing was going right.

"He agreed to meet with you, not to help. Not yet," Garrick warned.

"I'll convince him." Mylah was determined. Without Bellingham, it would be near impossible to pull off their prison break.

As they approached the lake, Bellingham fluttered into view. He cast his eyes about, checking to ensure they had not been followed.

"What a nice surprise," he said, loud enough for any prying ears to hear. "I must say, it is a particularly beautiful night."

"Indeed, it is. We're out for a stroll to the lake, care to join?" Garrick offered. Mylah found it all so preposterous, but she supposed it may be necessary. There was no telling what manner of creatures may be out there spying for the king.

"Thank you," Mylah murmured to Bellingham as he hovered by her shoulder.

"Let's hear it," he pressed, his eyes darting to their surroundings every few seconds.

"I haven't returned to stay," Mylah began. "I truly did come to retrieve the Book of Creation for the shreeve. It contains a spell that would reverse the one that created their entire race. Some may survive if it were to be used, but most would die."

"I see," Bellingham said, and Mylah took that as her cue to continue.

"I need your help to get into the castle so I can break out Torin and Elias. Then we'll be returning the book to Elowyn."

"I see," he repeated. "Why should I risk myself to help you and the shreeve?"

"Because we will be saving countless lives," Mylah said, hoping that was enough to convince him.

"And Garrick, you are caught up in this as well?" Bellingham moved between them.

"I am. I trust Mylah," Garrick said.

"It isn't about trusting Mylah, but the shreeve who gave her this information... I have to think about it," Bellingham pointed out.

"I understand," Mylah said. She understood what it was like to go against everything you'd believed in your entire life.

"Whether I help you or not, I will not betray your plans to the king. It is the least I can do, in case it turns out you are correct about the book."

"Thank you," Mylah let out a gasp of relief. "It means everything that you trust me at least that much. Whatever you decide, I will be there two days from now."

"I will inform you of my decision and the role I shall play before then," Bellingham promised. "In the meantime, I must return to the castle before the king notices my absence. Good luck to you both, and may no harm come to either of you."

"Same to you," Mylah and Garrick said in unison. Bellingham disappeared into the night while Mylah and Garrick finished their walk to the lake.

Thirty Six

The next morning, Mylah found a note beside her pillow. *I will help. West wing entrance, midnight.* Her heart soared as she read Bellingham's words. She may be able to pull off the near-impossible rescue after all.

A knock on the door stole her from her bed. Cassia stood on her doorstep, a bag of goodies in hand.

"I brought breakfast!" she sang as she shouldered her way past Mylah into the house. "Come, sit!" She made herself comfortable on the couch in the sitting room and patted the cushion beside her for Mylah to join.

"What's going on?" Mylah asked as she sat beside Cassia and grabbed a tart from the bag.

"What, as if I need an occasion to visit my best friend?" A smile remained plastered on her face, but her eyes shifted from left to right, and Mylah knew something was off. "I heard a rumor," Cassia whispered.

"These are delicious," Mylah said, leaning in closer to Cassia.

"The king has you under constant surveillance. I saw one of his men outside just now," Cassia informed her.

"I suspected as much. I felt them following me last night," Mylah said.

"That's not all," Cassia glanced around again as if expecting to see one of the king's men in a corner of the room. "They're planning to put you on trial again with the shreeve. One of the council members mentioned that they still had some doubts, and the king was all too willing to put you back on the chopping block."

"Do you think they'll ever believe me?" Mylah asked, even though it didn't matter if they wanted to interrogate her again, she'd be gone before the trial if everything went as planned. Cassia chewed her lip before she wrapped Mylah in a hug.

"You're not safe here," the waver in Cassia's voice betrayed her emotions. "How did it all go so wrong?"

"I'm sorry Cass," Mylah hugged her back. "I never meant for it all to turn out like this."

"Will you go back to Elowyn?" she asked, and Mylah turned hot. A sudden realization came over her as she hugged her best friend.

"Why would I do that?" Mylah pulled back and gave Cassia a skeptical look.

"I thought that maybe..." Cassia trailed off and her face flushed. "Don't hate me, Myles," she stood up from the couch.

"Why would I hate you? What's going on Cass?" Mylah stood beside her. Cassia pulled open her jacket and revealed a small button placed on her shirt. To anyone else it appeared to be the symbol of Adair, but Mylah knew that it had been enhanced with magic somehow.

What is that? she mouthed to Cassia.

I'm sorry, they're listening, Cassia mouthed back. Mylah threw her hands up in frustration.

"You're being ridiculous. I could never be mad at you," Mylah improvised.

"I was worried things had changed," Cassia said after mouthing, *Thank you.*

"This is my home, I could never leave," Mylah walked towards the window and peeked outside. She thought she saw movement among the trees. "The shreeve will get what they deserve, and I will prove myself loyal, once again."

"I know you will," Cassia said, joining her by the window. "I have to get going, my mother is expecting me." Cassia hugged Mylah again. "They have Crane," Cassia whispered in her ear low enough so those listening wouldn't hear. She pulled away and Mylah searched her face for any other information. Sadness and fear were all that she found.

"It will all be okay," Mylah said. Cassia left the house and Mylah walked out after her, scanning the area. As Cassia had told her, there was a figure watching from the trees. Mylah waved to him and continued to Garrick's house. "You're probably supposed to remain a bit more concealed," she called back to the king's man. He didn't respond, but he followed her down the road.

At Garrick's, Mylah knocked on the door and he ushered her inside.

"I guess you heard," he said as they entered the sitting room where Elena sobbed on the couch. "I received word this morning that Crane had been taken in for 'suspicious behavior.' In essence, if we try anything, he is the collateral." Garrick collapsed beside his wife on the couch and dropped his head into his hands.

"I understand if you can't help me anymore. I'll make sure to free him if I can." Mylah sat opposite them in the armchair.

"Oh," Elena lifted her head and wiped her tears. "Garrick's helping. If the king thinks," she took a breath, "that he can take *both* my boys away from me," she shuddered.

"Elena, I don't want to put Crane or Greyson at risk," Mylah countered. "If it's just me, the king will have no reason to believe either of you were involved and he'll let them go."

"If you think that, Myles, you know nothing of King Florian," Garrick said, shaking his head. "We've been blessed these past few years to have had him as a king, for sure. He's done many great things for our kingdom. But his past...there's a reason we have such a strained relationship with the shreeve. It started long before he became king. When he was a commander for his father's army, he did some terrible things."

Mylah's mind flashed to the journal she had read, and the mention of shreeve turning up dead near the border...*tortured and battered, before being dumped in our territory.* She shivered.

"He used to torture shreeve, didn't he?" Mylah whispered, closing her eyes, and trying not to picture what was happening to her friends in the dungeon.

"Yes. He and...and your grandfather," Garrick's voice grew quiet. Mylah's eyes flew open.

"My grandfather?" she questioned. She hadn't known any of her grandparents since they'd all died before she was born, or just after. Emil had talked about his parents sometimes, but Vita *never* mentioned her parents.

"Yes, your mother's father. He was a horrible man. He hated shreeve almost as much as King Florian," Garrick continued. "It's a wonder your mother turned out as sane as she did."

"You're going to give her a bad impression," Elena chided.

"No, I need to hear this," Mylah said. "What about my mother's mother? My grandmother?"

"She was lovely," Elena spoke over Garrick. "The poor thing lost her second child, though she *was* past the safe age to bear one at the time."

"Mother never told me that...though she never told me *anything* about her past." Mylah yearned to speak to her mother more than ever, but Elena and Garrick were the closest she could get.

"Well, she was ashamed of her father, rightfully so," Elena's voice quieted, and her gaze drifted down the floor. "Her father being who he was, and then her mother..."

"You said her mother was lovely," Mylah reminded her.

"Oh yes," Elena smiled but sadness dwelled in her eyes. "She was, but she had an affair." In that moment, everything clicked in Mylah's mind. The stories all meshed together, and it all made sense.

"With a shreeve," Mylah filled in the blanks, surprising Elena and Garrick.

"Yes," Elena said.

"The baby wasn't lost," Mylah said, talking more to herself, though Elena and Garrick hung on her every word. "*Jacinda* brought the baby to the father, General Ansel of Elowyn. The baby, Sascha, was raised in the Elowyn castle by a wonderful woman named Petra."

"So, she lives?" Elena smiled and Garrick laughed.

"No," Mylah winced as she spoke. "The king killed her because she and Castien had fallen in love."

"Castien...isn't that the new king?" Garrick asked and Mylah nodded. "And so, King Haldor created the monster..."

"He's not a monster!" Mylah snapped, surprising everyone, even herself.

"We know that, dear," Elena soothed Mylah, placing her hand on Mylah's arm. "Who are we to judge King Castien when our own king is..."

"Trying to commit a mass murder?" Mylah suggested. "He's known what was in the book all along, hasn't he?" Mylah said, realizing that all King Florian wanted was the translation so he could begin the spell to end the shreeve race.

"I didn't know it at the time," Garrick began. "But I suspect that he did. He wanted you to go into Elowyn and learn the translation and the elements needed for that spell. There is no reasoning with him, he wants to end the shreeve forever."

"Did..." Mylah gulped. "Did Pa know, too?" Her father had helped the shreeve in the past, but that didn't mean he wouldn't have translated the book for his king regardless of the consequences.

"No, Mylah. No one besides the king knew," Garrick said, placing his hand on her arm. "Your father was a good man and would never have put so many people in harm's way like that."

"Thank you," Mylah whispered. There was no telling whether Garrick was right, but in her heart, she knew; her father would have made the same decision she had made. To save the shreeve. "So, our breakout plan can't wait. There's no telling what King Florian's doing to Torin, Ana, and Elias..." Mylah's mind whirled with the possible horrors they were experiencing right at that moment.

"He won't hurt them anywhere the council will see. They believe him to be a just king, even with his history. But you're right. We can't wait. If we do, the king could find some reason to dispose of Crane before we can free him," the words brought tears to his eyes and Elena reached over to hold his hand.

"How can I let Bellingham know? He agreed to help," Mylah racked her brain. "He's unreachable in the castle. If either of us go near it..."

"I'll send a message, it will be coded, and there's no telling whether he'll see it or understand it, but it's all we can do," Garrick said, grabbing a quill and paper from the side table. He wrote,

> For Crane,
> I received word this morning that you have arrived at the castle. I am writing to ensure they are treating you well enough, and to find out when your trial shall be. If not tomorrow, then perhaps soon? I hope they don't keep you long. Your mother and I would like to see you as soon as possible. Perhaps they will allow us a visit tonight. Mylah wishes you well too and will be by our sides until we know you are safe.
> Love,
> Your father

"Do you think it's clear enough?" Garrick showed the note to Mylah.

"If Bellingham happens to see it, I think he'll understand, but I don't know how he will see it."

"This note will never reach Crane, of that, I'm sure. It's possible they will throw it away or burn it. I'm hoping that they're expecting me to send a coded message and will read it. Bellingham is one of their best decoders because he is so used to uncovering lies. If all goes well, this letter will end up in his hands."

"And if not..." Mylah trailed off.

"Then we're on our own," Garrick finished.

"Come on, let's draw up our plan." Mylah stood from the couch and knelt in front of the tea table, clearing the top of it. As she set up a makeshift castle using cups, quills, and other knick-knacks, Garrick went to the town messenger and requested his message be delivered to the castle right away. When he returned, Mylah and Elena were already strategizing.

"Take a seat, dear," Elena beckoned to him, and he sat beside her on the floor.

"We will execute our plan assuming that Bellingham will receive your note," Mylah explained. "Otherwise, we will improvise when we arrive." She pointed to a statue of one of the old kings on the table. "This is the west entrance where Bellingham told me to meet him at midnight. We can easily travel through the woods and remain unseen until we have to cross the castle grounds to the entrance."

"Which will be monitored from the tower," Garrick said, pointing to a miniature pony statue that represented the watchtower.

"I think that's why Bellingham wants us to arrive at midnight exactly. He must know when they will be monitoring which areas. But we will wear all black to blend in with the night, just in case." Mylah motioned to another statue and moved it to the center of the castle. "This is King Florian. We have no idea where his chambers are, or whether he will be in them. That is the one part of the castle that remains unknown."

"We can hazard a guess," Garrick cocked his head to the side. "Here are the council chambers, these are the gardens, here is the ballroom, the dungeons are below...he must be in one of the towers."

"That would be my guess as well, but which one?"

"Does it matter? We just need to get to the dungeons," Garrick pointed out.

"I'm worried that Elias isn't in the dungeons. Why else would Greyson be needed to guard him? I suspect he's being kept somewhere else." Mylah's eyes flicked between the two towers. "But we'll worry about that when we get inside. Bellingham may be able to tell us."

"Crane would most likely be in the dungeons, so I'll go there," Garrick decided.

"And I'll find Elias."

"Wait, you aren't going to be separating, that would be insane," Elena cut in, shaking her head.

"We have no choice," Mylah said, turning to Elena. "We can't waste a single second once we're inside. If anyone realizes that we're there, we're done for. Garrick and I can't take on a whole castle filled with guards." Elena still seemed unsure, but she said nothing more.

"We have to trust each other to make it out alone too," Mylah said as she realized it. "We can't be wandering around the castle trying to find one another. Garrick goes to the dungeon, freeing Crane, Ana, and Torin, and I find Elias. Once we accomplish our own tasks, we get out."

"I won't leave the castle until I know that you're safe," Garrick said, and tears welled in Mylah's eyes.

"You have to. If we both get caught, there's no one left to help the other," she smiled up at him. "You'll come with me, won't you?" She looked from Garrick to Elena. "Back to Elowyn with the others."

"After we do this, there'll be no place left for us here," Garrick answered and Mylah's heart leapt at the idea of being together with them all, safe in Elowyn.

"You'll love it there, I promise. It's nothing like home, but it has its perks." Mylah couldn't stop smiling.

"When we leave the house tonight," Garrick began, turning to Elena. "You must leave as well, my love."

"I'll come with you and wait in the forest," she said, but Garrick gave her a sad smile.

"I can't risk losing you," he kissed her cheek. "Head to the graveyard and wait for us there. If we don't show by first light, then run. Head to the border."

"There will be shreeve waiting at the border for us, they will help you. Tell them I sent you, and tell them to send help," Mylah added. She prayed that Sabine and Broderick hadn't given up on them.

"I won't leave without you," Elena held Garrick's hand tight in her own. "There is no life for me without you and our boys."

"Trust me, Elena, the shreeve will be able to help," Mylah tried to convince her, but she stayed firm.

"I will go to the graveyard and wait for you there, but I will not continue on without either of you."

"Very well," Garrick sighed. "We will just have to be sure to return to you then." At that moment, a soft tapping came from the window. Mylah's head snapped up and she grinned as she recognized Briar flitting there, waiting to be let in. Mylah ran to the window and opened it, careful not to hit Briar.

"Briar! You made it!" she exclaimed as the sprite zipped inside.

"I don't think I was seen," she huffed, trying to catch her breath.

"Garrick, Elena, this is Briar. She's a friend from Elowyn." Mylah sat back on the floor as Briar, Garrick, and Elena exchanged pleasantries.

"I delivered your message to Genevieve," Briar began but Garrick cut her off.

"Genevieve? What part does she play in all this?" he asked, intrigue lighting his eyes.

"She is going to help create a distraction at Snake Head Lake to draw some guards away from the village. It will help make our escape smoother," Mylah explained. A river ran from Snake Head Lake to the ocean, just as a river ran from the Lake of Anguish to the ocean. Genevieve and the other sirens would be able to travel that route in order to create their diversion. "But she doesn't know the day or time yet. That's where Briar comes in." Mylah relayed her new message to Briar, informing her of all the details Genevieve needed.

"I will be sure to get to her in time. I should go now, just to be safe." Briar touched Mylah's shoulder before flying out the window. She poked her head back inside once to say, "I'll see you soon!" Mylah waved and then she was gone.

Thirty Seven

Mylah and Garrick readied themselves as night fell. There was still someone keeping guard outside the house, but they already had a plan to lose them. Elena packed herself a bag with all their most precious items she could not leave behind. Mylah had given her the Book of Creation for safe keeping.

"I will meet you at the edge of the woods in twenty minutes," Mylah told Garrick as she headed for the door. "If I'm not there, go on without me. I'll catch up. One of us must be at the west entrance at midnight to meet Bellingham."

"Be careful," Elena said as she wrapped her arms around Mylah.

"I'll see you soon," Mylah said, hoping against all odds that she wasn't wrong. Elena ushered her out the door.

"Goodnight, dear. We shall see you in the morning," Elena said for the guard's benefit as she waved to Mylah. Mylah waved back and continued to her house. She acknowledged the guard watching her with a nod and hurried along.

Once in the safety of her house, she changed into her all-black outfit and armed herself with as many weapons as she could conceal in her skintight pants and top. Daggers scraped against her skin where she didn't have sheaths, but it was all necessary. Inside the castle she would need every weapon at her disposal. She pulled on her cloak to conceal her weapons.

Mylah strolled out the door, casually waving to the guard who stood out in the open. "Care for a stroll?" she asked, heading in the direction of the lake.

"You are not to go anywhere in the kingdom unattended," the guard protested.

"It's a good thing you're with me then, isn't it?" She walked on, putting her hands in her pockets. The guard muttered something to himself but followed her. "You can walk beside me; you don't have to lag behind like a stalker." He didn't respond, but Mylah noticed he closed the gap between them.

"What's your name?" she asked. "I don't recognize you from my time in the dungeons."

"Phillip," he said. Mylah noticed his hand rested on the hilt of his sword.

"Ah, Phillip." Mylah took note of his every move to try to find some weakness, as she'd been taught. "How did you wind up being a guard dog for the king?"

"I am a member of the royal guard, and you will treat me as such," he commanded, and Mylah barked out a laugh.

"Sorry, but I don't respond well to those who consider themselves better than me." She slowed her pace and grasped one of the daggers in her pocket. Garrick had told her how best to wield it to knock someone out. Mylah turned to Phillip as if she was about to ask a question. "I was wondering," she began. He stopped and turned to her. She struck out first with her hand, striking him in the throat and as he leaned forward, she came up with the dagger, slamming the butt of it against his temple and sending him sprawling to the ground.

"That worked better than I thought it would," Mylah laughed and shoved Phillip's body under a bush, tying his hands and feet together and shoving a piece of cloth into his mouth so he wouldn't be able to scream once he woke up. Once she'd finished, she turned and ran.

Garrick waited for her at the edge of the woods that lead to the castle. He grinned when he saw her.

"You did it!" He seemed as surprised as she was. He handed over the sword he had brought for her, and she looped the belt around her waist.

"Let's not get ahead of ourselves, the worst is yet to come," Mylah reminded him. Garrick had brought the horses as planned. They mounted them and took off through the woods. As they neared the castle, they decided to leave the horses to try and make less noise. From the position of the moon in the sky, it was nearing midnight. Mylah wasn't great at telling time by the sky, but Garrick made up for the skill she lacked.

"Come on, we can wait here and still see the entrance if Bellingham shows up," Garrick whispered, crouching down behind a bush. Mylah joined him. They remained silent as the seconds ticked by. Every time Mylah glanced at the door, she swore she saw movement, but it was gone before she could be sure.

Before long, they heard shouts coming from inside the castle. A line of guards streamed out the front gates on horses, heading in the direction of the village.

She heard someone shouting. *"The sirens are in the lake!"*

Mylah smirked. Genevieve had played her part.

Finally, the side door that they watched opened a crack and a tiny figure appeared, fluttering in the shadows.

"Now!" Garrick pulled Mylah to her feet, and they sprinted across the short expanse of open space between them and the doorway. Sliding through the cracked door, Mylah closed it without a sound behind them.

"Thank you," she whispered to Bellingham. "Do you know where Prince Elias is?"

"The north tower. But the king has placed a guard there."

"I will head there. Garrick, I'll see you on the outside," Mylah didn't waste any time. She hurried down the corridor towards the north tower.

Thirty Eight

Garrick watched Mylah run in the opposite direction of where he would be headed. His heart clenched at the thought of her facing any danger alone. He had to remind himself that she'd already proven herself strong enough to take on any formidable task, but it didn't change the fear that gripped him when he lost sight of her. He loved her as much as Greyson and Crane, and he couldn't stand the thought of losing her.

Garrick steeled himself and focused on the task at hand. "I have to get to the dungeon," he told Bellingham.

"That I can help with. Follow me." Bellingham led the way through the corridors, avoiding any guards on duty. They came to the dungeon, and he paused. "Wait here a moment." He disappeared and the longer he was gone, the more exposed Garrick felt. Someone could happen upon him at any moment.

"Okay," Bellingham said as he reappeared. "Quickly." Garrick followed him down the stairs into the dungeon and past empty cells.

"Here," Bellingham stopped in front of a cell and flitted between the bars. Garrick peered into the darkness and noticed a girl curled up in the corner. *Ana*, he thought. She roused when Bellingham landed on her shoulder.

"Have you come for me?" she asked, her voice weak and tired.

"Yes, dear," Bellingham spoke softly and coaxed her to stand.

"Any idea where the keys are?" Garrick asked, and Bellingham laughed.

"Keys? Oh, to be so powerless." Bellingham took something that looked like a metal pin from between a crack in the stone. He inserted it into the lock along with his arm. After a few seconds, there was a thunking sound and Bellingham removed the pin. Garrick stepped forward and pulled open the cell door. He helped Ana out of the cell, but once she found her footing, she seemed to be able to move fine on her own. Garrick was grateful she didn't seem too battered. He had been worried that the king would have caused the shreeve more harm in the time they'd been in the dungeon.

"Wait," a voice gasped from the cell beside them. A shockingly beautiful face appeared from underneath a hood and Garrick took a step back. "I can help you," the man offered.

"We don't have time for this," Bellingham warned.

"If you set me free, I will help you escape. I'm much more powerful than any human or shreeve in this place," the man, who Garrick realized was fae, said.

"Which is exactly why we won't be trusting you," Bellingham snapped, moving on down the row of cells.

"The girl, Mylah..." Garrick stopped in his tracks and turned back to the fae man.

"What do you know about her?" Garrick growled.

"I know that she is no match for King Florian. I know that if she is a part of this little escape plot, she is going to need my help," the man sneered, and Garrick cursed inwardly.

"Let him out," Garrick demanded, and Bellingham flew back to him.

"Are you crazy? He can't be trusted!" Bellingham said, but Garrick couldn't shake the feeling that Mylah was in danger, and if that were the case, then it was possible that the fae man was right and he would be able to help her.

"Let him out. He's obviously not on the king's side, since he's imprisoned, which means there's no harm in freeing him. He'll either make a run for it or help us." Garrick tried to reason with Bellingham who hovered beside him, debating his options.

"Fine. But if this backfires, it's on you." Bellingham unlocked the fae man's cell, just as he had done for Ana and then flew off before the man could even stand to find Torin or Crane. Garrick followed him, not waiting for the fae.

Towards the end of the cells, Garrick noticed Bellingham working on another lock.

Garrick approached the cell and realized who he was looking at. The general of Elowyn's army glared up at him.

"Come to have your shot at the shreeve?" he growled, baring his teeth. Garrick could see the marks on his body from whips and chains, along with the blue and green tattoo-like markings that pegged him as a shreeve.

"I'm here to break you out, so get ready to run," Garrick said as the lock thunked and the door swung open.

"Can you fly ahead and see if Crane is here?" Garrick asked Bellingham, who continued forward to check the rest of the cells.

"We need to hurry, come with me," Garrick held his hand out to the shreeve. "Torin, isn't it?"

The man bared his teeth again. "Do not speak my name," he hissed.

"Look, I don't have time to hash out old feuds and grievances. Mylah is saving your prince, and I was sent to retrieve you. So, either come with me now, or sit there and be executed in a few days," Garrick said, losing his patience with the general.

"Mylah..." he seemed conflicted. Ana walked into view and held her hand out to Torin.

"Come on, Mylah and Elias need us," she said, and Torin took her hand.

"Here, take these," Garrick handed Torin a sword and a dagger. "We may have to fight our way out." Torin responded with a grunt, but he took the weapons.

"Down here," Bellingham called from the final cell. "Hurry, the guards will return any second." Garrick ran to Bellingham and pulled open the cell door he had already unlocked. He fell to his knees beside Crane who was nearly unrecognizable beneath the swelling and discoloration in his face.

"My son," Garrick gasped out. "What have they done to you?" Crane groaned and rolled towards Garrick. Voices came from the other end of the dungeon and dread began to sink into Garrick. The guards had returned.

"Stay here, I will distract the guards. When I say, 'all is well' leave through that door," Bellingham said, pointing to the door closest to Crane's cell. "Until then, don't make a sound." Bellingham left and Garrick closed the cell door.

"We're going to have to carry him," Garrick said, and Torin turned incredulous eyes upon him.

"We? Why should I help you?"

"Please, he's only in here because the king knew I'd try to help Mylah save you." Torin didn't respond, but he also didn't say no, so Garrick took that as a good sign.

"What are you doing here, Bellingham?" one of the guards said. Garrick turned back to Crane and tried to maneuver him onto his feet. Crane groaned with every movement.

"Shut him up," Torin hissed. Garrick ignored him and put one of Crane's arms around his shoulders, supporting the full weight of him. Torin turned back to look at them and shook his head. He stepped up to the other side of Crane and took his other arm, placing it over his shoulders, lightening Garrick's burden.

"All is well, I assure you," Bellingham's voice echoed down to them. Garrick and Torin began moving in sync with Crane between them, while Ana led the way. She opened the cell door as quietly as possible and inched out. The guards' backs were to them. They hurried to the exit and opened the door.

"What the...hey!" Garrick's blood ran cold. He didn't bother turning, he knew they had been spotted. Instead, he propelled himself forward, pulling Crane and Torin with him through the door and slammed it shut. They moved as fast as they could, but Crane slowed them down. The guards were closing in fast.

"You go on, I'll hold them off," Garrick grunted, releasing himself from Crane's grasp.

"I don't know where I'm going," Torin said. "I'll fight with you." They didn't have time to argue anymore, the guards were upon them. There were two of them, clad in armor and wielding swords. Before Torin could make a move, Ana stepped in front of him.

"All is well," she spoke in a calming, trancelike, voice. A calmness overcame Garrick and his sense of urgency dissipated. The guards paused and cocked their heads to the side.

"The prisoners are escaping," one of them said.

"There is no reason to be here. You should return to the dungeons," Ana continued, and the guards began to turn away from them. "Return to the dungeons. All is well," she repeated. Once the guards were back behind the door, Ana turned back to the others. The calmness seemed to evaporate, and the direness of their situation returned.

"We should keep moving. Guards patrol these halls every hour," Bellingham said, and they jumped back into motion. Garrick and Torin anchored Crane between them and followed Bellingham as he led them back to the west entrance. Ana lagged behind to keep a lookout.

"Where is Mylah?" Torin asked as they neared the exit.

"She's in the north tower, saving your prince," Garrick huffed out. Supporting Crane was taking much more of his energy than he had realized. They made it to the exit without being noticed again and Garrick thought he could cry in relief.

Garrick pushed open the door and Bellingham went to scout and make sure the coast was clear. Torin removed Crane's arm from his shoulders and stepped away.

"My duty is to my prince," Torin said, backing away with his fist over his heart. "I hope we meet again." Before Garrick could say anything, Torin and Ana both took off running back down the corridor towards the north tower.

Thirty Nine

Mylah slowed as she heard voices up ahead. She drew her sword, preparing for a fight. As she inched forward, she came to a small alcove in the wall leading to another doorway which she took refuge in. She pressed herself up against the wall praying that whoever was walking her way would not notice her. It was dark enough she figured she would blend in with the shadows.

The voices drew closer, and she could make out what they were saying.

"Do you think the king will let them live? He can't, right?"

"They're *shreeve*. Of course not." One of them chuckled and Mylah scowled but remained hidden. They passed by without so much as a glance in her direction. *Some guards you are*, she thought. She waited a solid minute before leaving her hiding spot.

As she approached the north tower, she heard more voices. There were at least five or six guards. Mylah swore to herself. She hadn't expected the tower to be so heavily guarded. She peeked around the corner and surveyed the scene before her.

Two guards stood outside the door that would lead up the stairs of the tower, two more guarded the hallways leading away from the tower, and one stood back to Mylah, guarding the hallway she currently occupied. Five total. Mylah leaned back against the wall, racking her brain for any ideas. There was no way she could take them all on at once, but if she could draw them away from the tower, forcing them to file down the hallway, she could pick them off, one by one. She readied herself with her sword and steeled her nerves for what she was about to do. Before she could move, there was another voice.

"You're needed in the dungeons," a man said and there was the sound of armor creaking as the guards began to move. "You two, stay here," he added. A few moments later, Mylah heard feet running down the hallway to the right. Panic seized Mylah as she realized why extra guards would be needed in the dungeons...*Garrick*. She turned on her heel, but then stopped herself. No. She needed to focus on her task and trust that Garrick could handle himself.

Mylah peeked around the corner again and saw two guards remained, the two by the tower door. That she could handle. She strode around the corner and put on a grave face.

"They're attacking," she sputtered, stumbling for effect. "The shreeve..." The guards glanced at each other.

"What are you doing here?" one of them asked.

"I saw them coming from the town, I followed them here to help make sure they didn't get away." She kept taking steps closer to the guards. "They were headed for the south tower..." she gambled that it was in fact where the king's chambers were.

385

"The king," one of them mumbled. "But he ordered us to remain here, no matter what." They stood a little taller, confident in their decision to stay.

"Right, yes, that makes sense, the prince is their prize after all," Mylah said, coming within arm's reach of the guards. "Greyson is up there too, though, isn't he?"

"Yeah, but he couldn't take on a shreeve. He's barely able to take us on in training," they both laughed. Mylah didn't hesitate, she struck out with her sword, swiping low and knocking the guard on the right to the floor. In the same motion, she brought the sword up and stabbed the guard on the right in the shoulder, the only part of him, other than his head and arms, that armor was not covering. He howled in pain.

"Did you ever consider he needn't waste his time with fools like yourselves?" Mylah hissed as she removed her sword and braced herself for the retaliation.

The guard on the right stayed down. He'd hit his head when he fell and was either knocked out or dead. Mylah prayed for the former, she hadn't meant to kill anyone that night unless it was absolutely necessary. The guard on the left pulled out his sword as his right arm remained unmoving at his side.

"The king warned us about you, *traitor*," he sneered. "Swooning over a disgusting shreeve, how pathetic." Mylah struck out again, but the guard blocked her blow.

"You know nothing of me and what I've been through," she said, stepping back to allow herself some space to think and consider her movements.

"All I need to know is that you betrayed your kingdom and now you will pay for your crimes." He lunged forward, nearly slicing into Mylah's side, but she twisted away. Even with one arm, the guard kept up with Mylah's movements and attacks. She couldn't gain an advantage on him. She shuddered to think how easily he would have taken her down if he had use of both arms.

"Though it is quite entertaining dancing with you, I think I'll end this now," he said, pulling up his arm that Mylah thought she had taken out of commission. He smirked and quickened his movements to the point where it was all Mylah could do to stay out of his range and defend herself. It was too late when she realized he had backed her against a wall and was about to deal his final blow. Out of nowhere, a dagger flew through the air and stuck in his hand, making him drop his sword. Mylah let out a surprised squeak but wasted no time as she rolled across the wall, out of his way. Torin appeared from the center hallway and finished off the guard with a single blow, his sword cutting his head clean off. Mylah pinched her eyes shut and pressed her fist against her mouth to bite back her scream.

"Are you okay?" Torin's gruff voice asked, and she opened her eyes to see him standing before her. Tears leaked out of her eyes as she threw her arms around him. Ana ran into view and smiled when she saw them.

"Garrick did it," Mylah breathed. Torin made no move to hug her back.

"Let's go, we don't have much time. The other guards are beginning to catch wind of what's happening in the castle." Torin turned out of her grasp and opened the door, taking the stairs three at a time. Mylah followed as fast as she could. She couldn't let Torin face Greyson alone or else he would kill him.

"Torin, wait!" she called after him as she raced up the stairs. "Don't hurt him," she huffed as she reached the top of the stairs, out of breath. Torin already had Greyson pinned up against the wall with his sword at his throat. "STOP!" Mylah screamed. Torin and Greyson both turned to her. Ana appeared at the top of the stairs, stopping dead in her tracks as she took in the scene before her.

"We don't have time for mercy," Torin growled.

"Then go get Elias. I'll deal with Greyson," Mylah told him. Torin rolled his good eye but released Greyson and ran for the other door in the room, knocking it down with the force of his body. Ana seemed to be debating whether to help Mylah, but her allegiance to her kingdom won out and she followed Torin.

"What are you doing, Mylah?" Greyson's eyes filled with betrayal and anger.

"I can't let the king kill them," she told him, taking a step towards him. "It's not right, Greyson. The king wants to wipe out an entire race. I don't know his motives, but there are children and families who would be killed for no reason."

"That's not what's happening," Greyson shook his head. "Those shreeve invaded our territory to steal from us. They deserve to pay for their actions."

"We stole from them first!" Mylah cried out, exasperated. She didn't have time to argue with Greyson. *What is taking Torin so long?* she wondered.

"If you do this," Greyson began, but Mylah cut him off.

"I'm leaving, Greyson. Me and your family. We're all leaving. They had Crane in the dungeons, using him as a threat against your parents. Tell me you didn't know?" Mylah took another step towards him.

"I heard he was in the castle, but I didn't know where." He cast his gaze to the floor.

"But you assumed, and you did nothing." Mylah's lips curled in disgust. "You've changed, Greyson. I don't know who you are anymore."

"Just because I'm not the same lovesick idiot who would follow you to the ends of the Earth. You only ever knew me when I was living for *you*. I'm finally living for myself, and I'm sorry if that's not someone you want to be friends with anymore." Greyson's words brought tears to Mylah's eyes. There was movement behind her as Torin and Ana came stumbling out of the room supporting Elias.

"They must have drugged him or something," Torin said.

Mylah whipped back around to face Greyson. "What did they do to him?" She raised her sword and Greyson took a step towards her, placing his chest at the tip of her sword.

"You won't hurt me," he said.

"She may not hurt you, but I will," Torin growled, leaving Ana to support Elias alone, and storming across the room.

Mylah held her hand out to stop him. "You're right," she said as she lowered her sword. "I won't. So, please, tell me and we'll go. What did they give him?"

"Nothing serious, just a drug to keep him sedated. He kept trying to use magic to escape, it was all we could do to keep him contained. He'll wake up in an hour or so," Greyson explained, and Mylah let out a sigh of relief that as long as they got Elias out of the castle, he was going to be fine.

"We need to leave, now." Torin stalked back to Elias and helped Ana support him again. "It will be a miracle if we make it out of here alive." Mylah turned to him and in that moment, Greyson grabbed her from behind and pulled out his own sword, holding it against her throat.

"Don't move, or I'll kill her," he commanded, and Torin and Ana paused, clearly conflicted.

"Go," Mylah rasped out. "Let him kill me if he can."

"Don't test me," Greyson held the sword tighter against her throat and blood began to trickle down her neck, soaking into her shirt.

"Get Elias out of here," Mylah pleaded with Torin, Ana had already stepped away from Elias, making no move to leave. "If either of you stay here, you'll die."

"I –" Torin hesitated but then took a step towards the door. "My duty is to the prince. I swore a vow to protect him and my king." His expression was one of pain and regret, but he kept moving. Ana remained rooted to her spot, waiting for the signal to use her power, but Mylah didn't give it.

"Stop!" Greyson cried out. "I *will* kill her!"

Go, Mylah mouthed to Torin, and he was gone. Ana lingered. Greyson let out a noise that sounded like a sob and released Mylah.

"I can't do it." He doubled over. "Just go, I already failed my king."

"Come with me," Mylah held her hand out to him. "Come with me and the rest of your family."

"I can't do that either." He glanced up at her through his hair that was plastered to his face from sweat.

"Greyson, please." Mylah's eyes shifted to the exit. "We need to leave now."

"I can't go with you, just leave. I can take care of myself." Greyson stood upright again and took Mylah's hand. "I will always love you, Mylah." Tears filled his eyes and Mylah threw her arms around his neck, hugging him tightly. He hugged her back.

"I love you, Greyson. Stay safe." She kissed his cheek and sprinted to Ana's side, grabbing her hand, and leading her out the door. At the bottom of the stairs, there were more bodies of guards that Mylah assumed Torin had taken out on his way through. Mylah could hear the thunder of more guards coming towards them. She and Ana ran in the opposite direction, to the right. Tears streamed down Mylah's face making it hard to see as she forced herself to keep moving.

"I could have calmed him, made him release you without all the trouble," Ana said as they ran.

"I didn't need you to," Mylah said, wiping away her tears with her free hand. "I knew Greyson would let me leave."

"But what if he hadn't?" Ana asked, but before Mylah could answer, King Florian stepped out of a door in front of them, bringing them to a screeching halt.

"My, my, my," his words slithered over Mylah, leaving dread in their wake. "What do we have here?" he sneered.

"Ana," Mylah nudged Ana with her elbow.

"I'm trying," Ana said, sounding breathless. The king laughed, throwing his head back.

"Your little mind tricks won't work on me," he growled as his face changed from amusement to pure disgust. "No one can mess with my mind anymore." He took a step forward, reaching out to grab Mylah.

"Don't touch her," Ana snarled, grabbing his wrist. "Just because I can't change your mind doesn't mean I can't break your bones." Mylah could barely breathe as she realized that they were stuck. Guards were filing out into the hall behind the king. Ana dropped his wrist and put her arm in front of Mylah, pushing her backward with her.

"At least you were able to free your friends, right?" King Florian crossed his arms. "Maybe they will attempt another rescue, or maybe, they'll leave the traitor to rot. What do you think they'll choose?"

Mylah would feel fine giving up if Ana were not beside her. Mylah had brought Ana into this mess, and she couldn't accept that she had condemned her to a lifetime in a dungeon at best, or death at worst. Her mind ran through all possible escape routes, but the guards blocked every single one. There was no way they could get out of the castle alive.

"I'll make a deal with you," Mylah began when a force crashed into her from behind, sending her sprawling onto the floor. When she lifted her head, she saw that everyone had been sent flying. Ana lay beside her, dazed.

"What..." Ana tried to speak but she couldn't form the words. A hand gripped Mylah's arm and hauled her to her feet. She turned and came face to face with the fae man who had been in the dungeon with her.

"You," she gasped.

"Me," he grinned, pulling Ana up and forcing them both forward. "Best get a move on before your highness wakes up from his cat nap." Mylah didn't need to be told twice. She grabbed Ana's arm and pulled her along. Thankfully she was able to run, even though she still seemed a little put out from their fall.

"You can run but you can't hide from me, Mylah Orson!" King Florian's voice echoed through the halls after them.

"He recovers fast," the fae groaned. "Not to worry, we're almost there."

"Who are you?" Mylah asked as they ran. "And why are you helping us?"

"My name is Lachlan, and I owed someone a favor, now we're square." He winked before racing past them and out of sight.

"Hey, you!" Mylah heard someone call from behind them. She pushed herself to move faster, run harder. She and Ana veered left. Mylah hoped it would take them back to the west entrance. Footsteps pounded behind them, and Mylah could tell they were gaining on them.

"Mylah!" she heard a voice ahead of her and nearly cried out in relief as she saw Bellingham hovering before her. "Quick!" He beckoned her onward and she let out her last burst of speed to reach the door and throw herself outside. Ana followed shortly, slamming the door shut behind her. Mylah saw Torin making his way across the opening between the castle and the woods, *Too slow.* She ran to catch up to him with Bellingham on her shoulder. She grabbed Elias' other arm and helped Torin make it the rest of the way, but still not fast enough. By the time they reached the woods, guards were already spilling out of every entrance of the castle.

"We only have two horses," Mylah realized as they neared the others.

"You made it," Garrick wrapped Mylah in a hug and looked behind her expectantly.

"He wouldn't come," Mylah told him. "I'm sorry, I tried." Garrick set his jaw and straightened his posture.

"He made his decision," he ground out. Mylah knew he was holding back his disappointment and pain.

"We need to move, and fast. The guards are crossing the clearing now," Bellingham said. Mylah glanced around, realizing Lachlan had not joined them. She couldn't worry about him, though.

"Ana and I can run, we're faster than any of you," Torin said, and Ana nodded in agreement. "But someone needs to take Elias on a horse."

"I will," Mylah said, striding over to her horse. Garrick was already there, ready to help Torin put Elias on the horse. Mylah sat behind him with one arm around him to keep him steady and the other holding the reins. Torin helped Garrick with Crane next. Garrick mounted his horse and Torin boosted Crane up behind him. Thankfully, Crane was at least conscious so he could help a bit.

"Why are they stopping..." Bellingham asked as he watched the guards who had been approaching. "They're turning back, that doesn't make any sense. Unless...of course."

"What is it?" Mylah yelled.

"The king has a copy of the shreeve book. He doesn't need to stop you from taking the original," Bellingham explained, and Mylah's heart dropped.

"We can't worry about that now," Garrick said, snapping the reins of his horse. Mylah followed suit, though her heart still clenched, and pressure began to build in her head. They made their way back through the woods, moving faster than they should with Crane being injured and Elias unconscious. Torin and Ana ran behind them, almost able to keep up with the horses. Mylah marveled at their speed, obviously not inherited from their fae side.

As they rode, a glow rose towards the edge of the village. At first, they had no idea what it was, but as they neared it, they realized something was on fire. They continued towards it since it was in their path to the graveyard where they were meeting Elena.

"Oh no," Garrick murmured, and Mylah realized that the fire seemed to be in the exact spot her home had been.

"I need to see it," she said.

"Are you crazy?!" Torin cried out.

"It's too dangerous. It's gone, Mylah," Garrick tried to reason with her. But she needed to see her home one last time before it was reduced to nothing but ash.

"I'll be fine." Mylah beckoned to Torin to take over supporting Elias before she jumped down from the horse. "I'll meet you all at the graveyard. If I'm not there by daybreak, leave without me." She took off running before Garrick could stop her. Not that he would have been able to while Crane clung to him.

She made it to Garrick's house within a few minutes. From there, she could see the blaze that had engulfed her home. She fell to her knees as she watched the fire rage on. Everything she ever owned, mementos of her parents, were up in flames. Tears streamed down her face yet again. She remained hidden in the undergrowth as she watched her home burn.

Their houses were mostly made of stone, so most of the structure remained, but everything else; the roof, the doors, the interior, all went up in smoke. Time slipped by and she stayed rooted to her spot, mesmerized by the flames that had begun to slow.

"Mylah," a hand landed on her shoulder, and she barely flinched. "It's time to go." Garrick stood behind her and lifted her to her feet. She let him lead her away in a daze. They reached the horse he had brought back with him, and he boosted her up onto it. His cuff snagged Mylah's necklace, ripping it from her neck as the chain snapped. Mylah's hand flew to her bare throat, her eyes widening.

Garrick didn't notice and was about to mount the horse himself, when instead, he jolted forward, slamming into the horse's flank. An arrow protruded from his back. Mylah screamed. Heaving, Garrick turned to see their attacker when another arrow struck him in the chest with a sickening thud.

"Go!" he yelled with his last breath, throwing his weight against the horse again to force it to move. The horse took off running. Mylah turned back to see Garrick fall to the ground beside her necklace, his lifeless eyes staring at the sky.

Forty

Mylah screamed as the horse ran, unable to comprehend all that had happened. She tried pulling on the reins to turn back but the horse, still in flight mode from the impact of Garrick's body, wouldn't respond to her attempts

"Go back!" she screamed through the tears. "No, no, no," *this can't be happening.* Mylah closed her eyes and opened them again, expecting to find herself back kneeling on the ground in front of the fire, but all she saw were trees rushing past as the horse continued to run. She glanced back, trying to see if she was being followed by whomever had killed Garrick, but she saw nothing. Ahead of her Elena waited with Crane and Mylah would have to tell them what happened; that it was her fault that Garrick was dead because she couldn't accept that she had failed and lost her childhood home.

If only she had been able to walk away from her past, Garrick would still be alive. If only she hadn't lingered so long watching her house burn. If only...

A branch whipped Mylah off the horse. She fell on her back, and it knocked the wind out of her. Gasping, she scrambled to right herself, but black spots filled her vision. *Maybe this is what I deserve...* she thought as she remained lying on the ground. *The guards will find me here and kill me, and everything will be right again.*

Footsteps hurried towards her, and someone brushed the hair out of her face.

"She's just in shock," Elena's voice broke through to her. "Bring her over here," Elena instructed. Someone picked Mylah up into their arms and carried her to wherever Elena had indicated. Cool water splashed onto Mylah's skin and soothed her.

"She's waking up," Crane's voice, though muffled and hoarse, brought her back to consciousness.

"Crane?" Mylah's eyelids fluttered open, and his face filled her vision.

"There she is," he tried to smile, but his face was too swollen. "Where's Garrick?" he asked, and Mylah shook her head, closing her eyes once more.

"He didn't...they killed him," her voice cracked, and Elena cried out in agony. Crane remained stoic. "It's my fault," Mylah said through her sobs.

"No," Elena forced out as she returned to Mylah's side, tears streaming down her face. "No. None of this is your fault. This is King Florian's fault, and he will pay." Elena's eyes hardened and Mylah saw herself reflected in them. It was strange to see that same look on Elena's face that had haunted Mylah's own eyes for so long. A look she realized had disappeared while she had been in Elowyn. It was revenge that Elena sought, and Mylah would help her get it.

Mylah wandered away from the graveyard to where her parents were buried, giving Elena some space to grieve.

Flowers had sprung up around the gravestones despite the cool temperatures. Mylah knelt between her parents' graves and hung her head.

"Would you be proud of me?" she asked them, knowing they would never answer.

"It's nearly daybreak, we have to move," Torin's voice found her in the dark.

"How is Elias?" Mylah asked, rising from the ground, and wiping the dirt from her knees. She figured Elias should be awake.

"He's awake, but still groggy," Torin said, and Mylah sat up. The movement caused her head to throb and the muscles in her back to ache.

"Careful," Crane said as he placed his hand at her back to help support her.

"I'm fine," Mylah forced out through clenched teeth. She stood and made her way over to Elias who sat leaning against a tree.

"Let's ready ourselves," Torin told the others, giving Mylah and Elias some privacy.

"Elias," Mylah crouched down beside him and tried to take his hand, but he pulled it away.

"Don't touch me. You betrayed us," he said, and it felt like a slap in the face.

"No, I was only pretending so I could get out and save you!" Mylah protested.

"Not just in the castle, but this entire time. Did you not lie about your name and identity? Did you not warn them that we were coming? Did you not play me for a fool?" Anger was thick in his voice and Mylah understood. She had done everything he accused her of.

"You have to understand," she tried, but Elias put his hand up to stop her.

"I don't," Elias paused and then went on. "How did the king know?"

"Know what?" Mylah furrowed her brow.

"About my father." Mylah's eyes widened as realization dawned on her. "He called me 'king killer.' And there are only six people who know that, four of which are back in Elowyn."

"I didn't, Elias, I swear," she was about to tell him about how Greyson had betrayed them, but Torin appeared.

"It's time to go," he said as he reached down to help Elias to his feet. Mylah tried to help but Elias pushed her away.

"I'll ride with Torin," he said.

"I don't think these horses will be able to handle the weight of both of us, it's better if I ride with Ana," Torin pointed out. "These horses aren't enhanced with magic like ours. And you can't ride alone."

"So be it," Elias stated.

"I promise not to let you fall," Mylah told him bitterly. She'd lost too much to continue worrying about Elias' feelings any longer. If he was content to hate her, then as he said, *So be it.*

Elena and Crane were already on their horse, Torin and Ana took the horse that had been Garrick's, and Mylah and Elias sat together on her horse. The entire six-hour ride to the border, Elias remained silent. Mylah cursed their ordinary horses for being so slow. Elena sobbed most of the time while Crane tried to soothe her, and Torin chatted with Bellingham who rode on his shoulder. Mylah assumed

Bellingham had deemed it too dangerous to return to the castle because he had been seen helping them.

At the border, they crossed into Elowyn territory with a collective sigh of relief. They were immediately surrounded by Elowyn guards. Mylah cried out as she recognized some of them.

"Sabine! Broderick!"

"You made it!" Sabine grinned. "The king knew you would."

Elias scoffed. "What if she hadn't chosen to betray her people, and betrayed us again?"

"I didn't, and I got you both out," Mylah snapped, dismounting from the horse. Elias had enough of his strength back to keep himself stable. "I stuck to the plan *we* made."

"And yet we still failed," Elias snapped back.

"Wait, you didn't get the book?" Sabine asked, her brow wrinkled in confusion. "But that was the goal of the mission."

"I know! I know that was the goal of the mission. I have the book, but King Florian made a copy! What do you want me to say? I'm sorry I ruined everything and got people I loved killed? Because I am," Mylah gasped for air. "I'm sorry." She covered her face with her hands.

"We'll figure something else out," Broderick spoke up. "All that matters is that you're all safe." Mylah glanced up from her hands to see Broderick standing before her. He took her hand and squeezed it. "Don't blame yourself," he said.

Mylah was about to respond when Briar came into view, and everyone turned to her.

"Genevieve and the others all made it safely back to the ocean after their successful diversion," she filled them in.

"Thank you, Briar," Mylah said.

"We need to report to the king," Sabine called. "It's time to move out."

"I can ride with someone else from here," Elias said, and Mylah whipped around to face him.

"Am I honestly so retched to you that you can't even bear the thought of riding a horse with me for another few hours? I thought you'd be able to forgive me, after all I've done and given up for you and your people. Clearly, you're not the man I thought you were," Mylah said and noticed everyone stared at her.

"Clearly I'm not," Elias answered. "Sabine, Broderick, help me," he commanded. They lifted the prince from Mylah's horse and helped him onto Sabine's horse.

"What do we do with our horses?" Mylah asked Broderick who returned to her side after helping Elias.

"We should set them free and switch your people to some of our horses." Broderick motioned to the few remaining guards who dismounted and began the shuffle of rearranging so Crane, Elena, Ana, and Torin each had an enchanted horse. Torin was the only one who didn't need a guard with him since he already knew how the horses moved. Crane and Elena sat with guards behind them to brace them against the speed that would otherwise send them flying.

"Come on, Leylah," Broderick led her to his horse. Mylah flinched at the name but said nothing. Elias glared at her, and she worried he would reveal her secret, but he too remained silent. Castien had wanted her to keep that secret until after she returned to the castle, and so she would.

They reached the castle in a few hours, much to the shock of Crane and Elena who were not used to the enchanted horses. Their group was brought straight to the king who waited in his study with Korriane and Killian. As soon as they walked in, Castien was by Elias' side, helping him into a chair and fussing over him.

"What were you thinking?" he roared. "Leaving in your condition, you derailed our entire plan."

"You told me to go," Elias hissed and then groaned as he sat down.

"Obviously I didn't mean it! Did they hurt you?" Castien asked, looking to Torin and Mylah for answers.

"Of course they did!" Elias yelled, shaking his brother off. "They made sure not to leave any visible marks."

"If I weren't part fae, I'd look like that guy right about now," Torin said, pointing to Crane. "I assume they did the same to Elias." Mylah's stomach clenched at the thought of it. She turned to Ana, searching her face and realized the same must have been done to her. Ana gave her a small nod, affirming Mylah's fear, her gaze never leaving the floor.

"Mylah, tell me what happened," Castien demanded, turning to her. Apparently, he had already informed Korriane and Killian of her real name because they were unfazed.

"Well," she began, and relayed the last few days, ending with Garrick being killed and her getting away. Tears streamed down Elena's face as Mylah spoke and Crane kept his arm around her shoulders for comfort.

"So, a copy of the book is with the king," Castien groaned. "All that to lose our best chance at retrieving it." He pinched the bridge of his nose and closed his eyes. Mylah had expected a much bigger outburst from him, so this was welcome.

"I will return and retrieve it myself," Mylah said, but he cut her off.

"Don't be stupid. They'll kill you on sight," he waved the idea off.

"He's known all along what's in the book, why try so hard to decipher it now?" Mylah asked.

"I don't know for sure, but I think he's working with someone else," Crane spoke up. Everyone in the room turned their eyes towards him. "I overheard someone saying he's been meeting with someone. A woman."

"A consort no doubt," Castien snapped.

"No, they weren't alone. There were other council members included in the meetings. The guards I overheard said that she was the one who gave the king the means to capture the prince," Crane countered.

"You mean the drug that blocked my magic?" Elias asked, his jaw clenching.

"Yes, a potion of some sort," Crane confirmed.

"It must be a witch, he has witches that he works with," Mylah offered but Crane shook his head.

"No, they made it seem like she's someone much more important than one of the king's witches. Someone with a lot more power," Crane clarified, and Castien stiffened.

"Do you think..." Torin murmured, and the king cut him off.

"Queen Aveda," Castien said.

"The queen of Cyprian?" Mylah had heard of her but knew nothing more than her name.

"If he's working with her," Castien started, ignoring Mylah's question. "We'll need reinforcements as well. Killian, send word to Amaris. They will join forces with us, this affects them too," Castien commanded. "And write to our allies in Hyrdian."

"Yes, your majesty." Killian fled the room in search of a messenger.

"Everyone else, prepare yourselves. We're going to war."

Printed in Great Britain
by Amazon

14600066R00237